UNCHARMED

UNCHARMED

LUCY JANE WOOD

MACMILLAN

First published 2025 by Macmillan
an imprint of Pan Macmillan
The Smithson, 6 Briset Street, London EC1M 5NR
EU representative: Macmillan Publishers Ireland Ltd, 1st Floor,
The Liffey Trust Centre, 117–126 Sheriff Street Upper,
Dublin 1 D01 YC43
Associated companies throughout the world

ISBN 978-1-0350-4550-1 HB
ISBN 978-1-0350-4551-8 TPB

Copyright © Lucy Jane Wood 2025

The right of Lucy Jane Wood to be identified as the
author of this work has been asserted in accordance
with the Copyright, Designs and Patents Act 1988.

All rights reserved. No part of this publication may be reproduced,
stored in a retrieval system, or transmitted, in any form, or by any means
(including, without limitation, electronic, mechanical, photocopying, recording
or otherwise) without the prior written permission of the publisher.

Pan Macmillan does not have any control over, or any responsibility for,
any author or third party websites (including, without limitation, URLs,
emails and QR codes) referred to in or on this book.

3 5 7 9 8 6 4

A CIP catalogue record for this book is available from the British Library.

Typeset by Palimpsest Book Production Ltd, Falkirk, Stirlingshire
Printed and bound in the UK using 100% Renewable Electricity by
CPI Group (UK) Ltd

This book is sold subject to the condition that it shall not, by way of
trade or otherwise, be lent, hired out, or otherwise circulated without
the publisher's prior consent in any form of binding or cover other than
that in which it is published and without a similar condition including this
condition being imposed on the subsequent purchaser. The publisher does not
authorize the use or reproduction of any part of this book in any manner
for the purpose of training artificial intelligence technologies or systems.
The publisher expressly reserves this book from the Text and Data Mining
exception in accordance with Article 4(3) of the European Union
Digital Single Market Directive 2019/790.

Visit **www.panmacmillan.com** to read more about all our books
and to buy them.

*To the daughters who fix it all for everyone.
You deserve the same magic
that you give to others.*

AUTHOR'S NOTE

The events of *Uncharmed* take place prior to Belle's adventures in *Rewitched*, but both are standalone stories set in the Selcouth world.

Chapter One

SUGAR AND SORCERY

The promise and power of a little treat is perhaps the most magical concept that a mind can manifest. The potency that it holds, hovering just beyond arm's reach, is a gift that can lead to wonderful things. It is well-intentioned trickery and silent prayer. It is a mug of warm, silken coffee clutched between chilled hands, in exchange for waking up before the morning sun. The bright splashed palette of supermarket flowers for completing a tick list, the wrapper crinkling against a net of oranges, a squashed loaf of bread. Or the promise to one's self that a precious half-hour will be reserved amidst the madness, for peace and rest, reading and escape, everything else forbidden to interrupt while feet are tucked underneath legs and a blanket keeps the world away. A little treat can change it all.

Each small, bargaining vow holds equally compelling magic, but most folk would probably agree that their favourite treat is a sweet one – and the best of those could always be found at Celestial Bakehouse. Everyone who knew the bakery would bribe themselves with a trip. If only they could get through their pile of work, their demanding day-to-day, then the reward would be to follow the scent of toasted cinnamon sugar that trailed down the street until they reached the candy-striped canopy. An otherworldly charm seemed to float on the air at Celeste, as regulars had taken to calling it. The irresistible pull of the place, powder pink and pretty on the corner of London's Maple Row, might well have been explained by the treats inside. Then again, it might also have had something to do with the owner.

When Annie Wildwood first moved in and turned the place pink, the bakery had seemed to spring up overnight, appearing one morning as if from nowhere in a cloud of rosy spring light and foggy icing sugar. Word had spread in a matter of days, that Celeste and its charming proprietor were something special. Bewitching, even. The small fact that Annie was indeed a witch was almost by the by. Everything was crafted with love above all, but over her thirty-two years, Annie had come to discover that sugar and sorcery was a particularly compelling, delicious combination.

'I'm afraid Joe just got the last choux bun,' Annie said, gesturing to the older gentleman who was winking and waving on his way out of the shop, delighted at his luck. 'But there's one caramel éclair left with your name on it, Olive.'

'That'll do me, duck,' Olive said, tired eyes crinkling. The lady, her sandy hair tumbling out of a hasty bun, turned to the line of customers waiting behind her, beaming smugly for beating them to it. Not that they had much to worry about; Celeste had a habit of presenting its visitors with the very last one of their favourites at just the right time.

Spotting her moment while Olive was fumbling in her purse, Annie fluttered her fingers in the direction of the last éclair, the white chocolate topping shining like marble. A glint of pale-pink *Proprius Minutia* sparks sprinkled the air and the letters of 'Olive' began to ice themselves in a delicate loop across the glaze. From the moment she'd begun her days at the bakery five years ago, Annie had quickly noticed that customers were far too preoccupied with the reason for their sweet reward to realize that anything as insignificant as magic was afoot. Witchery in the non-wicche realm wasn't as tricky to conceal as one might think.

Strictly speaking, personalized goodies were not something Annie had time for these days. Since word had spread far and wide about Celeste, she had barely a spare second for the flourishes that she'd treasured at the start, but the little details were what made all the difference. She was not one to cut corners. Annie wanted every Celeste visit to be a special one.

'Had a good day?' Annie called back over her shoulder as she lifted the glass dome and took up the éclair with her tongs, a pop of fluffy gingerbread cream bursting through one side of the pastry. The early evening light was pouring through the shop's bay window, turning the whole place peach. September's young autumn had delivered a crackle of orange-peel leaves across the pavement outside and, as the door swung open and stirred them in a gust, they rustled in the background against the chatter of the packed cafe.

'Quiet chaos,' Olive shrugged. 'They're all quiet chaos these days.' Her smile faded to something more self-conscious at the confession, the glint in her eye dimming.

Annie faltered, sensing deep in her bones that she was needed – as she always could. It was a feeling that pulled at her, like a vine of ivy that wound its way around her ribs. She added in a slice of cinnamon apple crumble for good measure and wrapped it all up in its own little box with a ribbon tied around it. Olive took it carefully by the handle, as though the sweetness inside was a remedy. There was still a line of patient customers almost reaching the door, despite closing time hanging in the air. But Annie would find the time to spare, once they had all been served.

'Have you got time for a tea, Ol? I'm just closing up,' Annie said softly, leaning over the counter. 'You can help me finish this leftover banana bread.'

Olive looked delighted, then hesitated. 'I know you're a busy lady. You don't want to be wasting your exciting evening plans on me.'

'Where did you get these so-called "exciting evening plans" from? I think I'm good to take a rain check,' Annie replied, cheerfully batting away the suggestion. She ignored the twinge in her chest that longed for home after being on her feet since the early hours.

When Celeste eventually cleared out, she seized her chance to flip the pink sign from Open to Closed before anyone else could press their nose against the door with a pleading look. Annie had sent her co-workers Faye and Pari home hours ago (despite their protests), not wishing them to spend their precious evenings at the bakery. Annie knew how cherished that time should be and would never want to take it from them — not when she could get through things easily enough by herself.

Finally, armed with two forks and a doorstop slice of spiced, nutty loaf that tasted like Sunday afternoons in October, Annie joined Olive at the bay window, just as the first stars began to scatter outside.

'Tell me all about it.'

The marbled banana loaf was no accidental choice; Annie

had selected it especially. The brew of comfort concoction (chamomile, feather light, a gasp of butterfly breath, stir clockwise . . .) that she had melted into the salty-sweet caramel drizzle would bring a little bit of solace for the next few nights. Annie listened to how Olive's life had changed, busier and emptier all at once since she lost her husband, her childhood sweetheart. Annie poured out tea and comfort entwined and told her that she could only dream of finding a love like that. By the time Olive was done, a rare hour just for her, away from the children, her shoulders were higher for sharing the weight of her troubles. The shop's pearly sconces flared across the black and white tiles and a throw of crumbs dotted the scalloped tablecloth.

Encounters like this were not rare for Annie. Indeed, she seemed to unconsciously attract them. More importantly, she was never one to turn them away. Celeste was always supposed to be more than service with a smile; it was service with genuine friendship. She made sure to remember every detail of people's days – everything from appointments to kids, from redecorating to exam results. Annie always knew what to say to make it all a little brighter. No detail was too small to recall and no favour was too big to request. Her heart was soft and full for all.

Days at Celeste began very early and ended even later. The results of her hard work, because she had had no choice *but* to make it work when she had first opened that bakery door, lay behind the glass to admire. A patchwork of pastel-coloured macarons each morning, summoned in the kitchen from mixing bowl to oven to plate before sunrise. Cinnamon swirls curled like Catherine wheels. Immaculate fruit tarts glazed like stained glass. Chocolate so creamy that it conjured spun silk.

Delicate croissants shaped like seashells and pillowy pains au chocolat infused with the feeling and the taste of golden hour. Her flair for all things sugary or spellbound and her affinity for baking were something to behold. Ever since she was a girl, Annie had held an intimate understanding of the importance of a sweet treat; the way it could alter the worst of moods, brighten the darkest of days, bring a little bit of hope to a heavy heart.

'Who's the lucky gent tonight, then?' Olive asked, a knowing expression on her face as she gathered her tartan coat and stuffed a rogue children's toy back into her permanently overflowing handbag.

'I don't know what you're talking about.' Annie feigned innocence as she cleared away their empty plates and untied her frilly, flour-smeared pink pinny. Most things in her life were a shade of pink and she rarely strayed from it.

'It's like clockwork. Thursday, isn't it? And Thursday is always date night.' Olive waggled a knowing finger. 'Fridays are with your girls. Mondays are late-night Cake Club here, to brighten up everybody's start to the week. Tuesdays for your studies, Wednesday nights are left for spontaneous plans. I'm not sure what's spontaneous about planning your spontaneous plans in advance but . . .' Olive shook her head with a laugh. 'You're a marvel, Annie. When you find the time to sleep remains to be seen.'

'You know me,' Annie said, shrugging in good humour. 'I just like things to be organized.'

Olive clucked. 'There's organized and then there's the way you like to do things, lady. Whatever happened to going with the flow?'

Annie tried not to take this as a slight. It felt like one,

whenever people pointed out her need to consider things first. 'Everything's just better when it's wrapped up in a neat little bow, don't you think?' Hands on hips, she nodded pointedly towards the small box in Olive's grasp containing her éclair and crumble. The shine on its dusky pink ribbon winked back at just the right moment, as though it should have been accompanied by a high-pitched *ping*. Annie made a mental note to research adding magical *ping*s to her powers when she had a spare moment. It could be a very cute detail.

Olive tutted. 'Go easy on this one, will you? They're all hapless victims as soon as they see you. I've witnessed it in here first hand more times than I can count. Have to feel sorry for them, really. Poor chaps.'

Annie rolled her eyes affectionately. 'I'm only giving as good as I get.'

'It's that shampoo you're using, I think. Must get the brand from you next time,' Olive muttered as she turned to leave. *Splendor Coma* was a spell that Annie had mastered at her dressing table on day dot – the very same afternoon that she had come into her powers at fifteen years old, before her mother moved her on to more important things. Just the right amount of volume, a calculated projection of shine. A never-sickly fragrance that lingered when she turned, sweet coconut and fresh vanilla. Even in drizzly London weather, her hair never dropped.

Annie held the door as Olive left clutching the little box. A damp fog yawned out across the early night, coating the cobbled street with a misty rain that fizzed on contact with the cold air. 'Any time you need to talk, Ol, I'm always here.'

Olive paused for a second to wrap a hand around Annie's. 'You're a real diamond, Annie. What would we all do without you?' She shook her hand tightly and sincerely. 'I'll see you in the week, duck.'

Annie snicked the brass bolt shut and, with a deep breath, leaned her forehead against the front door. The conversation with Olive had been heavy; heartbreak and loss and sadness clung to the tips of her fingers, tingling against her magic like opposing forces. But Annie only allowed herself a second of quiet to swallow it down.

She glanced at the grandfather clock in the corner of the cafe and wiped a rogue smear of chocolate from the back of her hand onto the hem of her apron that still hung untied around her. She was a little short for time considering she still needed to close down for the night, freshen up, then make her way to the restaurant . . . Annie's mouth twitched into the slightest grimace as she ran through her nightly to-do list, but in the blink of an eye, the smile returned. Luckily, her specialism in Incantation had always lent itself well to transformative magic.

She picked up speed on her way to the back room, gliding the cafe's billowy curtains along the brass rails as she passed. A cascade of pink magic fell as they closed. A couple of remaining cups, saucers and plates left by satisfied customers soared through the air as Annie passed by with a flick of her hand, soaking themselves in a sink of warm water, before shaking off like a wet dog and sliding back onto the wooden shelves. A mop wrung itself around a soapy bucket, before twirling its way across the floor like a ballroom dancer, leaving frothy bubbles in its wake. The chairs shuffled neatly under the tables as the tablecloths shimmied to shake themselves down. This was another reason it was often easier to close up without Faye and Pari: Annie's magic could lend a keen, quick hand when she was alone.

UNCHARMED

The small room to the rear of the bakery functioned as a storeroom, staff room and dressing room all at once for their team of three. The space was, at any given time, covered in Faye's endless stacks of music magazines and DIY mixtapes recorded from the radio. Or Pari's impressive and extensive graveyard of craft projects, each of which she would grow an obsession with and entirely lose interest in three weeks later. September had been spent making tiny clay animals, which were now perched on every possible surface like little pastel-coloured gobstoppers. It was cosy, mismatched and chaotic, much like their combination of personalities as a trio. But Annie couldn't resist sending a nudge of magic across the room to at least tidy up as she passed the armchairs, alphabetizing mixtapes and colour-coding miniature clay bunnies.

Her own little corner was separate. Behind the pretty antique dressing screen, Annie tapped her chin thoughtfully. She gazed at the rail of clothes before her and scrolled her magic through the row of dresses, each fresh and fluffed for this exact purpose. Faye and Pari always laughed affectionately at her makeshift dressing room. 'I wouldn't trust anyone other than Annie Wildwood to keep pink silk and vintage organza next to tubs of dark chocolate spread,' Pari had recently pointed out.

The pink dress tonight. Well, the slightly paler shade of pink dress. There were four of them, all lined up on velvet coat hangers from light to dark on the dress rail, with high heels placed underneath each one. Each pair had been gently enchanted with *Calceus Commodus* to be extra comfortable — the higher the heel, the more the spell kicked in to pleasantly numb her toes. She was proud of that handiwork; gradual magic was a tricky talent to keep fixed in place. Important, though. Who had time for aching feet to ruin an outfit?

With a quick flick of a wrist to summon her magic, smudges of whipped cream, buttercream, miscellaneous-but-equally-delicious cream all vanished, leaving Annie somehow even more immaculate than before. The pale dress with a ruffle around the skirt glided from its hanger to the dressing mannequin, to be styled with the appropriate accessories. Satisfied with her choices, another subtle gesture of magic traded her hot-pink Celeste overalls for the mannequin's night-time ensemble. Her apron swooped by the strings to hang itself on the door and the wooden spoon that she'd wedged in her back pocket at some point flew back to the kitchen like a paper aeroplane.

Annie glanced at the mirror, a beautiful gilded piece that had been her mother's. She could immediately see Cressida Wildwood preening in front of it, memories from childhood rippling in the glass. Her mother would always be adding more hairspray or admiring some form of luxurious accessory while Annie was wrapped around the doorframe, unnoticed. She would watch and yearn in secret, supposed to be asleep while her mother and father got ready for their evening out. She wondered where they were going each night, so mysterious and glamorous, her father slipping a proud arm around her mother when she finally declared that she was ready. The mirror was a reminder, now that she was in on the secret, of how far she'd come and everything that had been left behind.

An entirely unnecessary smooth of her hair, a cautious check of her clinking bracelets, a quick practice of her smile. It looked genuine. Whispers of faint magic clung to her skin with a glitter. Andromeda Wildwood simply adored being a witch. Not only did it come in handy multiple times a day, woven through each element of her life like a golden thread, but it was such a cute look for her. Being a witch was bright and fun – and Annie loved to be both of those things for everybody.

She took a second to steel herself, a final glance in the mirror to check that everything was just as it should be. It was. It always was. Her heart thumped a little louder, as though it wanted to be noticed, to remind her it was still beating.

She whispered under her breath: 'Perfect.'

Chapter Two

ROSES ARE RED

The restaurant was all overhead lighting and not nearly enough crusty bread with butter for Annie's liking. Anywhere that didn't take their bread seriously was not the place for her. Her mind wandered with longing to her Celeste rosemary loaf, the crystals of special salt scattered across the golden crust. She made the topping herself, the salt shards chipped away from charged citrine, the sunshine stone and clear quartz for a sprinkle of good fortune. Eating bread was always a good idea, but an even better one when it was lucky.

Her own luck for the evening seemed to have expired rapidly. Annie had found herself sitting opposite Cedric Reuben and his very enthusiastically lacquered hair. She had spent half the evening unable to take her eyes off it, so pale blond and shiny that it looked as if it was made of plastic, like a doll. It literally reflected the candlelight. Annie wondered whether it would make a hollow noise if she knocked on the top and did her absolute level best to resist finding out. She had listened patiently as he spoke at length about his influential father, the supermodel ex-girlfriends. He paused a fraction too long to hear her laugh at his jokes and he'd talked a lot about hedge funds, but Annie knew nothing about gardening. Even *her* stubborn optimism was struggling. He hadn't asked her a single question, other than an empty 'yeah, you?' every once in a while. She'd nodded and smiled for most of the conversation.

Not that it really mattered. She'd never have offered up anything like the truth to Cedric anyway, but it would have been nice to have the opportunity to use her favourite versions on him.

Her girlfriends were determined to play matchmaker and had been excited about this one, so Annie had dared to let herself be the tiniest bit optimistic. They had turned it into some kind of game over the years, hunting down (allegedly) eligible bachelors for her – although their definition of the term was one that she didn't fully understand. If she could have sped up time to escape the company she'd found herself sitting across from, she would have. But she certainly wasn't one to meddle with the rules against bending time, rewinding the past or speeding through the future. Time manipulation was strictly against coven rules and she had a stellar reputation among London's wicchefolk to uphold. It definitely wasn't worth the risk of messing with the non-wicche realm's time structure to escape a bad date. Was it . . . ?

But sending one man's personal timepiece temporarily haywire, like a simple battery malfunction? That felt okay.

'You're so mysterious,' Cedric crooned at her, with a smug smile that edged to one side.

Dire dates called for desperate measures and she had to act if she wanted to get home with enough time for *The Spell*. Her spell.

Resting her chin on her right hand, Annie barely batted an eyelash (or no more than usual, anyway) as she swilled her glass of rosé to cover the movement towards Cedric's watch. A delicate cord of pale sparks flew from her fingers, scattering themselves across the table like rolled dice. Fortunately, magic required a reasonable amount of imagination to be visibly seen by a non-wicche, and men such as Cedric had less than none of that to put to use. The hands of his watch suddenly picked up speed, winding forwards three hours on the platinum face, and Annie continued her routine. She lifted her glass to politely cover a yawn. Right on cue, Cedric was encouraged to glance at his watch and she saw his eyebrows shoot up in surprise.

'What on earth . . .' He blinked, dumbstruck. 'I can't believe it . . .'

'Time flies, doesn't it? I'd better get going.' She beamed at him, her best side directly in his eyeline. She didn't even have to consider these movements any more, they just happened of their own accord after so many years – a combination of magic and muscle memory.

'I swear we just got here. We're only two glasses down. We'll miss the oysters,' Cedric said, baffled. He gave her a frustrated bottom-lip pout, which made her feel slightly queasy. 'Do you really have to go?'

The man could barely hide his desperation, stumbling as he shot to his feet. As she daintily slid out of the booth, Annie almost felt bad for him. Then she recalled the last hour of her life, which could have been spent doing something infinitely more helpful or productive or successful, instead of blankly smiling at this insufferable man. She willed the last remaining dregs of her patience to the surface and felt the spell – her deepest, longest-running, innermost enchantment – bubble brightly beneath her skin. She plucked determinedly at the positive, patient thoughts that strung themselves together like a paper chain.

He meant well. Surely. People usually did.

'Sorry,' she giggled, to a tune that was apologetic and light. She picked up her clutch from the table, along with the single red rose that Cedric had arrived with. 'I can't tell you what a wonderful time I've had. Really. We'll do it again some time.'

'Tomorrow?' He swallowed, voice breaking like a teenager.

'Not tomorrow. But soon,' she replied kindly.

Gentle and comforting, Annie's rehearsed departure speech slid off her tongue like warm honey. She balanced the compliments to flatter against the gentle excuse that he could pretend wasn't even there. The noncommittal second-date plans were hopeful enough to cushion the blow and the reality of her rejection wouldn't land until he arrived home without her. She always made sure to say the right thing, the spell igniting on cue, the words adding themselves together in a formula for the correct answer.

'Let me walk you home. Or . . .' Cedric interrupted his own train of thought, then tripped over a chair leg as he skipped to follow her through the restaurant, leaving his belongings behind. 'I'll join you in a cab. We can share a night cap.' He gave Annie what she assumed was supposed to be a look of seduction as his hand reached for her upper arm. But his voice betrayed him again, more strained with every last-ditch attempt to persuade her. She offered another patient, sympathetic smile.

'Not tonight. Big day at work tomorrow.' Annie sighed, as

though it was breaking her heart to hold herself back. 'I'll call you.'

Cedric had turned a little green around the gills. She tapped him generously on the satin lapel of his heinous velvet blazer and left him powerless to do anything except watch her leave. Normally she'd allow him to call her a taxi, one last gentlemanly gesture to let him think he'd been everything a woman could ask for. But the date had worn her patience to the bone, her energy had been sapped after a long day at Celeste and tiredness was starting to blunt her pinpoint decisions.

Plus she'd left it a little late. She was cutting it fine to get home in time.

She tinkled a wave as she left Cedric looking entirely lost and forlorn, then seized her chance to disappear from view and slip into the bathroom. Finally, she could breathe again. She turned to the wall-sized mirror above the sinks for a perfunctory check that her curls had remained where they were supposed to. They had, of course. She checked whether her lipstick had smudged. It hadn't. If her mascara was running, if she'd lost an earring, if her nail polish had chipped . . . Glancing down, she noticed her knuckles had turned white from gripping onto the edge of the basin.

Her smile burst through again as she spoke to the reflection of the girl who had just wandered in and was now re-sliding a pair of plastic butterfly clips into her hair. 'Oh, wow! I love your dress. You look gorgeous.'

The girl beamed, the ego boost visible and vivid even in low lighting. 'Oh, thank you! Just high street, can you believe it? Such a steal.'

'You're kidding! It was made for you. Fits you like a glove,' Annie replied to the girl's reflection. Being the friendly girl in the bathroom was a role that she loved to play. She liked the idea of this woman going home and telling her friends that she'd met the sweetest girl. How she'd absolutely made her day. Every time she wore that dress, the girl would remember Annie and she'd feel good about it.

When the girl was gone and the coast was clear for magic, Annie blotted her lips on a paper towel and threw one last glance back towards the door. She twitched her fore and middle finger together. A gentle plume of blushing sparks blossomed from her hand, cascading in a pink swirl around her for transference.

In a fraction of a moment, the soles of her heeled pumps made a smooth landing on the wooden floor of her own hallway. Her curls bounced on impact and Annie shook her head to clear away the sickly, tugging feeling of instant travel by magic.

Through the hustle and bustle of the day, Annie yearned for precious quiet at home. She thought longingly of her sofa, her books, her pyjamas . . . And, for a moment, the arrival did bring relief – a quiet sense of calm and joy. But quiet meant that there could be no more distractions.

The smile switched off, the upturned curve became a straight line. A sigh. Her shoulders dropped, as though a button had been pressed, and she reached for the base of her neck to stretch it out. She kicked off her heels and padded barefoot to the living room, dropping her coat to the floor in a heap and discarding her jewelled earrings, shedding layers like a snake as she moved. She stood in the darkness, to measure how it felt. Alone again.

With a flick followed by a bright flash of pink, the TV turned on to fill the room with the drone of an antiques show and immediately the white noise fuzzed everything a little at the edges, made it all feel less consuming. Annie fired her magic at the frosted table lamps to bring a stroke of light to the living room and sent a handful of tiny flames across the scattering of fresh cotton-scented candles, purposefully selected to smell like a home full of care and cosiness.

The answering machine flashed red on the telephone table. Her heart whirled up into her throat, wondering who needed her now, and she nervously fiddled with the star-shaped charm on her choker necklace.

'Annie, it's Viv. Are you there? Do you ever answer this damned thing? What's even the point if you're never home to pick it up? Well, excuse me for taking the time to check in, darling. I shan't bother next time. Look, I'm having a total wardrobe crisis and I need you to . . .'

Annie lurched forwards to press the large delete button immediately. Shutting off Vivienne's voice was like catching a spider in a cup. She would call her friend back, she really would – but she needed to be more prepared for that conversation. Perhaps don a suit of armour first.

A cloud of fluffiness wrapped itself silkily around her bare ankles and Annie sighed gratefully, scooping the bright white bundle into her arms. The little cloud let out a disapproving mew that sounded a lot like, 'What time do you call this?' Annie buried her face into the impossibly soft fur, inhaling that powdery-clean scent of safety and love and connection that never failed to greet her when she arrived back home. It carried an important reminder that loneliness at least came with a set of small pink paws on the side.

'I'm so sorry, lady. I'm a little late, aren't I? We can't have that, can we, Karma?'

UNCHARMED

The bundle of creamy fur nuzzled back with a high-pitched chirp, contentedly perched in Annie's arms as she was carried to the kitchen. Karma was largely above such menial tasks as walking to her own food bowl, preferring to be formally escorted whenever possible. The bell on the pink ribbon around her neck jangled as Annie conjured the food. Karma curled her downy tail around her body before eating with excellent manners – for a cat. Annie gave her beloved, beautiful familiar a gentle fuss behind the ears, the silky softness instantly grounding her.

The connection between a witch and her familiar was a precious thing and incomparable. Not that Karma would ever admit such an attachment to a human. But the snow-white cat, with ice-blue eyes and velvety rose ears, was never far away and always seemed to know when Annie needed her. If it weren't for her familiar, Annie sometimes wondered whether she would just freeze and maybe even disappear altogether.

Annie returned to perch on the arm of the sofa, then slid down into the cushions. She let her mind go deliciously blank in front of the television, the sound and light blaring out while everything else blurred around her. The cascading linen drapes, the pale pink couch, the glass surfaces charmed to remain free of fingerprints (and pawprints). Exquisite. Although very small and understated compared to her friends' palatial homes, Annie's place always looked immaculate. Like a show home or a catalogue photograph. She made sure of it – never a coaster, cushion or crystal ball out of place. Even her witchery equipment matched the carefully selected aesthetic that she had put together so attentively, a pale gold cauldron sat plump in the hearth, filled with white pillar candles and a bouquet of fluffy baby's breath. Her home looked the part, beautiful to anyone who caught a glance.

Now that she was sitting still, words from her day at the bakery came back to cloud her mind. As soon as she started to worry about others, it was as though Annie had knocked over a bottle of ink across a handwritten page. The plume of storm cloud spread itself over everything and there was nothing she could do to stop it or make it feel less imperious. It was all she could see.

Karma, sensing the spiral as Annie's thoughts grew roots, leapt onto her lap. A feathery tail was wafted directly into her face and across her lipgloss, a gesture Annie knew was intended as comfort. Finally, a headbutt to the chin and a purring soundtrack pulled her back to the present and Karma settled.

Annie reluctantly switched herself back on and looked at the clock. Half an hour until midnight. She debated if she had time to complete anything else before the spell, otherwise it would be a very late night, even for her. There were mountains of studies to be completed for the coven as part of her second-year apprenticeship – the scrolls of parchment were threatening to burst from the cupboard that she stowed them in. And she still needed an appropriate outfit for tomorrow night. That would mean pulling out her sewing machine to create something exciting enough for the girls not to notice a re-wear. They'd never let her live it down if they knew that she'd dared reach for a favourite again or restyled something old to keep up with their fatally fashionable ways. The girls were always quick to call her out on such silly decisions.

Your friends keep your standards high. They stop you from making a fool of yourself. They always know what's best for you.

A long day, even in enchanted shoes, had brought Annie's energy levels to a crashing low. She'd need an extra boost of some special ingredients to combat tomorrow's tiredness, to regain the equilibrium required. Cedric's rose caught her eye, deep red against the light table top where she'd discarded it.

Reaching for the flower, Annie lay back against the arm of the couch, without disturbing a softly snoring Karma, and began to snap each petal from the crimson head. The fracture of each leaf from the stem felt like a small, sharp shock, as though she could hear each tiny break. Red rose petals would be a useful addition tonight. A little extra passion or achievement or desire in any form never went amiss in the spell – as long as she balanced it correctly to counteract the negatives. Maybe a touch of valerian or powdered moonstone for added calmness, humility, patience . . . No one liked a woman who shone *too* brightly.

Carefully shifting Karma onto the sofa and earning a disgruntled scowl in return, Annie dragged herself up to begin again. Time for her nightly tasks – the next round of requirements that she placed upon herself.

She winced. A sharp thorn from the stem caught on her fingertip and brought a bright drop of blood to the surface. Annie pressed a rose petal firmly against it to stem the flow, red blending into red. Such careless mistakes meant that it was definitely time to turn to the spell.

Chapter Three

CURTAIN UP

'Which jam for the scone stacks today, Annie?' Faye called over her shoulder as she rattled around the pantry on their very precarious ladder, moving aside stacks of Halloween decorations to get to the tiered cake stands. 'These bloody awful pumpkin buckets should not be in here. In fact, we should probably burn them. I think they might be cursed.'

Annie gasped, mildly offended. She took great pleasure in hunting through flea markets and car-boot sales to add to the array of Halloween décor for the bakery. 'They are not awful and they are certainly not cursed. Trust me, I'd know.' She muttered the last part under her breath. 'I think you'll find that they are vintage, kitsch and adorable.'

Faye remained unconvinced, brandishing one of the buckets with a scowl. 'This creep is winking at me. Kind of sleazy.'

Annie huffed as she took the pumpkin buckets from Faye and placed them on the table. 'Well, there's no point putting them in the basement now, is there? We're approaching Code Orange. Time to turn this place into a Halloween dream.' She gasped again, slightly higher-pitched this time, her brain working at a million miles an hour as always. 'That reminds me. We need to decide our costumes as a matter of urgency.' Annie tapped her whisk against the side of the mixing bowl then used it as a pointer at Faye, raining Chantilly cream across the kitchen. 'We'll be staying open late for No Tricks, Just Treats, so excellent outfits are a must.'

'I have never known anyone in their right mind to take Halloween costumes as seriously as you,' Faye said, looking at the boss with complete bewilderment.

'Fancy dress is not a laughing matter. If you're not going to do it properly then you shouldn't do it at all,' Annie said, deathly serious.

'Can't we just do something easy?' Faye said with a groan. 'How about Dracula? I can chuck on a bin bag and gel my hair back. It could be a very hot look for me. Or three witches? Double, double, toil and trouble. Thunder, lightning, rain and all that.'

Annie couldn't help but twitch. The three famous words happened to be her coven's calling card. And she could not, in good faith, wear a witch costume. She was far too cautious and overthinking to ever risk committing magical exposure; such silliness would certainly be flying far too close to the sun. 'Don't you think witches are a little overdone?' she said, laughing. 'Our usual cafe theme makes so much more sense.'

'Well, I'm not going as streaky bacon again. That *wasn't* a good choice. I looked like a flesh wound.' Faye's cropped, bright crimson hair was supposed to have been the ketchup.

'No breakfast platter trio this year?' Annie lamented. 'But I made such a cute pancake with my little butter hat.'

Faye rolled her eyes, but then conceded somewhat reluctantly, as she nearly always did. 'Pari *did* really enjoy being a fried egg and I don't want to break your fragile heart either. Fine,' she grumbled. 'We can do breakfast again. Don't leave me stuck with something ugly though. I'm not being baked beans and definitely not a mushroom. You'll have a field day with the "fun-guy" jokes and it'll make me want to commit a crime.' She scowled again, turning back to the cake stands, forever lovingly exasperated by Annie and Pari's relentless joy. 'Maybe a blueberry?'

Annie clapped her hands, jumping up and down on the spot and showering the worktop in yet more Chantilly cream. 'Yes! You'll look sensational in indigo. We'll go for exotic, international waters this time with American breakfast instead. I have a little beret you can borrow that would be perfect for a blueberry.'

'And other normal sentences that are only said in this bakery,' Pari said as she stumbled into the back room, her vision blocked by a swaying stack of cupcake trays to put away, having filled up the counter with fresh goodies. 'Why are we talking about blueberry berets?'

'Isn't that a song?' Annie asked, pausing mid-whisk.

'Unbelievable,' Faye muttered under her breath.

'You mean raspberry,' Pari said. After years of working together so closely, their unlikely trio of strange brains understood the workings of each other in mysteriously interconnected ways.

'Inspired! In that case, we'll have raspberry jam today,' Annie said decidedly to Faye, puffing as she returned to ferociously beating the bowl of cream. In the morning's chaotic coffee rush, she'd forgotten to revive the crucial self-whipping *Dulce Lac Turben* charm on her whisk before Faye arrived and was now paying the price with aching arms. 'I do not have the upper-body strength for this job,' she whined with a foot stomp.

'You are pathetic. What would you do in a zombie apocalypse?' Faye replied.

'Die and be glad of it,' Annie said.

'Probably for the best. You wouldn't enjoy zombies and their flagrant disregard for personal hygiene and seasonal colour palettes,' Pari said, turning her attention to untangling some black cat bunting in the overflowing Halloween box.

Faye continued rummaging through the homemade jams that were her personal speciality, hunting out the checkered-lid jars. For a slightly grumpy, extremely svelte music-head, she was an unexpectedly keen jam maker. Undoubtedly the more serious member of the Celeste trio, Faye generally brought the other two back down to earth when they got carried away with excitable ideas that were either impossible to pull off (without being aware of the existence of magic, anyway) or insanely expensive to execute. The crops of blackberries, elderberries and gooseberries on her and Pari's patio, along with scientific theories for their cultivation, were among the only topics of conversation that ever brought out Faye's giddy side. Making jams to perfectly curated mixtapes was her ultimate stress reliever.

'We were just discussing Halloween,' Faye said to Pari, stacking up the jars in her arms. 'Annie is keen for us to reprise the iconic breakfast costumes. But, I hasten to add, we are going meat-free this year.'

'Ooh, please can I be the egg again?' Pari asked with elated clasped hands.

'What did I tell you?' Faye said. 'Making dreams come true one day at a time here at Celeste.'

Faye and Pari had come knocking at Celeste two weeks after opening, spotting the pink striped awning with a queue around the corner each morning and the blonde girl somehow juggling everything alone. They'd strolled in, hand in hand, having been made redundant from a local Italian deli that had recently closed down. They were both amateur but decent bakers and had their upcoming wedding to pay for. Annie had practically bitten their arms off for the help, asking right there and then if they wouldn't mind checking on the triple chocolate chip muffins that she suspected may be burning while she wrestled with the coffee machine. As though they had always been on her side, Faye had stepped straight in to create the perfect ultra-frothy cappuccino and Pari had skipped into the kitchen to rescue the muffins. Annie's intuition told her that they were something special, the ingredients to add a final sprinkle of sugar to her place.

It had been one of the best decisions she'd ever made. Faye managed the caffeine and logistics and was only thriving more and more with ambition as demand grew. Meanwhile, Pari's endlessly warm personality and chatterbox nature made her a firm customer favourite. A whirlwind of a human, maximum energy compacted into her tiny height, Pari would often be at the counter while Annie busied herself with final flourishes to bakes in the background. Faye and Pari, of course, knew nothing of the sorcery involved in Celeste's secrets, but Pari had shown a few signs over the years that she had become rather tuned into the presence of magic. Her nose would twitch, as though she could smell something more intriguing than just fresh bread and caramelized fruit in the air. Sometimes, her big brown eyes would hone in on a rogue spark of magic if it was left lying around for too long, as though she were watching a butterfly take first, fascinating flight. Annie had learned to be particularly careful with her powers when she and Pari were working in close quarters.

'How are the cinnamon bun supplies looking?' Annie asked Pari.

'A bit sad. There's a couple left, but the mums and babies group at the church will be letting out any moment, so we can wave goodbye to any and all pastries then. I swear some would choose the croissants over their own babies.'

'Who wouldn't,' Faye grumbled.

Annie flicked a splat of cream at her for that. 'But we did extra! I thought they'd last until at least lunch time.' She sighed and thumbed her forehead, recalibrating at speed as her to-do list multiplied. 'Let me finish up on these scones and then I'll see if I have enough time to throw in some more dough for proving.' She mopped her brow on her sleeve after all the whipping, then reached for the punnets of strawberries to begin slicing. Once the girls were out of the kitchen, she could knit some spellwork to lighten the load.

'Reminder that you have to take your lunch break today, Annie,' Pari added, before she headed back out into the cafe, gathering up the bundles of fairy lights to string across the ceiling as imitation cobwebs. 'And coffee does not count as a food group. I'll make you a toastie.'

'Seconded. You were in early again, so make sure you leave early, too,' Faye added, patting Annie on the back as she followed Pari out, chucking a tea towel over her shoulder in an enviably cool way. 'I know that technically you're the boss and, hey, I don't make the rules, but I'm in charge on this one, okay?'

'I'm fine,' Annie smiled weakly. 'All under control.'

It soon would be, at least – once she'd completed the fiddly bits and bobs for the scones and finished folding in the *Memoria Laetificus* blend of nostalgia dust into the icing sugar. Each of the scones, layered up with comfort cream and Faye's heartfelt, homemade jams, were perfectly finished with a final dusting of treasured memories to talk about while they were eaten. Each bite sparked a darling memory – favourite toys, treasured grandparents, happiest reunions – that kept conversation flowing, warm and precious.

'All under *your* control,' Faye said with her usual scepticism. She was constantly reminding, sometimes ordering, Annie to share the workload. 'Let us help you. It's literally what we're here for.'

It wasn't that she didn't want to. She was desperate to and she knew that their talents would thrive with fuller roles at Celeste. But, through her whole life, Annie had felt unable to share anything that felt tricky. Or burdensome. As though she wasn't allowed to take her foot off the pedal. Only she could solve her problems in just the right way and asking for help or delegating meant admitting defeat. She was not the girl who admitted defeat and she certainly never let go. She had never let go of anything. She was the one who continued to impress, to hold on and handle it all.

She returned her concentration to spooning cream into individual ceramic bowls.

'Having said that,' Faye called back into the kitchen, 'don't leave me to do any of the actual cooking. As long as you prefer our customers being of an alive disposition, anyway.'

After a mild threat involving a spatula and an undisclosed location where the sun don't shine from Faye, Annie reluctantly left her and Pari to close up the shop – but not before putting together a box of apple pie for them to take home as a thank you, braided with a caramel crust and tiny, bronze-tinted autumn leaves pressed into the pastry.

Friday nights were always reserved in her diary with doodles in pink pen and organizational stickers, but the occasion also brought a strange, slightly shadowed dread to the pit of Annie's stomach. It was certainly not the time for relaxing or letting her guard down. But that wasn't necessarily a reflection on the girls.

It was her own fault – just the way she was in social situations. Tightly wound and second-guessing her responses, reflecting on all the ways that she'd embarrassed herself as soon as she got home.

Leaving Celeste under the musical tinkle of her brass doorbell, Annie hurried across the street, puddles beneath her feet reflecting orange orbs from the early evening street lights. Magical transference would have been the easier option at any other time of day, but schools were still emptying and the busy row of shops was bustling. With so many children around, highly attuned to all kinds of witchery, it wasn't wise to whip out magic on a whim. Instead, she attempted to hail a black cab. It was a process that took some time; three cabs were taken by others who arrived after her and she gladly waved them away, insisting they take them. A surprisingly chilly wind bit sharply at her nose while she waited. Autumn had shifted across London, the last of summer hurried along with the leaves. She was relieved when she could eventually close a cab door behind her, blowing warmth into her hands against the numbness that the cold had gloved them in.

'Tempest Theatre, please,' Annie called to the driver. He turned back to give her a look as though she had entirely lost the plot.

'What d'you want that dump for? It's falling to bloody bits, you know,' he asked in a strong Cockney accent. 'Got an 'ard 'at and a bulldozer in that 'andbag of yours?'

'Of course, girl power!' Annie chimed, with added peace sign. 'And a safety vest, so don't you worry about me, sir. Luckily, neon yellow is one to watch this season.'

The drive across London gave Annie a rare chance to pause, unable to distract herself with much other than clicking buttons on her pager once or twice. The sight of the city wearing its coat had a calming effect on her mind. Shades of brown and burnt orange streaked past like a smeared paintbox behind the rain droplets on the cab window, splashes of mustard and buttercup yellow to fill in the tops of the burnished trees with thick, rich colour. The whole city smelt like cinnamon and fireworks, bonfire and black pepper, witchery and wonder. Perhaps the rain was unwelcome for most, but for Annie it brought a translucent cloak to the city, blurred it all a little and softened the sharp edges of every day. Autumn was a feeling she longed for all year. She drew a tiny heart in the condensation in the corner of the window and watched a single, determined raindrop slide through it.

A flush of chestnut brown and tangerine-coloured trees appeared across the horizon, the shapes bold against the sunset as they entered through the gate of Richmond Park, the pathways stippled by muddy wellies and even muddier dogs. The taxi veered towards a left-hand path, partially obscured by thick, overgrown knots of bracken and woodland. The uneven ground rattled the endless amount of lip products at the bottom of Annie's bag.

'Shame they let this place go to rubble and dust,' the cab driver said as they pulled up, peering his head out of the window for a better look. 'My grandad had some old photos of *his* grandfather arriving outside, would you believe? Proud as punch to have a ticket. It meant you'd made something of yourself, if you could say you'd been to the Tempest Theatre. Don't make 'em like that any more, do we?' He tutted and wound his window back up.

'Oh, isn't it just dreadful. I'd give anything to see it in all of its glory,' Annie said as she counted out a tip from her purse.

'Noise complaints all the time, o'course, but the police never find anything. Bloody kids. Or squatters, I imagine. You be careful in there, miss,' he said and gave a friendly beep on his horn as he drove away.

Hidden within the dense, tangled outskirts of the park, the Tempest Theatre reclined in the shadows of the sycamores, overlooking a grand, algae-laced pond that often went unnoticed on the park maps. Once a grand and favoured music hall, a polished jewel in London's history, the place had been beloved by anyone lucky enough to experience its centuries of performance and pleasure. But, as times changed and the concert experience fell from favour, the building had eventually been abandoned, left to tumble quietly into disrepair. Now, the ivy cascaded down its facade like one final leafy curtain drop; its pretty face bore scars of relentless British weather. The billboard across the front had once proudly listed talented acts and top shows in block letters that lit up the park each evening in Hollywood lighting. Now, in faded letters, it simply read 'NOTHING TO SEE'.

Annie knew that this wasn't strictly true, however.

She checked over her shoulder, but the handful of people nearby were all far too distracted by the miserable weather. Hoods were pulled in front of faces, soggy dogs with ears scooted back tugging them home. A flock of geese came in to land, splashing across the lake in a flurry of feathers, and, just beyond, a pair of deer butted their antlers together in a clash, putting on their own show before the theatre. The perfect distraction.

Cringing at the strained squeak of metal construction sheets and old hinges, Annie carefully pushed open the door.

Inside, dust and debris scattered the old foyer like a sprinkling of flour. The windows were boarded up and blocked any daylight from making its way in, as though the theatre herself were shy and couldn't possibly permit anyone to see her in such a state. Teetering in her heels with every careful step across splintered wood and chipped tiles, Annie made her way further in. Past the abandoned ticket booth, the gilded detail flaked away like worn make-up. Past the old cigarette machine, past the long-empty ice-cream stand and the peeling posters, all advertising upcoming concerts that were a hundred years ago. The click of her shoes pierced the quiet and, somewhere far above in the high rafters, a bird flapped its wings in a gust.

She held on tightly to the brass stair rail, its shine long dulled, and carefully made her way down into the main auditorium. Annie couldn't help but smile to herself every time she descended the crescent staircase. She found magic in it, a moment that made her want to gather her skirt like some kind of dramatic princess. In books and films, she'd be dressed in a ballgown that looked like an ornate cream cake, gliding her way towards a handsome prince with a hand outstretched. She had to stop a self-conscious, snorted giggle every time and settled for singing a nostalgic fairy-tale tune to herself as she headed down.

The concert hall was an eerie, cavernous space that seemed to breathe in and out all by itself, a curled-up dragon guarding hidden treasure, the place alive with the power of memories. It made Annie feel impossibly small, like a tiny spinning dancer set inside a music box. The silence made her want to shout into it, as loud as she could, almost to reassure herself that she was really there. She never did, of course. Rows and rows of crimson seating lined the stalls, each one balding and threadbare, coated in a layer of dust so thick Annie could have written her name in it. And above, remnants of a starry night sky painted in every shade of royal blue, navy and sapphire. Water damage sprawled and stained its way across the ceiling and an enormous, cobweb-coated mirrorball loomed at the centre.

Right on cue, there were the goosebumps. They chased one another across her skin, her heartbeat quickening as each of her senses began to ignite at what was to come. The taste of a coppery sweetness spread between her teeth from the stale, shadowy air. The earthy, musty scent mixed with burnt embers, probably damage somewhere by vandals – but a sweetness of toffee apple too that still lingered from the past. The Tempest Theatre always gave her the shivers.

Although, of course, that could just be the witches.

She reached the main concert stage. The piano sat plump and sprawling at the centre, the stage bowing under its vast weight. She lay her right hand across the keys, pink nails stark against the yellowing ivory, and tinkled them in the correct order. It was a melancholy sequence that she'd been taught years ago by her mother and father and would never forget, the combination always sounding so powerful. Magical.

With the final note, a sprinkling of magic sprayed from Annie's fingertips as though her powers were called forth from her body to the piano. The pink stars tumbled into the spaces between the keys, slipping through the cracks. For one exquisite moment following the music, it felt as though time stopped still, slowing even the dust that danced across her vision on the stagnant air, moths pirouetting in tiny movements.

Then, like clockwork, the painted stars in the ceiling fresco caught a glint of light that hadn't been there before. Each one twinkled in the blue darkness, one after the other, and carried the musical notes that Annie had just played through the room. Starry shapes cascaded across the seats below as the mirrorball began to spin. It sent new light across the theatre, illuminating every part of the music hall from the galleries to the foggy panes of glass in each door. The contrast from dark to light was almost blinding as it built. Squinting, a hand up against the glare, Annie saw the golds become gold again, extra dazzling. The crimson velvet returned to rich red. The stage was restored, piano polished to its former glory.

Then the seats across the stalls began to rearrange themselves, the neat rows spinning into separate, seated groups. Elegant tables shot up from the floor and were topped with emerald green glass lamps, ornate crystal drinkware, tiny bowls of plump olives, sparkling sugared nuts.

And in the final flashes of mirrorball light, the seats began to fill. Ghostly figures, each one changing from translucent, iridescent outlines that caught in the light, to fully formed people . . . Witches, warlocks and wicchefolk revealed.

Annie smiled, relieved as she was each time the magic of the theatre generously accepted her back into its arms. There it was, just as she left it. The Sorciety.

Chapter Four

GIRL TALK

The Sorciety was absolutely never to be confused with anything as common as a coven.

Selcouth, the coven of the United Kingdom to which Annie had been welcomed, was accepting and open to any and all witches, warlocks or wicchefolk. It was true that Selcouth had its own contentious methods of acceptance that it went to great pains to uphold for the purposes of tradition, namely a fifteen-year-long process of endarkenment that came to an end either successfully or unsuccessfully on a witch's thirtieth birthday. But the Sorciety was altogether a more underground, secretive affair. In fact, the average witch (riff-raff, as Sorciety members kindly referred to them) would look back with a blank expression if she were to ever be asked about its existence. Only a select few would know the signal; to simply call it 'fairy stories' and hum the opening notes of the Tempest Theatre under their breath.

Strictly reserved for those deemed worthy, wicchefolk within the Sorciety's closed club circle had long ago declared themselves the 'spellborn'. It was a title that, as far as Annie could tell, seemed to be dictated mostly by inherited magical influence, which, more often than not, came alongside inherited magical wealth. Prospective members were nominated and vetted only by existing members, before facing the long and magically taxing process of initiation – elaborate ceremonies, demanding interviews and considerable donations.

With its supernatural accumulation of magic and money, the club had centuries ago become a source of influence over the innermost fabric of the magic system. The fully fledged spellborn held knowledge and insight that was not to be shared openly among a standard coven and its undignified general-entry policy. Decisions were made at each full moon symposium that would eventually filter down to the lives of average wicchefolk. Wealth begets wealth, even within magical realms, and among the Sorciety's most prized secrets was the ability to invest their powers and create private, snowballing funds of magic to be distributed among their select few – and never shared elsewhere. From an accumulation of power only comes a need for more, so the snake had continued to consume its own tail for centuries.

'Annie, darling! How did it go with Cedric?'

Romily peered over her coupe glass as Annie finished making her way through the busy auditorium. Romily Whitlock was not a witch to waste time on small talk or pleasantries when there was fresh gossip to be harvested.

'Who?' Annie called, taking the spare seat in their ring of plush chairs. The five girls exchanged neat air kisses, one on each cheek, without actually touching. Never one to turn up empty-handed, Annie placed a box of immaculately iced biscuits, all decorated like autumn flowers, on the table and encouraged them to dive in.

'Last night? Constance's friend's cousin's associate? I know he's a non-wicche,' Romily continued, wrinkling her nose up at the last part. 'But, despite that blot against his record, she was confident that you two would make a gorgeous pair. He's in hedge funds – loaded apparently.'

'Annie, I knew things were dire for you, but do not tell me you dated a hedge witch,' Vivienne scoffed to Harmony, who shrieked a laugh at the idea. 'Frightful practice. Can you imagine choosing plants and actual dirt as the means to express your magic? Constant soil underneath your nails? So unchic.'

'No, it's magical investment and trading strategies, but, like, for non-wicche,' Romily explained, giving them a deeply judgemental side-eye as she swirled the dregs of her drink.

'Of course, Cedric.' Annie felt a guilty, jarring flashback from last night. She'd forgotten her time at the restaurant with him, what with everything else that was constantly fighting for her headspace. 'Right, right . . . He was lovely.'

Harmony prompted her, eyebrows high. 'But?'

Annie sighed. 'But . . .'

'There it is,' Romily huffed, chastising but at least entertained as she accepted one of the fresh cocktails promptly delivered by a waiter. Annie leapt to her feet to hand them out from the silver tray, making sure they each received their signature choice.

Annie had spent her childhood years with Romily as her very best, most precious friend, the pair of them growing up inside each other's velvet-lined pockets. They had made muddy pondwater potions at the bottom of their gardens together. Dressed up dolls in tiny witch hats, begged their fathers to enchant brooms on Sunday afternoons for them to fly about the attic. They had worn matching pyjamas and identical dressing gowns, waited on the landing and gawped together in secret at their beautiful parents gliding through life with matching cigarette holders and amber glassware. Their years of shared girlhood had been powerful enough to entwine them for a very long time. Annie still held the memories fondly, precious and delicate.

But something had altered in Romily's deepest chemistry when her teenage years reared their head and, with them, the arrival of real magic – and secondary school – to complicate things further. The hallways of Aconite Academy led her towards Vivienne Cinder and Harmony Morningstar, who had been altogether rather indifferent about Annie, but fawned over Romily's calm confidence, golden aura and familial reputation of wealth and importance. Her mother's supreme position at the Sorciety spoke for itself and earned untouchable status for her daughter. It had given Romily a new kind of poise and unwavering assurance, her youth and fragility vanishing in a moment. Next to Romily, Annie was simply someone ready to be moulded, happy to provide useful hair-related spell secrets that they could call upon. Even then, she was already eager to please. In return, the girls had tucked away their talons and swept her up under their silken wings. Through equal parts bitterness and reverence, their classmates had coined them the 'Fortune Four' and Romily in particular had revelled in the idea. The tag had stuck ever since.

They were her closest friends in the wicche realm and, after Annie's home life fell apart so unexpectedly a few years later, she remained endlessly grateful that they had not turned their backs on her.

Fortune Four nights had recently expanded to include a fresh member of the Sorciety: Ruby Wrathshade, whose family had moved from America and had been accepted thanks to their newly accumulated wealth in the modernized broomstick trade. They had deftly spotted a broom-shaped sales space in the freshly emerging so-called 'internet'. Ruby eyed her slushy, bright-blue, floral creation suspiciously, then promptly stuck her fingers in to fish out the floating thistle garnish and flick it from her fingertips. 'Do you guys have any coffee?' Ruby asked the waiter, but he simply twitched his skinny moustache and left with a haughty spin. Harmony, lifting a bubbling champagne flute, seemed repulsed by Ruby's every move and was doing a terrible job at hiding it. Her own drink was a loud neon yellow and fizzed with an over-enthusiastic ferocity as though it had got a little carried away with itself.

'I'm sorry. I know . . . I can't help it,' Annie said, batting her hand apologetically.

'Annie, we line up bachelor after bachelor for you, each more handsome than the last, and they're never good enough,' Romily continued.

'It's never that they're not good enough,' Annie replied, quick to justify her actions. 'They're all perfectly nice chaps, in their own ways. And I'm so grateful that you take such an interest in trying to set me up with someone special. I know you're all trying to help. It's just that . . .'

'It's just that they're not bloody *perfect*,' Vivienne groaned, never one to enjoy the softer, romantic angle of anything. Gossip was considerably less interesting to Vivienne Cinder when any genuine feelings were involved. 'I'd get a move on if I were you, Annie.' She sighed dramatically. 'No offence, it's not like you've reached hag status just yet. But there's always a younger witch just waiting to step out of the shadows and take your place – and your warlock. It was us once, right? Harmony's favourite hobby, in fact.'

'They're fun to play with,' Harmony giggled.

'You're dating, huh?' Ruby asked Annie as she began to rummage through the box of biscuits. Harmony continued to look entirely horrified by Ruby's existence, particularly as she took two biscuits before deciding to add a third for luck. 'What?' Ruby paused to ask Harmony indignantly. 'You said we were going for dinner. Cocktails do not equate to dinner, you know.' She turned back to Annie. 'The way these ladies talk, I was beginning to think that anyone single and over the age of twenty-five around here was resigned to the Old Crone shelf.'

'I shouldn't think you could call Annie's escapades *dating*,' Vivienne snorted.

'She tries her best,' Romily said with a pitying headshake.

'The folks around here aren't particularly appealing to me either. Unless you've got a thing for warlocks who wear cravats, you're screwed,' Ruby said. 'The guys all look like they're carved from soap. Or maybe grown in a lab. Are they the result of some sort of teenage dream boyfriend enchantment?'

'Annie's been desperately dreaming of her Mr Right since we all started at Aconite together,' Harmony said chirpily, as though sharing a fun fact.

'Alas, it's only ever Mr Fright,' Vivienne said.

'I'm sure Ruby doesn't want to hear about my utterly calamitous love life,' Annie laughed, waving away the subject before it could claw itself too firmly into the room. She was already starting to feel her face warm with embarrassment. She held the back of her hands against her skin to try to cool it down. 'Is it hot in here?'

'There's been a few warlocks over the years, but she always seems to end up with a broken heart, don't you, babe?' Vivienne said, not gentle in her tone or expression. 'And here we are, still no rock on that finger. It must be getting cold without one.'

'We're constantly trying to set her up with every gorgeous warlock we can think of. We've even moved on to non-wicche now – and still no luck,' Harmony said softly, pouting as she patted Annie on the knee, her own ring emblazoned with an obnoxiously massive emerald that caught the mirrorball lights. 'It's the least we can do. Planning weddings is honestly *such* fun. You're missing out, Annie. I don't know why you don't just find someone!'

Annie smiled serenely. 'I'm fine as I am. Everything is just fine.'

'It'll happen when you least expect it,' Romily said with a cool nod. She leaned back and swilled her frosted martini, studded with pale fruits that looked as though they were made of glass.

'One witch's spinsterhood is another witch's independence,' Vivienne said. 'But we totally admire your tenacity, Annie. You'll catch up. Who needs a hubs? Take mine, if you'd like. Half of the Sorciety seems to. Fortunately, his money and magic remain firmly mine if he wanders too far.'

'You're so brave,' Harmony said with wide eyes at Annie, surprisingly sincere with her condolences considering almost everything that left Harmony Morningstar's mouth was carved backhanded by a double-edged sword.

Annie laughed. 'Again, thanks, Harm. But I am the polar opposite of brave.'

'Look at you,' Harmony said admiringly. 'You're wearing suede in the winter months. You're totally brave.'

'She's right, Annie. To be on your own,' Vivienne said, 'especially with things still so . . . *precarious* for you.' She emphasized 'precarious' with a pointed eyebrow. Her voice dripped with so much white-hot pity that it felt like spots of acid rain that Annie should have thrown up an umbrella to.

'I wouldn't say precarious,' Annie said, inhaling to push down the flood of uncomfortable feelings that the conversation was starting to crack open.

They didn't mean it the way it sometimes felt. They loved her. She was always the first one at the end of the phone line on a bad day, when they needed to talk about their problems and offload them onto willing ears. She was part of the gang. They truly cared about her, were always so supportive.

The spell reminded her to keep herself in check when too much of their company started to make her skin itch.

'You know. Since your dad,' Harmony stage-whispered, as though she were embarrassed to say it out loud. Harmony's eyes darted to both Romily and Vivienne, tripping over herself at the prospect of opening up their favourite topic of conversation. It hurt, but Annie understood the interest. Scandals like theirs didn't happen often.

'Am I missing something? What'd your old man do?' Ruby asked after a loaded pause. She snapped another ginger biscuit in half and used it to point across the circle between them.

'It's nothing. All a very long time ago,' Annie replied, giving the girls a look she hoped would signal to steer the subject somewhere else.

Vivienne gave a dry laugh. 'Rubes is going to find out sooner or later. It gets brought up at practically every symposium, even after all these years. Annie's dad was . . . well, he's not exactly a revered and respected member of the Sorciety like the rest of our fathers.'

'Not a member of any kind. At all, in fact,' Harmony said between giggles and Vivienne spluttered in return, both covering their mouths as though to chastise themselves.

'Harm, don't be unkind,' Romily said. Harmony sulked with a flounce. 'It was terrible for Annie of course, wasn't it, babe? But the whole thing was maybe even more awful for the rest of us. I still can't believe what he put us all through, making the whole Sorciety suffer. And your poor mother. Just dreadful.'

'Sounds to me like complicated family stuff. Probably isn't anyone else's business,' Ruby said, directly to Annie rather than to the circle. Annie gave her a weak smile.

Vivienne interrupted. 'I'm afraid Griffin Wildwood made it *everybody's* business when he started gambling his supply of sacred magic, as though it were a handful of dirty pennies. Honestly, Annie, I still don't know how you've lived it down. The thought of him tossing his and your magic around in all those revolting wraith lairs. Mortifying, truly.' Vivienne rested her chin on her fist, a twinkle in her eye.

'Endless rumours, the Wildwoods' magic stocks rising and plummeting so sharply . . . Suspicions were raised. Even Selcouth knew something was afoot and we all know they're useless,' Harmony prattled on, leaning so far forwards into the circle that she was almost bent in half. 'Can you even imagine?

It put our whole existence at risk. The *coven* could have discovered us. We really had no choice. My own father worked on the case, he told me everything. All the gory details.'

'Much surveillance later and guess what? The Sorciety discovers that not only was he losing his own precious magic at careless, breakneck speed, but Cressida and Annie's, too,' Vivienne said.

Romily sipped calmly and quietly, as though she were lamenting the whole situation afresh. 'Gambling his own wife and daughter's magic. Can you even believe it? Such loser behaviour.'

Annie stayed quiet and picked at the iced detail on a biscuit marigold, the girls' voices muffled in her head as though she were hearing them from underwater. She crumbled a sugar petal between her fingers.

'His days here were numbered after that, of course,' Vivienne concluded, stirring her short, honey-coloured cocktail with her finger in mid-air. Although over ice, the drink smoked dangerously in her palm, like a fire had just been put out inside the glass.

'That's . . . Wow, that's awful,' Ruby said.

'Isn't it just? I mean imagine risking the Sorciety like that. Something so prestigious and sacred, that's been running the magical hierarchy for centuries. So reckless,' Romily replied. Although not quite so unbridled as the other two, even she was purring as the gossip sparked and caught fire.

Ruby gave Romily a baffled look. 'No, I mean awful for Annie. I'm sorry that happened to you.'

Annie shrugged it off, still smiling. 'No need to apologize. Not too much of my magic was lost, thankfully. The same can't be said for my mother's powers but . . .' She pushed down the bundle of memories that began to unravel itself. Stumbling, smashed glasses, slurred excuses, blurry apologies. 'Mum and I were used to things falling apart and having to build them back together. He was an unpredictable man at the best of times.'

Although she knew it wasn't her fault that her father had fled – she was a grownup who could acknowledge that other grownups made their own decisions of free will – Annie couldn't help but still feel a strange responsibility for Griffin's choices. It burdened her, even now, so many years later. It was a childlike part of her that she knew was formed from hurt, but that knowledge didn't make it any easier to ignore that tugging question: *What if?*

What if she had behaved differently, been a better daughter, a more impressive, perfectly polished apple of his eye? Perhaps he wouldn't have done the things he did. Perhaps she could have saved him, pulled him back from the brink. Years later, such an unanswered, whispered possibility clung to the walls of her mind like condensation in the cold.

'What happened to your mom?' Ruby asked.

The question that Annie always dreaded being asked – when she had to weigh up whether to lie or to dump the uncomfortable, ugly truth onto somebody she barely knew. 'Strange things happen to a witch whose magic is taken from her,' Annie said quietly. 'She tried her best, but she couldn't cope. She . . . she left to find him when I turned eighteen and never came back.'

Guilty by association with her husband's misdemeanours, Cressida had faced the chop from the Sorciety without so much as a chance to defend herself. She took it admirably well – at least publicly. Privately, she began to wither in all ways, a hollowed spirit of the radiant woman that Annie had been in awe of her whole life.

'That's rough,' Ruby replied gently, mouth squashed to the side in a diagonal line. 'Families are messy.'

'Speak for yourself,' Harmony said. 'My family is rather neat and tidy.'

'Blood is thicker than water,' Vivienne said smugly. 'And magic is thicker again.'

'Always hated that phrase – usually tossed around by people who've never been let down by someone who's supposed to put them above all else,' Ruby said, brushing biscuity hands on her jeans. 'From what I've learned over the years, families are never as shiny as they seem.'

The three witches looked at Ruby as though she had suddenly started speaking in tongues, a mixture of bewilderment and aversion on their faces. Annie heard Harmony mutter a quiet 'Ew'.

'Anyway,' Romily said firmly, twirling the stick of glass-like fruit in her drink. 'We've all moved on, haven't we, Annie? You've done such a wonderful job at rebuilding what they left of the tattered Wildwood reputation.'

'I don't know about that,' Annie winced, spinning her own frothy, shimmering pink cocktail by the stem of the glass. 'I'm just trying to not let anybody down. I'm forever grateful to still be welcome here and that you all stuck by me when you didn't have to.'

'As I keep telling you, patience is a virtue, babe,' Romily said and gave her a wink. 'You're doing so well in your role at Selcouth and everyone here enjoys you immensely. You'll earn your Crescent one of these days.'

Annie's ears pricked up. 'Is there any word on that? Has

your mother mentioned anything? I know you said you were going to try to put a word in . . .'

Of the six significant families who governed the club, the Whitlocks, Cinders and Morningstars were half of them and Romily's mother was the Supreme Herald at the helm of it all. They were yet to use their influence to help Annie win Crescent status at the Sorciety, the fully fledged membership that she was still desperate to secure to protect herself. As she spoke, all three seemed to flash their pins in unison, silver emblems of an overflowing cauldron wrapped in a pin-sharp crescent moon. Abundance and secrecy, the Sorciety's most precious values.

Romily pulled a sad face at Annie. 'Haven't had a chance, babe. Honestly, between the solstice cruise and planning the Sorciety fundraisers for All Hallows, I've been run off my feet. I'm seeing Mummy for lunch next week so I'll try again then, if she's in a good mood.'

Annie was embarrassed to admit it now at thirty-two, but she had never questioned the Sorciety's existence while growing up wrapped in its enticing caress. It was only when the Wildwoods fell dramatically from favour that it had opened her eyes, made her question its nature – and whether the claims of the spellborn could truly be considered fair.

As a child, she (often hand in hand with Romily) had dreamed of the night that her mother and father would include her in their surreptitious evenings. Alongside the Whitlocks, they would disappear for nights in their finery, leaving the girls with a nanny and a kiss on the head. There was never any explanation of where they were going. Her mother only ever whispered one clue to her, over and over, that had inked itself into Annie's young mind: 'To where everything is perfect.'

When she had finally been allowed to peer behind the curtain and join them in the Sorciety, Annie had blindly fallen in love with the beauty of it all, the way everything shone, the splendour matching up to her mother's promise. Being included and accepted was too fragile a feeling to tinker with. Now that she was older and (allegedly) wiser, it was one of several problems with the magic system that felt unsettling.

But she was tangled in a sticky velvet spiderweb, one that kept her trapped within delicate silver strings, but still ensured she felt held and supported. The Sorciety was the closest thing she had to a family. Its fickle world could often leave her feeling lonely, but without it, she was truly alone. She owed them everything. She couldn't let them down.

Annie just smiled.

'You know we always do what's best for you, Annie. Apart from all of that nonsense in the past, you're absolutely perfect,' Romily added, raising her glass.

'I didn't think the Sorciety had room for much compassion. How come they let you stay after all that crap with your parents?' Ruby asked. Before Annie could answer, Vivienne jumped in on her behalf.

'Annie's a useful girl to have around the place, aren't you?' Now it was Vivienne's turn to wink at Annie. 'They just love her over at the coven, so she's a handy contact for the Sorciety. Keeps an eye on things for us, new witches and warlocks who make themselves known, any changes in stance or unrest beginning to rise – we're the first to know. She's our very own super sleuth sorceress.'

It all felt precariously interlinked, like a dainty paperchain; its beauty was reliant on her perfect performance.

Romily smiled fondly. 'Never one to let us down, are you, babe?'

Annie smiled, pleased to have found herself firmly on their good side. No, she wasn't.

Chapter Five

A PERFECT PACT

'There you are, girls.'

Annie's gaze shot around from her conversation with Ruby about dabbling with the idea of her very first broomstick – was there ample luggage space? Plenty of the Sorciety had stopped by over the course of the evening, the charms of the Fortune Four always drawing a crowd to flirt and to share stories at their table, but this was the voice that every club member hoped to hear all evening. It was the one that proved that you truly mattered.

'Mummy!' Romily sprang to her feet and promptly placed a kiss on each of her mother's cheeks, squeezing her upper arms fondly. 'They were out of the punch you like, but I ordered you a cherry liquor instead, which I think . . .'

'I loathe cherry, darling. Why in all realms did you get that?'

She dismissed her daughter to turn back to the circle with a dazzling smile. Annie caught the trail of Romily's hurt and disappointment like smoke for a fraction of a moment, before she shook it off as Glory Whitlock joined their table, her presence so overwhelmingly magnetic that Annie could almost feel her body pull physically towards her.

Knowing Glory since she was a child, she had always experienced this side effect of a witch who held such vast magic. As one of the most longstanding magical families, the Whitlocks' power investments were prodigious and electric, their wealth outstripping any of the other five Herald families. Glory walked the forceful and mighty line of being equal parts wildly charismatic, classically gorgeous and absolutely terrifying. Being on her good side felt like stepping into a circle of sunlight; her bad side felt like the coldest, darkest shadow.

'How was the Heralds' meet, Glory?' Annie asked.

Glory stroked Romily's hair into place as though she were a doll. 'Oh, they're all frightful bores. Harmony, you really must tell that father of yours that parties are about more than just logistics and operations, darling. These warlocks love nothing more than the sound of their own voices while they drone on and on about the magic budget.'

'That sounds like Daddy alright,' Harmony said with a conspiratorial smirk. Her father, Barnaby Morningstar, was a sallow, weasel-like man who worked as numeromancer for the Sorciety. He was the quieter half of the Morningstars, alongside Harmony's mother, Alette, a beguiling and beautiful part-witch-part-siren who outshone him in every way possible. In well over a decade of membership, Annie had only ever heard him speak about either the grand cosmic budget or Harmony crashing his car.

'I don't think he's quite forgiven me for last year,' Glory replied. 'The scale of the Halloween fireworks alone had to be covered up with magic that almost wiped out the supply across London for weeks. But that's not my problem. That's what I'm paying them to handle.'

UNCHARMED

'But the Samhain Ball, Mummy?' Romily asked hopefully.

Glory tutted. 'Well, obviously, darling. You girls know you can rely on me to make sure that it's celebrated in style. Why bother at all if you're not going to go bigger and better than last year?' She gestured for the girls to lean in closer, as though keeping a great secret. 'And between us, I'm planning something very, very special for All Hallows. The forecasts are showing unrivalled magical potency this Halloween, the likes of which haven't been seen for centuries. We shall be sure to make the most of it. No expense spared. A treat for us all to indulge in.'

'Oh!' Annie exclaimed, clapping her hands. 'That's so exciting.'

'I know you know the importance of a treat, Annie. And this one will be sensational,' Glory said with a glint in her eye. 'Come on then, tell me about the wonderful things you're all doing.'

'We've been to visit the spa spirits, universe knows it was needed. Apart from Annie, of course. She's been working *very* hard at her menial labour,' Vivienne said, sarcasm dripping as she peered across the circle.

'So determined, aren't you, Annie?' Glory declared. 'Admirable in this day and age to find that in a witch. You're very like your father in that way, something to prove to the world.'

Annie froze and let her eyes flutter closed as she took a breath. That was the only line that ever made her truly falter. The one stretch of her miraculous levels of patience that made them snap back into place like a tight elastic band.

People don't know how much it hurts to hear. It's not their fault. You're overreacting.

'Anything we can do to help with the plans, Glory. Please just let us know,' Annie said.

Glory sighed as though the weight of the world were resting on her. In some ways, at least in the magical realm, it was. 'You just make sure you're keeping us ahead of the curve with that coven, Annie. Being aware of their movements has never been so crucial. If it were up to me, you know I wouldn't make you mingle with all that cursed riff-raff at Hecate House, but I hear they have a new watchman in place who could royally ruin things for us if he were to glance in the wrong direction. So for the good of the Sorciety . . .'

'You don't need to worry about that. I wouldn't let you down,' Annie said. 'I know you're relying on me.'

Over the many years of Annie's friendship with Romily, Glory had in many ways provided a second home to her. She had watched over her when Annie's parents had left her behind, and Annie had grown up under her gaze, albeit a distant one. She would always be grateful to Glory for that.

Glory reached out a motherly palm, gentle against Annie's cheek, and her expression softened fondly. 'You're a good girl, Annie.'

Annie left after a second cocktail. Tiredness was beginning to seep into her shoulders, the spell fading in potency. It was far too late to wait for a taxi in the midst of Richmond Park. Fortunately, magic could step in to carry the load and her home's pink front door was behind her in a moment. She tried to remind herself that it wasn't so bad to be alone when the silence wrapped itself around her in a thick scarf. She'd be wishing for it once the spell began again.

UNCHARMED

Once Karma had been suitably fussed, fed and escorted to the window to begin her viewing of the foxes who liked to stalk the pavement, Annie could begin her own nighttime ritual.

She closed the bathroom door to ensure that the cat wouldn't follow behind her. The one and only time that Karma had inadvertently seen the spell in motion, she'd started to hiss as soon as the steam rose in its ghostly tendrils, unsure of what was unfolding, but her feline instincts certain that it wasn't good news. Before Annie could comfort or reassure her, Karma had retreated under the bed with her back arched, her already enormous white tail puffed out to three times its volume. Once the spell was over and Annie had seen the final dregs drain safely away, it had taken an entire spoonful of custard to coax Karma out from under the bed and win back her love. She rarely set paw in the bathroom any more.

Every witch needed her altar – a purposeful place for her craft – and this was hers, where no one else was allowed. An uncharacteristic décor choice for Annie, decidedly non-pink nor fluffy, the bathroom was a darker space. The walls were lined from floor to ceiling with wooden apothecary cabinets, the glass doors stained in moody colours that depicted a tangle of spiked bracken and winter flowers, poppies and hellebores. Each cupboard door was firmly locked against visitors, doubled down with both security magic and a physical key that could only be summoned from her mind – a nifty incantation that she'd recreated from the coven's own security measures. An antique chandelier of glassy droplets hung from the ceiling above the bathtub. Annie cast her magic towards it to grant each candle branch a tiny flame. She took a moment to breathe, leaning against the door, reassuring herself that she didn't need to rush. Things would soon be back under control.

She padded over to the sink, lighting the rest of the candles around the room, and cast *Venustas Tergeo*, an incantation she'd perfected as a teenager to remove her make-up instantaneously. Her self-care ritual was the most sacred part of her day, glossing and plumping herself to a mirror glaze that would rival the sugar donuts at Celeste. Annie took a moment to examine her face as closely as she could in the mirror, pulling the skin tighter at the sides, lifting her brow a fraction higher to where it used to be. It was one of the stranger parts of getting older; the moments of realization that her face really was starting to change, teenage features fading while faint pencil lines began to sketch themselves around her eyes and forehead. That was, at least, when the spell began to wear off. She would rarely go long enough between topping it up to allow these things to fully take effect.

Eager to begin, to feel *right* again, Annie turned on the brass taps of the bathtub. A heady, fragrant mist plumed from the hot water as it flowed, the whole room fogging around her. Each cabinet was bursting to the brim with lotions and potions, pots and powders, bubbles and broths, like a blooming flower field for her to reach into and choose from. It felt a lot like picking flowers, knitting the spell together, snapping stems and plucking petals that were perhaps best left well alone. A flower picked for its perfection would soon begin to wilt, fading in a carefully considered bouquet made to be admired.

But every time that doubt crept in, she remembered her mother. The spell was a rite of passage among the Wildwood women through history. Cressida had been keen to induct her daughter as soon as her magic came to blossom, determined that Annie wouldn't spoil all that she had spent her life curating. She thought her young daughter had a habit of ruining things with silly slip-ups.

Annie dabbled and debated between bottles of nectars and vials of elixirs, pulling out refined combinations of favourites while putting others back in as she changed her mind on the night's mix. The recipe needed tweaking every now and again, usually in synchronicity with the full moon. Whenever the moon sat particularly plump among the clouds as she left the monthly Sorciety symposium, she knew it would be time to revise her alchemy. Time to take stock of where she needed to distil and define the qualities of herself. Her current blend would certainly need modifying for the coming month. Magic often went awry in October. The air was supercharged.

'Rose petals, pearl dust, opal quartz . . .' Annie muttered to herself, tucking the pastel-coloured trio of ingredients under her arm, the colours of a bursting summer dawn. The glasses clinked in a satisfying melody. 'Adder's tongue, fox scream, heather and feather. Maybe crow tonight . . .' The dark shades of jet, smoke-grey and rust looked stark against her first choices. They made for an unsettling combination.

'All people are a contrast,' she said quietly, reasoning her decisions.

With a flourish, a pair of glasses appeared at the end of her nose, her vision a little less than perfect with the spell wearing off for the day. She held the ingredients up to the soft candlelight, checking that each looked as it should in texture and colour. The slightest flaw could really scupper things in the precise potion balance that she craved. They had to be the best of the best. Annie appreciated hallmarks of quality, promises of longevity, something to assure her that they wouldn't let her down. Whether ingredients or shoes, handbags or people, those things were rare and important.

Satisfied with her decisions, Annie sent the selection of stoppered bottles, vessels and mysterious, miniature boxes cascading through the air, over the dark green floor tiles to levitate just above the full bathtub. The burgeoning heat from the water had brought a bloom of steam across the mirrors and a dampness to her cheeks. With concentration and methodical precision led by her magic, like a conductor stirring her orchestra to a final crescendo, each vial tipped its required amount into the water one after another. Gradually, the combination turned the water from a pale, crystalline blue to an intense, cardinal red.

Annie slipped off her clothes and dipped a toe to test it. She inhaled sharply through her teeth. She had found that increased heat made the most potent result, brought out the best in her. It was worth the pain, to be the best that she could be.

Some of the spell's results were surface-level. Immaculate hair of course, long lashes, excellent teeth, unsmudgeable make-up, a hypnotizing scent, a dazzling smile.

But the spell ran deeper, too. Stiffly unwavering patience. Endless generosity with her time. A selflessness that made most decisions on her behalf. Always conscientious, welcoming and warm. Almost no sleep ever required. A supernatural problem-solving streak that anyone could call upon whenever they needed to.

Stepping into the potion was a path to perfection.

UNCHARMED

Annie stared determinedly at the chandelier, which blurred to a watery glow. She lay back against the tub, wincing just for one more second, before the scalding water finally brought its welcome numbness and she succumbed to it. When it felt comfortable, Annie slipped fully underneath the surface. Emerging again, pushing her wet hair away from her face, droplets of crimson water clinging to her lashes, she steeled herself to whisper the incantation. The water burst and bubbled between her lips as she spoke:

> *Fair price to pay for those who wish it.*
> *A ghostly shadow to solicit.*
> *No gift is free so here in smoke,*
> *The dark mistakes of wicchefolk.*
> *Surrounding whispers of their sadness,*
> *Feel the stroke of regret's madness.*
> *Exchange the balance for my shine,*
> *A pact that makes perfection mine.*

They had been waiting patiently, poised for their cue. Wisps of steam that emanated from the hot water began to rise towards her voice. The curls of vapour moved upwards in hypnotizing movements for her to inhale, stretched smoke carrying up from the potion to the ceiling and fading into the bathroom's cocooning warmth. The trails of spectral steam swayed and morphed like flames, until they blended into a smoke screen that engulfed Annie almost entirely.

It was hard to make out any specific features among them, but so much time spent with the spell meant that Annie had grown very familiar with the voices of the ghosts who came to visit her. Every night, when knitting the spell – the hex – together, she recognized their cries, their faces pulled in and out of focus, but never quite enough to see definitively. Figures amid the grey smoke were there one moment, barely visible, then gone. Before they could reveal themselves as more than an eerie blur, the mist blended faces and figures together into a drizzly grey.

She didn't know their stories in detail, but she knew all about their mistakes. The pain that came from imperfection. That was the pact that Annie made for it all. *Splendidus Infernum.*

Annie gave a full-body shiver as the hot water turned ice-cold and the hex began. The figures around the tub always changed, impossible to pin down, but she knew the most haunted regulars and their faintest outlines. There was the cloudy image of the man with wire-rimmed glasses who cried to himself in secret, willing his breath to steady and stop the flow before anybody saw, terrified they'd find out his truth. The faceless lady with the thick plait swung over her shoulder, so plagued with guilt that she was confident it would be best to fade away entirely, to unburden the world. The young woman so filled with troubled, unanswered questions, wondering if she'd done the right thing, certain that she hadn't, unable to ever come to terms with her decision.

As the enchantment spelled out explicitly, no gift ever came for free – and Annie could never say that she hadn't known the price to pay. It was only fair and right that the exchange for her perfection was a heavy cost. The trade meant that she willingly took on the most imperfect moments of others, haunted by their sadness and regret every time she came to do the deal, taking on the weight of their feelings and hurt so heavily that she didn't ever really stop thinking about them. Highly attuned to all emotions around her thanks to the longstanding Wildwood hex, Annie felt it all, all of the time, as though it could burst from her like barrels of thunder that she must silently keep hold of. The cost of pleasing everybody was one that she paid alone and she found herself in a spiralling, bottomless debt of it.

But it was worth it. She had to make sure she wasn't disappointing anybody and this was the way to be sure of it. She had to be perfect. She could cling to the safe familiarity she knew and nothing would change; no one else would leave her behind. It would mean she wouldn't fail. Look at the wonderful life it had made for her. Everybody was delighted by it.

Annie's mother had never struggled with the cost; other people's emotions weren't something that held a lot of weight with her. But to Annie they meant everything.

The midnight of her fifteenth birthday was spent meeting ghosts for the very first time. Cressida had pushed her to continue, insisting it would get easier, but still Annie carried them all, her heart like a locket bursting at its delicate hinges with the burdens of others. Like a nocturnal creature that burrowed down when the sun rose, worry wove its way through the tunnels of Annie's heart under the moon at midnight and barbed itself into the softness.

Thirteen minutes passed and sparks of magic began to spit from the dark red potion, smoking like ashes as they fell to the surface again. The ghosts and their struggles seeped into her soul as she breathed them in. She could feel every regret they carried, the weight of their history, all the mistakes that kept them chained to the wicche world when it had long since been their time to pass through onto the next. The spell came to its conclusion – restoring her and destroying her all at once – and, as she furiously wiped away a tear that threatened to hit the water and upset the balance of her careful concoction, Annie wondered why, if she was doing everything so right, it all still felt so wrong.

Chapter Six

THE STRAY

The chaotic mid-afternoon rush, when customers could no longer fight the distraction of their sweet tooth and were pulled by the tempting call of a little treat, was a daily occurrence at Celeste. Faye had dubbed it 'power hour', digging deep for gladiator-style motivation, and had invented their daily tradition of a 2 p.m. espresso shot with a ceremonial sleeve-rolling of their matching pink overalls. Pari, meanwhile, affectionately referred to it as 'hell o'clock', because she loved to be the tiniest bit theatrical at any opportunity and had invented her own extremely enthusiastic, devil-inspired cheerleading routine for the occasion, which used two strawberries as horns and dishcloths as pom poms.

Annie, sensing in the pricking of her thumbs that it was going to be a popular Monday for the cherry buns in particular, had taken herself off to the kitchen to whip up another tray of the favourites in preparation. As soon as customers spotted them behind the counter, studded with plump currants and coated in their glistening snowdrift of icing, they were (understandably) powerless to resist. It may also have had something to do with the nifty cosiness enchantment that

Annie folded into the flour, the pillowy dough leaving customers comforted as every soft mouthful conjured the precise sensation of being wrapped up in a duvet on a cold winter's night.

The freshly baked buns were warm and yellow gold. Annie summoned the enormous punnet of cherries from the cupboard to finish each one with a flourish of shiny red, like a kiss. But before she could place the first gem into the icing, her attention was caught by a speck of rogue magic in the corner of her eye, skipping its way across the countertop like a rolling penny. It wasn't her own; it didn't reflect pink. Funnily enough, her first thought was Pari.

Wherever it came from, the spark of magic halted at the tub of cherries. She squinted more closely, feeling slightly like she was going mad, but they really were moving. Quivering, little blurred dashes of polished red that trembled in the tub like shaken marbles. The cherries began to levitate and flew across the wooden worktop to scatter themselves across the buns. They hopped to and fro, before settling with purpose. Eventually, Annie understood. They spelled out a distinct, red message in the white icing.

Hecate House requests you.

The coven.

As Selcouth's communication went, it was relatively subtle, which Annie was grateful for. She had warned the communications department several times that their delivery was often ill-timed and inconsiderate to a witch based in this non-wicche realm. In the past, Selcouth had scrawled messages with levitating chalk across the Celeste menu board in front of a bustling cafe. Annie had caused mild disaster, diving across the counter at breakneck speed to grab the chalk for herself. They'd made messages appear in scatterings of flour while Faye was helping her bake, stamped the star-shaped crest through baguettes like sticks of rock, even animated a gingerbread man once to pass on their request. That one had required all of Annie's most skilled powers of distraction, bursting into very loud song to divert everyone's eyes from a tiny iced gentleman shouting into his biscuit megaphone.

'I wonder what they could want,' Annie muttered to herself, picking off the cherries and moving them to where they were supposed to sit in the centre of the buns. An unexplained summons from anyone always set fire to the embers of her anxieties, reinforcing that constant, smarting feeling that she was in trouble for something, but one from the coven was particularly unnerving.

She wiped her fingers absent-mindedly on her apron. As far as she could calculate and as far as she could rely on the spell, she hadn't done anything wrong – even if it felt like she must have done. Selcouth had a tendency to err on the side of dramatic, but whatever the reason, a coven summons meant a long night ahead. She glanced up at the clock and calculated how best to split her time for the rest of the day. She had just about finished the buns in time for the rush, but she couldn't clock off yet, Faye and Pari would be run off their feet. What felt like days ago, she had stopped to inhale a lunchtime sandwich in a matter of seconds, while she juggled the eggs delivery (thankfully not literally) and navigated the celebration cake collections simultaneously. And she'd promised a tray of cupcakes to Mrs Harris for her daughter's birthday . . . A little bit of magic could speed up that process, at least.

A flicker of pink sparks sent equipment flying through the air to ready itself in front of her, while rows of paper cake cases lined up neatly in rainbow order. A box of eggs landed to her left and each one waited patiently on the edge of her mixing bowl to dive in gracefully like synchronized swimmers. A heavy sack of sugar huffed and wheezed its way across the kitchen with great effort, clutching onto the edge of the stool at the halfway point to take a breather. Annie could leave those ingredients to work while Faye and Pari were occupied and, luckily, she kept her coven uniform stowed neatly beside her dress rack, hidden underneath the pie dishes for safe keeping.

The lilac dusk had turned into night across the city and Annie could finally take notice of the summons. It was much later than she'd intended to set off for Hecate House and she knew that the delay would not be well received. But the perfection that *Splendidus Infernum* provided did not extend any further than affecting her own self, which meant the inevitable, imperfect ways of life could not always be avoided.

A huddle of teenage girls had rocked up to Celeste after school and nursed thick, frothy strawberry milkshakes for hours while they filled the cafe with laughter. Annie didn't want to rush them, watching from the corner of her eye with a wistful smile. They seemed to melt into one another, the girls speaking a different language of inside jokes and references that anybody else would struggle to understand. It felt impossible to think that she could ever be so relaxed with her friends, so herself around anybody. Precious moments of girlhood like that were not something to be rushed, so she'd let them stay in the bay window until they dragged themselves home for dinner. She sent each of them away with one of her sprinkle-covered, wish-laced sugar cookies for good measure and, in a fair exchange, they'd told her that they liked her shimmery eyeshadow.

Annie wrapped her arms around herself tightly. Her breath bloomed in front of her, patent heels catching the orange bursts of streetlights as she walked. She passed the local bookshop where she would often drop in samples for the booksellers, the newsagents that always saved a copy of her favourite fashion magazine, the only dry cleaners that she ever trusted with her jackets. Even magic couldn't fluff up feathered cuffs like they did.

The latest incarnation of the London entrance to Hecate House, changing every full moon to prevent discovery by non-wicchefolk, had proven to be a handy one that month, just a short walk from Celeste to the local playground of all places. The entry gate, plump carved pumpkins adorning either side and Halloween bunting strung through the railings, was locked at night, but a quick spell made light work of that.

Everything around felt earthy and damp, the flowerbeds all swollen with rain. Crisp leaves freshly shaken down had softened to a chocolate cake mixture underfoot, so Annie picked her way carefully along to avoid her heels slipping. The playground was deserted but for a skinny fox who was nuzzling his way through the bin. He debated scarpering when Annie set foot inside, but his senses evidently picked up on the safe presence of magic and he returned to his treasure hunt. As a gust of wind breathed through the chestnut trees, the roundabout circled in a slow churn and two swings swayed back and forth, their rusty chains clinking. Annie ducked her head underneath the climbing frame, feeling the cold, flaking paint beneath her fingers.

She stepped towards the hopscotch, but stopped short of placing her feet inside the first square to pull the cloak and hat from her bag. Both were neatly folded in dust bags and she unfurled each item of Selcouth uniform with great care. The pointed coven hat would never be her accessory of choice, but she had made the best of it, adding a billowing pink organza ribbon to the brim, which she fastened in a neat bow beneath her chin. The coven cloak, however, was a thing of beauty. Whoever had first designed it all those years ago had Annie's full seal of approval in sorcery style. A billowing piece of velvet that reached the floor, it made her feel somewhere between a celestial witch and a woodland princess. Traditionally purple, she had subtly tinkered with hers to have, of course, more of a pink tinge to its glimmer. The fabric was embroidered with the most delicate details of the night sky's constellations, so finely sewn that it looked like a scattering of starlight itself. She had always felt that starlight was powerful. Each witch, warlock or wicche's cloak was their own bespoke design, so that the pattern revealed the night sky's alignment at the moment of their birth. Annie had plenty of beloved pieces sitting pretty in her wardrobe, but the cloak trounced them all.

Fastening it at her collarbone with the mother of pearl brooch that she had added, Annie gave a determined and high-pitched *'hmm'*. It was time to enter Hecate House.

'Three.'

She muttered it to herself as she stretched her right leg across the hopscotch with an inelegant jump, skipping the first two boxes entirely. Her heels landed on the chalked tarmac with a clip-clop. Coordination was not her strong suit and she was glad that nobody was around to witness it.

'Seven, then nine,' she reminded herself with a wobbly leap into the seventh box, teetering in her shoes as she stretched to land safely inside of it, then took a step into number nine.

'And thirteen.'

Her feet landed side by side inside the final box of the drawing on the ground. For a fraction of a moment, nothing happened at all. Just the right amount of incidental, paused time passed for a child to hop straight out of the final box, if they happened to follow that same unlikely sequence with their feet. Enough time for them to safely jump out of the drawing before they would ever notice how the paint suddenly shone with a magical reflection of the moonlight. And how the words *Tonitru, Fulgur, Pluvia* twinkled back at the stars in an iridescent patch of puddled water.

Thunder, Lightning, Rain.

'Come on, come on,' Annie said with a pained expression.

She knew exactly what was coming. Her heart began to quicken. She just about had time to tuck her hair behind her ears and lock her arms across her chest to brace before the asphalt beneath her feet unlatched itself. The thirteenth square swung open like a trapdoor and Annie couldn't help but squeal as she plummeted through the playground floor. Her hair whipped upwards and behind her and she clung to the ribbon that secured her hat to her head.

After what she assumed must be a slow-motion charm to cushion the fall, Annie lost her footing only ever so slightly on the eventual landing. Gracefully, she caught her balance against the pale stone walls, then smoothed her hair and gave the curls a perfunctory bounce, exhaling with triumph. At least that dreaded plummet was over for another little while. She peered way up at the entry just in time to see the tiny, far-off trapdoor close itself and shut off the last of the moonlight.

Annie headed further in, through the foyer to arrive at the atrium. Selcouth's headquarters boasted an array of beautiful décor, as was only appropriate for the home of the United Kingdom's esteemed coven, but the atrium in particular could steal any witch's breath. The mosaic beneath her feet, depicting an otherworldly sun and moon, spanned the enormous round room. Its domed roof was equally beautiful, lined with a blanket of radiant physical magic, as though each spark were stitched together in an iridescent quilt. Annie couldn't help but take a moment to admire it, quietly counting her blessings on every visit. The cerulean blue of the tiles below provided a stunning clash to her fuchsia heels, she appreciated, and she waved at a cluster of witches who were passing by with greetings.

Pressed into the walls of the atrium were twelve doors and each bore its own giant bronze zodiac figure above, fastidiously guarding whatever lay behind it. One wooden door was arched in a sharp point and a monstrous bronze scorpion was poised above, its pincers and tail curled into a threatening stance. Annie softly waved a hand towards the middle of the door and a metallic clanging rang out through the hall as though she'd used an invisible door knocker.

'Enter.' A voice from within, after a thoroughly disapproving sigh, that sounded rather like it would prefer that whoever it was did the opposite of accepting their invitation.

'Only me,' Annie called brightly. She slipped off her coat from under the cloak and placed it on the hatstand, which bowed like a butler as it accepted her goods onto its arm. Against the sombre, dark wood and gothic feel of the office, the pastel pink of her coat (and the rest of her ensemble) looked like some kind of universe malfunction.

'There you are. I was beginning to wonder whether you'd been mauled by wild dogs.'

'I'm not sure we get many of those around here, Morena. Mostly Labradors and spaniels, as far as I've noticed. Although I'm still not convinced that a children's playground was the safest choice for the House to reincarnate itself.'

Annie glanced at the moon dial in the corner of Morena Gowden's office. A leaking patch of pale moonlight that waned through a gap in the high ceilings showed that it was precisely on the hour of eight. Tiredness tapped behind Annie's eyes. Her feet tingled and her lower back grumbled, but she shook it off as quickly as the spell would allow. She was grateful as ever for the extra energy that *Splendidus Infernum* provided to supernaturally maximize her productivity.

She made a beeline for the corner desk that sat adjacent to Morena's own and took her seat behind it. She lined up her fluffy pen, pink notebook and a marshmallow-scented candle at perfect, perpendicular angles. She lit the candle with a point of magic, then swept up a mountain of scrolls that had been added to the desk since her last visit. Most importantly, she tucked the fluffy pen behind her ear to get into the spirit.

'Quite on the contrary. Children don't bat an eyelid when a fairy comes to remove a tooth previously lodged within their own skull, right from underneath their pillow as they sleep. The little miscreants are alarmingly relaxed with all manner of the supernatural.'

'Oddly enough, that does make sense,' Annie conceded.

'And,' Morena continued, not even glancing up from her work, 'the cherry on top of the cauldron comes in the form of opportunity to scare the living daylights out of any little blighters who do fall in. I shall be appearing in their nightmares for years to come with any luck.' Morena gave a rare smile at the thought.

Everything about the tall, spindly witch who Annie was apprentice to was razor sharp and intimidatingly immaculate, from the cut of her high cheekbones to the mathematically precise, silver-grey victory curl beneath the brim of her hat. Her unfaltering, dark stare and the ghostly contrast of her deep burgundy lipstick gave Morena a sort of elegantly haunted look, which Annie had always considered extremely chic, if not slightly terrifying. While the rest of the coven seemed to quake in their cloaks when Morena entered the room, Annie had always held an inexplicable soft spot for her.

It was Morena's sister and fellow Sage Witch, Bronwyn, who Annie tried to avoid at all costs, a little sceptical of her always-cheery disposition. Her impossibly good nature felt somehow superhuman, strangely untrustworthy to Annie. Either that or there was some sort of complicated, questionable spell afoot – something she knew about all too well.

Annie squinted cautiously as she unfurled the first of her papers. Now in her second year of apprenticeship, having sailed through Selcouth's endarkenment trial, her time at Hecate House was largely spent buried underneath mountains of ancient books for research, with Morena as her counsel. Most of the work was done remotely to fit around her hectic Celeste schedule, visiting Hecate House only when she was summoned, but Tuesday nights usually took her to the depths of the library to turn page after dusty page, sometimes even triggering unexpected incantations. Last week, she'd almost been hit square in the forehead by an ageing curse. She'd squealed so loudly and suddenly that Morena had come flying in and thrown a protection spell across the room, smack-bang into the face of her own portrait above the fireplace. She was furious about the damage and had decided that it was Annie's fault entirely. Annie was privately touched that she had leapt to her defence, but didn't dare say it. It would give Morena an aneurysm to think that she had inadvertently offered a kind gesture.

'Speaking of nightmares . . .' Morena looked up. 'Don't start on all of that yet, Andromeda.'

Annie swallowed. That was never a good conversation starter.

'You're probably curious as to the reason for your unscheduled summoning. I fear our usual order of proceedings may have been halted for a time.' Morena tented her spindly fingers together, leaning on her desk. Her left eyebrow was so sharply pointed that it almost pierced her hairline. 'We have . . . a stray.'

Annie paused. Her pointing finger hovered in mid-air while magically rifling through the scrolls. As her concentration broke, the papers dropped into a heap. 'A stray?'

'So to speak. A girl. The poor waif has come into her magic and doesn't know what to do with it. It seems to be causing rather a . . . predicament.'

'The first of her family? That's unusual,' Annie replied cautiously.

'Highly unusual,' Morena said. 'We haven't had a new kindling of magical lineage for some time and we were certainly not anticipating one. Regrettably, we find ourselves rather ill prepared.'

'That's never good,' Annie said nervously. It was very unlike Morena to miss a trick. She was usually full of tricks in fact, while Annie provided the treats. It was a partnership that was neatly witchy in that way.

'The girl is an orphan. She currently resides in a foster home under the care of an elderly couple, non-wicche. In a rather inconvenient set of circumstances, the gentleman is now in hospital after she accidentally set the net curtains on fire.'

Annie gasped.

'Not as dramatic as it sounds. The shock brought on a particularly nasty bout of angina for him.'

'Were we not monitoring her development? I'm sure I remember a girl up north having her debut fairly recently . . .' Annie's mind wandered and she rifled through her top drawer to find the records that the coven kept of newly debuted wicchefolk.

'Yes, we first became aware of her when her powers emerged only months ago. But accurate monitoring for an unknown is nigh on impossible, until their magic starts to come to fruition more clearly. No known magical lineage means no pattern to be mindful of, no expectation to work from. Bronwyn and I did visit on her fifteenth orbital completion for the usual endarkenment debut, but we hoped that she would take to the powers better than she evidently has. She was a creature of few words and we are now seeing what appears to be a complete lack of magical control.'

At this, Morena tutted unsympathetically, as though a fifteen-year-old girl should know how to behave when she found the infinite potential of real-life magic at her fingertips. Annie, on the other hand, felt the flutter of affinity in her heart, imagining the loneliness, the isolation, the fear of stumbling through early magic. It was difficult enough to experience with a support circle in place.

'I can't imagine it's safe to leave her to fend for herself. It could cause chaos,' Annie considered, tapping lightly on her chin. Morena smoothed an invisible crease on her cream shirt sleeve.

'That's rather why I've summoned you here, Andromeda. I have something of a proposition for you. Or, should I say, the coven at large has a proposition for you.'

Right on cue, the flame of the spell took charge. Annie's heart tweaked a little, the feeling of a problem to be solved itching in her bones, needing to be scratched. The aching, addictive sense that she was needed. She kept a straight, calm face.

'Whatever I can do to help serve the coven, of course. Although I'm not sure I'm . . .'

'I'll be frank, Ms Wildwood.' Morena rose from her desk and strode towards the roaring fireplace with her hands latched behind her back, pointed boots clicking on the pale stone. 'It's no secret that we're excited by your future at Selcouth. It's evident to any witch, warlock or wicche with two brain cells to rub together – although that is not as many here as you may think – that you exude a natural affinity. There's intuition and an ambition that I personally like to see in a young witch rising through the ranks.'

Annie beamed.

'You are, however, also rather soft at times,' Morena continued. Annie's smile vanished, her shoulders slumping in the face of even a mild criticism. 'But I imagine that your . . . *amiable* nature could be beneficial to a youngster in need of guidance.'

'Like you say, I'm far too soft,' Annie conceded. 'I wouldn't have a clue where to even begin.'

'It's hardly rocket science, Andromeda. What do they enjoy these days? I'm fairly sure it begins and ends at rock music and Satanism. Some ghastly application of eyeliner thrown in for good measure,' Morena said, shrugging.

'I don't think I could prove much use to her,' Annie said, doubting herself like a reflex. Morena gave her a huff in return and a silence fell long enough for Annie to feel obliged to fill it. 'But . . . maybe she could come into the bakery with me? She could even have a flair for sugar sorcery,' Annie said, feeling a bubble of excitement form as her imagination kicked in.

Her mind was now wandering off to tempting possibilities of a mini-me to take under her wing, to carve into the most immaculate, promising witch that Selcouth had seen since, well . . . since herself. Fluffy pens that moved in unison, matching magical flourishes in their hands and wrists. Identical quirks in their potion brewing, simultaneously bursting bubblegum as they turned over tarot cards. The prospect of coordinated cloaks, guaranteed to delight the coven each time she presented her own protégée . . .

'Selcouth has a rich history of mentoring through the magic system,' Morena said. 'The grimoire encourages shared knowledge and experience. But, due to the nature of the student, her youth and her naivety to our world, the job will doubtless pose its own unique, demanding challenges.'

Annie faltered. She hoped it was imperceptible, even to Morena's astute gaze. Realistically, it couldn't be done, could it? The bakery, the Sorciety and her friends, her coven work . . . It would be frankly impossible to juggle it all alongside tutoring a troubled teenage witch. She was already exhausted, struggling to keep up with everything. There was simply no way. She would run herself into the ground.

UNCHARMED

The right answer spilled from her lips as the spell kicked in. 'Whatever you need,' she replied, a placid, tolerant smile stretched across her face. She felt it tug at her cheeks, aching. 'I can make myself available.'

'Marvellous,' Morena said, with a satisfied nod. She picked up a gilded hand mirror from a side table and neatened the edge of her lipstick with the point of her nail.

Annie swallowed hard, unable to quell her curiosity for any longer. 'So, who is she?'

With an open palm that brought a cascade of sparks descending over its pages, Morena flipped the cover of the tattered, official coven grimoire on top of her desk to reveal the member register that was scrawled within the back pages. Annie raised her eyebrows in silent request to approach the ancient text. The Sage Witch gestured approval. Peering over the desk, Annie scanned the most recent entry.

'Maeve Cadmus. Cute,' Annie shrugged. Other than her name, the rest of Maeve's credentials on the page remained empty; heritage, gesture, specialism, all a series of blanks for Annie to fill on the coven's behalf. 'I can't wait to meet her.'

'Splendid,' Morena said. 'I'll ask Sybil down in the library to send up the forms. You shall begin promptly and rather aptly on the first of October.' She crossed the room in an elegant sweep and reached for the black telephone receiver that was balanced on the wings of a huge taxidermy crow.

'Oh, and, Annie . . .'

With a last caress of the victory curl that lay beneath the brim of her hat, Morena looked back over her shoulder to Annie.

'While I do not doubt your ability to ensure this runs smoothly, I must make it clear that we cannot afford for trouble to make itself known. You must inform me immediately of anything from Miss Cadmus that could be considered particularly . . . unusual. Unwanted attention, strangeness, anomalies . . . These are never welcome things at Selcouth.'

Chapter Seven

MAEVE

'What do you think?' Annie asked over her shoulder, chewing on the inside of her cheek as she checked her outfit from every possible angle in the mirror.

Faye stood with hands on hips behind Annie and spoke to her reflection. 'It's a bit much for the school run, isn't it?'

'Okay, maybe I've panicked. Is the blazer a little over the top? I *am* going to pick her up from school, though. It's a formal, academic environment, isn't it? I don't want to embarrass her by turning up and looking like a slob,' Annie said, examining the length of the skirt again.

'Where the hell did *you* go when you were a kid?' Faye said, bemused. 'This is a British state secondary school, Annie. I'd lose the corsage, for starters.'

'You don't like it?' Annie said, sounding entirely dejected as she removed the enormous floral corsage from her lapel before smoothing down her blouse.

'That'll do it. Yeah, now it all looks very laid back and normal, actually,' Faye said, deadpan. After much deliberation, Annie had finally settled on the exact opposite of laid back and normal for anybody other than herself: a flamingo-pink skirt suit with a pencil silhouette and enormous power shoulders in the matching blazer. The coordinated pink pumps and ruffle-bow blouse had resulted in an alarmingly bright finish, which she hadn't entirely intended on. Nonetheless, she had decided to roll with it as some kind of feminist statement that a modern teenager was sure to appreciate.

'She'll like the whole retro thing, right? It makes me seem fun,' Annie asked, flouncing the bow to give it a bit more life. Faye quickly turned away and busied herself with flipping through a few mixtapes. Annie gulped. 'Right?'

'Absolutely. There's nothing the kids love more than power suits. But,' Faye sighed, folding her arms, 'whether Maeve thinks your outfit is truly excellent or frankly insane is irrelevant. She's going to love you for you and this is an amazing thing that you're doing.'

Pari poked her head around the doorway. 'Woah. Your outfits get jazzier by the day, Annie. It's very children's TV presenter or maybe a weather girl?'

'She's going to collect the kid,' Faye explained.

'Of course, that's today!' Pari whooped. 'I still can't believe you're going ahead with it. As if you don't have a frantic enough schedule already, you decide to throw some volunteer work in the mix with an actual, real-life teenager.'

Annie had told Faye and Pari that she'd signed up for a local after-school scheme. As far as they understood it, she was to help Maeve with homework, encourage her about the future and offer up some work experience in a female-led, independent business. The small details about nurturing supernatural powers and managing potentially explosive magical mishaps would have to remain just between her and Maeve. The mental image of the lovely cafe curtains being set ablaze was one she tried not to dwell on.

'Wish me luck.' Annie pulled down the hem of her blazer firmly.

'Luck, luck, luck!' Pari sang, bundling her into a cuddle.

'I wish you an abundance of luck. In fact, I wish you a miracle and, more than anything, I wish that your sanity returns to you in due course,' Faye said grimly.

Annie landed with a shower of sparks in the middle of a pansy-covered roundabout. Stepping out of the flowerbed, she assessed the quaint, quiet village, finding a crossroads of three different residential roads to take. In a blur of fuchsia pink against the neat rows of brown terraced houses and a very grey northern sky, she put down her briefcase as she took in her surroundings with an optimistic smile. Small gardens in front of each house, porches full of winter coats and a couple of cats sleeping on doorsteps, one of which had startled awake on Annie's arrival. With a big stretch, he wandered towards her and immediately laced his way through her ankles. Attracting the attention of any neighbourhood cat within a five-mile radius was natural to a witch's animal affinity.

'What a warm welcome. Do you know where I can find Maeve?' She bent down to give the cat a stroke and, if she hadn't been paying attention, she might have missed the way he used his tail to point down one of the streets. A sign on the grass read Heath Road and a little way further loomed a large building, which Annie assumed to be the school. There wasn't much similarity to the boarding school that she'd attended with Romily, Vivienne and Harmony – considerably fewer turrets and drawbridges, for starters. This building was a slightly puzzling mix of intricate, old architecture, long-ignored 'Girls Entrance' and 'Boys Entrance' signs carved into the stone above the doorways, while modern prefab extensions were stuck against the sides. It was as though the school couldn't quite decide which century to belong to.

'Aha! Thank you, sir, you've been a big help,' Annie told the cat, conjuring him a small pile of treats in return for his assistance, before scooping her briefcase back up and waving thanks to a car that halted to let her cross. Unable to hold back an excited grin, she trotted towards the school, approaching its blue railings.

Morena had arranged for Annie to collect Maeve from the canteen and escort her to Celeste, where they could get to know each other over hot chocolate with extra cream. Annie had pictured their moment of meeting over and over, imagining her mini-me as a slightly shy but absolutely charming go-getter.

Annie had decided that the occasion called for ice-breaker brownies, so she carried a ribbon-tied box of them under one arm. Her other hand clutched the pink vintage briefcase, which was only full of the bare essentials for when they inevitably stayed up all night talking: fluffy slipper socks, feather-trimmed pyjamas, face masks. She could conjure anything else fun once they'd found their feet.

The bell had yet to ring for the end of the day. Searching for a place to wait, Annie spotted a bench across the road where an elderly man was sitting quietly alone, clutching a striped bag of sweets. His knee bobbed up and down, Annie noticed as she sat down – a small giveaway that he was nervous.

'Are you waiting for someone?' she asked brightly.

'My granddaughter. I collect her when her mum is working late. My favourite days of the week,' he said, unable to contain a sheepish smile at the mention of his grandchild.

'That's lovely.' Annie made sure that her own smile stayed put, even though her heart pinched. 'I always wished I had a grandparent that I was close to, but I never really knew mine. She's very lucky to have you.'

'Nonsense, I'm the lucky one. The light of my life, she is,' he said proudly, then jiggled the bag in his hand. 'We share a bag of strawberry creams while we walk.'

Another pinch. 'You must be very proud of her.'

'Proud like you wouldn't believe. She's eleven. I know it's only a matter of time until she's too old to be seen walking home with her Gramps, but never mind, eh? I'll treasure it while it lasts,' he said while he stared determinedly at the school doors.

As the bittersweet softness of his words entered the air, Annie was overwhelmed with empathy, touched by the genuine care laced between them. Then it began to dull, like an old injury that kicked up in the rain and cold. A greyness leaked into the golden feeling, a longing for an unconditional family love that fitted together so simply, something that she had never known but coveted more than anything.

A shrill bell tolled, snapping Annie from her thoughts, and the school doors burst open. A short girl came bounding over in a blazer that was three sizes too big for her and the old man raised himself with difficulty to meet her with open arms, before producing the bag of chocolates for her like a magic trick. They walked away and he turned back to give Annie a small wave. She hurried to wipe away a stray tear and rose to cross the road. As she waited at the zebra crossing, she couldn't resist sending a dusky pink twirl towards their bag of sweets; the same nostalgia enchantment that she added to the scone stacks at Celeste, which would help the girl to treasure the precious moment, now and on a far-off day to come.

A crowd of students had gathered inside the canteen, laughter and shouting muffled behind the glass. She approached the closed canteen doors, with a renewed spring in her step at the infectious buzz for the end of the school day, and knocked on the window to catch someone's attention. The group closest to the window spun their heads towards the interruption and each of their jaws promptly dropped. A moment later, they all burst into a fit of shared giggles, one boy shouting something across the room that Annie failed to quite make out. She couldn't think what was so funny. Eventually, one of the more well-mannered ones of the bunch came to open the door.

'Hello there!' Annie said excitedly. 'I'm looking for Maeve?'

The boy, a smattering of swollen acne across his chin and a fluff of moustache on his top lip, sniffed in response.

'Maeve Cadmus?' Annie went on. 'She goes here . . . To your school, I mean. At least, I think she does?' Annie, wide-eyed, tried to encourage him to respond. Perhaps he was shy.

'Someone actually wants to speak to Grave Sadness?' A tall, lanky girl poked her head around the door, chewing and popping on gum, with lips covered in concealer and eyebrows that had been plucked line-thin. Annie marvelled at how it was evidently the thing for some teenagers to make themselves as orange as possible. 'What do you want with her miserable arse?'

Annie did a double take, first at the girl's arrival, then again when she heard the boy mutter an even more vulgar version of what seemed to be an endless collection of nicknames for Maeve. So much for well-mannered and shy.

'I'm her cousin,' Annie answered with a curt smile. 'Just here to collect her for a family shindig that we have this weekend. Should be a lovely reunion.'

The girl snorted. 'Grave doesn't have any family, everybody knows that. Even her fake family didn't want her any more because she's such a freak.'

Annie blinked. Perhaps this school was a fan of the tough love approach. Morena had mentioned that it may be a difficult environment. Or . . . was she missing the joke? Was this . . . social awkwardness? Why wasn't she flourishing, as she usually did?

'Excuse me, please.' Annie shouldered her way past them both with a slight flounce.

'Careful she doesn't curse you,' the girl shouted over her shoulder at Annie, which only sparked more confusion and a vague touch of panic. Surely Maeve hadn't gone public with her magic?

As Annie clip-clopped through the canteen, smelling the rather unpleasant combination of reheated food, super-sweet body spray and teenage boys in general, every single head turned towards her. Not an unfamiliar feeling in itself, but within the school it felt much more . . . hostile. There was none of the usual admiration that she was used to, which touched her skin like sunlight and reassured her that she was doing everything right. Instead, this attention was a strange mix of gawping and muttering, burst with the occasional yelled laugh. It was making her feel curiously self-conscious . . . an unfamiliar feeling, one that made her want to scratch at the skin on her upper arms. Annie fought against crossing them over her chest. She tried to keep her chin up.

But, as she thought about it, a little bubble of dread forming at the back of her throat, she slowly began to remember her mother warning her about something like this. That the perfection spell had a tendency to glitch when it came to the opinions of . . . teenagers. *Oh no.* Annie cleared her throat and a small squeak came out.

They could all see straight through it. Everybody knew that teenagers had impossibly high standards and very little belief in perfection as a concept – aside from a certain tier of pop star or celebrity. During her school days, Annie's mother, Cressida, had worked meticulously to ensure that the alchemy had been balanced for her school friends. But Annie hadn't had much use for impressing teenagers since then and evidently her usual draught didn't cut it. This would make things extra difficult with Maeve.

She tucked her hair behind her ear, attempted to smile at each of the students. But, oddly, Annie found she wasn't entirely sure how to walk properly or where her hands should be in relation to the rest of her body. She was horrified to realize that she even felt unsure about her outfit choice. Annie felt a sudden, desperate urge to find a large hole in the earth and dive head first into it.

Her own teenage years had not looked like this. There had been no plastic trays, no boomboxes, no short striped ties against unbuttoned shirts. Forcing herself to get a grip, reminding herself that she was actually the adult in this situation, even if it didn't feel like it, Annie shook off the squeeze of embarrassment. Finally, after navigating what felt like an endless sea of side ponytails and hair gel spikes, the hostile shouting and pointing helped her to locate Maeve.

Tucked away in the furthest corner of the canteen, with a stack of books built around her like a fortress, a girl was sitting alone. Pencil in hand, she hadn't so much as looked up at the chaos and noise, only giving a cursory glance of aversion when one of the boys threw a balled-up burger wrapper directly at her head. She wore thick, black-rimmed glasses that blended into her long dark hair and she chewed on the sleeve of her school jumper while she focused on her drawing.

Not quite what Annie had imagined – almost the opposite in fact. But the girl had lovely shiny hair and an adorable smattering of freckles all over her face. Of course she was a little reserved – who wouldn't be when faced with this zoo for six hours a day? Deciding to remain as optimistic as she had been earlier, Annie took a preparatory breath, ready for the first magical meeting with her mini-me. A moment that neither of them would ever forget.

Approaching the table, she cleared her throat. There was no reaction.

'Maeve?' Annie tried again.

Maeve remained completely focused on the sketchbook in front of her, so Annie leaned over to tap the girl on the shoulder. She leapt back with a yelp when Maeve jumped about fifty foot out of her seat, breaking her concentration with a sharp jolt.

'Sorry, sorry. Hi, hello! It's me, Annie!' she grinned. 'Wow, I'm so excited to meet you.' She clapped her hands together. 'Yay, this is going to be so much fun. Are you ready to go?'

Maeve stared at her like a rabbit in headlights.

'Oh no, don't be scared. Did I come on too strongly? I tend

to do that sometimes. I'm just so delighted about all of this. A whole new adventure for both of us, right?' Annie was still clapping very fast. She wasn't sure why.

Maeve's dark brown eyes darted from Annie to the crowd in the canteen behind her, as though to check whether she was safe to engage. Fortunately, the zoo had already lost interest in the new arrival. Then her gaze fell to the pink briefcase that had been placed on top of the table and the box of brownies next to it, which was decorated with a ribbon so enormous that Annie now regretted opting for so much frou-frou. She didn't want Maeve to think that she was *entirely* ridiculous.

Annie decided to adjust her approach. Giving Maeve a conspiratorial wink, and with a gesture so subtle that it could be missed with a blink, she sent a small stream of pink sparks towards the ribbon to unlace it. The box opened and slid its way shyly across the table to reveal its contents. The drizzle of caramel she'd poured across the rich, gooey brownies looked treasure-like against the grey canteen and smelled impossibly good. Maeve remained uncertain, her mouth pushed to the side in a distinct, diagonal frown.

'Go on. Try one,' Annie nodded keenly.

As unable to resist delicious brownies as any normal being, magical or otherwise, Maeve tentatively reached out to break off a corner, the pillowy chocolate squashing between her fingertips. As she popped it in her mouth and chewed thoughtfully, Annie noticed Maeve's posture change the slightest fraction, her shoulders dropping down an inch or two, her chin raising a little. Annie allowed herself a moment of inner celebration for choosing the dark chocolate chunks coated in a touch of soothing enchantment. Yes, she had *maybe* banked on the calming properties being useful for too much excitement when they discovered they were fated best friends, rather than the frankly startled and slightly spooky feeling that was currently emanating from Maeve, but nevertheless . . .

'Better?' Annie chanced.

Maeve swallowed, then reached for more brownie. 'These are really good.'

'Thanks! I don't know how much information Morena has passed on, but I run a bakery. Well, it's kind of a bakery, kind of a cafe, but I also sell some flowers and we do book club and we do painting nights and it's such a beautiful spot, although right now it's covered in Halloween decorations, but in a cute way, you know? And . . . wait, do you actually know who Morena is? Silly me, maybe you're not familiar with the coven roles yet or . . .'

Annie saw Maeve's eyes widen again, so she firmly pursed her lips together to stop talking. With *Splendidus Infernum* evidently taking a smug rest in this environment, it felt like she was short-circuiting. She pulled out one of the plastic chairs, brushed off the layer of miscellaneous crumbs that covered the seat and sighed. She was taking entirely the wrong approach. This poor young girl was evidently shy and unsure of herself. Annie would have to tread carefully.

'Sorry, I'm being a little crazy,' Annie said softly. 'I think I'm . . . nervous?' A pause passed between them, then seemed to settle as they both took a matching breath.

'Me too,' Maeve admitted reluctantly.

'You don't need to be, I promise. This isn't a test; it's not something you can pass or fail. We're going to have a great time,' Annie said, then offered what she hoped was a reassuring smile, dimming down her dazzle a few degrees so as not to be quite so blinding. It occurred to her that without

Splendidus Infernum carefully adding a suitable, likeable filter, she might be a little . . . much?

Maeve frowned again, then nodded. 'I don't have any of my things with me, only my book bag,' she mumbled, heaving a large backpack covered in patches, pins and felt-tip doodles up from underneath the table.

Annie's brows shot up. 'That's just books?'

Maeve, Annie noticed, did not hold back an eye-roll, which surprised her. 'There's no such thing as *just books*,' Maeve said, stretching the sleeves down on her jumper. 'You might have gathered that the conversation around here isn't exactly stimulating so . . .' She shrugged.

'You don't spend a lot of time hanging out with your classmates, I take it?'

'Would you?' Maeve said, before giving another eye-roll so cutting that Annie was strongly reminded of Morena. Annie turned to see what had earned such a reaction from Maeve and her hands flew to her mouth as one of the boys pulled down his trousers and pressed his entire bare backside against the glass windows.

'If you have a spell to successfully pluck my eyeballs from my skull, I'd appreciate prioritizing that one,' Maeve said coolly, closing her sketchbook and leaning both elbows on the thick cover to rest her chin on her hands.

'Are they always like this?' Annie hissed, entirely horrified.

'Oh no,' Maeve said calmly. 'They're actually being far more gentlemanly than usual. You have to feel sorry for them really. This is them genuinely trying their absolute level best to impress you.'

'But they're . . . awful,' Annie said in disbelief.

'Yes. They're teenage boys,' Maeve said. 'What did you

expect? Having said that, the girls aren't much better. I'm telling you, this school is dishing out lobotomies for free somewhere. Just waiting on my invitation to arrive any day now.'

Annie blinked at her. Maybe this girl wasn't quite as unsure of herself as she had first thought. 'It's starting to make sense now why you build a book barrier.'

'It's generally considered embarrassing to be publicly literate at this school, so I try to remind them as often as possible. It helps ensure they all maintain a wide berth.'

'Can't say I blame you,' Annie said, reaching for a brownie herself now. 'So you're a bookworm, hey?'

Maeve tugged down her sleeves again. 'Reading or drawing, most of the time.'

'Maybe you can give me some recommendations, seeing as we've got a fair bit of time to spend together?' Annie said softly, feeling triumphant when she earned an uncertain but slightly proud nod in return.

'Sure, I can do that.'

'Great! I thought we'd go back to Celeste – that's my bakery in London – and have hot chocolates while we chat about how this is going to work and how you'd like to approach . . . you know, the m-word.' Annie silently mouthed 'magic' just in case of confusion, to which Maeve gave her a slow, obvious nod. 'How does that sound?'

Maeve faltered. 'How will we get there?'

'Don't you worry about that – magical transference is a wonderful invention. I can carry your bag for you, if you like?'

'That's okay. I long ago resigned myself to future back problems.'

'Seriously, pass it here,' Annie insisted, tugging the hefty backpack towards her. She reached for her briefcase and unclipped the golden fastenings so that it sprung open. It was jam-packed with various cosy fleece materials adorned with feathers, a few iridescent skincare products in fancy-looking glass bottles, a sequinned notebook . . . Essentials. With a huff, she plonked Maeve's backpack on top of it all, then closed the case. Under the weight of the lid, the backpack compressed down like a deflating balloon that exhaled a stream of pink sparks, until it was flattened to paper-thin with the rest of her things and Annie snapped it shut easily. Maeve shot to her feet, peering awestruck over the top of her glasses.

'How did you . . .'

Annie gave her a smug smile. 'Magic.'

Maeve looked as though she was daring herself to say something. 'Can you . . . Can you teach me how to do that?'

'Sure! That's actually a pretty easy one, a simple *Leve Bona* incantation that I sprinkle onto . . . well, every handbag I think I've ever carried, actually. I'm not really one for travelling light; I like to have options. Do you want to put those in too?' Annie gestured towards the stack of sketchbooks that were at Maeve's elbow. Maeve hurriedly gathered them in her arms and clutched them close to her chest.

'No, thank you, I can carry these.'

'Okay! In that case, shall we make a move?' Annie said as she rose from the table and gave Maeve what she hoped would be an encouraging nod. Things were already proving a lot dicier to navigate without the spell in place to make sure that she could always say the right thing. At least the brownies were working, though.

This time, with fewer eyes on her, it felt lighter to walk through the crowded canteen. She turned to make a joke about it with Maeve, pleased that they'd all lost interest, and only then realized that Maeve had fallen behind. A gang of girls had closed in on her and blocked her path, one of them asking loudly who her new friend was.

'Can't get any of your own around here, so you have to hire some old woman in to be your mate? That's actually embarrassing,' that same orange girl said.

Old? Annie was about to protest when Maeve immediately bit back.

'Jessica, I don't know when you found the impetus to organize your very own Moronic Ignoramus convention, but congratulations, I'm glad to see it was a roaring success. It's about time they gave you a promotion in the field,' Maeve said. She was bolder than Annie was expecting, jutting out her chin as she spoke.

Jessica looked at her blankly. 'What are you on about, Sadness? Using big words again to make up for the fact you chat shit.'

Maeve sighed and tried to shoulder her way past the girls, but one shoved her hard and sent her sketchbooks tumbling to the floor. Annie darted to pick them up, but Maeve immediately shot her a warning look, which she knew meant to stay out of it.

Jessica snorted. 'Drop a few more things on the floor, freak.'

'Anything else valuable to add to my evening or can I go now?' Maeve said as she stood with a completely unmoved expression. Jessica faltered, clearly running out of ideas for how to earn a laugh from her friends.

'Erm . . . Your hair looks crap,' she shouted as a last resort. 'Did you wash it in the chip pan?'

Maeve held her gaze, stony-faced. 'Yes. I simply love to wash my hair in vegetable oil.'

'Going back to your coffin tonight?' another girl chimed in.

'How would I live in a coffin? Where would I keep the chip pan?' Maeve turned to ask with a look of confusion.

At this, Jessica faltered again. 'It's 'cos you're so pale,' she said.

'I gathered that much,' Maeve nodded. 'I can't say I take that as much of an insult, though, when the only thing that could make you look pale would be the literal sun. You are tangerine. Is it intentional or are you trying to help air traffic control?'

Annie's feet were glued in place, her arms frozen mid-swing, unsure whether she was supposed to step in. The spell was proving wholly useless. In its absence, she glanced around for a teacher, but it seemed that the canteen was a kind of declared no-man's land. Maeve was holding her own and was evidently well practised at it, but the scene was making Annie's chest ache. She longed to save her.

'What's in the books, Sadness?' Jessica said, finally noticing a weak spot – the spray of open sketchbooks that had tumbled from Maeve's arms. She reached for them, but Maeve was quicker and lunged to scoop them up, elbowing her out of the way. Still, Jessica managed to snatch the top one from the stack.

'Don't touch that,' Maeve blurted out. She snatched for it back, the words coming before she could keep her well-checked composure.

Jessica scoffed, opening one of the pages and showing it to everybody in the circle. 'What freaky stuff have you been drawing, Sadness? Are these the plans for all the demon worshipping you do at home? In between your vampire-hunting shifts? Gonna put a curse on us all? Hang on, who's this?'

Annie only caught a glimpse, but saw that it was an impressive sketch of a girl.

'Have you got a secret girlfriend? Or is this meant to be you? You wish you were that pretty, Sadness.'

'Give it back,' Maeve called, her rehearsed calmness shrinking by the second. A bloom of visible red embarrassment had spread behind her freckles and Annie found her heart tuning into Maeve's anger, brewing in the air. She sensed it easily, her heightened empathy latching on. It was hanging like a storm cloud over the canteen, dark and intense and overpowering.

Jessica ripped out the page from the book and waved it over her head. 'Everyone watch out, Sadness has been perving on us all and drawing us in secret. She's probably getting off on it,' she shrieked.

Annie's own eyes filled when she noticed that Maeve was fighting back tears now, struggling as the other girls blocked her while Jessica shoved the sketches towards anyone who cared enough to look. Annie couldn't stand it any more – even if it did make Maeve furious. Her desperate need to help took over. She marched towards the bundle of girls and tried to break a couple of them apart to pull Maeve out, a fiery protectiveness sparking at the pit of her stomach like kindling.

'Stop it! It's no one! That's mine!' Maeve shouted, oblivious to Annie. Her whole body was tense, her face screwed up as she tried to snatch her art away. 'Give it back!' She was straining to be heard over their cruel laughter that filled the whole canteen, more and more students joining the crowd when they noticed the trouble.

Maeve was yelling, elbows flying in every direction around her. 'Why can't you just leave me alone? I've never done anything to you.' On the final word, she flung an accusatory finger in Jessica's direction.

A streak of flames shot through the air like a bolt from the blue. The jet of fire only narrowly missed the very top of Jessica's high ponytail and she yelped as it scorched her scrunchie, leaving a smoking trail behind it. All in the huddle that had been tightly formed around Maeve leapt back, the group dispersed as though electrocuted. The fire landed with a slam into the canteen wall, on a poster reminding students that kindness was always the coolest choice. The paper immediately burst into ash and embers, leaving the grey wall covered in just a giant black scorch mark. For one short second, nobody moved.

Then the floor began to shake – a low rumble pushing up from underneath the building, as though the foundations were being rattled – and the shutters across each window slammed in unison with a deafeningly loud, metallic crash. The fluorescent canteen lights cut out. The whole room was plunged into darkness and that soon broke the spell of silence. The canteen erupted into screams, everyone flapping hysterically. Annie felt the hairs on the back of her neck stand to attention. She knew exactly what had caused the power surge.

Magic. Wild, strong magic.

'Maeve . . .' Annie called over the chaos, a slight edge of a warning tone that sounded unfamiliar in its adultness. She stepped towards what she recognized as Maeve's silhouette in the pitch black.

'I didn't . . . I didn't mean to . . .'

Annie reached for what she could just about make out as Maeve's hand, to take it and lead her as quickly as possible away from the scene. But she jumped when she took it, finding something unexpected wrapped tightly in the palm of Maeve's hand. With a few pink sparks, Annie cast out a small burst of torchlight to see it.

Maeve unfurled her fingers to reveal a perfect, round orange. A crackle of magic burst across the small green leaves.

'Why do you have an . . . Oh no, is that . . . Is that Jessica?' Annie whispered sharply.

Maeve peered up at her and just about managed a nod.

Annie nodded back in unison, a perfectly serene smile slowly appearing across her face – her default reaction in a crisis. 'Okay. This is fine. This is absolutely fine. You bring your little friend there . . . and I will fix all of this. Somehow.' Her smile twitched ever so slightly.

'But . . . I just turned Jessica into an orange,' Maeve replied, a little too loudly. Annie counted her lucky stars that the room was still raucous. Nobody seemed to have noticed in the darkness that Jessica had suddenly vanished with a distinct scent of smoke and citrus fruit.

'Shhh. Yes, it would appear that you have indeed managed that. But that's okay. That's fine,' Annie said calmly, placing a hand on Maeve's shoulder to steer her. 'Let's get you out of here.'

Fortunately, in her stupor, Maeve blindly followed.

In the dark canteen, Annie was thankful that nobody seemed to notice the woman in the hot-pink power suit and the teenage girl clutching an orange striding towards the exit. Annie didn't pay any of them much mind any more, focused only on making sure that Maeve was safely away.

Still, Annie couldn't help but notice the boy who'd muttered the deplorable nicknames for Maeve. He was busy shoving another poor boy into a headlock, taking full advantage of the chance to get away with whatever he wanted. He earned a very sharp scowl, along with an almost imperceptible turn of a wrist. Without *Splendidus Infernum* to quiet her emotions, to take the sting out of something as imperfect as anger, for instance, the decision was made before Annie could talk herself out of it.

It was unfortunate that the poor boy would find himself with uncontrollable itching in the most unideal of orifices for the next couple of weeks, but it simply couldn't be helped. Magic worked in such unpredictable ways.

Chapter Eight

CHANGE OF PLAN

'I can fix all of this.'

Annie sounded a little shriller than she'd intended as she walked the same twenty paces over and over. She had herded Maeve sharply away from the school and guided her by the shoulders down a quiet residential road. Removing evidently-more-out-of-control-than-realized teenage powers from a busy scene seemed like the first priority. Annie knew exactly what came next, but was avoiding it for as long as celestially possible. Selcouth needed to know about this. Maeve, meanwhile, was still unable to look away from the orange in her hand and had been babbling away frantically ever since.

'I can't believe I did that . . . Did you see it?' Maeve said, stumbling over her words.

'Which part?' Annie replied, still pacing. 'The accidental transfigurative magic on a non-wicche? The spontaneous sorcery fire? The low-level earthquake in a sleepy village in northern England?'

'This magic stuff . . . It's crazy! Or am *I* crazy? Is this really happening?' Maeve removed her glasses and rubbed at her eyes.

'You're not crazy, sweetheart,' Annie said, softening slightly. 'But you are a little out of control, to say the least.'

'That was . . . that was . . .' Maeve looked as though she were about to profusely vomit at any moment, so Annie rubbed her back gently to try to bring her back down to earth.

'I don't mean that in a bad way,' Annie carried on. 'No need to worry. It's all easily fixed and I can fix anything, trust me. It's kind of my specialist subject. You haven't done anything wrong. We can just . . .'

'That was the coolest thing that has ever happened in the entire history of the universe.'

Annie stumbled back as Maeve burst into overjoyed laughter and leapt into the air, brandishing the orange as though it was a victory trophy.

'I knew magic was going to have its upsides, but oh, wow, this is unbelievable. Can I turn the whole lot of them into fruit? In fact, fruit is too good. Why did I go for an orange when I could have turned Jessica into anything?' Maeve was talking at superhuman speed, laughing frantically in between sentences as the adrenaline coursed through her. 'Can we try it again? A newt? How about I turn her into a scabby pigeon or a bin?'

Annie sighed and threw her hands onto her hips. 'No bins. No pigeons, rats, raccoons or whatever else you might be inclined to conjure,' she said, listing the options off on her fingers. 'Setting fire to the curtains at home we can handle, but accidental transfigurative incantation and almost wiping out a canteen full of kids was not what I had in mind for us on this mild October afternoon.'

'You're being dramatic,' Maeve said, sagging a little and

mirroring Annie's unimpressed body language. 'I didn't hurt anyone. I just . . . orange-ified her a bit.'

'A bit?' Annie said, eyes pointedly fixed on the very fully formed orange. 'Maeve, you threw fire. Actual sorcery fire, from the palm of your hand no less.'

'Sounds pretty impressive when you put it like that,' Maeve said, unable to hide a proud smirk.

'Oh, it would be extremely impressive – *if* you were intentional in your magic use. But there's nothing impressive about chucking it around willy-nilly. You're supposed to control your magic, not the other way around.'

Maeve shrugged indignantly. 'Maybe I don't actually need any help with magic at all. Seems like it's working pretty well to me.'

Annie scoffed, remembering how this feisty girl had seemed like such a gentle wallflower on first impressions. 'Don't go getting too big for your boots, young lady.' She immediately hated how adult she sounded, using the phrase 'young lady'. *She* was the young lady, wasn't she? When did this happen? She shook back her curls to clear her head. 'Uncontrolled magic is not cool.'

'Yes, you seem like someone with her finger on the pulse of "cool",' Maeve said acidly. 'They deserved it,' she added as she pushed her glasses up the bridge of her nose.

Annie, having witnessed the way they'd treated Maeve, found she couldn't exactly argue with that. 'Maybe they did . . . But it's not just about a one-off dabble in Incantation on your school bully. There's the small matter of risking the exposure of wicchekind, Maeve. Do you know how tricky it's going to be to wipe so many memories of your escapades back there?'

Maeve chewed at her bottom lip, then huffed. 'Okay, maybe I didn't think about that part. Luckily, that lot would never even consider the possible existence of magic. They're all far too boring to think big. Don't stress about it. They'll just see it as more proof of how weird I am.'

Annie exhaled loudly, tapping her foot as she began to think. 'Maeve, not to be a total bore, but I am going to have to tell the coven about this. They're not great fans of anomalies in the magic system and you certainly are a rare one.'

'Is that your polite way of calling me a pain in the . . .'

'I think it's the best thing to do here,' Annie spoke loudly over her, hoping that assertiveness would give the illusion that she knew what she was doing. 'I'm not sure they realize quite how haywire your magic is. She's not going to like it, but . . .'

Annie paused for a moment, wriggled her shoulder pads back into place and closed her eyes in concentration. A crackle of magic popped between her fingers and, moments later, Morena appeared like a storm cloud in front of a flowering red rhododendron to their right. Maeve stumbled back into the bushes with shock, hand flying to her mouth.

'Shit!'

Morena squinted slightly at the brightness and, once she'd adjusted to her new location, stared stony-faced from Annie to Maeve and back again.

'Thank you for that most bracing welcome, Miss Cadmus. I shall be sure to greet you in the same way next time our paths cross,' Morena said as she adjusted her cloak over her crisp shirt. She turned her attention to Annie with raised eyebrows. 'Well?'

Annie rushed to her. 'Morena, you know I would never,

ever request a summoned transference from you unless it was absolutely necessary.'

'I should hope not. And to this universe-forsaken realm, of all of them? This had better be very, very good, Andromeda.'

'It's more the direct opposite.' Annie hesitated. 'I fear this may be very, very bad.'

'I know you,' Maeve interrupted as she approached Morena with a pointed finger, the orange-shaped Jessica clutched in her other hand. 'You bought me that big old book for my birthday, with your small sister.'

'Yes, I'm rather like a fairy godmother in that way, aren't I?' Morena's mouth pursed so tightly that her lipstick turned to a small circle. 'Except you would never catch me dead in that atrocious uniform. Andromeda, what exactly is the quandary here?'

Annie froze, unsure of where to start, then gave a breathy laugh. 'Honestly, you're never going to believe it . . .'

'I set the canteen on fire, cut the power, caused an earthquake and then turned Jessica into an orange,' Maeve interrupted, handing the piece of fruit over to Morena.

Morena didn't move for a moment, then with a resigned sigh took a pair of glasses from the inside pocket of her cloak and placed them on the end of her nose. She accepted the orange to examine it in fine detail. 'Andromeda, do you mean to tell me that this citrus fruit is in fact a non-wicche student?'

'Like I said, she deserved it,' Maeve muttered under her breath.

'She's not entirely wrong about that,' Annie said, glowing when she received a small, secretive smile from Maeve for her camaraderie, which almost made the whole thing worth it. 'And, looking back, it was a rather impressive series of events, if not an ideal one. We may have quite a special witch on our hands.'

At that, Maeve beamed.

'A special witch is of absolutely no use to me if she is going to give Selcouth days' worth of complex and dreary memory reset work. Not to mention the fact that teenagers are particularly tricky to magically manipulate, what with all the hormones flying around,' Morena drawled.

'What can I do to help?' Annie asked, a hand to her forehead. 'Morena, it's all my fault. I should have removed Maeve more quickly, as soon as I sensed that things were going south. My intuition was a little . . . squiffy at the school.'

'Squiffy indeed. Miss Cadmus, will you excuse us for a moment? Take your orange for a walk,' Morena said, handing Jessica back. Maeve wandered a few paces away with a sniff and a scuff of her shoes against the pavement.

Morena turned to Annie with a flourish of her cloak. 'To be frank, Andromeda, the most helpful thing that can be done about this mess is to swiftly remove Miss Cadmus. Not only is it highly dangerous to her, particularly if there seems to be some sort of affinity towards fire of all things,' she tutted. 'But there remains a huge exposure risk until her powers are under control.'

'I can take her to my house?' Annie offered, but instantly regretted it. It was a habit of hers, suggesting solutions that she then prayed would not be accepted. She thought of her bathroom, stocked to the rafters with highly potent potion ingredients, not to mention her midnight *Splendidus Infernum* ritual, which, for all she knew, could run amok with an unpredictable magical presence in the vicinity. Plus there was Karma, who hated spontaneous visitors and would have to be bribed with inordinate amounts of custard. Annie felt a tidal wave of relief when Morena shook her head.

'Absolutely not. London is far too populated. And neutral ground is a better choice, given the unpredictability of her powers. Selcouth will provide emergency accommodation for the two of you.'

Annie's heart began to patter at an unsteady rhythm. 'Accommodation? For us both?' Panic started to lace its way through her veins with a cold, icy trail.

'I regret to say that this shall be more of a nannying role than initially anticipated. A live-in companionship for the time being, so that you may monitor her closely,' Morena said, pacing while she considered. 'It may be a rather all-encompassing role. I personally cannot think of anything more frightful.' She visibly shuddered.

Being sent away, somewhere unknown, with full responsibility for Maeve, felt terrifying for many, many reasons. Annie actually felt a wave of nausea at the prospect. Her thoughts began to run away from her. Being away from home, her finely tuned routine thrown into disarray, her diary descending into chaos. Dates began to jumble, plans began to criss-cross, her head ached. How would she keep everything running perfectly, just as it was supposed to? What would she have to let go of?

'For how long?' Annie gulped, earning only an unconcerned shrug in return.

'Until we see satisfactory improvements.'

There was Celeste to think about – although at least she could trust Faye and Pari to man the fort temporarily. Perhaps she could bake at long distance, transfer the goods by magic? But her precious, important time spent at the Sorciety would surely have to be put on hold. As she saw her Crescent status fade further into the distance, Annie felt as though she was dangling from a ladder above a vortex and each rung at her feet was beginning to break away.

As though sensing the waves of panic beginning to emanate from her apprentice and the rare possibility that Annie may actually be preparing herself to say no, Morena cleared her throat.

'A pertinent reminder, Ms Wildwood. This situation would be a perfect chance to impress and prove oneself. Rising in the face of adversity, stepping up when the coven is in need . . . The sort of act that doesn't go unnoticed by Selcouth.'

Annie frantically twiddled a curl of her hair, then smoothed it back into place before twiddling again. She attempted to surrender to *Splendidus Infernum*, to allow it to readjust her thinking and to uncover the positives. People needed her once again. Acknowledging the thought stirred the spell at every nerve ending.

Impressing at Selcouth would also secure her further at the Sorciety. Glory Whitlock would be thrilled, proud to hear that Annie was moving closer to the inner eye of the storm. She was needed. Morena needed her, the coven needed her and . . .

She glanced around to Maeve, who was now playing keepy-up with the orange.

Maybe this young girl needed her, too.

Magic bubbled at the ends of her fingers, behind her eyes, at the base of her skull, connecting the dots and firing up the neurons. Rose-coloured glasses were all very well and good, but Annie's rose-coloured magic was even more effective. Perhaps the opportunity could be considerably chicer than she'd first thought. Images of a beautiful, wintery chalet flashed across her mind. Or a luxury river-side apartment, where they could share fruit platters on the balcony. Everything began to feel a touch brighter, the edges of her world turning pink again.

Morena tapped her foot. 'Well? Can I count on you to fix this, Andromeda?'

As if she had a choice. As if she could say no.

'Of course, Morena,' Annie smiled. 'I'll be like an even more magical Mary Poppins.'

Morena looked appalled. 'Pop in where?'

'Never mind.'

Morena gave a quick, satisfied '*hmm*'. 'Well, now that I'm here, I'd better do what I do best and follow the faint sounds of screaming. I shall rectify this situation as best I can.' She began to gather up the hem of her cloak, beckoning Maeve back. 'Ta-ta for now, Miss Cadmus. You shall remain at a safe house, under the care of Ms Wildwood for the foreseeable future. Would you give me that?' she asked, gesturing to the orange.

Maeve reluctantly threw the fruit underarm to Morena, who caught it smoothly in one hand as if it were a baseball. 'Andromeda, expect to hear from me when this has settled down to the coven's satisfaction.'

'Absolutely. We'll have a wonderful time, won't we, Maeve?' Annie found that she was bobbing up and down a little, grinning far too enthusiastically and . . . yes, she was clapping again. Her natural optimism, combined with the push and pull of the fractured spell, were causing strange, extremely annoying reactions. The girl only shrugged back in response.

On that note, Morena turned on her heel with a final dramatic flourish of her cloak, the deep purple flashing richly.

Annie called after her. 'Morena? You haven't told us where we're going. Morena . . . !'

Without even a glance backwards, Morena only raised a hand with an open palm and a wordless gesture of magic. The Sage Witch's transferral spell had knitted itself together before Annie could get an answer. A lash of whipping wind gathered her up with the girl and sent them away in a quick, thrumming vortex of time and space and speed.

'Woah.' Maeve staggered and Annie lunged to catch her.

'Poor thing, it really is rotten the first few times,' Annie said kindly. 'We ought to prioritize some kind of soft version of transference for first-timers. Now, where in the world . . .'

Under Morena's incantation, the transferral spell had taken them to what could only be described as the middle of nowhere, a small woodland clearing that felt as though it were painted in sepia. The bustle of London and even Maeve's quiet village felt a world away as a dense silence fell suddenly around them, save for the rustling of leaves and some chirpy bird song. Slim, silver-barked trunks towered above, as though they were stretched straight from the sky, and nearly bare branches knotted together like an intricate birdcage, the last of their golden brown treasure sprinkling over the witches with the breeze. The air was fresh with a nutty, earthy scent – damp soil, sleeping animals and the ripe, bursting blackberries that were smattered across the tangles of lower brambles.

Something bleated faintly in the distance.

'Was that a . . . sheep?' Annie blurted out at an extremely high pitch.

Maeve snorted. 'Don't worry, I'll protect you. Maybe we're camping? That could be fun.'

Annie let out a horrified noise, somewhere between a gasp and a death rattle. 'Maeve, don't joke about such things. Still,' she went on, not allowing herself to falter too long, 'we can make the best of a little adventure, can't we?' She scooped up her briefcase, shook back her hair and marched forwards with renewed purpose, even in the face of what she could only describe as . . . nature.

'Do you actually know the way?' Maeve asked, sounding sceptical. She shielded her eyes from the dappled golden hour light that was leaking into the forest like melted butter, pouring onto the skirt of fallen leaves kicking up at their feet.

'Not exactly. But it can't be far and I know a spell to help us,' Annie said. She popped her briefcase back on the ground, careful to avoid any particularly muddy patches, and flexed her wrist. A flow of *Iter Rectio* sparks flew from her fingers towards it, catching the sunlight as they circled. The briefcase began to rattle, as though something inside were clamouring to escape. She picked it back up and the case promptly lurched forwards, dragging her arm with it like an untrained puppy on a lead. She beckoned back over her shoulder to Maeve to follow as the briefcase led the way.

'Keep up!' Annie called as her arm was tugged forwards, hop-skipping over tree roots in her high heels. 'Any second now, we'll break through these woods and there'll be a beautiful park-side townhouse waiting for us. I just know it. Maybe Georgian or Edwardian. I bet there's a balcony and a reading room. An amazing potions pantry. Oh, and I hadn't even thought about the kitchen . . . Probably a giant cast-iron stove and a larder, one of those lovely new mixing machines,' she said dreamily. 'Every modern and magical convenience you can think of. Maybe we can try some new recipes tonight, some soothing autumn comfort food to settle ourselves in. And dessert. Are you hungry?'

'I guess,' Maeve muttered, power-walking to keep up.

'Little sweet treats are so important, don't you think?' Annie pushed aside a few rogue branches and hopped over a bunch of sticky weeds. 'Anyway, what's been your favourite thing about your magic so far?' The unexpected question sent Maeve careering back into her shell. It was going to be a long road, memorizing which questions were entirely mortifying to a teenager and which were slightly more acceptable.

'I dunno. Stuff.'

'Stuff is wonderful. I love all kinds of stuff, too,' Annie replied, desperate to not let the conversation die completely. Maeve's confidence seemed to flare and shrink with the flip of a coin. But, despite Annie's best efforts, the two witches continued their unplanned hike in silence, until the briefcase eventually fell to the floor with a sudden thud.

'Are we here?' Maeve peered around Annie's side.

Annie let out a small, disturbed squeak. Unwelcome visions of a two-man polyester tent grew stronger. She recalled Faye once telling her all about a weekend camping trip when they'd had to use a tiny portable stove to heat a tin of beans and suddenly Annie felt as though she might cry.

She willed herself to find a solution, looking for some kind of signal from Morena that they had reached their destination. Anything would be reassuring. It was almost entirely . . . leafy. And orange. And brown. Autumnal certainly, but she couldn't concentrate on the cosiness potential at a time like this. The October evening light was quickly dwindling. What was Selcouth thinking, sending them to the middle of nowhere on a whim, with no further help or even some kind of treasure map? What kind of covert magical organization didn't at least leave a treasure map lying around? She'd be having words with the admin department, that was for sure.

'There, look.' Maeve pointed.

Through the gaps in the dense trees, a single glow of lemon-yellow fell just ahead of them, like a singular firefly to guide their eyes. The place was well disguised from prying eyes, a blanket of enchantments knotted together tightly to keep it from view. Only a very particular angle of light and shadow, as if caught and trapped through a prism, revealed where to look through the thickets. Each step closer brought it more clearly into view and, when Maeve parted the foliage, an open, dusk-drenched glade was tucked away and waiting quietly. Annie gave a sigh of relief, waiting for the manifestation to complete itself. A gorgeous lakehouse would suit them nicely. Maybe a sprawling luxury farmhouse. Or a classic castle, freshly renovated for the modern witch's requirements.

Instead, exactly in the centre of the meadow and framed in the orange of the woodland, sat a tiny, shabby cottage.

Chapter Nine

SALTED CARAMEL

'Oh no.' Annie's voice was barely more than a whisper. Even from a distance, the cottage looked as run-down and dishevelled as if it had been rudely awoken from a long, unintentional nap, one that had only left it even sleepier than before. Its sandy thatched roof stuck up at all angles like ruffled, sleep-styled hair, trails of moss as thick as pistachio cream lined the gutters, and the wooden slats of the walls were a hodge-podge of wonky angles and slipped lines. A crowd of tangled greenery wound its way up the building, one crooked window peeping through the leaves, with red gingham curtains just about visible behind the murky glass like an embarrassed blush. It was a pocket-sized, abandoned trinket left behind, as though someone had left their most prized possession hidden away to come back and collect later, but moved on and forgotten all about it.

'Come on then,' Maeve called, already skipping ahead through the tawny long grass.

'Mmmhmm,' Annie replied through pursed lips. In her admittedly unsuitable footwear choice, she delicately followed Maeve who had already reached the porch, chasing the winding path towards the burgundy front door. The circle of woodland around the meadow blazed with autumn colours and encased the cottage in a backdrop of fiery oranges, rich scarlets and buttery yellows. As she approached the boarded porch, which housed a broken swing that blew in the breeze, Annie spotted clusters of polka-dot red mushrooms nestled in the beige grass, bursts of soft heather and bunny ears like cream-coloured, fluffy fountains. And, she had to admit, the wildflowers in lavender and blue that bloomed through were beautiful and matched the evening sky perfectly, as though the meadow had decided a handful of sprinkles would be a suitable finishing touch.

'Well, this is . . . quaint. Rustic. Um, pastoral?' she said, mustering her last drop of positivity as she stepped straight into a muddy puddle. *Splendidus Infernum* was being tested to its limits. The hex would need considerable attention this evening. Her stomach plummeted even further as she realized – the spell. Would she even be able to manage it here? Did filthy, abandoned cottages come equipped with large bathtubs and a full arsenal of quality alchemy ingredients to peruse? Annie let out a squeal and karate-chopped the air as a persistent dragonfly began to circle her head, accidentally wobbling the string of lanterns that hung along the breadth of the porch. She cursed her signature sweet vanilla scent.

Maeve on the other hand had perked up dramatically, impressed by the reveal of her first ever magically disclosed secret location. She did a terrible job at suppressing a loud laugh as Annie battled the dragonfly, then excitedly discovered the front door was already unlocked after rattling the handle. They stood side by side as it swung back with a pained squeak, as though its bones were aching and hadn't been moved for quite some time. Maeve was quick to hop inside and gave a little shiver as she stepped across the threshold. It was chilly — colder inside the place than out, having evidently been left empty for quite some time.

'Home sweet home,' Maeve laughed as she rushed into the kitchen, clearly finding the whole thing hilarious.

Annie laughed too and her hands flew to her hips. 'There must be some mistake.' The heel of her shoe promptly slipped through a gap between the floorboards as she followed the girl inside. She clung onto the doorframe to wrestle herself free. 'They can't possibly expect us to . . .'

'This is the right place. Look, that stamp is from the coven, isn't it? I recognize it from the paperwork the sisters gave me at my endarkenment,' Maeve said. She had picked up a black envelope, adorned with an intricate silver star illustration. It was addressed to Andromeda Wildwood and had been lying patiently on a simple square dining table for her to find. She took it from Maeve and began to read, the copperplate handwriting lighting up with an amber glow as her eyes scanned the page. Magical correspondence always glowed whenever it was read by the eyes of wicchefolk.

Andromeda,

I trust you shall find your accommodation satisfactory. We were in somewhat of a pinch to house you and your ward in such last-minute circumstances, as most of the coven's usual options were already reserved for October. It is of course busy season in this line of work and wicchefolk do enjoy their inane mini breaks for Samhain celebrations. Most inconvenient, if you ask me.

Arden Place belongs to a trusted and acclaimed coven

member but has remained unused for some time, so the cottage is yours for the task at hand. I thought its understated, solitary nature would provide a suitable and safe blank canvas for you and young Maeve to become comrades. There may be a minor issue with the hot water,* but surely nothing that a little magic can't fix. You'll find the wood supply out back (I imagine you are a dab hand with an axe), along with the bathroom facilities.

I shall be monitoring closely and aim to be in touch in due course when Maeve's magic has settled to something more harmonious. I would ask you to remember your esteemed duties to the coven above all else and, as previously agreed, to report trouble to me immediately. Strays can be unpredictable and Selcouth does not appreciate anomalies.

Have jolly good fun and do send a postcard. Address it to Bronwyn, as I shan't care to read it.

Morena

* See also, the electrics, the heating, the lights, the locks. There may also be rather a lot of creatures about the place. I cannot confirm any further details than that, for fear that you may leave and never return.

'Bathroom facilities? Out back?' Annie spluttered.

She sprinted to the rear window and smeared a clearing through the grime with her sleeve to press her face against, leaving a touch of lipstick on the glass. True enough, a small wooden outhouse stood in the garden – which was in fact just more meadow, surrounded by even more woodland. She spotted the basic facilities: a water closet, a free-standing sink, a silver metal tub and simple shower system, all behind a movable wooden privacy screen and directly beneath the stars. A small, babbling stream of periwinkle blue wrapped around it all like a ribbon. She gulped so hard that it may have been audible, as Maeve stepped closer looking concerned.

'Everything alright?' Maeve peered through the window next to Annie, her glasses slipping and clinking against the glass.

'Absolutely. Couldn't be better,' Annie rushed to reply. Her grin stretched a little madly. 'Well, you were right. This really is the place.' She had to force herself to turn back around and face the girl. The pair stood in silence for a moment with matching, uncertain expressions – Annie's slightly maniacal, Maeve more intrigued, as they took in their unexpected new home.

To one side of the cottage was a small open kitchen, everything made from rough-hewn wood and worn brass. A line of well-used copper pots and pans was hanging from a rack above the stove range and a rusting, scratched-up cauldron had been left to the side, an encrusted layer of something dark green and over-stewed sitting in the bottom. Bunches of old dried herbs hung with damp-stained string from the ceiling beams. The few shelves were packed with a clumsy clutter of half-empty jars. The kitchen's one saving grace was the wide window above the sink, which, although filthy and framed with frankly offensive lace curtains, offered up a view of the glade outside.

The other side comprised the living room: a flattened sofa, one threadbare armchair with stuffing weeping through the seams, a rocking chair. The hearth was covered in a thick layer of soot and feathers that had tumbled down the chimney. Crowded bookshelves flanked the fireplace, but were thick with dust.

Even as someone with a terrible habit of landing herself in unwanted situations to keep others happy, this one had to take the biscuit. And the cake. And the cinnamon bun, too. What had she gotten herself into? The pair of them clearly had next to nothing in common, polar opposites in all ways. That fact alone was guaranteed to make it next to impossible for Annie to have any kind of breakthrough or teach anything of value. The girl clearly thought she was hopeless and would take no notice of her if she attempted any discipline or learning. It was like adding unwanted sugar to a distinctly savoury recipe, two different flavours that clashed dramatically.

Although – Annie's optimism elbowed its way through as *Splendidus Infernum* fired up – someone *had* invented salted caramel with entirely excellent results, she contemplated. And ketchup, as a concept. And apple sauce, specifically on a roast dinner. Perhaps she and Maeve could be a similar unexpectedly sweet combination.

She clapped her hands together decidedly, making Maeve jump. 'New plan. This place needs a magical makeover and, if there's one thing I know, it's makeovers,' Annie chimed. 'It'll be like we're on one of those home-renovation shows. An extreme deep clean, a lick of paint, some throw cushions, a drastic and immediate change of curtains . . . This place will be gorgeous. Right?' Her fingers waggled as her imagination began to awaken and a spray of pink sparks glittered around her waist.

Maeve laughed. 'Gorgeous might be a bit strong. Why does it feel like you're about to turn this dump into your Malibu dream house?'

'You think there's dream house potential?' Annie said, firing a wink in Maeve's direction.

She spun on the spot and delivered a swirl of magic in the direction of the wooden ceiling beams. A dainty floral pattern chased its way along the wood, chains of hand-drawn bluebells, daisies and lilacs painted across each one by an invisible brush.

'It just needs a witch's touch . . .'

Annie's magic conjured more alterations. The sofa changed to a pale blush pink, a whole assortment of soft throws and floral cushions springing up to match like marshmallows on the top. The threadbare rug turned fluffy under their feet, making their toes wriggle and Maeve cackle as it tickled. Vintage teacups appeared with a rattle on the simple coffee table, a roll of floral wallpaper unfurled itself above the fireplace and a wreath of pink roses and baby's breath wove itself around the pane in the front door. Finally and most crucially, she summoned a duster, a dishcloth and a mop and set them to work, feathers and suds flying to tackle the cobwebbed nooks and crannies.

'This feels like the part in a kid's film when you're supposed to be singing a catchy song with a talking badger or something,' Maeve said with a stubborn eye-roll. But Annie noticed that even she couldn't hide a childlike glint of delight in her eyes as the transformations unfolded, a sparkling twirl of incantation surrounding them.

Perhaps not quite a dream house just yet, but it was clean and the soft colours made Annie feel more at ease. She itched to go wild with her visions for the place, but she held herself back, realizing that the transformative incantations would be some of the most overt displays of magic that Maeve had ever seen. It should be a gradual process – she didn't want to completely overwhelm the girl, who already thought that she was too much.

'Much better,' Annie said triumphantly, dusting off her hands. 'Never let it be said that I can't make the best of a bad situation. Do you want to help me do something about these ghastly net curtains next?'

Maeve flinched with a shiver and her smile dropped a fraction. Annie cursed herself for not being thoughtful enough to immediately light a fire. A string of pink sparks towards the hearth rectified that immediately, roaring flames springing up behind the grate with a crackle.

Maeve just shrugged again and turned to face away. 'I think I'll probably just get an early night.'

'Oh.' Annie's shoulders sagged, taken aback by the sudden flip. Teenagers really were as unpredictable as everybody said. 'I thought we could do face masks. I packed us a few.'

'I have sensitive skin,' Maeve mumbled.

'But . . . they're fruity?'

'And homework to do, so I should probably just . . .'

'Well, afterwards? How about I conjure us some pizzas and a Halloween video and you can tell me about how you've been finding your magic so far? Is it just oranges you're dabbling in? Or have you ventured into pineapples yet? Considerably more spikes involved, so I guess the health and safety aspect is questionable.'

Annie could have punched the air when an almost imperceptible twitchy smile came back to Maeve's face for a second, but the girl quickly caught it. 'Thanks, but like you said, I've brought you enough of a bad situation to handle today. Sorry to be a burden. It's kind of just what I always do. Besides, I'm not really hungry. I think I'll just . . .'

Frowning, Maeve scooped up her sketchbooks from the dining table and headed over to the one separate downstairs room. It was slotted next to the narrow, winding staircase at the back of the cottage. In her mini makeover, Annie had conjured a delicate script of purple and blue to paint 'Maeve's room' in looped letters on the door. Maeve peered around it, noted the simple bed frame, bare mattress and side table and rocked back on her heels, waiting for permission to leave.

'Right. You go relax, decompress, of course it's been a big day for you. Sorry, I shouldn't have assumed, I just . . .'

'It's fine,' Maeve replied, their words clashing, that early wall of awkwardness between them building itself back up tenfold.

'Well, goodnight,' Annie said, her voice uncomfortably high. 'I'll be right upstairs if you need me. If you need anything. In fact, silly me . . .' She flicked her wrist and more sparkles glided around the bedroom door. 'There. I've made up your bed and you'll find some new pyjamas, plus a full drawer of my favourite toiletries. That should be everything you need, at least for tonight? We can get a bit more organized in the morning.'

Maeve nodded, chewing on her bottom lip. Annie, for some inexplicable reason, gave an enthusiastic wave and immediately regretted it as Maeve raised her eyebrows. Just as the door was about to close, Annie couldn't help but blurt out a final thought. 'Maeve?' She cringed, adjusted her volume a little. 'You are never, ever a burden, okay? Not with anybody, but especially not with me. I'm so pleased to be here with you.'

At that, Maeve peered back around the door and frowned for a moment, as though confused by how to respond. She only gave a tiny nod, then shut the door behind her with a click.

Annie felt her entire skeleton sigh as the tension broke. She hadn't realized how tightly wound she'd been all day. Tightly wound was her normal state, a familiar rigidity that ensured nothing could go wrong. But today, it hadn't worked. Everything was entirely out of her control and she had found herself in the middle of nowhere, with a difficult teenager who thought her new guardian was a ridiculous cupcake of a witch. Which, perhaps, she was a bit.

Her head fell into her hands and she cursed herself for every single silly decision she'd made throughout the day. With *Splendidus Infernum* entirely redundant when it came to her relationship with Maeve, Annie was already making huge mistakes: stumbling over her words, endlessly awkward, putting her foot in it over and over without even understanding how or why. Being here with Maeve meant that Annie's real self was going to be more on display than she had allowed in forever. She wasn't even sure she knew what – or who – that was any more. What *was* abundantly clear was that Maeve didn't seem to like her much – and Annie didn't blame her in the slightest. This was going to be a long, long stay at Arden Place.

'What have I done?' Annie asked herself in a whisper.

Darkness had descended outside and was spilling into the cottage, stealing away the temporary feeling of comfort and cosiness that she naively thought she had managed to create. It was going to take more than a few superficial tweaks. Maybe it wasn't possible for her to make a happy home at all, having not known one herself in a very long time.

Annie sighed and glanced back at the herbs hanging from the beams of the kitchen ceiling. With Maeve having chosen an early night (or, she suspected, just removing herself as soon as possible from Annie's company), she should turn her attention to the most pressing problem.

'Lavender for creativity, compassion, calming, new ideas,' Annie said to herself.

The spell wouldn't work on her relationship with Maeve, and she would have to accept that, but Annie could still maintain as much balance across the board as she possibly could – think more efficiently, gain control of the situation, shine up her outlook to something more polished. All she had to do was be perfect again. She would be letting everyone down if she buckled.

Standing on her tiptoes, Annie snapped off a stem of the lavender and crushed it in her palm to a fragrant powder. She headed to the back door and quietly snicked it open, steeling herself as she always had to for what was to come. Regrets, mistakes, heartbreak . . . Her heart cowered.

A bath would help.

Chapter Ten

THE PRACTICE OF MAGIC

Annie began the first day at Arden Place before the birds had even awoken. Rummaging through the kitchen cupboards in the dark to find anything more than one single mug and one single plate, she promptly admitted defeat and conjured her pink moka pot and a fresh bag of industrial-strength coffee beans. Caffeine was always the best place to start and, as she took the first, rocket-fuelled sip, it felt as though she had pushed up the central lever in an abandoned factory, fluorescent lights flickering on and whirring sounds starting up. It was time to make magic happen.

There was no point sulking. She had to make the best of the situation like she always did, as she could always be relied on to do. This mess wasn't about her. In fact, she had been selfish to centre herself in this, to let her positivity waver so dramatically yesterday. No more.

While the first rays of morning light spilled through the lace curtains from creamy clouds, the sound of birdsong was scattering across the pink-to-blue sky. The rundown cottage was certainly not what she'd had in mind and her heart already longed for London's rush and routine, but Annie had to admit to herself that this moment of peace, as she sipped and schemed, leaning against the countertop to look out onto the meadow, was not entirely terrible. Each blade of bristling grass was gilded, as though it had been dipped in honey, with autumn sunlight, which spilled into the cottage with a soft, romantic glow.

After successfully managing to conduct *Splendidus Infernum* in the outdoor tub with a patchwork of make-do ingredients from the meadow, the spell had been boosted and a vague plan was falling into place. As all good plans did, it began with breakfast. A little treat or two would make everything better and, if she couldn't head to Celeste, Annie would simply have to bring Celeste to the cottage. The Arden Place kitchen was looking distinctly pinker than before. She had stocked it full of produce and filled the kitchen shelves with an abundance of ingredients, along with her favourite cookbooks (and her personal grimoire). The small dining table now wore a mint-green silk-trimmed tablecloth and a vase stuffed with frilly dahlias.

She matched the birdsong with the clatter of a whisk that was working of its own accord in the fluffiest pancake mix. There was the sizzle of fat popping in one of the copper pans while sunny golden yolks cooked, alongside browning sausages and crisping bacon. Annie spun from cooker to countertop while a feast came together in a cloud of her most natural magic. Best of all, she assumed that either her singing or the sugar-sweet scents must have been responsible for attracting the interest of various woodland dwellers. A young deer peered through the window with greedy eyes. Just above the sink, two rabbits had leapt up onto the sill and were sitting either side of the tap. A whole family of chaffinches with plump orange cheeks had taken it upon themselves to fill an empty milk bottle with a purple wildflower arrangement.

Annie poured a stream of velvety chocolate into a jug, to pair with the pancakes, which were multiplying at a rate that felt ever so slightly out of control. The heavenly smells were finally beginning to replace the airless, musty scent of the cottage that had greeted them the night before.

She turned to reach for the icing sugar, then screamed. Maeve, having appeared from nowhere and making no noticeable sound, was watching every move with a slightly agape mouth. Annie toppled backwards against the countertop and clutched at her heart.

'Maeve! Good morning! You caught me by surprise there. Don't worry, I didn't need a functioning heart anyway. Overrated, if you ask me,' Annie laughed, re-twisting her hair, which had tumbled in the fright. She fastened it back with her pencil and tightened the waist bow of her apron.

'I just wondered what smelled so good.'

'You didn't witness me singing into the wooden spoon, did you? Because if you did, I will pay you to keep that a secret between us.'

Maeve snorted. 'I might have done.'

'Great. You'll never respect me as your leader now,' Annie lamented, then turned back to flip the pancakes. They soared so high with the bounce from her magic that they grazed the ceiling, then plopped back into the pan with a smattering of buttery bubbles. 'What can I get you? You must be starving.'

'Can I just get a cup of coffee?'

'Maeve.' Annie's hands went to her hips and she scowled. 'You need to eat for brain power. Otherwise how will I impart centuries of magical wisdom and expert guidance?' This earned another snort-laugh from Maeve. 'Come on, I made . . . Well, I made everything. I wasn't sure what you'd like. Come and help yourself.'

Maeve shuffled over, clutching a book as always.

'Do we secretly have seven jewel miners, an evil queen and a forest-dwelling huntsman coming to join us this morning? This is insane,' Maeve said, as a pair of sparrows flew to her shoulders with a napkin between their beaks and tucked it into the collar of her pyjama top. Yawning, she flopped a couple of pancakes onto her plate, along with a giant spoonful of fresh strawberries and a very generous drizzle of chocolate that formed a moat around her food. 'Okay, maybe I am hungry . . .'

'What are you reading?' Annie asked, aiming for casual while she finished off arranging the selection of pastries that she'd summoned straight from Celeste's counter. Faye would be far too busy with the coffee orders to notice and she could only hope that Pari would still be too sleepy to see them vanish. Fortunately, both of them had been absolutely over the moon when Annie had used the rusty, rotary dial phone by the cottage door to call, imparting the surprising news that she'd be away for a while at a 'recreation centre' for 'team building' on her 'scheme'. Faye had encouraged her to try bouldering if they had a climbing wall, and Pari told her to watch out for black cats and faceless figures wearing cowboy hats, because she'd had a strange dream – and that was that. Perhaps asking them for help wasn't the completely mortifying, world-ending task that she always built it up to be. In fact, it had been very easy.

Maeve reached for one of the pains au chocolat and dunked

the end into a scoop of Faye's plum jam. Maeve slid the book across the table to Annie, a copy of *Feral Familiars: Tame Them All, From Black Widow to Mole Rat*.

'I found it on the bookshelf when I couldn't sleep. This place has tons of animal books. Do you think . . . Do you think I'll be able to have a familiar?' Maeve asked, her brows stitched together in a very serious expression. Annie felt a fizzing in her chest and for once it wasn't driven by anxiety. It was a second-hand thrill for everything that lay ahead for Maeve and her magic. This scenario was not what either of them had been expecting. But magic was supposed to be fun – otherwise, what was the point at all? That was something that she hadn't taken much notice of for a while.

This was a project. A messy starting point for her to unpick the knots and restitch into something that felt familiar and neat and right. A recipe that needing tweaking, extra sugar and spices to find the balance.

'It's kind of a package deal,' Annie explained as she poured herself a fresh cup, then hesitated over a second mug. 'Are you old enough to drink coffee?' Maeve glared in response, so she poured her one, too. 'If an animal familiar hasn't made themselves known to you already, then it's imminent. One of the branches of magic is Animal Affinity – and that means having a familiar in your life, whether you like it or not. Judging by that lot, I don't think you'll be having any trouble.'

Annie gestured towards the window full of woodland creatures, who all seemed to have forgotten about the pancakes on offer and were instead peering intently at Maeve as she scooped another spoonful of berries onto her plate. Annie glanced from the menagerie to Maeve and back again, a strange thought springing to mind. Had it been Maeve they were interested in all along, rather than her or her sweet-scented baking?

'I've never had a pet of my own before, but I've always wanted one,' Maeve said. 'There was a toad once, which I caught and kept in my room for a while. He kept trying to escape though, so I felt bad and set him free. He came back to visit every so often; I'd wake up and find him sitting on the end of my bed. Slimy, but cute.'

'In that case, we'll make a special effort to look out for any potential familiar pairings. There's no better place than in the middle of the countryside. Maybe you'll get something particularly cool.' Annie glanced back at the full cast of creatures intently watching them eat breakfast.

'I hope it's not a toad,' Maeve said with a grimace. 'What have you got?'

'A cat,' Annie smiled proudly, dusting pastry flakes off her fingers. 'Cliché, I know, but she's perfect. In fact, I'd better summon her, she'll be wondering what's taking so long.' She stood up from the table and headed over to the couch, then began to wriggle a stream of sparks from her finger like water. She paused. 'You're not allergic, are you?'

Maeve shook her head and folded her legs underneath her on the wooden chair, evidently excited, and that was all the encouragement Annie needed. Karma appeared on one of the blankets, arriving on a petal-pink cloud of magic. She let out a tiny mew and trotted straight over to give Annie a pleased headbutt on the hip from the arm of the sofa. Annie scooped her up into her arms and carried her over to Maeve.

'Karma, I'd like you to meet someone very special. I know you're not one for unfamiliar company, but please be nice,' Annie said desperately. She tried not to recall the times that

Karma had encountered ex-boyfriends, Romily, Vivienne, Harmony, Glory . . . All had resulted in at least one minor injury, with Karma refusing to warm to any of them and reasonably concluding that their forearms deserved a personalized combination of kicks, bites and scratches.

'Aren't you just the prettiest girl I've ever seen,' Maeve said in an unusually sweet voice. Before Annie could take a tighter hold, Karma wriggled from her grasp and immediately leapt at Maeve. Annie lunged, but the snowy cat simply picked her way through the plates, rested her front paws on Maeve's shoulder and nuzzled her with a trilling purr and a flick of her outrageously fluffy tail.

'She likes you!' Annie said, astonished. This whole scenario continued to get stranger by the second. 'I'm going to take that as a very good omen for our first day of exploring your magic. It's time we figured out what makes it tick, besides the idiots at school. Are you excited?'

Maeve shrugged, which Annie was starting to learn was a reflexive means of communicating 'yes' rather than indifference.

'Good enough for me. I thought we could start with some kind of—'

'What were you doing last night?' Maeve blurted out.

'What?'

'I saw you go outside when I went to find a book. Just before midnight – and you were gone for a while. Was it some kind of witchy moon ritual? Did you sacrifice something? Can I join in?'

Annie blanched. She was certain that she'd waited long enough for Maeve to be fast asleep before she began the spell, leaving it until the very last few minutes before midnight.

How careless of her not to have triple checked. She forced herself to laugh it off. 'Oh, I just had a bath. Sorry if I was noisy, I was really trying my best not to wake you.'

Maeve gave Karma a scratch under her chin, which seemed to be sending her to another planet. 'I thought I heard voices. I thought there might have been other people around.'

Annie's stomach jolted into her throat.

The spirits within the hex. The way they spoke to her, wailing and whispering through the thirteen minutes of the spell . . . But there was no way that Maeve could have heard them. The ghosts that shared their regrets and mistakes in Annie's ears were for her to hear and her alone. That was the pact. They weren't a real, physical manifestation that could be seen or heard by others. She had been sure to keep her own voice low, too, uttering the incantation into the water at barely even a whisper, silently fretting and worrying for all of them until the water ran ice-cold. Quiet, efficient crying was something that she had mastered long ago to get through the bad days. Maeve must have particularly good hearing.

'I do sing to myself in the bath,' Annie laughed casually, gathering up their now-empty plates. 'That must be what you heard.'

'Maybe,' Maeve nodded uncertainly. Fortunately, her curiosity was distracted by Karma, who had rolled onto her back, showing off her tummy in a most undignified fashion that she would never normally resort to. 'Or maybe the woods are haunted by the spirits of the damned.'

'Do you think?' Annie held a hand to her chest at the mere idea.

'I hope so,' Maeve grinned. 'We'd probably get on well, me

and the damned. Does magic mean I can communicate with them, if there do happen to be any hanging around out there?'

'Technically, yes,' Annie admitted reluctantly as she stacked their plates. 'Necromancy is another of the branches of magic that you'll dabble with in time, along with Animal Affinity, Incantation, Earth Sorcery, Alchemy, Clairvoyancy. But Necromancy is certainly not my favourite; it gives me the heebie-jeebies. I think for now we'll focus on the living, if it's all the same to you.'

Privately, Annie worried about how Necromancy magic would interact with her use of *Splendidus Infernum*, so she did her level best to avoid that particular branch of the craft whenever possible. There were already numerous spirits, ghosts and presences that haunted her tied up in the hex. Inviting further communication with the dead on top of that was certain to cause chaos. Not to mention the fact that it was all very creepy.

Annie clapped her hands together, then stood to shimmy Maeve's chair out with her still sitting on it. 'Up you get. It's the first day of your new life as a talented, knowledgeable, in-control witch, Maeve. A little enthusiasm, please.'

Maeve scowled and sighed as she scooted her chair backwards, but Annie was pleased to note the tiniest fraction of an upturned smile being promptly pulled back under wraps. Her positivity might be frightfully uncool, but it seemed to be making progress.

'Welcome to Witchery 101.'

Annie was never one to trust the process, but she had been left with little other option than to follow her instincts on how one spent time with a teenage witch. She was determined to be the perfect teacher, but their first session was off to a . . . testing start.

Maeve had not reacted well to what Annie had thought would be an inspiring and motivational academic setup: a small wooden desk for Maeve in the living space, along with a full matching set of kitschy, witchy stationery that Annie felt was a dead cert for magically academic success. She had also manifested a framed, rolling chalkboard just in front of the fireplace, with a full rainbow of fat chalks that wrote by themselves, a shiny red apple resting on the ledge, as any self-respecting teacher would add, and a wind-up pencil sharpener attached to the side.

'What the heck is this?' Maeve scowled, holding up her new broomstick-shaped pencil case.

'Oh, it's nothing, really,' said Annie, mistaking abject horror for gratitude. 'Everybody knows that any kind of productivity is at least 75 per cent reliant on the appropriate notebook and pen selection. It's the least I can do. Now don't hold back, okay? I myself would list starting a brand new notebook as one of my greatest fears in life. What if I make a mess on the first page, ruin the whole thing with ugly handwriting or bad spelling? Don't even get me started on saving sticker sheets or not using my favourite colours in a pen set. But I want you to know that this is a safe space, Maeve. Let your magic *and* your mistakes run free here!'

Maeve only blinked hard and her dark eyebrows stitched themselves together in a crease.

'Now, let me take attendance,' Annie continued importantly, conjuring a clipboard. 'Maeve Cadmus?'

Maeve glanced around the room. 'Are we expecting someone else?' she asked, stony-faced.

'Well . . . no, but you can never be too prepared. So, I suppose you're present!' She gave the list of one single name a perfunctory tick with her fluffiest pen and smoothed out her skirt as she cleared her throat. 'And you can call me Miss Wildwood.'

'But I've been calling you Annie this whole time.'

Annie's smile jerked a fraction. 'Well, alright then.'

As always, her magic had been in its upmost element when she'd conjured the outfit – a pink pinafore dress covered in a sweet print of various magical shapes – tarot cards and crystals and cat faces – with an immaculate white shirt and a pink tie underneath for a little professionalism. In her patent pink heels, she approached Maeve's desk.

'Can you consciously summon your magic yet, Maeve? Or does it still just sort of, appear, when it wants to?'

'Of course I can,' Maeve said sulkily, as though Annie were silly to even ask. The two witches simultaneously moved to summon their magic, Annie raising her wrist to create a small flourish, Maeve squeezing her hand together in a fist before bursting her fingers open to send out a stream of sparks. Magic was accommodating that way – happy to oblige and bend at will to any gesture that a witch, warlock or wicche might be drawn to at fifteen years old. Annie had always thought it interesting how the choice seemed to reveal a lot about the wicchefolk themselves – whether they were bold or shy, expressive or subtle by nature. Maeve's bursting palm suggested a slightly frantic but determined approach, which Annie could definitely work with.

'An old friend of my mother's who . . . yes, perhaps *was* eventually exposed as a rather nefarious character, determined to raise an army of vampires to his whim, but I always thought his personal choice of simply raising his left eyebrow to knit a spell was a very smooth selection. In fact, on reflection, that choice should probably have been a villainous red flag to the coven from the outset . . .' Annie rambled.

'He sounds cool. Can't *he* teach me?'

'Anyway, look at you, magic on demand. Off to a wonderful start!' Annie carried on, determinedly ignoring the stream of snark. 'Now, I know you were very interested in Incantation, so . . .'

'I told you, Necromancy,' Maeve whined, her head falling back to stare at the ceiling.

' . . . So a little transfigurative practice sounds like it could see us right, don't you think? I thought we'd start with some basic enchantment, with a touch of girly sparkle. After all, what's magic without sparkle?'

'Unbelievable,' Maeve grumbled, folding her arms emphatically.

'Thank you! I thought perhaps we'd begin with something inspired by some of the most precious, celebrated magic of all time.'

At that, Maeve's ears pricked up. 'Well, alright . . . now we're talking,' she said, surprised. But her excitement quickly waned when Annie gestured to two large, fat pumpkins that she'd gathered (with a lot of struggle) from the garden, almost tumbling backwards into the stream when she lifted them. Maeve slumped back down into her seat in a huff.

'You're about to tell me we're putting my extraordinary, otherworldly powers to good use by making vegetable soup, aren't you?'

Annie simply gave her an excitable wink. With a flutter of her left hand, one of the pumpkins began to transform from bright orange to a paler, almost crystal-like surface. The sprout changed from natural to metallic, twisting into an elegant swirl. Finally four spindled wheels popped from beneath the pumpkin, along with a heart-shaped window on either side of what was now a small, finely crafted carriage. Annie gave a delighted 'yay!'

Maeve simply sniffed.

'You don't like it?' Annie asked, dejected.

'I'm not really one for princesses,' Maeve shrugged. 'But my transfigurative magic worked okay yesterday . . . Alright, let me have a go, then.'

'Excellent! I love your enthusiasm,' Annie chirped, returning to Maeve's side so that she could attempt to give some further guidance.

'Now, you'll need to recite the spell verbally while you cast, seeing as you're new to all of this. Once you've performed it perfectly, your witchcraft will be able to recall the spell silently in the future. But, for now, we need a very clear and succinct *"Puella Magi Iter"*. That recitation refers to a girl's magical journey – you see how that sums the spell up nicely? It's all about personal intention. Do you think you can remember that?'

Maeve blew her hair out of her face and pushed up her glasses determinedly, glaring at Annie. Annie cleared her throat and shuffled a little as she tuned into the emotions that began to cloud the air above them. Irritation, a spark of anger. She cursed herself for taking the wrong tone.

'*Puell* . . . What was it again?' Maeve asked.

'Make sure you're . . . Not quite, more like . . . You must hold out your leading magic hand as you speak,' Annie interrupted, noticing Maeve's hand was off target. 'Are you concentrating properly? Focusing on guiding your powers towards the object as you . . .'

'I am, look! I'm pointing, aren't I?'

'Yes, but it's not . . .' Annie leaned across Maeve and held her arm up at the slightest, most fractionally different angle. The spell tuned in sharply to more unrest in the air. Impatience, resentment, a roughly bristled pride that felt like an electric shock . . .

'That's exactly what I just did!' Maeve shrugged off Annie's hand with a shove. 'Let me—'

'On second thoughts, maybe I'd better . . .' Annie tried again to encourage Maeve's arm down a fraction. She felt her heart quicken when she spotted a crackle of magic snap between Maeve's fingers. 'Let's take a moment to—'

'I can do it!' Maeve said stubbornly and a little louder. The squeezing, fiery feelings prickled at the back of Annie's neck, sent a panicky feeling up into her throat.

'It's my fault. I'm getting carried away with myself,' Annie rushed to say, keen to placate the rising temper. 'You're not ready just yet and that's fine.'

'Of course I'm ready! That's literally why we're here!'

Now it was fury, a deep sense of injustice, yelling furiously at Annie from inside Maeve – emotions that felt dark and dangerous and unpredictable. Annie kept desperately trying to calm the girl's rising emotions. 'Let's go back to some much more basic theory, Maeve. If you'll take out your notebook instead—'

'Just let me have a go, will you? You're not listening to me! You're not trusting me!'

'Let me give you another example to—'

'*Puella Magic Eater!*' Maeve shouted.

UNCHARMED

The pumpkin exploded. Slushy, bright orange guts flew in every direction, splattering the entire cottage in an alarming volume of wet mush that smelt distinctly and horribly of very, very burned pumpkin. Karma, who had been peacefully snoozing on the couch, let out a furious yowl as a splat of pumpkin landed directly on her tiny soft head. Both witches froze. A few moments passed before Annie finally moved to wipe a few inches of pumpkin from the ends of her hair.

'Puella Magic Eater? Are you serious?' Annie said in a dangerously calm voice.

Maeve used her forefingers to clear her glasses like windscreen wipers. 'Well, it was worth a try. You weren't giving me a chance.'

'You're not taking this seriously enough, Maeve.'

'Me? *You* made a princess carriage from a pumpkin. I want to do real magic!' Maeve jumped to her feet to measure up face to face with Annie. The pair of witches glared at each other, covered in soggy pumpkin guts.

'*All* magic is real magic, Maeve. Especially the fun and joyful kind. You don't have anything to prove here,' Annie said as she shoved her hands onto her hips. 'I already know you're talented. But power without control leads to chaos,' she said with a sigh, flicking away more mush from her fingers.

'I'm not a kid. I don't need you controlling me or my magic,' Maeve bit back. 'And I definitely do not need a nanny.'

'Oh, I can see that. But your magic might need one. You seem highly capable and very clever, but your magic can't go around sending flames every which way towards curtains and canteens whenever your emotions catch fire.'

'Those were accidents,' Maeve said angrily.

'Exactly. I think the coven would be less concerned if you

had meant to do it, if you were committing purposeful arson. Then we could just punish you for it and that would be that. How do you expect me to trust you if you keep being so reckless and messy with your magic?' Annie hoped that the question would be enough for Maeve to reluctantly admit that she was right. Instead, her words seemed to stoke more fire.

'And how do you expect me to respect you if you keep being such a ridiculous, people-pleasing pushover?'

Annie tried her very best not to burst into tears at that. Maeve glared at her, fists balled at her sides, knuckles coated in a crackle of magic. And yet Annie noticed the slightest twitch in her resolve, as though she had surprised herself by blurting out the words and was forcing herself to stick to her guns. But the brief flash was gone in a moment.

'I can't believe I'm stuck with you,' Maeve fumed. A slop of pumpkin fell from her shoulder to the floor with a wet splat, which sounded horribly loud in the silence that hung between them. 'Leave me alone.'

With that, the girl stormed into her room and slammed the door behind her, leaving Annie frazzled and defeated, dripping in pumpkin and wondering what on earth had just happened.

Chapter Eleven

PICTURE PERFECT

Annie had come to the fundamental conclusion at around three o'clock in the morning that she was simply a terrible person. After little to no sleep, tossing and turning on the pokey single bedframe upstairs, she threw aside the duvet with defeat. As always, the regrets of the *Splendidus Infernum* spirits haunted her dreams and waking moments alike, but now they were combined with her own cruel uncertainty. Without her usual routine to follow like a tightrope, she felt untethered and the reality of her and Maeve's situation kept bursting her bubble of optimism with a sharp pin.

Naturally, she had agonized all night over everything she had said to Maeve, her own regrets combined with those of her ghost companions. All of this was so messy and unconsidered, not at all like her. But the fact was this was about the girl's happiness and the girl's future and making her feel comfortable during their time together, so that she could come to understand her sacred powers.

'I think we got off on the wrong foot yesterday,' Annie said as she took a seat at the other end of the sofa from Maeve, who so far had sulkily accepted a single cup of coffee without a word and pointedly ignored that morning's peace offering pancake buffet – although Annie caught her glimpsing back at them several times. 'And the day before.'

Maeve, of course, just shrugged and stared determinedly at Karma, who was selflessly keeping her feet warm in a sleepy bundle. Annie barrelled on determinedly. 'You were mature enough to tell me I was doing something wrong, to communicate that, and I ignored it. I'm very sorry for the way I reacted. It was the wrong approach. I should have understood that you're just keen to get stuck in. Magic is so exciting and you deserve to explore it in your own way.'

A quiet passed between them while Annie debated with herself what might be the next right thing to say. She was surprised when it was Maeve who relented and broke the silence first.

'I meant it, you know. I don't need a nanny,' she said.

'Alright, alright. Can we please not use the term nanny?' Annie said, exasperated. 'It makes me sound like I should have a blue rinse and a pension. I am in fact still the right side of one hundred years old, even if you're not convinced I am. I'm not here to control you and I'm not here to be a nanny.'

The girls paused their bickering for a moment as they caught eyes – one side glaring and one side browbeaten – both still attempting to figure out how to prowl around one another. Maeve pushed up her glasses and shrugged again. 'What are you, then?'

Annie sighed. 'Can I just start with being a friend?'

Maeve hesitated, then gave an almost imperceptible nod, which Annie somehow knew was best interpreted as the closest version of an apology that Maeve had to offer. 'I suppose that would be alright.'

Annie exhaled with relief, grateful for finding a reluctant truce if nothing more. She was struck by how one moment this girl was wise beyond her years, and the next she was still so soft and young to be out and alone in the world. That familiar nip of empathy gave a merciless squeeze around her heart. She would look after Maeve whether she wanted to be looked after or not.

'Can we try again?' The timid voice that came with Maeve's request caught Annie off guard. 'Or have I blown it?'

Annie smiled at her in return. 'You're allowed to try as many times as you like in this house, Maeve. You haven't blown anything. Well, apart from the pumpkin. That was very much blown up.'

At that, they both let out matching reluctant snort-laughs, Maeve wincing with regret. It felt as though the glacier of yesterday finally began to melt an inch. Annie, pleased with the progress, raised her mug to cheers Maeve.

'To fresh starts,' Annie said decidedly. 'I have a much better idea up my sleeve for today.'

The sleeve in question was an enormous, ballooning artist smock that she conjured for each of them. Annie had decided at some point during her sleepless night that, with the stack of sketchbooks in mind, she had gone about this all wrong. This wasn't a test to be passed. Maeve wasn't here to tick boxes or impress anybody, and she certainly didn't want to be reminded of school. Rather than an academic approach with no room for error and an intense spotlight on the girl's naivety to this new world, it made much more sense that Maeve's magic would naturally express itself through creativity. Annie was initially tempted to start in the kitchen, but reminded herself that this was not about her own magical passions.

The artist smocks were accompanied by matching berets and even some optional twiddly black moustaches. Armed with two large wooden easels, a pair of palettes and an enchanted paint box, Annie arranged their studio in the living room. As soon as Maeve saw the paint box, her eyes lit up.

'I get to use this?'

'Absolutely, it's for you! The paints are enchanted with a little *Pigmentum Captura* spell that you'll harness for yourself with time and practice. It allows you to capture colours from the world around you and extract them for your paintbox.'

Each shade in the palette had an enticing, technicolour reflect of iridescence, like spilled oil. The vibrant orange-red came from the smattering of wild poppies that peppered a patch of meadow by the path. The vivid turquoise came from the wings of a butterfly that had landed on the handle of Maeve's mug. The dreamy pink was, of course, colour matched precisely to Annie's favourite lipstick. Colour catching was a nifty spell she often used for icing celebration cakes, to extract the essence of a colour and the emotions sparked by a memory to match.

So, Maeve and Annie spent the day making a mess. But, Annie was forced to tell herself, over and over again as her fingers itched and twitched to make it prettier, it was a beautiful mess. There was such a thing.

'This is the coolest thing I've ever done,' Maeve said, as she stretched out her fingers to send a stripe of banana-captured yellow towards her canvas. The flickers of her magic carried the colour like a shooting star through the cottage and it splatted onto the stretched fabric in a satisfying splash like a bursting water balloon. The only hard and fast rule to Maeve's painting session had been no tools, to allow her magic to freely lead the way. Maeve's canvas was quickly turning into an experimental masterpiece that looked as though it belonged in an expensive gallery, something the Sorciety would try to purchase. Annie, mostly worried about whether the purple paint that she flicked on her dress with all of her enthusiasm would be easily removed, had insisted on using a paintbrush to keep things neat – and then started again three times anyway. She had taken herself off to make them a cup of tea when she got embarrassed that her painting wasn't very good.

She offered out the steaming mug of strawberry lemonade tea, zesty and sweet and bright, and stood a few paces back behind Maeve, to watch as she launched more colours in a free-spirited way. Sunshine streamed through the gingham curtains of the cottage, with a red tinge from the fabric. It gave the whole scene a dreamlike quality that soothed both witches' uncertainty.

'I don't know how you do that,' Annie said, marvelling at the way that Maeve cast colours this way and that. A lucid orange, inspired by the marmalade on the kitchen counter (and memories of Jessica), landed in a dash across the canvas.

'Do what?' Maeve called back.

'You just dive in and . . . make stuff. Without freezing. Without overthinking it or questioning whether it's going to be any good.'

'Well,' Maeve said distractedly, contemplating the paint-box for her next move. 'It doesn't really matter, does it? Can't it just be a complete mess? You said that none of this was a test.'

'Right,' Annie faltered. 'It's absolutely not.'

'I'm just enjoying myself,' Maeve said simply. 'Doesn't have to be perfect.'

Annie had to look away from the painting, mortified to find her eyes were smarting as she watched the paint fly. Maeve's take could not have been a sharper opposite to her own. It occurred to Annie that perhaps she spent her whole life feeling as though everything was a test, one that had to be passed to prove something. But somehow, it was always a test that she hadn't prepared hard enough for. She existed with a feeling that she was constantly in trouble – except she didn't know with whom or why – and she was always trying to earn her way back into their good books. She was relieved and somewhat amazed to think that Maeve did not live that way. That it was even possible to do so. Maeve trusted herself enough to believe that something magical might come from the mess she made.

With one final blast of a dazzling azure blue, a colour that they had given to the paintbox from the bright midday sky, Maeve's hand finally dropped to her side. She shook out her wrist and winced a little.

'Continuous magic practice when you're not used to it can really wipe your stamina,' Annie said, noticing the first telltale signs. 'Let's have a biscuit. I'll summon a couple of the jam and cream sandwiches from Celeste.'

In synchronized exhaustion, Annie and Maeve flumped down onto the couch side by side, Annie smartly crossing one leg over the other while Maeve slid down into a diagonal slope, half hanging off the cushions. She pulled the two sides of her biscuit apart and scraped off the filling with her front teeth, while Annie dunked hers in her cup of tea.

'Do you have a boyfriend?' Maeve said through a mouthful of biscuit, a few crumbs flying out onto her chest as she spoke. Annie choked on her tea. She decided that it was probably best to put down the scalding-hot liquid before entering into this conversation.

'What made you ask that?'

Maeve shrugged, which wasn't easy with her shoulders already squashed into her ears against the back of the couch. 'I just figured you probably do. You look like you'd date guys with jawlines that could decapitate a woman.'

'Well, no. I don't have a boyfriend,' Annie said, awkwardly stiff. Talking about close relationships often made her feel on edge, like hovering over the risk of getting a paper cut. Was it supposed to feel like that?

'Why not? You're nice and pretty.'

'Oh, thank you,' Annie smiled self-consciously. 'But I'm just very busy. I don't have a lot of time for anything like that.'

'Time for what? Love? You should probably prioritize that honestly, I hear it's good for you.' Fortunately, Maeve dove into another question before Annie could quite work out the answer to that one. 'Do you have a lot of friends?'

Annie pondered the odd, direct question. 'Not as many as you might think.'

'You said you're busy all the time, though.'

'That's for sure. I certainly know a lot of people. But true friends are a rare prize.'

'Ahh. So you mostly hang around with terrible people, then,' Maeve nodded, eyeing up her guardian. 'I could have guessed that.'

Annie scoffed at the brusque assessment. 'What makes you think that?'

'Well, you're a people-pleaser. Otherwise, you would have turned down this – no offence – absolutely crap situation to babysit me for the foreseeable future in the middle of nowhere. Just saying. So by my early calculations, you're probably always saying yes to things you don't really want to do. And therefore probably stuck with the wrong people, too,' Maeve said matter-of-factly. 'And that's fine. I don't really have any either. Friends, I mean,' she added. There wasn't an ounce of self pity in her tone; she said it all as though reading a non-fiction book aloud.

Annie was a little taken aback by the frank and unexpected character assassination. She tucked her hair behind her ear, a reflex to regather herself. 'I'm sure that's not true.'

'I don't lie,' Maeve shot back.

'Oh, I didn't mean to suggest that—'

'It's not a big deal. Luckily, I like my own company. I have to say though, magic isn't very helpful when trying to just be a normal person who people might actually want to hang out with,' Maeve continued. As though suddenly aware of her thoughts being heard aloud, she shrank even further back against the sofa cushions. 'From what I can tell, magic and friends don't mix particularly well.'

'Well, hopefully we're about to change that,' Annie said gently. Ironically, two of the easiest relationships of her life were Faye and Pari, the two non-wicche people who she could drop an inch of her guard down around. It was the friendships that magic openly accompanied that were anything but easy. The thought trickled down her back in an uncomfortably cold trail.

'Not that I actually want to be friends with any of them at school,' Maeve carried on, oblivious to Annie's internal monologue. 'They have the combined verbal skills of an onion. I'm waiting until university to start again and meet cool people. Or I could move to the wicche realm?'

'Sounds like a plan,' Annie said with a soft smile. She tried to remember whether her younger self had ever operated with such a lack of self-doubt or anxiety for the future, but it seemed impossible. 'And am I allowed to ask you some of these deeply personal questions now?' she asked. 'How much experience do you have in the complicated world of love, to offer up such sage wisdom?'

'Less than zero. I just read a lot of books. Can I do some more painting?' Maeve went to rise from the couch, but Annie swiftly batted her back down with a frilly scatter cushion to the shoulder.

'Hang on a second, you're not getting away with it that easily. It's only fair. You tell me your secrets now.'

'There's nothing to tell.' Maeve finished her biscuit, then dusted her hands together before reaching to stroke Karma. The cat had settled on the top of the sofa behind her head like her own personal cartoon cloud. 'Did you somehow miss that everyone at school thinks I was born into the circus with three heads?'

Annie stuck her tongue out at Maeve. 'I'm sure they're not all as bad as you think they are. You're not exactly inviting anyone to share your sandwiches, are you? Maybe you just need to try a bit harder? Make more of an effort with them.'

Maeve froze and gave an uncomfortable shiver. She wriggled herself upright and further away, pressing herself up against the sofa arm as the relaxed ease in her eyes vanished again. 'You don't know what it's like.'

Immediately, Annie knew that she had said the wrong thing; she had killed the delicately repaired connection between them. She squeezed her eyes shut, furious with herself.

'Maeve, you're right. That was insensitive, I—'

'You actually don't know a single thing about me,' Maeve said quietly. 'No one ever does, so stop pretending that you do.'

'I'm sorry, I only thought that—'

'What? That I'm the freak everyone thinks I am and that I'm asking for everyone to hate me? That you can swoop in and mould me into someone else who fits in better, who won't be a pain in everyone's life and, most importantly, will let you look like you saved the misunderstood, troubled witch?'

'Maeve, that's not what I—' Annie's mind raced at a million miles an hour, trying to piece the smashed moment back together as quickly as she could. But none of the pieces fitted together; she could barely keep up. Maeve's mood swings were so erratic, it was like something came over her in the blink of an eye.

'I really thought you seemed nice,' Maeve snarled, jumping to her feet. Her face was screwed up tightly, her dark brows in a low, furious scowl. 'But you're just like everyone else, aren't you?'

Karma peeped one eye open to see what the racket was about.

'Maeve, I—'

'This is all just to make *you* feel better about yourself. You might think I'm a complete joke, but guess what? I think *you* are.'

Maeve's fingers sparked like tinder. Hearing the crackle of

uncertain magic, Karma's ears scooted back and she meowed dubiously. Her claws flexed into the soft fabric of the cushion, aware that trouble was brewing.

The overhead light flickered. Annie's eyes darted to the ceiling. 'Woah, woah. Let's just take a breather, we can have another biscuit.'

'I don't want a bloody biscuit. Don't tell me what to do. You don't know me. You don't know anything about me!'

Both witches spun around to the kitchen, but quicker than their eyes could carry, the contents of the cauldron that Annie had left simmering for dinner burst into a blindingly bright blue flame. A sudden jet of fire flared across the length of the stove. It lit up the whole downstairs with a jet-propelled whoosh and hot embers flew in a streak to the hems of the gingham curtains. They burst into flames.

Karma jumped up with a yowl, the tip of her tail almost reaching the ceiling at the shock. Paws skittering across the floor, she bolted from the back of the sofa straight out of the open front door. Frantic claws scratched across the wooden porch and landed with a thud into the meadow.

'Karma!' Annie scrambled around the sofa, tea spilling everywhere. She quickly shot a spell to extinguish the flames as she moved, but it was barely a second thought.

She was chasing after her familiar before she could even allow two logical thoughts to chain themselves together. Hidden entirely by the long grass, Karma had already vanished. But Annie's feet kept moving. Somewhere, she registered a thudding beat onto the wet, muddy ground. Her own bare feet. She willed herself to run faster, chasing a distant rustle in the grass ahead. Her vision blurred. The meadow was a smear of tickling grass and clouds, the skyline of the woodland a smashed amber glass, streaks of orange and red and brown somewhere in her periphery. Nothing felt real. She could only feel fear and confusion and dread – maybe her own or maybe Karma's. Maybe there wasn't any difference. She had to find her.

Chapter Twelve

SWEET KARMA

Annie was not much of a runner. Endorphins could allegedly make her happy, but she firmly believed that a slice of cake could normally make her much happier. But if anything was going to make her run, it was the need to find her familiar. She would run to the ends of the earth if she needed to, if it meant that she could protect her heart's link. Annie broke through the trees and left the meadow behind for the woodland, with no choice but to trust that her affinity would take her the right way. Eventually, she had to stop, folding over to rest her hands on her knees and catch her breath.

'Annie, I'm sorry. I'm so sorry.' Maeve came sprinting behind her, much less winded by the exertion but maybe even more visibly upset. She fiercely wiped at her wet cheeks. 'Did you see which way she went?'

'She bolted somewhere up there,' Annie said, fighting to get her breath back. 'Maeve, wait . . .' Before she could finish, Maeve ran off to blindly follow the direction of Annie's vague pointing, quickly vanishing into the trees. Annie winced and pulled herself back up to rejoin the desperate search party.

'Maeve, please hang on a second.' She caught up and tugged at Maeve's dungarees strap to make her stop. 'I shouldn't have pelted after her like that. It probably only made her more scared. If we stop for a moment, I can tune into our affinity and listen properly to my instincts. But I do need to be able to breathe to do that.'

Maeve, now gasping for air, too, nodded as she tightened her ponytail and pushed her glasses back up her nose. They slid straight back down with the sheen of sweat across her skin. Annie inhaled deeply to reset, the sharpness of cold air filling her nose. Another, slowly in and out. A gust of wind breathed through the chestnut trees that canopied above, sending her hair flying back and a smattering of auburn leaves fluttering down like a whisper. Gradually, it grounded her. Then, after making space in her mind, she caught it faintly on the breeze: that sweet, powdery scent that could always soothe her soul, the one that smelt like home.

'This way,' Annie said softly. It could have been their intrinsic familiar connection or maybe it was all the magic that she had felt carrying on the air around the cottage, but something told her that she didn't need to panic. All four paws had stepped into a safe space. Her heartbeat regulated the smallest amount. The aura around the woodland seemed to change from red to amber, to a gentler gold as she thought of Karma. It was vast and labyrinth-like and unwelcoming to a prim and proper house cat, but her heart knew as they began to walk that Karma was okay. It was just a matter of time until they found her. She gestured to Maeve to follow her, heading in the direction that the magic tugged her towards.

'Do you know where she is?' Maeve asked quietly after some time.

'No, but I know she's okay. The sense of danger has dropped,' Annie replied gently. 'She won't be happy with you that she's had to get her paws muddy, but I promise we'll find her and she'll be fine.'

Maeve sniffed and wiped her nose with her wrist. 'I really am sorry, Annie.'

'I know.'

'I didn't mean to scare her. I would never want to do that.'

'I know that, too.'

'I'm sorry for loads of stuff, actually. Yesterday. And today. And now this. I just . . .' Maeve broke off whatever it was that she was pushing herself to share, swallowing it down to keep to herself. Annie only nodded, sensing the regret, then gestured with her chin for them to keep walking. The pair walked side by side in silence, occasionally clicking and calling for Karma as their bare feet scuffed through the dirt. It said a lot that Annie was too focused on finding her familiar to be disgusted by the state of her filthy pedicure.

'You can tell me,' Annie said softly after a time, reaching out to put a gentle arm around Maeve's shoulder. For the first time, she didn't flinch away. In fact, she leaned into it, needing to be held.

'It'll sound stupid,' Maeve muttered.

'Sweetheart, if we don't start being honest with one another about how this feels, we're never going to make any progress. It's just going to be exploding pumpkins and me driving you to the edge of insanity until the coven decides that we're both officially and categorically useless.'

Maeve gave an emphatic sigh. 'I just feel so much, all at once. Everything feels massive, all of the time. And I don't know where to put any of it. It bursts out of me before I can figure out how to shrink it back down again. It's like everything is just expanding inside of me until, before I know it, I've blown something up or set fire to something and ruined it. I've always blown up in one way or another, but it used to just be my temper acting alone. Now there's bloody magic involved to make it happen literally, too.'

Annie found that she related so acutely in many ways to the revelation that she wasn't sure whether she could even admit to it out loud. Annie knew what it was to feel. Even when she felt nothing, it was still an enormous kind of nothing. A huge, cavernous, swallowing nothing.

'You know, it might seem like we're very different types of people, Maeve. But I do understand what you mean,' Annie said, resisting turning her head to look at the girl. The magic of walking side by side was that people could tumble into their own thoughts while sharing them, more for themselves than the other. Eye contact risked snapping that careful, fragile bridge.

'Oh, please. There's no way that you, Ms Perfect, have ever had any kind of outburst that someone's had to, like . . . fill in a form about. My whole life is documented in forms. Meanwhile, you're the most calm and collected person I've ever met. Your reaction to my absolute disaster at school? And yesterday? It's kind of terrifying, actually. I wouldn't be all that surprised if you told me you'd killed a man.'

Annie laughed. She didn't take Maeve's dismissal as an insult. Any fifteen-year-old would assume that they are the only person to have ever felt the things they feel and, in a way, they weren't wrong. After a lifetime of listening, she had learned that everyone sipped at their own entirely unique concoction of experiences and responses.

'Calm and collected? Me?' she replied. 'I've always thought I'm a bit like a swan: calm on the surface but frantically kicking underneath – except my swan is doing an aquatic Irish jig. I spend most of my day trying to decide which thing to ruin next with worry and overthinking. I guess we show and process them in different ways, but I feel the big things, too, Maeve. I'm tying myself in knots most of the time.'

Maeve's eyebrows spoke for her as they jolted up in doubt.

'It's true, I swear. I feel things so hard and so much, just like you, that sometimes it's like they're going to stop me from breathing,' Annie said. She thought about the spell and what it did to her. 'I feel it all on everyone else's behalf without them even asking me to, they all take up so much space that there's barely any room for me to figure out my own thoughts.'

An owl hooted softly above them, welcoming in the early evening and the first streak of pearly moonlight behind the clouds.

'You might feel as though your feelings and your powers are bigger than you are, but at least you express them, Maeve. At least you let them out and you fight back against them and you show them who's boss – or who will be boss eventually. That's strength in itself. I really admire that about you, your bravery. Even if it does explode in ways that you're not expecting sometimes.'

For the first time, Maeve looked properly at Annie as they walked, her mouth squashed into a frown. 'What do you do with yours? All your feelings, I mean. I'm all ears for suggestions.'

Annie thought about it for a moment. 'Nothing,' she answered truthfully.

She laughed a breath through her nose as her mouth stretched into a line, but it couldn't be classed as a smile. What *did* she do with her true feelings, to honour them or consider them or even acknowledge them? She had trained that out of herself long ago. That was where the spell stepped in, so that she could remain as perfect as she willed.

'What, like, ever?'

'No. I just find a way to make them feel smaller and controlled again and then I can move on.' Annie had never been honest with anybody like this before; something about the girl's vulnerability brought it out of her. If she expected Maeve to be honest with her, then it was only fair. Or maybe it was just because nobody had ever asked her before. It felt like splitting open a rock to reveal a fossil inside, the shape of the truth inside so strange and old that she was unsure of what it was really exposing.

Maeve gave her a baffled look, as though Annie were an alien that she'd just encountered in the middle of the woods. 'What, so you don't ever just . . . scream? Or yell? Or chuck something across the room and embarrass yourself a bit, but then feel better for it afterwards?'

Now it was Annie's turn to shrug, feeling self-conscious. As though some kind of secret shortcoming had just been pointed out, even though she didn't think Maeve meant it to feel like that. The girl seemed genuinely fascinated.

Maeve turned suddenly to Annie with a glint in her eye, a bubble of a mischievous grin unable to keep itself under wraps any longer.

'Do a big shout.'

Annie spluttered. 'What?'

'Yeah, go on,' Maeve said, laughing at her own dare.

Annie hesitated, giggling. 'Right now?'

'Right now. Just do a massive, ugly scream. Like you're the

hopeless blonde who's about to be the first one murdered in a horror movie. No offence, by the way, but that would definitely be you. Shout as loud as you can.' Leaning back with effort, Maeve let out a proud yell, right from the back of her throat that echoed monstrously through the canopy of leaves above. Birds erupted from the tree above in a gust of wings, startled by the noise. It made Annie jump, clutching at her heart. Maeve grinned wickedly, sinking her hands back into her dungarees pockets. 'Like that.'

'I can't do that,' Annie laughed, incredulous.

'Course you can.'

Annie's mouth pressed into a flat line, somewhere between a frown and a smirk. 'Ahh,' she squeaked in a fractionally louder voice, adding jazz hands into the effort for some impossibly confusing reason. It sounded more like a deflating balloon than anything else.

Maeve pulled an unimpressed face and crossed her arms. 'Is that really the best you've got?'

'Sorry, sorry.' Annie felt as though she was failing at something again. 'I'm not very good at . . . letting go. It makes me embarrassed to be seen like that.'

'Even by me?'

Annie nodded. 'I don't know why. I felt it with the painting, too. It's like a switch that I can't turn off. It's just not me. I can't be that way.'

Maeve snorted, then sighed. 'You're so perfect. It must be exhausting to be you.'

Usually, when Annie heard that she was perfect or even that she was good, it felt like a compliment. A pat on the head or a squeeze of her shoulder that provided enough sustenance for her to live off for a little while. She would stow it away like a treasure and permit herself small glances until it vanished and the supply needed restoring. But from Maeve, she could guarantee that it wasn't intended that way.

'Well, thank you,' Annie said uncertainly. 'Yes, maybe it is hard work to live like this. But I'm not sure what happens if I stop being that way.'

Maeve rolled her eyes. 'I don't think the world ends, you know.'

'*The* world might not end, but mine could.'

Annie was taken aback even to hear herself say it. It came out before she could consider whether she meant it or not, whether she *should* say it or not. But, as the words unlatched from her tongue and floated down to the floor, dropping at her feet, she knew that it was true. Everything would fall apart if she allowed herself to rest, even just for a second. 'I have a lot of people that depend on me to keep showing up as best I can.'

'But why do you feel like you owe some kind of version of yourself to anybody? Like your friends, just to make them feel more comfortable. No thanks,' Maeve said, sniffing. 'If you ask me, the whole point of life – and maybe the whole point of magic too – is that you're supposed to just be yourself and see who sticks around. Granted, it's not working all that well for me so far.' She let out a funny bark of a laugh and squinted at Annie, waiting to see whether she had a response, then shook her head when one didn't come. 'You really are just as much of a weirdo as I am.'

Annie detected a faint tone of admiration or maybe wonderment in there somewhere. She knew that this was a real compliment, coming from Maeve, and felt strangely proud about it. 'Maybe I am.'

'So it *is* possible we might have been friends at school, then. If you were like thirty years younger, anyway. I bet I can predict exactly what your reports used to say . . .' Maeve adapted her voice to a formal teacher. '*A pleasure to teach and a very bright girl. But she must try to speak up more.*'

'How did you know that?'

'Mine always say that, too. We're the same, but different.'

Once again, Annie had to laugh at the frankness of Maeve's opinions, which she was starting to learn came entirely de-bubble-wrapped, no matter the sensitivity of the topic. It was either rude or refreshing, she hadn't quite decided yet.

Eventually, they reached a clearing in the woodland and Annie felt a tingle stipple its way down her spine, as though she had brushed something electrified. Her magic was tingling, the affinity sparking like a flint trying to catch light. Karma had to be close by.

It could have been the light playing tricks. A scattering of pale flowers, maybe a cotton-coloured puff of creamy hydrangeas . . . In the middle of the woods, in early October? Annie squinted at the splash of white.

Tail curled up neatly around her candyfloss-like shape, Karma was sat directly in the middle of a fairy ring. The circle of mushrooms sprung up from the ground like jutting jewels, bright caps of red rubies and creamy mother of pearl.

'Karma!' Maeve sprinted forward with a cry of relief.

'Wait! Don't step inside,' Annie called quickly, darting to catch up. Maeve recoiled backwards with a stumble. 'Fairy rings can be a little unpredictable.' The ring of mushrooms was a large one, maybe fifteen feet wide, and Karma was right in the centre licking her front paw to wash behind her ear. The little pink bell on her bow jingled as she moved.

'That's so strange. Do they grow like that or is it a magic thing?' Maeve asked.

'A little bit of each. Impressive, isn't it?'

Finally acknowledging her rescuers, Karma gave a quiet *'mrow'*, distinctly unimpressed that it had taken them so long to track her down, as though it hadn't been her own choice to bolt into the unknown. She scampered forwards as Annie knelt down beside the edge of the fairy ring. Delivering a prompt headbutt to the knee, she began to purr at an impressive volume when Annie scooped her up and Maeve stroked her with profuse apologies.

'You found the protective magic to keep you safe, Karma. Clever girl,' Annie said softly, planting a kiss directly on top of the cat's head and leaving behind a lipstick mark.

'I've never seen one of these before,' Maeve said, still fascinated by the fairy ring. She toed her shoe against one of the mushrooms curiously, until Annie warned her again.

'Seriously, don't. They're fickle things; you can never quite know whether one has benevolent or sinister intention. In other countries' folklore, they're known as witches' rings – *Hexenring* in German, I think – and anyone with magical blood is normally safe to step inside, but you can never truly tell if you're permitted. It's non-wicchefolk who mostly need to worry about the consequences, but a lot of wicchefolk think they're dangerous and best avoided.'

'Dangerous? A bunch of mushrooms?'

'There are all sorts of myths about fairies dancing non-wicchefolk to death after they've accidentally stumbled inside.

And they turn them invisible so that no one can see that they need help.'

Maeve let out a low whistle. 'That's so dark,' she said, sounding unmistakeably impressed by the grisly legend.

'Isn't it? There's some horrible tales through history. I much prefer the idea that they're just using the mushrooms as dining tables. Can you imagine how tiny their teacups must be? So adorable.'

Maeve rolled her eyes. 'Boring. Can we talk more about the death dancing instead? I have a lot of questions.' Annie tutted at her tendency towards the morbid. 'Anyway, ours must be safe — definitely a witches' ring, since Karma clearly decided that it was a safe bet.'

'I've always suspected that my beautiful cat is probably a genius; this all but confirms it,' Annie said proudly, before turning her attention back to the circle and studying it closely. 'There — see the way there's a very faint glimmer in the air inside it? That's protection. It makes sense that a witches' ring would help a familiar, especially, and us in turn to find her.'

Maeve tugged at her sleeves uncertainly. 'Does she hate me now?' Right on cue, Karma trilled a chirp and stretched out a paw to Maeve. 'I'm sorry I scared you, Karma. I scare myself all the time, so I get it.' Karma stretched her neck towards her, indicating that she would willingly accept a further scritch behind the ears as an apology.

'I've never seen this cat take so thoroughly to anybody,' Annie marvelled. 'She really loves you.'

Maeve grinned proudly. 'Why did you call her Karma?'

'I thought that was obvious,' Annie said with a smug look. 'I love all things sweet.'

'Well, cheers, fairies, witches, gnomes, pixies, whoever else happens to be hanging out around here . . .' Maeve said, saluting the circle of mushrooms. 'Thanks for looking after the cat and for not dancing us to death. That would be a really embarrassing way for me to go.'

'Come on, if I don't have a bubbling foot spa within the next three minutes, I think reality will set in and I'll never stop screaming. And, while I handle the fire aftermath, you've got the washing-up to do that painting distracted me from,' Annie said brightly as they turned to head back to the cottage, an arm around Maeve's shoulder where Karma was balanced like a parrot.

Maeve's mouth fell open.

'Are you joking? There's enough washing-up to keep me at the sink until I'm ready for an old people's home. You practically opened up a pancake cafe, I'm not . . .'

'Oh, I think you'll find you are . . .'

Their gentle bickering and laughter caught and carried along on the wind. The sound, a soft and distinctly precious one, something new and special to Arden Place, whipped into a swirl of crackling leaves like caramel through cake and folded itself around the witches' ring to mingle with the rest of the whispers that wound through the woods.

Chapter Thirteen

AN UNEXPECTED ARRIVAL

Although small, it felt like there had been a breakthrough. Maeve seemed more relaxed or at least less immediately bristling each time Annie opened her mouth to speak, while Annie was coming to discover that the girl only really seemed to need a gentle kind of encouragement – small boosts of reassurance that she was doing okay. Perhaps there had just been no one else to provide that until now.

In fact, she didn't want to push her luck or get carried away as she usually did, but Annie was fairly confident that Maeve even seemed to be . . . warming to her. The girl had to be practically forced to go to bed at night. She would shuffle grumpily to her room, in the fluffy socks that Annie had finally convinced her to wear, and was reluctant to spend much time by herself in there, constantly asking instead whether they could stay up to talk about magic lore or dabble with a new enchantment she'd read about. A few days after their walk through the woods and things were a world away from their initial night at Arden Place. They ended their first week at the cottage as friends.

'Will you put that thing away?' Annie called as she gathered together stacks of equipment in her arms from various cupboards around the cottage. She was referring to the copy of *Dynamic Draughting: Experimental Alchemy for the Spirited Warlock* that Maeve had found lurking on the shelves. She had then temporarily imposed a mute spell on Maeve's voice until she stopped insisting that she could definitely make a competent invisibility brew on first try, no problem. Her peace didn't last long, Maeve quickly figured out how to flip the spell onto Annie instead.

Late in the night, while the hex and its ghosts kept Annie awake long enough to see the sun coming up over the meadow, an idea had come to her that she couldn't resist bringing to life. Thankfully, Maeve seemed to have accepted that, when Annie had an idea, she committed to the delivery wholeheartedly, so she was becoming less and less surprised each morning by whatever scene greeted her when she groggily opened her bedroom door. This time, it was a row of identical ice-cream sundae glasses lined up next to the cauldron, complete with stripy straws.

'We're making ice-cream floats! Magical ones. Isn't that fun?' Annie beamed with a round of applause so enthusiastic that a spurt of rogue pink sparks tumbled from her fingertips. Maeve, still in a sleepy stupor, scowled as Annie shoved a paper busboy's hat on top of her head. 'Look at my shoes!' Annie spun on the spot and her fluffy slippers transformed in a pink haze into a pair of roller skates to match her diner girl attire.

'I hate this.'

'No, you don't. No one hates ice-cream floats.'

'I do, especially at this time in the morning. Where's the coffee?'

'Coming up, sweet cheeks.' Annie wielded the giant coffee pot at great height over a huge diner mug and skated towards Maeve (with a slight stumble) to hand it over with an exaggerated wink.

'I thought we were trying potions today, not bringing all of my worst nightmares to life. That's for the Necromancy spells, isn't it?'

'Wrong, my cantankerous friend,' Annie said, waggling a finger. 'I came to the important realization last night, after being awake for almost twenty-four hours – which is when you know it's an inspired idea – that ice-cream floats are kind of like very basic potions, aren't they? One of my more genius moments, I'm sure you'll agree.'

'I'll take your word for it,' Maeve said, clutching onto her coffee as though it needed to bring a miracle with its first sip. 'You should consider more early nights.'

They began with fun, silly recipes: basic, joyful enchantments that Annie remembered mixing chaotically in her dormitory at school. There was the cackle brew, with layers of peppermint dust (suitably peppy), cornflower petals (to banish the blues), a handful of pistachios (to make the drinker feel a little nuts). She reached for the jar of pumpkin flowers to pluck the stamens and sprinkle them on top like sugar, then encouraged Maeve to use her magic to stir while thinking of the funniest thing she could remember.

'Watching you singing into the wooden spoon over breakfast the other day,' Maeve decided, much to Annie's mortification. A swirl of red sparks ran through the ice-cream glass like strawberry sauce and, with a vortex spin, the glass rattled to a standstill.

'Et voilà. One potion float,' she said proudly, handing the

glass over to Maeve, who dove in with a tablespoon. The moment the sweetness touched her lips, she spluttered out a loud laugh that was equal parts pitchy and iconically witchy, sending a spray of melted pink milk flying everywhere. She couldn't stop cackling and Annie soon joined her, the pair of them bent double and clutching onto the countertop, sounding like Hollywood witches.

'This is so stupid,' Maeve wheezed between cackles. 'But very fun.' The words were a sugar boost to Annie's soul.

Before long, melted ice cream coated the kitchen. Maeve was a particularly big fan of the combination of double cream and liquid shadows – not only impossibly rich and chocolatey, but also successful in temporarily bestowing her a pair of sleek black cat ears. Annie favoured the extremely fizzy ginger-beer float, covered in popping candy, which had let them both levitate about a foot above the ground for bursts of a few seconds. The two witches agreed that the blend of dried dragon scale and crispy kale, which left them speaking in rhyme, was the absolute worst of the bunch, in both taste and result.

'Have you had enough for now? Perhaps one more if you'll allow? I mean . . . Ugh, do you want to make another one?' Annie asked, shaking her head to try to ditch the last of the terrible rhyming couplets stuck in her throat.

'I need a break,' Maeve said. She flexed the fingers of her right hand, stretching out the muscles that had been firing up magic and draining it dry for hours. 'Not to mention I feel like I might vom. Turns out there is such a thing as too much ice cream after all.'

'Right, sorry. Cup of sugary tea incoming,' Annie called out as she bustled around. It looked as though there'd been a minor explosion in the kitchen, puddles of overflowing melted ice cream and effervescent ingredients spilled everywhere.

'No more sugar. And make it a coffee, please. I hate tea,' Maeve said as she collapsed in an undignified heap onto the rug in front of the fire. Karma promptly moved from rocking chair to teenage lap, beginning her hard work of making biscuits on Maeve's stomach as she slumped.

'You're a witch, you can't hate tea,' Annie called, enchanting a cloth to mop at a pool of potion that dripped down the cupboard. 'Your coffee habit is concerning. You're too young to have so much caffeine flooding your veins. That's to carry you through your thirties.'

Maeve gave her an unimpressed look. 'Come and sit down. You need a rest, too. You're always flapping.'

Maybe the cleaning up could wait an hour or two. It was a grubby task, beginning to get to grips with Alchemy, but for one reason or another, it felt unusually fine to leave the chaos just as it was, something to revisit later. Maybe the mess could stick around — for a little while at least. Annie sat herself on the floor next to Maeve and handed over a mug.

'That's what my mother always used to say to me. I thought she was being dramatic, but it must be true if you think so, too.'

Sipping her coffee, Annie rubbed a finger gently down Karma's nose and was surprised to realize, in the rare moment of relaxation, that the distant feeling of the city wasn't something that she longed for. In fact, she rather liked thinking of it being so far way, like something in a memory. Precious pauses like this never made themselves known in her London life.

'What's she like?'

'Who? My mother?'

Maeve nodded, running her thumbs up and down the handle of the cup as she clasped it between both hands and savoured the warmth. Annie sighed and wondered where to even begin with describing Cressida Wildwood to someone who had never encountered her.

'Well, she was . . . complicated,' she said, settling safely on the facts.

'Was? Is she dead?'

'No, I don't think so, but I haven't heard from her in a long time,' Annie said quietly with a soft smile. It was always a strange line to walk whenever anyone asked her about her family – it unravelled conversations at rapid speed. 'It's a confusing kind of thing.'

'You can say that again,' Maeve said with her eyebrows raised.

Annie sighed. Griffin's betrayal had set Cressida on a path that left her almost unrecognizable. She seemed to fade before Annie's eyes, growing more translucent, obsessed with the Sorciety that pushed her out and, more importantly, how she might get back in. The idea of her fellow witches discussing her, picking apart the details of her personal life and how her pride had crumbled, proved impossible to ignore. As time went on, her pretence at interest in anything else – even her own daughter – vanished entirely, along with her grip on reality, but Annie had done her best to ignore that. Annie was skilled at ignoring all the right things when it was required of her.

Her mother's fall had not been through any fault of Cressida's own, her magic caught up in the mess that Griffin left behind, so Annie practised sympathy for the bitterness and animosity that her mother had harboured. When Griffin Wildwood abandoned not only his morals, his senses and his decency, but his family, too, Cressida and Annie were left bound in a kind of poisonous rope: a bind that held them together while causing more damage as it tightened; a woven confusion and wonder at where he'd gone and how they had been so oblivious to it coming.

These feelings weren't fair of her, after everything Cressida had been through. Her mother only wanted what was best for her. She meant well. And she owed her so much. Everything she'd lost had been a step in Annie's gain.

Fortunately, the spell was the one thing that her mother had left behind for her daughter. It dulled anger down to keep her reactions in check. Anger was not a pretty feeling.

Annie dragged her mind back to the here and now.

'So where'd she go?' Maeve asked. Annie was strangely touched to notice a fraction of tactful softness in her tone.

One day on her usual errands for her mother, Annie had arrived home to find a cigarette still burning and a note scrawled in haste. The words were so brief and thoughtless, yet managed to confirm everything that Annie had already begun to believe. At some point, everybody left her sooner or later. She wasn't worth staying for.

Gone to find your father. You understand x

'Your guess is as good as mine, sweetheart. The Christmas cards stopped a long time ago and my communication spells have always bounced back. She's a complicated woman who's been through a lot,' Annie said sadly, shyly treading her way around memories of the people that she tried not to think about. 'But, before all of that, she appreciated beautiful, exquisite things. She needed looking after and loved to feel special. She enjoyed spending her fortune on nothing in particular . . .'

Maeve inhaled a sharp breath. 'Fortune? Wait, you're telling me this whole time we've been cooped up in this place but you're rich? Why aren't we on an all-powerful witch yacht right now?'

'Wrong. I *was* rich,' Annie laughed. 'Growing up, yes, my father was an important warlock who mixed with other, even more important warlocks. My mother had a huge inheritance, our family moved in the right circles . . . Our circumstances changed.'

'More complications,' Maeve said with raised eyebrows. 'For someone who seems so perfect, you sure come with a bit of baggage, don't you?'

At that, Annie laughed again. 'That's one word for it. But I don't think any family relationships are straightforward, do you?'

'I wouldn't know much about them.'

Annie stiffened. Why had she asked that?

'Do you remember your mother?' she asked tentatively. They were growing closer now that they were coming to somewhat understand one another, but the subject of Maeve's family was one that neither witch had dared to broach until this unfortunate mutual ground had revealed itself. She wasn't sure how the question, burrowing a little deeper than they had done so far, would be received. Annie prepared for a blast of sorcery fire to make its way somewhere between her eyebrows.

Instead, Maeve swilled the black coffee around in her cup, determinedly focused on the inky contents. 'Mine left me behind, too. I don't remember much about her. Hardly anything at all actually.'

Annie let Maeve sit with her words for a moment. Outside, a beat of rain had started to strike against the window frames, the sound like a smattering of pebbles on the glass and the cushioned thatched roof. Inside, the heart of the cottage felt warm and safe.

'She was young, so it's not all that surprising that she left me,' Maeve ventured. 'I used to be so angry at her for it. But I don't hold it against her any more. You have to be pretty desperate and clueless to abandon a kid, don't you? I figure she must have been having a hard time.'

The vivid picture of a little, lonely version of Maeve being abandoned was one that felt acutely devastating, a prick so sharp and sad against Annie's heart that she almost buckled. A ferocious, stormy defensiveness whipped itself up inside her like a hurricane, with an overwhelming wish that she could go back in time and protect that little girl. She would settle for looking after her just as she was now.

'There's no question that she must have been frightened,' Annie said. 'But I'm sure you were, too.'

Maeve took a sip of coffee. 'It's actually a really weird story. I was only found because the bloody postman heard me calling out for her. I snuck a look at my records once and they said that the house was empty, as though she and anyone else around had just vanished. Everything was as though she left quickly and meant to come back, teacups on the table, half-eaten bowls of porridge in the kitchen . . . Isn't that crazy? And I was sitting at the bottom of a closed wardrobe, playing with a doll. I've always assumed that she got herself into trouble and she had to run, but . . . pretty bleak stuff, isn't it?'

Annie could only nod at the top of Maeve's bowed head.

'I seem to attract . . . bad things. Dark things,' Maeve said with a breathy laugh, quieter now. She began to tug at the skin around her nails again, but promptly picked herself up. 'Like I said, I don't have many memories because I was a baby. Only about four. But somewhere in the back of my mind, I know that she was kind. And she'd draw really good pictures for me to colour in when we woke up early. I guess that's where I get it from.'

'Maybe you're like her in lots of ways. Probably more than you know.'

Maeve made a *'hmm'* sound, twiddling the end of Karma's tail. 'I can't say whether that would be a good thing or not, so I'll just claim the art for now. Are you anything like your mum?'

'I hope not,' Annie said before she could stop herself. Her hand shot to her mouth and both girls giggled at the revelation. 'I just mean we've never had a lot in common,' she hastened to add. 'Apart from our appreciation for the importance of the right handbag. She could be a bit . . . ruthless.'

'Ruthless?' Maeve said, surprised. 'The total opposite to you, then.'

Annie squared her shoulders. 'I can be ruthless if I want to be.'

Maeve rolled her eyes while draining the last of her coffee. 'We've only known each other for a few days and I've already seen you cry maybe one hundred thousand times.'

'A witch can cry a lot and still be a tough cookie.'

'Sure she can, but *you* cried when I managed to successfully brew a cat-ears potion, Annie. You're the most sensitive, compassionate person I've ever met. I don't know how you ever get anything done.'

'It does get in the way a bit,' Annie admitted. 'I do sometimes wonder what life would look like if I didn't pay so much mind to what anybody else was thinking or feeling.'

'Maybe it would look like it was your own.'

It was a revelation to hear aloud, so earnest and simple.

'Don't look so surprised,' Maeve went on. 'You've admitted it all in bits and pieces. Exhibit A, you're working too hard at your bakery. Which is great, obviously, but you're allowed to let it go and watch it float away if it's not making you happy.'

Annie squinted at Maeve, eyeing her up suspiciously. 'Are you sure you're fifteen and not a wizened old warlock in a particularly convincing disguise?'

'It's just not that deep. I let things go all the time,' Maeve said with a lolloping stretch against the side of the armchair. 'It's like grabbing a balloon at the fun fair. You enjoy it for a while, but then it becomes this annoying, cumbersome thing wrapped around your wrist that bashes you on the head all the time as you're trying to walk along. Sometimes it's better to untie the bow and let it go.'

'Maeve, it's not that easy.' Annie's gaze fell onto their matching fluffy socks, bright orange and leaf-patterned, resting either side of the long, stretched-out cat.

'Why not?'

'Because letting people down is the worst feeling in the world,' Annie replied in a quiet voice. Even saying it out loud brought a pebble-sized lump to her throat. It was supposed to be her teaching things to the girl, not the other way around.

'But this is *your* life and you're letting people make you unhappy in it,' Maeve said, her voice rising in such a passion that Karma squinted one unimpressed eye open. 'Just because you're not doing what they expect of you. Keeping everyone happy, pleasing everyone all the time . . . It's just a thankless game of putting out fires, one after another.' Karma let out a passive-aggressive sigh, displeased that Maeve's rant had resulted in a lack of continued strokes. 'It's pointless, isn't it, Karma? Stoke your own fire instead.'

Life with Maeve Cadmus was one reality check after another. Annie exhaled deeply, then reached for a sofa cushion and gently batted Maeve around the head with it.

'What was that for?'

'For being too smart for your own good, little witch.'

'Not fair,' Maeve added, her grumpy tone firmly returning. 'And yes, I do realize the irony of me talking about fires, when it's exactly what has led to us both being stuck here.'

It was late. After the nightly battle with Maeve over the fact that, yes, she did have to go to bed at a half-reasonable hour and, no, they could not pull an all-nighter, a dense lick of darkness covered the meadow and its surrounding woodlands in a sooty black. Annie towelled off behind the privacy screen that wrapped around the tin bathtub, the last of her tears still lingering on the back of her hand. Stars studded the sky like scattered dice; the moon had shyly tucked itself in, only a thin scratch of silver peeping up from the blanket of night.

A tiredness hung heavy across Annie's shoulders, the exhausting weight of the spell's familiar voices seeping through her body, before the kick of endless energy had arrived in the magic. Cloudy, spectral shimmers of a whole range of visitors had appeared, desperate to share their secrets, leaving their burdens behind on Annie's shoulders. She was exhausted from listening.

UNCHARMED

She closed her eyes in half-sleep as she wrung out her wet hair. The noise of the droplets tumbling into the draining tin tub sounded impossibly loud against the garden, an orchestra of crickets hidden in the grass flooding the open air as she wrapped up the ritual. She watched the last of the crimson liquid drain safely away into secrecy, then gathered up her ingredients to stow them away, casting a simple *Caecus Abscondo* invisibility enchantment over each of the bottles and stowing them beneath an empty crate for good measure.

She was drying her hair into plaits with *Capillus Aura*, when a loud rustle caught her attention. Among the long grass, it sounded fuzzy and coarse. Annie faltered, straining to tune back into the specific sound, which had passed as quickly as it came. Then there it was again. Something big. Likely a deer or a fox slinking past. There had been an almost constant stream of woodland wildlife since they'd arrived at Arden Place, further ensured by the fact that Maeve insisted on leaving out plates of leftover dinner for them each night.

But this time the rustling had changed — fractionally closer now and more of a shuffle. The grass was brushing up against something over and over. Like heavy legs, wading through. It was making its way towards the front of the house, growing closer, louder with each sweep against the meadow.

A dense dragging along the ground. And . . . was that a grunting? Were there . . . bears in the English countryside? Annie liked to imagine that bears were just adorable big babies and could be tempted out of any situation with enough pots of honey, like Karma and her custard, but it wasn't something she wanted to put to the test.

A voice. Deep and rough. She definitely heard it.

The hex was complete, the residual spirits had all departed

with the dregs of the drained potion, and it wasn't Maeve pottering out of bed this time. The voice was much too gruff. It sounded surly, only just audible from this side of the cottage. Annie was frozen to the spot, unsure of what to do. They were so vulnerable here. No one knew where they were, other than Morena. Even Annie couldn't be exactly sure where Arden Place was, tucked away from the 'real' world.

One thing was certain: she couldn't very well fight an intruder in her fluffy white towel, so she tiptoed with haste back into the cottage, moving extra slowly to ensure that the squeaking hinges didn't give her away. Silently, she dipped behind the curtains and hurriedly threw on the only thing that she had taken outside to change into – her buttoned, pumpkin latte-print pyjamas were not the most threatening choice for battling an intruder, but they would have to do in a pinch.

Annie gasped sharply as the cascade of lanterns around the front of the cottage shook, casting just enough light along the porch to reveal a silhouette. Someone was trying to peer through the window. A large hand came up to the glass. A man's hand, the darkness obscuring everything else. Annie tried to remain calm, but intense fear clipped her breath.

Her heart was in her throat as she stayed hidden behind the curtain, not daring to move while her mind raced. Her only clear thought was keeping Maeve safe. She wondered how to get herself across to the bedroom without revealing her whereabouts to the intruder. And she would have to wake Maeve up gently so as not to frighten her. Maybe she could tell her that there'd been an emergency, that they had to transfer quickly, right away. She wouldn't even have to know that someone was trying to get inside.

'Do you hear that?'

Maeve hissed through the darkness, standing in the dark kitchen clutching a glass of water. Annie leapt in the air with a stifled squeal, clutching at her chest from the fright.

'I thought you were asleep! Of course I hear that. I was trying to make sure that *you* didn't hear that,' Annie whispered back dramatically.

'I don't sleep much here. I hear stuff outside all the time. But that's . . .'

'A man? A real-life man?' Annie said, wide-eyed.

'Right,' Maeve nodded slowly, looking distinctly less sure of herself than usual. Her eyes darted from Annie to the front door and back again. She gulped. 'What do we do?'

Hesitating for only a second longer, Annie dashed over to the kitchen in an awkward, hobbling crouch and pulled out her favourite wooden spoon from the cupcake-shaped utensil holder. She lunged in front of Maeve and wrapped a protective arm backwards around her.

'Get behind me,' Annie wheezed.

'What are you . . .'

'I'll protect us. I might not look particularly tough, but I am,' Annie said, flicking her ribboned, bedtime pigtails back and sounding as though she was trying to convince herself of the fact more than anything. Holding Maeve behind her as they shuffled into the living room together, she brandished the wooden spoon out in front.

Heavy footsteps pounded the length of the porch and something else cumbersome thudded against the edges of the wooden steps, over and over, being dragged with great effort towards the door.

'Do you think that's a body?'

'Maeve! Don't say that!'

Annie and Maeve both let out involuntary gasps when the handle rattled once, then again more wildly.

'This feels quite bad,' Maeve admitted, swallowing hard.

'We can take him,' Annie said with an unconvincing, quivering voice. 'We're witches. We might not have weapons, but we do have spells. Loads of them.'

'I don't know any spells!' Maeve seethed. 'What am *I* going to do? Paint him into submission? Milkshake him to smithereens?'

Annie's pigtails shook decidedly once again. 'On the count of three, I'm going to open the door . . .' she said calmly.

'What? No, don't do that! Why are you politely opening the door for someone who's trying to kill us?'

'One, two . . .'

'Annie, no!'

'Three!'

Channelling the wooden spoon as a temporary wand for dramatic emphasis, Annie fired her magic towards the front door and a crescendo of brave and extra hot-pink sparks shot through the cottage. The hinges blew off and the door came crashing to the hallway floor in a (hopefully) controlled explosion. She and Maeve quickly crouched down together behind the sofa, Annie shielding the girl with her body, Maeve flinging her hands over her ears.

Against the night sky, a shadow filled the doorway, tall enough that he had to duck his head to be able to come inside, broad shoulders intimidating against the small frame of the cottage. He lugged an enormous sack over his shoulder and dumped it over the threshold with a final groan of effort.

'Who the bloody hell are you?' he said.

UNCHARMED

Annie shot to her feet, still wielding the spoon wand. Maeve stayed crouched, unsure whether she was supposed to follow for moral support or remain hidden, as Annie leapt around the side of the sofa to confront the intruder.

'I should ask you the very same thing, you scoundrel! Who do you think you are, barging into my house like this? Get out. Right now. Or I'll . . .'

'You'll what, spoon me to death?'

'I will do no such thing, brigand!' Annie shouted, horrified by the assumption.

'Not like that, I mean . . . Oh, will you please put that thing down before you take my eye out, waving it around like that? And I think you'll find that this is *my* house.'

Chapter Fourteen

THE BANCROFT COMPROMISE

Annie's eyes darted to Maeve's, silently asking whether she understood what in all the realms the man was talking about. The girl, still hiding behind the sofa, looked equally stumped, but she gestured her head towards the man, encouraging Annie to keep pressing on with the interrogation.

'What do you mean, this is *your* house? I think you'll find that this house belongs to Selcouth, the esteemed coven of the United Kingdom.'

'Oh does it, indeed? Who told you that, hey? Bloody Morena Gowden, was it? I bet. I swear to the zodiac and back . . .'

'You're telling me you *live* here?' Annie's voice was supposed to sound strong and certain, but was in fact only getting squeakier.

'Too bloody right I live here. I go away for a few months and come back just wanting a decent kip and a nice dinner to find . . . What in the hell and high waters have you done to my living room? Everything's bloody pink.'

As he stepped a little further out of the shadows, Annie

could just about make out a few of his defining features in the last of the candlelight. His scowling face was rugged and a little weathered, deep lines across his forehead and furrows between his brows, a scattering of freckles that hinted at time spent outside. A slightly crooked nose, dark green eyes, which were scrutinizing her closely, and an unkempt beard that looked brown until he stepped further into the light and revealed the slightest red tint. He shoved back the long, dishevelled hair that was falling into his eyes. The furious look across his face softened a fraction as he took a step closer towards her, but Annie promptly mirrored it by taking one back. She noted that his clothes were dirty, his boots caked in mud, and she crinkled her nose at the sight.

'Well, then. There's clearly been some kind of . . . administration error,' she said.

The man gave a resigned sigh, thumbing at his eyebrow in exasperation. 'No, there hasn't. I should have known that Morena would have revenge planned. She's furious with me for not coming back sooner, for refusing to be at her ludicrous beck and call. This is her reminding me who's in charge at that bloody coven, whether I like it or not.'

Annie squinted. 'You . . . you work at the coven?' she stuttered.

'Aye.' Not only did this man look like some kind of lumbering . . . lumberjack, perhaps crossed with a cowboy-pirate, he spoke like one, too. Annie purposefully forced a more intimidating scowl back on her face.

'Then why have I never seen you at Hecate House before? I spend a lot of time there,' she said importantly. He had to be lying. For various reasons that she didn't allow herself to contemplate because they were highly inappropriate when she was trying to be menacing, she would *definitely* have noticed this man before, if they had ever crossed paths.

'Because I try to spend as little time at that fate-forsaken place as possible,' he replied grumpily. 'Mostly thanks to Bronwyn, always asking me to join her crochet club or set me up on a date with some witch or other. And if it's not *her* meddling in things, then it's Morena telling me that field work is a waste of time and that she'll land me in a paperwork role before next Halloween.'

Annie still refused to drop her weapon spoon. 'I don't believe you.'

The man breathed out deeply through his nose with closed eyes, seemingly willing himself to find patience. He shrugged off his jacket to hang on the heart-shaped hook next to the door that, until Annie's redecoration, had been a nail jutting out of the wall. He paused, scowled at it, then turned back to her with his hands on his hips. 'Suit yourself. Either way, this is still my house.'

'And we're staying in it. Aren't squatters' rights a thing, Annie?' Maeve bolted up to her feet from behind the sofa.

The man jumped and muttered a curse under his breath. 'Where the bloody hell did you come from? There's two of you, is there? Any more uninvited witches lurking behind my curtains?'

Annie decided that nobody needed to know that she had indeed been hiding behind the curtains earlier. Instead, she folded her arms crossly.

'Who are you?' She eyed him with suspicion. He firmed his jaw, then took a deep breath again, apparently relenting a small fraction of his surly demeanour with the dawning realization that it wasn't getting him many answers.

'Hal,' he said, in a softer voice now. 'Well, Harry. But no one's called me that since I was wearing babygrows.'

'Couple of years ago, then?' Maeve said. He glowered at her.

'Hal Bancroft?' Annie asked, the name coming to light. She'd seen it countless times in coven records and always wondered why she'd never bumped into the mystery warlock in question, seeing as she made it her business to be firm friends with anyone and everyone at Hecate House. All she knew was that he headed up Selcouth's work within the Mythical Beasts department and, from what she'd heard, he much preferred the company of animals to other wicchefolk. Now that she thought about it, she had also definitely heard Bronwyn mention numerous times what a 'handsome devil' he was. Annie made sure to scowl even more enthusiastically at the devil in question.

'Right. And you? I got as far as Annie, but didn't catch much else,' he said, arms folding.

'I am Andromeda Wildwood,' she said, puffing her chest out a little to assert her dominance of the situation. He simply gave her a slow, single nod in return.

'And your sidekick?'

'Oi,' Maeve said, smoke practically projecting from her ears at that.

'That's Maeve Cadmus, our newest Selcouth recruit. We're staying here for a while to get her magic under control, until the coven is confident that she's got hold of her amazing abilities.'

'Brilliant. Very nice of Morena to offer up my home to an out-of-control kid and the Babysitters' Club.'

'Who do you think you're calling . . .'

'Maeve,' Annie said sternly, holding her back with an arm

as she lunged towards the man over the top of the sofa. 'It's very late. Why don't you go back to bed and let me handle this, okay?'

'But . . .' Maeve rolled her eyes, sensing that she was fighting a losing battle if she bothered to protest. 'Fine. Seeing as he's clearly not a troll or a minotaur or something else cool, this all just became a lot less interesting. But I won't be sleeping, so come and get me if this bozo makes you walk the plank or starts asking where the treasure is.'

Annie couldn't be sure in the low light, but she was almost certain that the cutting assessment earned a wry smirk from Hal. She offered Maeve a reassuring smile in the hopes that it would seem as though everything was under control, but knew already that she'd pay for shutting her out in the morning. Annie waited until the bedroom door was closed before she turned her attention back to Hal.

'Look, this certainly isn't ideal,' she said. 'And I apologize for . . .'

He grunted. 'I'll sleep on the porch. We'll sort this out in the morning.'

'What?'

'Look, Andromeda Wildwood. I've crossed four realms today and you don't even want to know how long it's been since I had a shower. But, even so, I'm hardly going to kick you out and send the kid packing, am I? We'll sort this out tomorrow, when my head isn't pounding and my eyes aren't about to fall shut.'

'The porch? You can't sleep outside on the porch,' Annie scoffed.

'Oh yeah? You'd rather a strange man was in here with you, would you? I know that bed isn't fitting us both in it,' he said.

Even in the dark, his eyes glimmered green. Annie blushed crossly. He bent down to pick up the heavy sack of belongings that he'd dumped on the floor, a sleeping bag, what appeared to be horse reins, a cracked glass lantern spilling out of it. He groaned at the weight as he threw it all back over his shoulder. 'Obviously. It goes without saying. I'll sleep outside.'

'Well.' Annie relented an inch, slightly baffled by how considerate he was. For a ruffian. 'That is very understanding of you.'

Hal grunted again. 'Don't mention it. The Bancroft Compromise; why *wouldn't* there be two strange witches having a sleepover in my house, after I've spent three months in a French shed monitoring the nocturnal patterns of banshees?'

He turned and reached for the handle of the front door, before realizing with a start that there wasn't one any more. Hal flexed his magic for the first time, sending a quick and graceful burst of bronze-tinged sparks to lift the smashed front door, bring the panels back together and set it into place. Looking back over his shoulder, he gave Annie a lazy, one-fingered salute.

'Nice pyjamas, by the way.'

Annie shoved her arms into a fold across the cartoon latte cups and scowled once more for luck, her most determined yet. When the door closed behind Hal, she made sure to fire a double-locking spell across all the doors and windows. Just in case.

Annie rose early again, barely allowing her eyelids to close before springing back up out of bed. The spirits of the hex had been particularly vocal, tormenting her with dreams of painful wrong decisions. But she had to put their troubles aside as best as she could and confront the immediate problem, which, she saw from the bedroom window, was currently lounging on the porch swing with a partially undone shirt and a grubby Stetson pulled over his face against the dawn. What kind of self-respecting warlock wore a Stetson?

Annie was determined that she would deal with this. Not that she doubted for a second that Maeve could handle herself and would reality-check the man into questioning his own existential worth, but it was unthinkable. Part of her was even slightly grateful for an interaction where she could rely on the spell again, to navigate things successfully in a perfectly polite and friendly manner. At least it had come back to help her last night; Hal had backed down so quickly, the effects of renewed *Splendidus Infernum* helping to defuse the tension of her spoon-based threats.

The memory of Hal's snarky comment about her pyjamas ensured that she dressed quickly and made herself look more put-together, conjuring jeans and a pink shirt and sweeping her hair into a curly ponytail and headscarf before heading downstairs to make a coffee-based peace offering. He had, albeit unwillingly, given them his home after all.

Manoeuvring the front door open with her hip, she tiptoed out onto the porch with two mugs of her favourite maple spice blend, placing one down on the wooden boards next to the swing. Hal was still fast asleep on his back, an arm swung lazily behind his head to rest on. He hadn't even bothered to conjure himself a pillow or a blanket, covering himself with his heavy, sheepskin jacket instead. He was at least two foot too long to even be attempting to sleep on the swing. Somehow he'd managed it though; he was clearly used to sleeping uncomfortably for his field work.

Leaning on the porch rail, watching his chest rise and fall in a slow rhythm of sleep, Annie took the chance to size him up a little better than she'd been able to in the dark. He was, she noted with a wrinkled nose, still filthy from head to toe and, judging by the way that he'd managed to fall asleep in such a ridiculous position, he must have been roughing it while out on his banshee scouting. But, beneath all of the caked-on mud and smudges of grubbiness, he did have nice hair, she had to admit. Long and scruffy to his shoulders, pushed back but stubbornly still falling into his face while he slept. Long, thick eyelashes that were wasted on a warlock, a slightly crooked nose and, behind the tangle of beard, she could see a strong, square jawline.

'Stop watching me sleep.'

Hal lifted his hat and lazily opened one green eye. His surly voice croaked extra deep with his first words of the morning and Annie startled backwards in her slippers.

'Stop pretending to be asleep!' she retorted, embarrassed to be caught out.

He closed his eyes again and shifted his body with a grimace. 'I wasn't pretending. But the smell of my first decent cup of coffee in three months would be enough to wake me from the grave.'

'In that case, special delivery,' Annie said, gesturing to the cup she'd left beside him. It felt a little like she'd taken a chance with feeding a wild animal and then returned to a safe distance. He peered through one eye again and then glanced back at her from under his brow.

'Room service, hey?'

'It's probably the least I can do.' She leaned against the porch post and moved her weight onto her other leg, trying to appear nonchalant. Hal leaned down to pick up the mug and swung his legs over to a seated position with a groan. Holding the coffee in one hand, he used his other to push down his shoulders and adjust his neck muscles.

'Actually, you're right,' he groaned. 'You're on coffee duty for the foreseeable.'

'That seems fair, seeing as we've accidentally invaded your home. Sorry about that, by the way.'

He looked at her for a moment over the top of his mug while he blew on the steam, then gestured with a nod towards the wicker armchair at the end of the porch. It had previously been splintered and unbraided, covered in cobwebs and animal droppings, but Annie had made light work of the transformation. Now it was a gleaming brown, with a red gingham cushion to match the curtains. He brought it a foot closer towards him with quick magic and she accepted the wordless invitation to join him.

'Early riser, then, huh?' Hal asked, taking a first tentative sip and then leaning back with his eyes closed and a low hum of pleasure. Annie, mortified to find that she was staring, turned fixedly out onto the meadow. Thankfully her attention was stolen by a whole family of hares lolloping their way through the rustling grass, the dawn dew catching the tops of their ears. A hedgehog was snuffling its way along the shallow steps of the porch and a pair of bats swooped low enough to skim the tops of the wildflowers. A hush of lemon-meringue clouds in the pink and pale-blue sky was just starting to brighten behind the band of trees.

'I'm not a big sleeper,' Annie said.

'Yet somehow you look as well rested as a woman who just got back from an all-expenses-paid trip to paradise. Lucky girl,' he said, eyes still closed with his head resting back on the top of the swinging bench. She blamed her own paranoia for the possible tone of scepticism in his voice.

'I take my skincare very seriously,' she said casually. 'Now, where do we start in our negotiations?'

'I don't know about any negotiations. Let's just start with what you're actually doing here, shall we?' Every time Hal looked at her, his gaze lingered a second longer than would have been considered polite, as though he had to force himself to look away. The spell was working and she felt the relief of it. It did feel strange, somehow more potent than usual, but Annie had been holed up with Maeve and had felt none of the usual response to her perfection for days on end. Sometimes she forgot how powerful it could be.

'It's simple. I'm here until Maeve doesn't need me any more. She's only fifteen. This is all very new to her and she's showing certain . . . tendencies that aren't safe to be left to flower around non-wicchefolk.'

'Tendencies.' Hal nodded with a smirk. 'I'm assuming that's your gracious way of saying the kid loves to blow stuff up. So glad my house could be of service for that particular habit.'

'I haven't seen her explode a single thing,' Annie said defensively, circling the rim of her mug with a thoughtful finger. 'Oh, actually . . .' She recalled the pumpkin. 'Generally, it tends to be more . . . flame-related.'

'Brilliant.'

'But we're making progress already. We're on day . . .' Annie bit down on her lip as she calculated on one hand, '. . . seven of no spontaneous fires around the place, so you really have to admire the development there, at least.'

'Seven whole days? Now I'll rest easy.'

'Oh, wait . . . I forgot about the kitchen.'

'That explains my singed curtains. Can I ask where her parents are?'

'She doesn't know her father; her mother left a long time ago. Selcouth picked up on the arrival of her magic, but have no tracings of heritage to work with, not a single wicche relative to help uncover its nature. They decided to step in when she accidentally caused flamey chaos at her foster home.'

'And that's where you come into all of this?'

'For one reason or another, Morena thought we'd be a good fit. I think it's just about having someone here with her, to give her a safe space so that she can spend some time away from normal life and experiment. Throw her magic around a little, see what makes it soar.'

Hal gave her an upside-down smile. 'Very poetic.'

'Thank you. But, as you can see, we are now in a pickle.'

'And I'm sensing that I don't get a whole lot of choice in this pickle. What if I'm not a pickle guy?'

'Well, then you are wrong, because pickles make everything better. Besides, it's coven orders. Can't argue with that.' Annie shrugged innocently, paired with her best and most angelic smile.

'Is that so?' He paused. 'Alright, a man knows when he's defeated.'

'Ha,' Annie said triumphantly, leaning back in her chair with her arms folded.

'No need to look so pleased about it. Obviously I'm not going to turf you out. If you both need a place to stay, then so be it. I can set myself up out here until Selcouth says it's time for you to go. Got a tent in my rucksack.'

'We can't ask you to do that. This is your house. There must be . . .' Annie struggled to think of a counter-offer.

'It's not a problem. Haven't exactly got the room in this

place for conjuring new furniture. Like you said, this is about Maeve – I don't want to make either of you feel weird about some guy being here.'

Hal smiled and continued: 'Consider it the Bancroft Compromise. My dad always used to say that for when my mum got her way and it involved absolutely no compromise in the slightest.' His half-smile quickly turned into a frown, as though he wasn't sure why he'd just shared that. 'I am however saying this on the assumption that it won't be for too much longer. If you're still here for New Year then I might have to set a banshee on you.'

'I don't *think* it will be for that long, but . . . Look, if Maeve is comfortable with it – and I mean genuinely comfortable; trust me, I'll know if she's lying – then you should at least sleep on the sofa.'

He leaned back again, stretching an arm over the top of the swing. 'This bed isn't so bad.'

'Unless you happen to be a secret contortionist, then that's not true. I've heard plenty of wicchefolk vouch for you before. And I'm confident that no warlock who's ever encountered Morena Gowden would dare to upset her charges. Take the couch,' Annie insisted.

Hal stared at her through thoughtful eyes, fixed as though trying to read her better, then slapped the thighs of his trousers to close the matter. 'So, the girl,' he said gruffly. 'She's probably only encountered the Sage Witches so far, right? Why you for the job, instead of them?'

'Good question. It was Morena's call. I think she just knew that I wouldn't say no.'

'Ahh,' he smirked. 'So we can *both* blame Morena for screwing us over. Now it all makes sense.'

'Excuse me, I haven't been screwed over. I'm having a very good time with Maeve,' Annie said, affronted by his bluntness. She wasn't used to being around men like this. The ones she knew from the Sorciety were always so proper, with well-measured reactions to everything. Although perhaps 'well-measured' was her own optimistic code for . . . dishonest, complicated, even manipulative.

'Come on,' Hal chuckled. 'Morena is definitely getting a kick out of putting a princess like you out here, just as much as she's relishing the fact that I've come home to a candyfloss utopia. She knew exactly what she was doing. You're telling me that you're genuinely delighted to be here, putting your life on hold for the kid? You don't exactly strike me as a gnarled old counsellor who thrives in the great outdoors, mentoring the chosen one.'

'And what do I strike you as, exactly?' She swung one leg over the other and tapped a foot up and down impatiently.

Hal furrowed his brow, considering her carefully. 'I haven't quite worked it out yet. To be honest with you, the Little Miss Perfect thing . . . it's a little disconcerting.'

Annie faltered. That wasn't the adjective that she'd been expecting. She had felt assured by the knowledge that the spell was working fastidiously in the background, but the safety net of mouldable, placated satisfaction that it normally provided didn't seem to be there. Instead, Hal seemed as unsure of her as she was of him.

'Well, you've got me wrong,' she said, bristling. 'And you've got Maeve wrong, too, so you need to work on your character reading.'

'I haven't said a word about the kid. I like her. She seems pretty fearless. Plus she called me a pirate and I'll always take that as a compliment.' For the first time, Hal failed at keeping his smile controlled in a tight line and it flooded out of his face into a cheeky, bright grin. Annie blinked hard. She forced herself to remain focused on the matter at hand.

'You called her "the chosen one",' she said with an added sarcastic impression of his deep voice. 'I didn't like your tone,' she snipped.

'No tone included,' he said matter-of-factly, draining the last dregs of his mug then returning it to the porch floor. He kicked off gently on the swing, sending it into a slow pendulum. 'I meant it sincerely. You're telling me you haven't noticed?'

'I've been trying to get her to like me since we first met. There's very little I haven't noticed about Maeve.'

'And yet you think all of this is normal, do you?' He gestured with a nod out towards the meadow, where a bundle of wolf cubs had just come scampering out of the woods and towards the cottage, followed by their mother, who was doing her best to herd them and give each one a grooming lick on the head. They glanced over to the cottage with twitching snouts, as though they were drawn to the scent of it, intrigued by what might lay inside.

Hal leaned towards Annie, forearms on his thighs to close the space between them, a glint in his eye and an intrigue in his smile that hadn't been there before. 'Because I gotta tell you, Blondie. That isn't normal.'

Annie laughed. 'You're being a little dramatic. We're witches, we're in the woods, we're using concentrated, active magic – rather lovely magic, too, may I add. There's always going to be animals drawn to that.' She faltered. 'Isn't there?'

'Sure, there's creatures and critters around here all the time – it's part of why I set up camp at Arden Place myself. But this many? All at once?' Hal rose from the swing and, after stretching out his chest, turned and leaned over the railing that ran around the porch to peer past the side of the house. He beckoned her over.

Annie stood up to join him, her hands holding onto the rail next to his. She clocked Hal's scent for the first time, buried beneath the nature and outdoors that clung to his muddy clothes. An enveloping sort of scent, a crackling fireplace in winter, woody and amber, clove and chestnuts. She was mortified to realize that she'd unintentionally shifted closer to him as she tried to decipher it. She took an emphatic step away to counteract that.

Sure enough, a pair of fawns were gazing into the open window of Maeve's bedroom. Her arm, strung with her stacks of beaded bracelets, was reaching over the sill to offer them slices of apple and a stroke on the snout. They nuzzled happily into her touch, although they were fighting for prime position against Karma, who had joined the window meeting to claim her own strokes as rightful priority. She kept whipping the fawns in the face with her tail to make sure they knew it.

'Animals will always be drawn to magic, sure enough. But make no mistake: they're not interested in your witchcraft or mine,' Hal said, tapping his hands on the railing as though he were satisfied to have been proven right. 'It's her they're drawn to. You need to keep an eye on that kid.'

Chapter Fifteen

SILVER SECRETS

Annie returned inside to deliver a coffee to Maeve, but more importantly to assess how the girl felt about the prospect of this unscheduled arrival sleeping on the couch. Their couch. His couch? She wasn't quite sure how she felt about it herself, caught off guard by his odd combination of easy kindness and general scowling. But uprooting Maeve again, just when it was starting to feel like an understanding had settled between them, was not the right solution either. Annie was comforted by how many times she had heard other Selcouth members sing Hal's praises. She had once even heard Morena reluctantly admit that he was 'irritatingly considerate' and 'offensively decent', apart from the way that he insisted on traipsing mud through the entirety of Hecate House on every visit.

Maeve told Annie that she couldn't give two hoots (in slightly less polite terms) where Hal slept, providing that he'd give her an insight into some of his adventures. Even a slightly sullen teenager could not resist a tale of exploring various realms, sleeping under the stars among some of its most legendary beasts.

A result of Maeve's eager interest in Hal's fieldwork, her first question being whether he'd ever slain a vampire, the unlikely trio spent the morning getting to know each other. If not entirely broken, it did at least melt the ice of their first encounter. Annie, between flapping to make sure that everybody had the breakfast they wanted, was learning that Hal seemed to mostly prefer communicating in grunts and low hums about almost everything – apart from his lifelong love for animals. Sharing memories of his voyages lit a fire behind his eyes, the green turning richer as he got carried away on a tidal wave of nostalgia and adventure. She had to catch herself once or twice when she realized that she was watching his face tell the story almost too intently, resting her chin on her hand while he recalled the time he had been tasked with tagging a flight of young dragons for the coven to monitor.

'But that must be, like, insanely dangerous. Weren't you scared?' Maeve asked, wide-eyed.

'Of course I was scared, especially after one of the adults broke my nose a few years ago. Anyone who says they don't get scared is an idiot. These are really good by the way,' he said off-handedly, ripping apart a pecan and pistachio croissant from Celeste's supply. His table manners were, frankly, atrocious and Annie made sure to focus on that fact while he carelessly licked the remainders of the filling off his fingers one by one. 'But I did also happen to know that a dragon's favourite treat, aside from the roasted flesh of man, is . . . Any ideas?'

'Roasted flesh of literally anything else?' Maeve chanced.

'It's actually a scotch egg.'

Maeve looked disgusted. 'That might be even grosser than the roasted flesh of man.'

'Dragons love scotch eggs. Can't get enough of them when they're babies. So I laced a whole packet of them with a dozing draught, trailed them through the forest, waited until they were all fast asleep after the feast and then tagged them all on the ear with no bother. Even managed to give most of them a little stroke on the beard for good measure. Dragons are pretty cute when they're sleeping. Just big puppies really.'

Maeve slumped at the anti-climax of the story. 'Scotch eggs? That's the worst conclusion to a dragon-hunting story I've ever heard.'

'Heard a lot of them, have you?' Hal grinned, popping the last of the croissant in his mouth and dusting the crumbs off his hands over the tablecloth.

'Right, come on, you. There's witchery to do,' Annie said, attempting to coax Maeve away from the tantalizing conversation, as much as she wanted to sit and listen to more of it herself. 'I thought we'd try some more Incantation today. I remembered this nifty little trick from when I was your age of scribbling spells onto parchment, crumpling them up and making them burst into glitter. You won't believe how . . .'

'Absolutely not. No glitter,' Hal said. He looked accusatorially at Annie. 'If your magic is anything to go by, that damn stuff will get absolutely everywhere and I'll never see the end of it. I've already noticed yours, hanging everywhere around the place.'

'You don't like it?' Annie said, genuinely baffled. As a firm believer in extra sparkle at all times, she had tinkered with her own magic to ensure the glitter lingered a little longer than the average.

Hal cleared his throat. 'Well, it's not that I don't like it. It's just . . . Oh, do what you want. Best believe I'll be charging

Morena a redecorating fee when you're done, anyway.' He took his plate to the kitchen and refolded the ends of his shirt sleeves, which were pushed up past his forearms. Annie had noticed his forearms. Now that they were clean (she had purposefully kept herself busy while he was out back in the tub), she could see that they were tanned. And large.

'I'll leave you two to do . . . whatever it is that you do, exactly, but I'll be back later,' Hal said as he tugged on his boots, dropping shards of mud around the cottage. 'Thanks for the cake – or whatever that was. Not exactly bacon and eggs, but it was . . . well, delicious, actually. Any more going spare?'

'You mean a croissant . . . ?' Annie reminded him, although she suspected that she might as well be telling him it was an aubergine. She sent a broom sweeping after him as she folded another croissant into a napkin and handed it over. 'Oh, I probably should have mentioned that the raspberry compote had a few confidence currants added into the syrup. They're a Celeste recipe, helpful to shake off any self-consciousness in Maeve's magic exploration, but if you feel extra fabulous today, you know why.'

She smiled angelically and earned an incredulous glare from Hal in return. He picked up his jacket from the hook and, as he opened the front door to leave, she noticed him toss his overgrown hair over his shoulder with a particularly superb flourish. He froze. 'Bloody berries.' He turned back to shoot her a final scowl and closed the door behind him.

'Where do you think he's off to?' Annie asked, watching him stride across the meadow into the woods. Maeve was poking her head around her bedroom door as she brushed her teeth. With her magic beginning to flourish, she wasn't even bothering to hold the toothbrush for herself. It levitated smartly in her mouth while a hairbrush simultaneously tugged by itself at her long, dark hair. Annie couldn't help but snort at the sight.

Maeve shrugged and spoke with a mouthful of toothpaste. 'Probably off to lasso a griffin or something.'

The next few days flew by in a brume of raindrops and smoky silver clouds as October folded in over Arden Place, as though holding it carefully inside warm hands. Time was spent reading and baking and crafting and making – a current of magic crackling from Maeve as she grew in confidence and calmness. Hal spent his days outdoors, returning for dinner and sleep each evening, while Annie kept the fireplace roaring at the cottage and the extra silky hot chocolate flowing. Her secret recipe always involved stirring in at least one wish from the tiny velvet drawstring bag of them that she'd purchased from a useful elf contact.

On a particularly balmy evening, noting that Halloween was less than three weeks away, Annie was keen to harness the increasing enchanted energy that lay in wait, and carry on the positive improvements she'd been witnessing each day in Maeve's magic. It was growing at impressive speed and, after Hal's early comment about the way Maeve seemed to be attracting all things magical within the local radius, Annie was starting to wonder whether he might be onto something. Not that she would be letting *him* know that. But she wanted to challenge Maeve, to push her magic further than just ice-cream sundaes and rainbow paintboxes.

'Now, I don't want you to get down on yourself if your

spell doesn't knit quite as you intend it to,' Annie said, loading up Maeve's arms with a pink tasselled picnic blanket, a pink hamper full of picky bits to split for dinner and Karma's favourite pink cushion, plus two telescopes. Disappointingly, these were not pink. 'This is very tricky magic; a lot of witches inside Hecate House would struggle with this one.'

Maeve simply gave her a look. 'Try me.'

With Hal yet to return from wherever it was that he'd slunk off to, the witches headed out into the sprawling meadow at the front of the house, night drenching the long grass in a silvery hue that made the whole garden feel as though it was painted in streaks of watery moonlight. It was that precise idea that had inspired Annie's plans for the evening. Since they'd arrived at the isolated cottage, the sky had felt like it contained their own personal constellations each night – stars that no one else could see – and it was time to put that to good use.

'We're going to try something sparkly.'

'Oh, not again,' Maeve whined. 'Didn't you get the message when I exploded your princess pumpkin?'

'I think this might be a little more up your alley. Maeve, I want you to harness the stars.' Annie tried to keep a straight face as she said it, but her heart did an excited skip at how Maeve's face immediately lit up.

'Stars? You mean like actual, proper stars? How do I . . . What do we . . . ? I suppose that sounds pretty cool,' Maeve said, a gigantic smile almost splitting her face in two.

Both witches lay on their backs, side by side on the blanket, with Karma settling happily around Maeve's neck as though to make herself as inconvenient as physically possible. When night had fully rolled in, with its intricate pattern of sapphire sky sprawled above, Annie handed Maeve a pencil.

'It's straight from your pencil case.'

'It is? I don't recognize it.'

'Okay, so I might have turned it pink. But that was an accidental, happy side effect of the enchantment, I promise. I've threaded a spell of *Caelum Adambratio* inside of it to get us started, to bestow the lead with pure, silver starlight into the tip. And now all you have to do is . . .'

Annie stretched up her hand towards the sky and against the darkness and tried a quick, extremely terrible sketch of herself, which she tried and failed to not be embarrassed about. A line of silver trailed behind wherever she moved the pencil, etching her drawing into the sky. 'Obviously I'm rubbish at this, don't look at it. But I have a feeling that *you're* about to do something wonderful.'

With no hesitation and only pure delight, Maeve took the pencil for herself and spent the next handful of hours joining the dots of the stars to paint the night sky with her own illustrations. Handily learning the alignment of the stars, moons and planets as they drew, it was as though the constellations came to life. Maeve filled every inch of the vast space above with her drawings, lost in her own world as well as the sky.

'How does this even work? It's incredible,' Maeve said, her tongue poking out slightly as she concentrated intently on her drawings.

'Nifty, isn't it?' Annie said, thoroughly pleased with herself for finding something that showcased the nature of Maeve's magic so well. 'If she so chooses, a witch can bequeath her powers into an object. She might wish to for lots of different reasons – maybe leaving a little protection behind for loved ones when she crosses over or if she's keen to use a wand rather than a physical gesture. Obviously, those reasons are more permanent, but it can be temporary, too.'

'Like the other night when Hal arrived and you were waving a wooden spoon around?'

Annie blushed. 'Exactly. I didn't entirely intend upon bewitching a wooden spoon — not my smoothest decision — but I was just swept up in the moment and it pulled on my magic. You're borrowing magic from the stars, it'll be replaced when you've finished, but the pencil becomes a kind of wand to channel them. Which feels very fitting for you and your many talents. I have to say, though, it's tough magic, I wasn't expecting you'd take to this so easily.'

The stars seemed to whisper Maeve's stories, her sketches of liquid silver and magic decorating the sky like lace. Annie could have burst with pride seeing them strung together with the girl's spellwork and art. She buzzed with the realization that it only reinforced their suspicions that Maeve's magic was a unique, promising treasure.

Eventually, Hal returned.

'I wondered if you two were responsible for these masterpieces,' he said admiringly, dropping his satchel to the ground to join them. He leaned back into the grass, both hands behind his head, to watch as Maeve finished an impressive drawing of Karma batting a ball of yarn that unravelled into Orion's Belt.

'I can't take any credit. It's all Maeve,' Annie said, watching contentedly as the silver trail from the pencil sailed over her head like a shooting star.

The three of them had melted quickly into an easy companionship. Annie was most surprised to find that she felt, perhaps not entirely relaxed, but at least 10 per cent more so around Hal's calming presence. Almost every man she encountered in her normal life made her feel the exact opposite: uncomfortable and rigid, overly self-aware. But she found herself relieved and excited to see him come back safely to the cottage, just as he promised each morning. Plus she supposed that any man who allowed Karma to sit on his head like a Russian winter hat was probably a decent sort of warlock.

While Maeve was distracted with an intricate portrait of the four of them among the stars, Annie noticed that Hal was silently trying to catch her attention. His brows shot up and his eyes widened. She could read the meaning easily, even before he mouthed the words 'the kid' with a wink that was obviously intended to be encouraging, but conversely made Annie sort of flail a bit and feel as though her stomach might be eating itself. He was encouraging her to raise the topic with Maeve.

Since Hal's 'chosen one' comment, Annie had been actively avoiding the prospect of frank conversation with Maeve about the strangely magnetic qualities that her magic was exhibiting. On the surface, it seemed foolish to let a teenager know that they may or may not be in possession of any kind of unusually strong early abilities. But after getting to know the girl so well in a short space of time, Annie knew that there wasn't a presumptuous, arrogant ego to worry about. And why shouldn't a young girl be told that she was, in fact, rather amazing? It wasn't a dangerous concept. Annie would have sold her soul for someone to have ever said that to her and to have truly meant it. Maeve deserved to know that she was even more special than they had first suspected. She gave Hal a small, subtle nod.

'Maeve,' Annie said, rolling onto her front so that she could look directly at her. 'This is brilliant. Your magic . . . I'm starting to realize that it's rather strong. Really strong, in fact.'

Predictably, and as Annie should have known would happen, Maeve simply shrugged. 'I know.'

'You do?'

'Course,' the girl said dismissively, keeping all of her concentration on the portraits, finishing the finer details of Annie's nose and Hal's facial hair. 'I've been telling that to anyone who'd pay attention since they came in. That's the problem, though, people just don't listen to me. I told you that it all felt huge.'

'Right, you did.' Annie recalled their walk in the woods. 'But I assumed we were just talking about your emotions.'

'Emotions? No, Annie,' Maeve said, rolling her eyes. 'My emotions are all over the place, but they're just emotions. They come and go; it's part of the deal of being fifteen. It's the *magic* that's big.' She said it as though it were entirely obvious, as though Annie should have figured it all out days ago.

'Oh, well . . . That's wonderful, good for you. And I've been thinking,' Annie decided to chance.

'Don't pull a muscle,' Maeve said with a snort.

Annie gave her a sarcastic look, then plucked a dandelion from the edge of the picnic blanket and passed a finger over the downy clock. 'Maybe I should get in touch with the coven to tell them how we're doing. I know we're supposed to be waiting for them to give you the all-clear, but I really think they'd be interested to know that . . .'

'No.' Maeve's hand jerked in mid-air, the pencil dragging an unplanned, silver scratch across the sky.

'Maeve, you don't even know what I'm suggesting yet,'

Annie laughed. 'If the coven knew that your magic was this extraordinary and improving so rapidly, they might . . .'

'They might what? Throw me a party? Put me in charge?'

Maeve dropped the pencil to the blanket. Her beautiful sky art faded as the spell unravelled, as though someone had taken an eraser to it all. The feelings coming from Maeve changed within the pit of Annie's chest as she tuned into them; a quiet, growing sense of worry and dread that mingled with a quick anger, which Annie inhaled with the chilly meadow air.

Maeve shook her head and her eyes moved from the sky to her nails, which she began to rip at. 'Come on, Annie, even you're not naive enough to think that strangeness is something that's ever celebrated. Even in the wicche world, I don't fit in.'

Annie blinked, confused. She shook it away with a disbelieving laugh. 'The whole purpose of the coven is to celebrate magic in all its forms. They'd be delighted to see how special you are, just like Hal and I have been. So far, all of my suggestions have felt like giving dot-to-dot homework sheets to a genius. You're too good! They might have ideas of how we could work on your magic even further, really push your talents.'

This time, Maeve's indignant snort was echoed by a matching one from Hal. Annie shot him a glare and he quickly returned to silently staring at the sky. Though he knew it wasn't his place to contribute, he was evidently listening and had opinions that matched Maeve's.

'See? Even the cowboy knows I'm right.'

'Don't you two start ganging up on me. Maeve, they could challenge you better than I can.'

'But I want to stay here,' Maeve said, a hint of vulnerability in her voice. It didn't linger, promptly replaced by confidence again. 'You're telling me that a magical coven would be thrilled to hear that a fifteen-year-old girl has extraordinary powers? That they'd be chuffed for me and want to help me to channel them and test them as much as I can?' Maeve shook her head, as though she pitied Annie's innocent mind. 'Yes, that's what always happens in stories like mine, isn't it? It always works out so well for the weirdo, doesn't it?'

Hearing the suggestion aloud made Annie pause. And, frustratingly, she could tell just from Hal's cocked eyebrow that he was in agreement. He had technically remained silent, but had leaned up on his elbows. Annie could hear exactly what he was trying to say without taking sides in business that wasn't his: 'the kid's right'. She tutted at him, despite the fact he hadn't actually said anything out loud.

'I know that Morena will want to know how wonderful you are,' Annie said coaxingly.

'Morena has never thought anything was wonderful in her life,' Hal said. 'Except maybe medieval torture techniques. She told me she'd revel in putting me in the stocks once.' Annie shot him a look that made his eyebrows shoot up in innocence. He reached for his Stetson and plonked it on top of his face as he lay back down in resignation. 'Alright, butting out.'

The coven would absolutely want to hear about her findings with Maeve. But Annie also felt the creeping scratch of a realization that the Sorciety would expect her to share this information with them, too. The idea made her bristle, a strange wave of nausea taking hold at the prospect.

'I just don't really know why it's any of their business,' Maeve said sullenly. 'At least not yet.'

Annie considered Maeve and Hal's prediction: the possibility that the coven wouldn't be as excited as she thought to celebrate an up-and-coming protégée. That instead they might take no delight whatsoever in a spark of fresh potential. The elder wicchefolk might be threatened and concerned. Maeve would be nothing but their latest red flag. Selcouth had always made it crystal-clear that it did not appreciate anomalies in the system and spikes in the use of magic usually led to intense, controversial debate. Annie had even heard tell of powers being removed altogether.

Unwanted attention, strangeness, anomalies . . . These are never welcome things at Selcouth. It had never been something that she had considered before, but Selcouth's determination to cap these things was not necessarily a bold and brave one. Maybe it was cowardice.

Annie thought back on what she'd seen of Maeve's magic. Wonderful things. Beautiful, impressive things, full of colour and life, youth and joy. And the possibilities that it seemed to hold – so many that it felt fizzing, overflowing, sugary and wild. Maeve's magic was too special to allow them to seize it, just as it was beginning to blossom into something beautiful. That especially applied to Glory and the Sorciety, too.

Something within Annie told her that, if she was ever going to break the rules, perhaps now was the time to try it, to go against what she knew she was absolutely supposed to do and choose what felt right to her instead. She had Hal here now, a talented and respected warlock who could provide assistance. And Maeve was always telling her to stop pleasing everyone. Maybe the kid . . . Maeve, was rubbing off on her.

Annie released a deep-seated, healing sigh. Being bad just once in a lifetime felt surprisingly good.

'Your secret's safe with us,' she said, pulling Maeve into a hug. She felt Maeve's shoulders sag with relief and it was the only sign that Annie needed to feel confident in her decision. At least for now. She was competent enough to monitor Maeve's magic while in a place that the girl felt confident and relaxed. They could slow down, take time to learn more about it, understand its nature before the coven came barrelling in. Hal gave a satisfied, triumphant hum and, without even removing his Stetson from his face, held up a hand for the girl to high five. Their loud clap against the quiet brought a sudden, more pressing thought into Annie's brain.

The moon swung heavily above them, like the polished pendulum on a sky clock. Surely it couldn't be that late.

'What time is it?' Annie asked shakily, swallowing hard.

'Just after midnight, judging by the moon,' Hal said, lifting his hat to squint at her through the darkness, the three of them only lit to one side by the porch lanterns. 'Why?'

Annie shot to her feet, spilling her drink across the last of the breadsticks as she frantically dusted dry grass off her jeans. She turned to Hal and Maeve, barely even registering their baffled expressions. 'I have to take a bath.'

'You don't smell that bad,' Maeve said.

'No, no, you don't understand. It's . . .' Annie stumbled over her words, holding her forehead. 'Hair wash night. Of course! Can't upset my hair wash schedule,' she called back far too loudly, followed by a slightly hysterical giggle as she turned to run. She saw Maeve and Hal share a baffled side-eye, but she didn't have time for that now. She ran back to the blanket. 'In fact, it's way past bedtime. Everybody inside.'

Annie promptly hustled them back inside the cottage, hastily snatching up a bundle of dandelions that were growing in front of the porch as she coaxed them in. She was fairly sure dandelions had some worthwhile qualities? Perfect digestion, at least. They would have to do for tonight's spell. It had already slipped and paled, judging by her rash decisions to be bold and bad. She couldn't let it fade any further.

Chapter Sixteen

BRIGHTER THAN THIS

Soon, the unexpected arrangement at Arden Place saw mid-October arrive and the trio fell further into a strangely comfortable, pleasant routine. One corner of the triangle was sugary sweet, the second all eye-rolls and curtains of dark hair, the third a perpetually dishevelled grumbler. But each of them had to admit that their triple combination of Annie's optimism and positivity, Maeve's straight-talking determination and Hal's calming presence seemed to balance their counterparts surprisingly well. Like all marvellous potions, each ingredient was understated alone, but made something unexpectedly magical when combined.

After an arduous day of tackling deeper levels of Incantation theory (arduous only because Maeve kept asking extremely complex questions that Annie didn't know the answers to), Maeve's confidence burned brightly. After she successfully managed to conjure fire on demand for the very first time, using a gentle brume of *Ignis Candela* to light every candle around the cottage, rather than allowing it to be explosively dictated by her temper, Annie declared that her progress called for a celebration.

UNCHARMED

All day, she had been dreaming up an enormous roast dinner, with a showstopping dessert to follow, and she let her magic flow freely around the kitchen as it did best. Annie hummed at the stove with the radio on, sparks flying to keep spoons stirring in saucepans and trays shuffling inside the oven while a pot of spiced apple cider simmered at her side. A wonderful smell of stewed pumpkin combined with maple-glazed vegetables flooded the cottage, along with the faint wood smoke from the fireplace.

The three of them sat down at the table together (Hal only joining once he had scrubbed from head to toe, following Annie's insistence that he would not touch her white table-cloth otherwise) and tucked into towering plates. They were loaded with herbed carrots glazed to a sweet shine, roast potatoes so golden and crispy that they crunched under their forks, and a rich, dark gravy at the perfect consistency. The latter was Hal's contribution, who insisted that he didn't trust anyone else to make it right – even Annie. Maeve had been given the all-important task of using her newly harnessed sorcery fire to char a handful of marshmallows for the pudding.

'I'll never eat again,' Hal said, leaning back in his chair and cradling his stomach after dinner.

'Pudding?' Annie asked brightly.

'Go on then.'

Unable to contain a bursting smile, knowing that she'd done herself proud, Annie brought out the masterpiece that had taken hours and satiated her magic pleasantly – a towering chocolate cake so tall that it genuinely swayed as she levitated it towards the table. The midnight-coloured cocoa was iced so delicately and so intricately that Maeve declared it should officially be considered Annie's magnum opus. Swirls of deep purple buttercream cascaded across each tier and enchanted edible flowers bloomed one by one around the edges. Miniature chocolate stars were scattered across the top, in tribute to Maeve's successful starlight spell, and surrounded an enchanted chocolate cauldron that poured out warm, white chocolate in a velvety river. Solely for extra cuteness, tiny chocolate pumpkins adorned the bottom tier, while Maeve's expertly charred marshmallows made for perfect little ghosts.

'Too much?' Annie asked, suddenly self-conscious. Maeve was already diving in with the cake slice, her brow furrowed with the pressure of making the first cut.

'Never,' Hal said, looking momentarily baffled by the whole situation, but very impressed nonetheless. She gave him a shy smile of appreciation for that.

Later, each of them sipped at black coffees and picked up chocolatey crumbs on their fingers.

'I can see why that bakery of yours is such a success story. And why everyone at Hecate House is tripping over themselves to get to the leftovers,' Hal said, pulling the napkin out of his collar and balling it onto the table in final defeat. 'Your friends must be stopping by all the time to sample everything you make.'

Annie laughed quietly. 'My non-wicche friends are right there with me. The others . . . They're not quite so convinced.'

'Well then,' he said gruffly, interpreting the awkward silence when she didn't elaborate. 'They don't know how lucky they are, do they?' He scratched at his beard, avoiding eye contact at all costs.

Maeve was the first to leave the table. 'Annie's the best,' she said simply, as she flexed her magic to stack up their cake plates. Annie blushed furiously, but gave her a delighted round of applause for the effortless levitation spell. Even Hal gave her a 'Not bad, kid,' before she excused herself for time with her pencils, sketchbooks, Karma and, incredibly, a snack plate.

Annie and Hal began to clear the rest of the table, neither saying a lot, and found themselves standing together awkwardly at the sink.

'You wash, I'll dry,' Hal muttered. Annie wasn't entirely sure why they'd both opted to be side by side, washing up together, when cleaning dishes was statistically proven to be magic's most common use. All she did know was that she felt calm. Safe. Was she . . . relaxed? The shocking thought immediately undid that possibility as a bewildered tension at the idea laced her back together.

'The kid seems happy,' Hal said. 'Never met anyone quite like her. Either of you, actually.'

'I could say the same to you,' Annie laughed. 'She's finding her feet. It's funny to be around someone who sees straight through it all.'

'Sees through what?' Hal asked. For a fraction of a moment, Annie almost dared herself to say it all. To confess, to split open the dark secret that *Splendidus Infernum* took priority over anything and everything.

'Nothing. You're similar in that way, how you both seem content out here,' she said, willing a change in conversation. 'I've been meaning to ask, how *did* you end up all the way out here? In the literal middle of nowhere, only the animals for company.'

He laughed at that. 'They're my kind of conversationalists.' Seeing that she was waiting for a real answer, he sighed. 'My dad died a few years ago. He was my whole world. I kept a close eye on him and his broken heart when we lost my mum. Then, when he was gone, too, I just needed to start again. Figure out what was right for me, for the first time in a while.'

He slowed down the tea towel against the plate that he was drying, then cleared his throat, pulling himself back together.

'I like the peace here, having room to think and live slow. And the animals are always glad to have me around when humans sometimes aren't. This place called to me right from the start; the meadow sits on crossing ley lines so there's potent magic in the air, meaning . . .'

'Your own personal magical menagerie,' Annie chimed in.

'Exactly. I just feel more at home somewhere where the sky is wide open and the ground feels solid. I can get on with my research, immersed in all these incredible creatures. It's safer here if I bring back any unpredictable beasts from my travels. And I can leave for a long time and know that no one will come knocking – at least, until you arrived.'

He gave her a side-glance and Annie gave him a sheepish smile that made him lose his train of thought.

'Y'know, it's a damn shame that your friends back home don't seem to appreciate you the way they should.'

Annie's hands stopped of their own accord, still in the soapy water. She tried her best to explain. 'They do, I know they do. Different parts of my life just exist in different boxes and it's best to keep it that way.'

'Boxes, hey? And which box do you like the best?'

'Maybe time at Hecate House. Although honestly, I've put too much pressure on myself there because I'm always trying to impress the coven . . . Or the bakery . . . well, actually I put too much pressure on that, too. Probably girls' nights, then, I guess, but they can be a little . . .' She caught herself rambling. 'I can tell you that it's *not* my dating life, that's for sure.'

'So nothing's bringing you all that much happiness these days, then,' Hal said, re-rolling the damp end of his sleeve before chancing another glance at her.

'The past couple of weeks have been the first time in a long time I've had anything that's felt like real happiness, I think? I feel kind of . . . free.'

The confession spilled out of Annie so quickly that she swore she could feel the spell reel back, a little shocked that it hadn't been able to filter things first, as though she'd snatched permission away from it. Conversations at Arden Place kept bringing down her guard in ways she didn't think were possible.

'It's so different to be around people who I don't ever have to second-guess. It feels like you're both taking care of me sometimes, even though I'm supposed to be the one that's doing the caretaking. I don't have to tread quite so lightly around here.' Annie tried to laugh it off even as she said it. She kept her eyes determinedly focused on the sink full of bubbles.

Hal, too, seemed to be inordinately fascinated by his already-dry plate. 'I'd say that's the least you deserve.'

A small silence passed. 'And you're welcome to tread wherever and however hard you like in this house,' he carried on. 'Although my housemate is pretty strict about taking your boots off first.' She flicked a bunch of soapy bubbles up at him and he quickly returned the attack. 'Rules are rules. I'm just the lodger.'

Annie laughed. 'My friend Vivienne said once that if I found myself in a situation without rules, I'd make some up anyway, just to make myself feel better.'

Hal did a double take. 'Vivienne? As in Vivienne Cinder?'

'You know her?'

'Absolutely not. I made it a personal mission to ensure I never knew her after she asked whether I was the stable boy at her endarkenment ceremony. Demanded that I fetch her a cab and an unsweetened tea and that I do something about fixing the draught in the foyer. A draught – in an ancient, underground, magical headquarters,' he said, stony-faced. Annie cringed and gave him an apologetic smile on Vivienne's behalf.

'I'm not sure any of my wicche friends would be your cup of tea. They live very different lives to yours,' she laughed, but the words felt like dropping a glass on the floor. She hated how she sounded as soon as she heard them.

Hal cleared his throat, focused determinedly on the tray that he'd already dried to within an inch of its life. 'I bet.'

'Mmhmm,' Annie replied, keeping a placid smile on her face so as not to reveal the fact she felt like smacking a soapy hand directly to her forehead. The realization that she had said the wrong thing sat heavy in her chest; the spell had faltered and stalled, all of the magic in the air after the day's incantations was upsetting the balance.

'Not that it's better or worse,' Annie rambled on, desperate to patch over the awkwardness she'd accidentally created. 'Just different. They wouldn't understand the appeal of this place.'

'It's that bad, huh?'

'Oh no, not at all,' Annie muddled. 'I just mean that . . . Well, you and I. We're so opposite, aren't we? It's funny! We don't go together, we hardly belong under one roof, in such close proximity.'

'Right,' he swallowed. 'That's true enough.'

The splashes of water against the sink sides and a very faint snuffling of some kind of creature on the porch were the only noises, until Hal spoke again.

'Nice change of pace for you here, though – with me and the kid. You needed a break, but you'll be glad to get back to your shiny world,' he said bluntly. Annie shook her head as she placed a plate onto the rack and flicked the bubbles off her hands.

'Hal, that wasn't supposed to sound how it did. This is a very special place. It feels wild and beautiful. It's the biggest adventure I've ever had. Well, the only adventure, but . . .'

'But not exactly pretty and polished up to your standards. No chandeliers, no sparkling champagne towers, no grand fireworks – apart from when something accidentally explodes while I'm cooking at the cauldron . . . or if the kid has anything to do with it,' Hal laughed under his breath. 'Your world is somewhere brighter than this place. You need all that stuff.'

Annie watched him closely, giving up entirely on the dishes. 'You think so?'

'Sure seems that way.'

Privately, she had started to wonder over the past few days whether that really was the case. Her life had been a series of designated, polished paths that led to glittered rooms. She had assumed that she belonged neatly among them. But barely a moment had gone by at Arden Place when she'd even felt a pang of longing for any part of that world.

'I'm doing okay at this, aren't I?' she asked hesitantly. 'Yes, it might have been a bit of a shock to find myself with a toilet that I have to cross a literal stream to get to, but . . . I stayed, I'm seeing it out.'

'You're doing great. Especially with Maeve,' Hal said with a resigned smile. 'But you'll leave, too,' he added, 'as you should, because you deserve the best.' He sniffed. 'Like keeping a swan in a chicken coop,' he grumbled to himself. It made her laugh.

'I'm learning that your world has its own kind of brightness,' she said quietly. A beat of silence thrummed while Annie tried to figure out what to say next. Why wasn't the spell taking charge of this messy, complicated moment for her?

'You couldn't see yourself leaving it all behind, starting again?' Hal asked, surveying her with soft eyes. She willed the spell to formulate her next move, the right answer, the correct response, but nothing seemed to come. Her mind was blank. Why was it failing? Annie opened her lips before she'd quite figured out the right answer, just as Maeve swung herself around the kitchen corner. Annie and Hal took simultaneous steps apart.

'Annie, Karma won't take her enormous head out of my custard tart,' Maeve whinged, holding out her snack plate at arm's length. 'I saved it since breakfast to have in bed while I was drawing and she's . . . Oh.' Maeve did a double take, the cat dangling over her shoulder and shoving a paw into her face to try to steal the custard for her own whiskered chops. 'Sorry. Didn't realize I was interrupting.'

'You're not! Never. Absolutely not, of course not, not at all,' Annie said frantically. She spun around quickly to lean against the sink, snapping the moment. Her face must have been approximately as bright as her neon pink slippers. Even Karma had stilled, sensing the tension.

'We're running low on wood for the stove. Better go top us up,' Hal muttered to excuse himself, giving both Maeve and

Karma matching scruffs on the top of the head as he shifted past. He grabbed his jacket from the hook and the front door swung behind him with a bounce before Annie could ask if he needed any help.

Although, now that she thought about it, they had loads of firewood. Annie remembered seeing him chopping it earlier in the afternoon. It had been extremely distracting.

Chapter Seventeen

MAEVE'S CONFESSION

The heady, perfumed bathwater clung to Annie's skin in a damp sheen, flushing her face and making her eyelids droop closed. Damp tendrils of hair clung to her forehead and she wiped them to the side along with the last few tears that sprung from the hex. It had been a particularly difficult burst of the spell. It all felt so much more extreme out here in the open than at home in her bathroom. Even so, she had made sure to double down on certain potion ingredients to strengthen it as best she could, after the spell had failed her so many times with Hal earlier that evening.

Splendidus Infernum was often unpredictable that way. Sometimes the spirits would feel even more regretful than usual and, with Halloween looming, their passions were strengthened as the veil between the living and the dead grew thinner. Tonight Annie had found herself haunted by a young woman who regularly visited, the stars blurring behind her tearful eyes as she listened to reams of overpowering, unfinished business. Her most imperfect decision, the purest of irreparable heartbreak.

Annie needed to drag herself upstairs and at least try to get a burst of genuine sleep. As a compromise to get the girl to go to bed, she had promised Maeve that they would dabble with short-distance transference in the woods tomorrow. Annie suspected that her terrible sense of direction combined with Maeve's travel sickness might make for a challenging lesson. It was comforting to know that Hal was nearby to help fix things, if she needed him.

She scooped a handful of the water into her hands and watched the maroon liquid trickle between her fingers like red wine, ripples flooding the surface one after another. There was still the sound of crying lingering on the meadow's air, a child-like, sorrowful sound.

It took Annie a moment to come around from the spell's drowsy lull to realize that the crying was not residual from the visiting spirits. It was coming from inside the cottage, drifting through an open window. Annie had never left the bathtub so quickly. She grabbed for her dressing gown, threw it on and sped inside, slipping and sliding on wet feet as she careered through the cottage and into Maeve's room.

'Maeve? What's wrong?'

Maeve was sitting up in bed, her back rigid against the headboard while she hugged her legs and rested her forehead on her knees. A crackle of rogue magic clung to her pyjamas and the crown of her head and she batted away the sparks as she realized that Annie had discovered her. She glanced up with swollen eyes that matched Annie's own.

'I didn't want to tell you.' Her voice didn't sound like Maeve at all. She sounded afraid.

'You can tell me anything,' Annie said instinctively, as she rushed to the edge of the bed and held out a hand to Maeve's, who accepted it gratefully.

'There's someone here.'

Annie shook her head. 'Did you have a bad dream? Hal's sleeping out in the living room, remember? I'm sure you just heard him tossing and turning.'

Maeve wiped at her eyes crossly with the backs of her hands and sniffed. 'It's not Hal and it's not you. I . . . I feel something here, Annie. In this place.'

There was a gruff throat-clear from the side of the room. Hal was leaning against the doorframe. 'Sorry, I don't want to interrupt. I heard the back door fly open and just wanted to see if you were both okay. Do you want me to go?'

Annie gave him a grateful half-smile, but turned back to Maeve to let her make the decision.

Maeve shook her head. 'You can stay. Maybe you know something that we don't.'

Annie rubbed Maeve's forearm, which was still wrapped tightly around her legs. 'Can you try to explain what it is that you're feeling?'

Maeve still looked reluctant to share, but took a deep breath. 'I know I'm about to sound completely mental, that's why I haven't wanted to say anything but . . . I can sense something. At night – every night, since we got here.'

'You should have told me,' Annie said, pulling Maeve into a hug straight away without any more questions. 'I'm sorry you've been holding onto this all by yourself.'

Maeve leaned her head against Annie's shoulder. 'Someone . . . or maybe even more than just one someone . . . it's keeping me up at night and it's creeping me out.' She sounded frustrated, annoyed with herself for letting it get the better of her. 'As soon as bedtime starts to roll around, I feel sick.' She mumbled the last part as though she were embarrassed to admit it.

'Since when?' Annie asked.

'I felt it the moment we walked in the front door for the first time, like my instincts suddenly sharpened. It was like stepping into a cold shower.'

Annie had a flashback to their arrival at Arden Place. She had been so distracted by the unexpected sights that greeted them, but not enough to miss the full-body shiver that Maeve had given as she stepped over the threshold. Her sudden, unpredictable mood swings. The constant begging to stay up as late as she could possibly get away with. Annie had pinned it on typical teenage behaviour, but perhaps there was something more sinister at play.

'I thought you liked it here. I'm so sorry, Maeve.'

'I do! I'm so happy here – at least in the day. I've tried to ignore it and tell myself I'm being a stupid baby, but it hasn't gone away. I can still hear them and feel them. All the time. It's like a presence or something.' Maeve wrapped her arms even more tightly around herself.

'You hear someone? They speak to you?' Hal asked, curiosity and concern both audible in his voice as he took a few steps closer to the bed.

Maeve nodded, then tucked her hair behind her ear to glance at Annie for reassurance, as though she were trying to weigh up whether she was being taken seriously or not, whether it was a safe place for her to remain honest and vulnerable.

'Yeah, I hear them,' Maeve said. 'Occasionally I sense they're nearby in the daytime, too. And then tonight, for the first time, I . . . I swear I saw them, someone sitting at the end of my bed. As though whatever it is is getting stronger. Right where you're sitting, Annie. It's always the same time,' she said quietly. 'Just after midnight.'

Annie felt ice flood her veins, but her face flashed burning hot. A coincidence. It had to be.

There was no possible way that Maeve could be feeling any kind of repercussions from the spell – a spell that had absolutely nothing to do with her and no malevolent intention towards her. *Splendidus Infernum* was a tightly bound, immaculately practised routine of necromancy that Annie had mastered over years upon years of discipline and rules. There was no way that it could be interfering where it wasn't welcome.

'It's just your magic settling in,' Hal said calmly. 'It can do strange things to you at the beginning. Being fifteen is tough at the best of times, kid, but throw magic into the mix too and it's bound to be unsettling.'

'I think it's more than that. There's this breeze. It rushes in through my window from the garden and clings to me, even when I'm under the covers. Every single midnight. I can't shake it. It makes me feel dreadful, as though I'll never be happy again. All they ever want to do is tell me how sorry they are for the mistakes they've made. It's exhausting,' Maeve confessed, plucking at a thread on her patchwork quilt. 'I haven't been sleeping much.'

So it was true. Annie couldn't keep eye contact with either of them. Thoughts twisted themselves into uncertain shapes. Brewing the potion in unfamiliar surroundings, she had been careless. And with everything that Hal had noted about Maeve's powers after only a matter of hours around her, it would unfortunately make sense that Maeve was attracting elements of Annie's own magic to her, like a magnet. That could absolutely include the haunted, regretful spirits that lingered in her *Splendidus Infernum* bargain.

'That sounds horrible, Maeve,' Annie said, swallowing a throat full of dread so solid that the words came out thick and suffocating. She felt sick with inky black guilt. 'I'm so sorry.'

She caught Hal's eye. He was staring at her, a loaded look in his green eyes. Did he know that she knew something more? That was impossible, surely; the spell would ensure that her words always sounded believable and appealing to him. As far as Hal was concerned, the hex would pick up the weight of her secret and cleverly keep it hidden.

'I am happy, I am. I'm having such a good time here,' Maeve was quick to add. 'But this feeling comes every night to ruin it and then, when the murmuring stops and I can eventually sleep, I spend the day feeling like I'm trying to remember a dream. All I can remember is the sadness from their voice and it stays with me all the time.'

'You're brave to tell us,' Hal said, tenderness in his deep voice. 'I promise you though, this is a safe place. There are so many protective enchantments around Arden Place. Mostly to keep people out in general, because, well . . . I hate people – but especially any kind of dark magic. I keep a close eye on things around here,' he said, catching Annie's eye, too.

Maeve shrugged and stretched her pyjama sleeves over her hands. 'Like I said, I don't really understand what it is. Do you think this place is haunted or something? That would be cool.'

'No one's being haunted on my watch, kid.' Hal shot a wink in Maeve's direction.

Annie gave the girl a weak smile and wrapped a soothing hand around the fist that was still frantically tugging at blanket threads.

'Are you going to make me leave?' Maeve asked quietly. It was as though she'd been daring herself to ask, steeling herself to hear an answer that she didn't want. Annie felt Maeve's apprehension tighten itself like a boned corset around her own ribs.

'I'm not going to make you do anything you don't want to do,' Annie said. 'Please don't worry about this, okay? You leave that to me. I'll do the worrying for the both of us.'

'How about I do it for all three of us?' Hal added.

Annie knew what Maeve's revelation meant. A terrifying realization had cemented itself in her mind and she knew what had to be done. She would have to give it up. After so many years of it controlling every aspect of her life, tampering with her strings like a marionette master, permitting her to remain in the confines of perfectionism to keep everybody happy . . .

The spell would have to end.

Chapter Eighteen

FAMILIAR SCENES

Maeve woke up tired and cranky, but Annie knew that it was only because she was smarting from the embarrassment of being so vulnerable – not a trait that came naturally to the girl. Annie had heard her up even before she was, treading the creaky floorboards to make snacks and sit outside on the porch as the dawn broke. She had turned down the offer of short-distance transference and even trying her first tarot-card pull, which was when Annie knew there was something really wrong. Instead, she seemed compelled to just draw. Maeve set up camp at the dining table with her sketchbooks and pencils, drawing with a fervour as though her arms were separate from the rest of her body, head bent low over the table so that her dark hair hid her work. It was only when she resurfaced, leaned back against her chair to stretch her wrist and assess her art, that Annie caught a glimpse of the drawing. It was the same character again that Maeve seemed to draw for comfort, the dark-haired girl who always cropped up in her work.

Annie busied herself with the butter and sugar that she had begun to work on while Maeve was content. It was quiet across the cottage and its meadow. Annie too felt insular and reticent, a little shocked by the realization that she had come to about her future without *Splendidus Infernum*. A little treat was the only answer for it all. It felt good to sink her hands into the sandy mixture, to be baking for pleasure, not under pressure. Time seemed to stand still and watch on with a small, secretive smile at Arden Place.

'You drew that?' Hal asked, stopping as he passed through the house with a giant bucket of freshly picked, extra shiny red apples slotted onto his shoulder. Maeve only nodded, flexing her fingers around her pencil. He raised his eyebrows to silently ask for permission and, when Maeve didn't object, he raised the sketchbook and held it towards the window to admire it more closely. 'That settles it,' he said gruffly. 'We're sending you out onto the streets to earn your keep, kid. You'll make us millions.'

Maeve blushed at the Hal-style compliment and let out a self-conscious snort of a laugh. It was the first smile she'd shown all day. Something about Hal's relaxed, comfortable nature had clicked for her as much as it had for Annie. Maeve dropped the secrecy around her art whenever he asked about it. He had already insisted on hanging above the fireplace the canvas she had created with her paint magic, and asked her to recreate the sky sketches she'd produced among the stars. Having come to understand his strange, thoughtful candour a little more, Annie was grateful for it. It seemed to wrap a blanket around her own anxious, tightly wound presence, softening her sharpest edges in ways that she hadn't known she needed.

'A friend of yours?' Hal asked, tapping the sketch as he returned it to Maeve.

'Sort of. I guess she is,' Maeve replied. He didn't push it, only giving his signature *'hmm'* in return. He shuffled the bucket of apples back onto his shoulder, shooting Annie a lingering, pensive look before he left, which made her pause. 'We should talk,' he called to her decidedly while stepping out onto the porch. She gave him a small nod from the kitchen, which he returned with a hat tip as he marched off across the meadow.

Annie glanced back to Maeve, who was tapping the pencil rapidly as she contemplated her work from all angles. The suffocating guilt from her realization that the hex was wreaking havoc with Maeve still clung hotly.

For the first time since beginning her pact with *Splendidus Infernum*, when she was just Maeve's age herself, Annie had vowed not to take a bath before bed. The looming prospect was already making her feel slightly sick, rather ironically filling her with an anxiety that matched the level of worry she normally felt on everybody else's behalf *because* of the spell. The possibilities of what this might really mean, who she might become and what might come crashing down around her, were too vast to allow herself to consider. Who was she if she allowed herself not to be perfect? What even was the alternative? She crumbled the butter and added an extra generous dash from her jar of serendipity cinnamon. She would need all the good fortune she could get.

'What are you making?' While Annie's thoughts dragged her to a far-off place, Maeve wandered into the kitchen and leaned in beside her.

'Friendship fancies. They're mainly to cheer you up, but I also thought they might be useful in getting to know Hal a little better. He still feels like a bit of a mystery, don't you think?'

'Not really,' Maeve said with a shrug.

'Oh. Well. They look very pretty on a doily, but the drizzle is also my secret alchemy blend to strengthen a friendship. Grains of paradise, rose quartz reflection, moonlight milk for ease and harmony . . .' Maeve pulled a face. 'Don't worry, it still tastes of chocolate,' Annie explained. 'It just helps to bring out the potential of a blossoming bond. He's such a closed book, but this should help. We don't even know where the warlock wanders off to every day.' She gave a determined nod, pleased with herself for the idea.

'I know,' Maeve said. 'He goes to the stables.'

Annie hesitated. 'He does?' Then hesitated again. 'We have stables?'

Maeve didn't seem to be listening too closely, more concerned with dunking a teaspoon into the bowl full of fondant icing. 'Are these like the French ones? I like the pink ones best.'

Annie smiled, unable to not take that as a personal compliment. 'Me too.'

They worked together in a comfortable, caffeine-accompanied silence, the scent of coffee and vanilla sponge stitching together sweetly. Maeve occasionally piped up with an undiplomatic question out of the blue. How would it feel to walk into Hecate House? Scary, but spellbinding. What were Annie's friends really like? Funny. High maintenance. Unpredictable. Did she miss her parents? Every day. Was she going to go back to the bakery? Of course. She loved working with Faye and Pari, though she was constantly chasing her tail. Why did she keep working there, then? Because she couldn't just start all over again. Of course she could, Maeve reasoned. Annie didn't have a comeback for that.

'Come on, enough of the interrogation for today,' Annie said, giving Maeve a gentle shoulder shove. 'Let's take these out to the resident lumberjack pirate cowboy. He likes you better than he likes me.'

Maeve raised a sceptical eyebrow, as though Annie had said something entirely obtuse. 'Oh, you're serious? You're even more oblivious than I thought, then.'

'Oblivious to what?'

Maeve blew her lips together in a scoff, then shoved a whole friendship fancy into her mouth whole. She held her hands up, as though she couldn't possibly answer with a mouthful of cake, and wandered off back to her artwork with a grin.

Balancing a tiny pink saucer of tiny pink cakes on a tiny pink doily, Annie carefully made her way out to the stables, after Maeve helpfully pointed out their location as somewhere between the stream and . . . well, trees. Annie picked her way through the long grass, squealing every few moments when her ballet pumps encountered a muddy puddle, until she gave up and used a quick dash of magic to switch to her pink wellies instead. After a small run-in with an army of toads at the stream, which almost sent her running straight back to London, Annie discovered that Maeve was right.

The small, rickety stables of Arden Place were tucked well away and woven into the woods. Nestled within the trunks of two impossibly large, hollowed-out oak trees, the stables were surrounded by thick, knotted roots, which formed a fence that opened up onto the back of the meadow as strings of flame-like will-o'-the-wisps cast a calming, supernatural glow between the surrounding silver birches. Drinking contentedly from a crystal-clear thread of stream that looped around the stables was a beautiful, dappled red-brown horse, the colour of conkers and identical to Hal's hair.

She soon found the warlock, too. Hal was slumped back in a camping chair, one leg slung over the other, Stetson pulled low over his face. Annie watched as he chewed on a mouthful of apple while he read a book, then held out the same apple for the horse to snaffle the rest of it. It seemed to be a finely tuned routine that they'd repeat every few minutes. When the stallion returned for the next snack, Hal gave him an absent-minded stroke on his muzzle. It was such a contented scene that Annie felt reluctant to disturb it. She let it hold for a precious moment, appreciating it, capturing it for herself, before she cleared her throat.

Hal immediately threw the book away and leapt to his feet so suddenly that the horse reared back onto its hind legs with a startled whinny. Realizing it was Annie, Hal dropped his defences and gave a gruff throat-clear. He turned to soothe the horse.

'Sorry, I didn't mean to interrupt Boys' Club,' she said. 'I come bearing gifts.'

'Didn't anyone ever tell you it's a bad idea to creep up on a warlock and his familiar? You're asking for trouble.'

Annie didn't know what she'd anticipated Hal's familiar to be (an ill-tempered honey badger, maybe, or a slightly cantankerous ass), but a majestic, noble stallion was not it. '*This* is your familiar?' She took a few uncertain steps closer.

'Not sure what cursed, past-life adventure I fell into to earn such a big dope, but yes. This is Mage. He might be bloody handsome and a show-off, but he's also a big chicken. Aren't you, pal?'

Hal took another apple from the pocket of the scuffed leather waistcoat he was wearing over his shirt and tossed it into the air just high enough for the horse to give a small jump to catch it. Pleased with his skill, Mage shook out his burgundy mane, obviously boasting in front of Annie.

'Why don't you bring him closer to the cottage?' she asked, admiring how Mage's coat caught the shine of sunlight through the trees. 'He's all alone out here, aren't you, Mage?' His tail flicked out dramatically.

'Normally you'd see him out in the meadow all of the time. He has the run of the place if he wants it. And he has been known to come in through the back door once or twice when he smells gravy. But I think he's a bit put out that there're so many other creatures flooding his meadow to see Maeve,' Hal said, stroking his thumb across the bridge of Mage's nose. 'Sulking, aren't you, Mage? Plus he's scared of cats, so he will have spotted Karma from a mile off.'

'Can I?' Annie asked, feeling shyer than usual as she extended a careful hand out towards Mage's huge shoulder. Hal gestured to go ahead, taking a step back so that she could give the horse a pat on his velvety coat. Mage gave a contented, relaxed blow of approval at her touch.

'Mage, you are quite the beauty. What are you doing hanging around with this guy and his silly hat?'

Hal smirked. 'Now that introductions are out of the way, to what do I owe the pleasure?' he asked gruffly, throwing his hat onto the low wooden stable post and pushing back his hair.

It was only then that Annie realized Mage had swiped two of the three friendship fancies straight from the plate. That explained why he'd taken to her so quickly.

'I thought you might like a treat,' Annie said with a sigh,

holding out the singular, miniature cake towards Hal. It looked like an exceptionally pathetic offering all on its own.

'Sure you can spare it?' he laughed, picking it up between two fingers and eating it in one go. He and Maeve were two sides of the same coin. 'Thank you,' he said with a grin through a mouthful of cake that made a dimple pop on one side of his face.

Annie laughed, too. 'Any time. Besides, you said a little ominously that we should talk.'

'Right, that I did,' Hal said. His forearms were bare again, the sleeves of his shirt pushed up to his elbows. Annie tore her eyes back to Mage, who was giving her an attention-seeking nuzzle on the shoulder, keen for more fuss or possibly more apples.

'I wanted to know what you thought of Maeve's revelations. You were keen to get to bed before we had much chance to discuss it. It all but confirmed our suspicions that she's attracting magic, pulling supernatural energy to herself. It's extraordinary. No wonder the kid has had trouble keeping it to herself,' he continued, picking up the book from the floor that he'd discarded and shoving it back into his satchel. Annie recognized the title, *Elixirs Most Eldritch*, as one she'd borrowed herself a few times from Hecate House library to aid with amending the hex.

'She's a very special girl,' Annie said, hiding her face from Hal's curious eyes by staying turned in towards Mage.

'I know it. But you have to admit, all that spooky spirit stuff is a strange one. Never known a glimmer of trouble at Arden Place in all my years.' Hal leaned his back against the stable door with his arms folded, a bent leg scooched up the wide tree trunk. 'And it got me thinking.'

'Don't pull a muscle,' Annie said. She'd stolen that one from Maeve.

'Have you noticed anything like that yourself around here?' Hal went on, bending a little to try to steer her gaze back to him. 'Is there anything that *you'd* like to tell the class? You know, while we're all getting things off our chests.'

Annie, purposefully avoiding eye contact, made an extra effort to keep her face blank and her laugh bemused. 'Me? What secrets would I have to share? If you hadn't already noticed, I'm a very uncomplicated person.'

'Oh, I have to disagree with you there,' Hal said, an arcane smile tugging at that same dimple that Annie had only just noticed for the first time.

'It's true. Sugar, spice and all things nice. That's all there is to know,' she said indignantly, finally turning around to face him now that she felt the need to defend herself.

Hal gave her his gravelly '*hmmm*' in return, but it sounded a fraction more dubious than usual. 'Granted, most of my magic and intuition is tuned into the nature of animals and beasts, but there's something about you, Annie Wildwood. I can't put my finger on it yet, but . . .' He waggled a finger, studying her face. His eyes raked over her, a little bolder. '. . . I will. I'll figure it out. Something about you is . . .' He shrugged off the rest of his thought.

Annie cursed the quiet flutter that her heart stupidly gave. She knew exactly what he was referring to; the alluring effects of *Splendidus Infernum* ensured that there was always an appealing air around her. The magnetism that caught everyone's attention and shoved her into the best possible light to perform. The compliment slid straight off her, feeling hollow. Starting tomorrow, he would feel very differently.

'And I don't mean that just because you're beautiful,' Hal said unexpectedly. An uncharacteristic blush formed at the tops of his cheeks the moment he said it. He squeezed his eyes shut, exposing his embarrassment. 'Obviously, you are. You know that. I don't need to tell you. But you are. Not that it matters. Anyway.'

She burst out laughing, feeling a not-entirely-unpleasant awkwardness bloom between them. She shook her head. 'Thank you? I think.'

'Back to the kid. I thought we should probably talk about it. Especially because . . . Well, before she got upset last night, I heard her talking back to them.'

Annie stiffened. Her smile popped like a balloon.

'I know you'll have the same first thoughts as me about that, given that we both know the inner workings of Selcouth well enough,' Hal said, lowering his voice and taking a step closer to speak under his breath. He joined her in leaning on the short stable door that was half swung open, both of them folding their arms on the top of the wood and staring ahead into the stable, watching as Mage returned to his hay bundle now that apples were off the menu. 'A kid talking to spirits, holding her own accidental seance, potent necromancy at the ripe age of fifteen . . . Not a recipe that's going to go over too well with the elders.'

Annie glanced wordlessly across at him, her heart pounding. Did he know something?

'A teenage girl sensing an otherworldly presence is not something to write home about,' Hal continued, as though he were contemplating his own thoughts as they tumbled out. 'But if they're communicating *back* with her? Using her as a mouth piece or channelling through her? Something's going on here. Pardon the pun, but . . . well, that spells trouble.'

Annie's breath hitched as she tried to formulate what to say next, how to quell Hal's suspicions as quickly as possible. But she couldn't rally her imagination quick enough to fix it. She felt like a moth flying dangerously close to a flame, frantically flapping her wings to stay afloat without touching the fire.

The spell was already failing – maybe her decision to end its hold had already affected its potency. Instead of an appeasing answer to fix things, Annie only found herself firing up, irked and defensive at the suspicion in his voice. None of this was a reflection on Maeve; she owed it to the girl to make that abundantly clear.

'Maeve is not trouble,' she said firmly. The one, singular fierce flare of anger felt unfamiliar in its heat.

Hal faltered at her thunderous expression. 'I'm not saying she is. She's a good kid.'

'Then what are you saying? What do you suggest? Why do I feel as though you're about to come bounding in with some kind of grand plan?'

He looked a little startled. 'I didn't mean it that way, I didn't mean that *she's* trouble. I meant that it spells trouble, for us. Here. If we don't figure out how to protect her properly.'

Annie blinked. 'We're an us?'

Hal's cheeks flushed again and he shrugged, embarrassed. 'Not an us, but . . . I don't know. I just thought I'd ask whether you wanted somebody to talk to about it. From my perspective, it's looking like a lot of pressure and responsibility on your shoulders to make this right, all by yourself. Sometimes it's easier to fix things as an "us".'

Annie seemed to have frozen in body and mind. A tumble of tangled thoughts flooded her head, so unfamiliar that she wasn't sure how to translate them. But somewhere in the mess she could recognize that, most of all, she felt relief. There it was. An offer of support. A comfort so curious, but so entirely enveloping in its gentleness and sincerity, that she thought her knees might buckle. Instead, she squeezed the top of the stable door tightly, feeling her nails sink into the damp wood. She forced her gaze up to the tops of the trees and took a breath as her eyes and nose burned.

'I'm not much of a talker,' Hal said gruffly, apparently realizing that it was down to him to fill the silence a little further. 'As you might have noticed by now. But I am a listener. Think that's why the animals took a shining to me ever since I was a boy. So . . . Not saying that you need to, of course. But if you want to.' He turned his head to face her and his hand hovered as though he were debating putting it over hers. Instead, he gave his signature, conclusive tap to the top of the fence. 'You can talk to me. I'd like to support you. Whatever's going on here, it's a lot, but we'll fix it together.'

Annie couldn't find any words that wouldn't open undammable floodgates. Instead she settled for a silent nod and hoped with all her heart that Hal would understand what she meant by that. Life without the fading spell to promptly blunt the spikier feelings, to soften the landing of big thoughts, was already proving tough to navigate and it hadn't even left her system yet.

'Anyway, Mage needs a brushing and I know he's eyeing up your braiding skills for that handsome tail of his. Can't say mine are up to scratch. How about it? He might even let you add a few flowers if there's apples to be paid.'

Hal dug into his satchel and pulled out a grooming brush, then offered it out to Annie. Their fingertips grazed with the slightest touch.

'Thank you,' she whispered under her breath. Firstly to him for the brush, and secondly to whichever supernatural forces had been at play in ensuring those friendship fancies had been quite such a potent recipe.

Chapter Nineteen

A BAD DAY

Annie awoke the next morning with a startle that made her whole body twitch. She flung out an arm with a violent jerk and bashed the bedside lamp from table to floor. Half asleep, she snuffled a mini snore and bolted upright. She licked her lips, finding them dry and a little chapped. Lip balm, immediately. She smacked them together, noticing a slightly stale feeling in her mouth that tasted worse for wear. Water, too. She could hear faint conversation and laughter downstairs between Maeve and Hal and the jangle of pots and pans being moved around the kitchen. Had she really slept in? That almost never happened. In fact, she couldn't remember the last time that it had. Annie was always the first awake, the one who made sure that everybody else's day started perfectly. Something wasn't right. Her brow crumpled and she gave a small hiccough of a burp when she stretched. Her hand shot to her mouth, mortified by the noise, and that was when she noticed.

The polish on her pinky finger was chipped. Genuinely, really chipped. A shard of the hot-pink paint completely missing in a jagged streak across her nail. Annie gasped.

Her hand moved to the top of her head and she touched her hair tenderly all over. She could feel that it wasn't where it was supposed to be. It was . . . messy? And unkempt? Her neat French braid had unravelled, flyaways sticking up every which way. And there was . . . frizz. A lot of it. Her nose wrinkled and she faltered before taking an uncertain sniff of her pyjamas. An actual, genuine, human-like scent emanated from her raised arm. It certainly wasn't vanilla or sugar or coconut.

'Oh . . . no,' Annie said, horrified. She scrambled out of bed, shoving the quilt to the floor, tripping over her own feet as she shot to the mirror. Her hands flew to the drawers below and she gripped the edge to steady herself as an awful, nauseating realization began to dawn.

'Please, please. No, no no . . .'

She poked and prodded at her face. Streaks of purple had appeared in crescents under her eyes, days and months and years of almost no sleep revealing themselves. Faint traces of worry lines had etched their way across her forehead, at her temples, between her mouth and nose. Her eyes looked a little bloodshot, crumbs of sleepy dust settled into the corners. Small flakes of mascara lined the lower lashes and, for the first time since she had been fifteen years old and immediately implemented *Cutis Lumen* magic on the case, one singular red spot had reared its head on the top of her left cheek.

Annie hadn't expected it to change things so drastically or so quickly. One measly evening cold turkey from the spell and she was already . . . imperfect? It was so unfair. Worse than imperfect – as if her body were making up for lost time as the spell drained from her system. She was a complete mess. She let out a low, mournful wail that sounded slightly like a wounded animal. She could not let Maeve or Hal see her like this.

Peering over the banister to scope out their whereabouts, Annie crept as quietly as she could downstairs, avoiding the specific steps she had noted as being exceptionally loud and creaky during midnight trips from the bathtub. She could just about make out the blurry heads of Maeve and Hal sitting out on the porch together in the late morning sunshine. They seemed to be scruffing the head of some kind of furry creature that had come to join their conversation. She couldn't quite focus on whatever it was, her usual 20/20 vision failing her. Reluctantly, she fired her magic back towards the bedroom to summon her glasses.

'Ow!'

One of the arms poked her straight in the eye as they flew into place. At least her magic still worked, she supposed.

Attempting to creep past unnoticed, Annie continued her silent descent of the stairs – until it wasn't quite so silent. Her fluffy socks slipped on the wood and she fell down the last few steps, making such a racket that Hal and Maeve's heads spun towards the cottage. They shot to their feet and sprinted inside, to find Annie clambering to her feet like a baby deer on ice. She gripped the banister and forced her usual beaming smile onto her face.

'Morning! I had a lovely trip, thank you for asking,' she prattled, doing her level best to make everything seem as normal as possible. Maeve gawped very unsubtly.

'Are you alright?' Hal asked with a single raised eyebrow.

'Mmmhmm,' she chirped. 'Wonderful, in fact. I can't believe I slept in, can you believe that? I'm so sorry you guys had to sort out your own breakfast this morning. Did you manage?'

'Luckily I'm very skilled in the fine art of cornflakes. And you're not here to wait on us. You're not working on shift, you know,' Hal answered. 'You sure you're doing okay? You look a little . . .'

'Different? Right. Woke up on the wrong side of bed, I think. Maybe a little peaky. Under the weather. Nothing that a lovely hot shower won't fix,' Annie said, darting as quickly as she could to the bathroom outside, leaving Hal and Maeve sharing an unspoken, baffled glance.

She bolted to the bathroom and dove straight underneath the running water. 'Oh my . . .' she squealed. Annie shot backwards away from the ice-cold stream, stumbled and reached for the edge of the tub to steady herself, but managed to tug down almost the entire shower curtain from the rail and wrap herself in it while she desperately clung on to find her balance. 'This cannot be happening.'

'Annie, what's going on out there?' Hal called through the back door, opening it a fraction. She panicked and grabbed in a hurry the towel draped over the privacy screen. 'I heard a crash. Do you need help? Did you fall again?' Her hair was hanging in wet rat-tails around her shoulders, bright blotches across her skin from the violent water temperature. She flailed, cursing under her breath while sort of tiptoeing on the spot as she panicked about where to go and what to do. Nothing came to her. The spell had turned its back on her entirely.

'I'm coming out there,' Hal called. She heard his heavy steps tread the path down to the bathroom. He rapped his knuckles on the privacy screen and gave it a moment before peering his head around to the bathing area. 'Annie?'

Annie breathed out an awkward, sharp laugh and, for some inexplicable reason, tinkled a wave. Terrible idea. A moment later, she darted to keep her towel held up.

'Oh, sorry, sorry.' He shot a hand up to cover his eyes. 'I just . . . I didn't . . . I mean . . .'

'No, it's okay, I just slipped. And then accidentally . . . And then I didn't . . . . And I just . . .'

Both of them reddened at their clashing words, avoiding eye contact in all possible ways they could muster. Hal raised his eyes to the skies and Annie steadied herself by taking a long breath.

'Do you need any help or . . .'

'I'm good,' she said, her voice squeaking awkwardly.

He nodded, pushed back his unkempt hair and turned to leave for the cottage again. 'I'll just . . .'

'Right, absolutely.'

'Great.'

Once Hal had vacated the vicinity, Annie decided that she should probably rely on magic to save her dignity – or at least what was left of it. She quickly cast her ever-reliable dressing spell to transform the towel into an outfit that would make her feel better.

One of her favourite dresses appeared on her body, reliable and comfortable, a cute floral slip that she'd had for years. But something wasn't right. The white T-shirt underneath was terribly wrinkled, as though it hadn't seen an iron for years, like something plucked from a heap in a rush. It smelt of last week's perfume and there was a slightly disconcerting, unidentified splodge on the dress, too, something spilled that had gone unnoticed, maybe? The fuzzy velvet hat should have been a fun statement, a perfect finishing touch, but instead felt, to put it plainly, mortifying. The outfit had been perfect in her mind's eye, but now that she saw it in reality . . . Well, it wasn't right at all. It had looked so much better in her head.

Annie was stumped. Another usually reliable, fashionably astute spell had failed her.

'Have you had some kind of breakdown overnight?' Maeve had ventured out to take Hal's place.

'No! Don't be so rude,' Annie scolded. 'I'm . . . trying out a new look.'

'Well . . .' Maeve sunk her hands into her jeans pockets and shrugged. 'At least the hat's not pink. That's a fun change for you. I just came to ask if you were baking this morning.'

Finally, something that couldn't go wrong. 'Absolutely I am. I'm making anything and everything you can possibly request and it will all be sensational. And I will do it while wearing this very fun hat,' Annie said decidedly. 'I'm pulling it off, aren't I?'

'That's exactly what you *should* do with it,' Maeve mumbled.

Baking would make everything feel better again. It was the thing that made sense when nothing else did. Annie promptly lost herself in the task at hand, relieved to finally have some way to prove that her perfection did not entirely rely on *Splendidus Infernum*. Some of her magical abilities were genuinely her own talent and that was very much the case when it came to making little treats. There was nothing that she couldn't do when it came to sugar-dusted sorcery.

Having beaten the dough to a pillowy pulp (which in itself helped to vent her fears and frustrations), she shaped cinnamon buns along with a loaf of fresh pumpkin sourdough bread and prepared the batter for sugar strand donuts. Then she fired her magic back towards the stove to start heating the oil. Maeve, who had stolen the hat for herself and had been observing the scene over a stack of sketchbooks and pencils scattered across the dining table, let out a yelp.

'What's wrong?' Annie asked absent-mindedly, before noting Maeve frantically pointing at the stove. They both screamed.

The entire pan had burst into flames, licking at the walls of the kitchen and blowing menacingly towards the gingham curtains. Again. Maeve darted over to yank Annie out of the kitchen, while Hal came sprinting in from the porch to magically extinguish the flames. All three of them stood in shocked silence for a moment, watching a cloud of black smoke float from the bottom of the curtains and out the window.

'I think I'm having a bad day,' Annie said matter-of-factly, a rogue tendril of hair flopping into her face as she spoke.

'I didn't know you had those,' Hal said, mopping his brow on his rolled-up sleeve.

'Isn't it my job to be setting things on fire around here?' Maeve asked dryly, looking decidedly smug.

Hal insisted that Annie abandon anything hot-oil related, including sugar strand donuts, and take a seat at the table, while he made her a steaming mug of strong tea. She sat bolt upright with her hands on her lap, in shock at the events so far. She was a walking disaster.

Meanwhile, Maeve chattered away, evidently unfazed – even enjoying the switch-up to their usual routine. Something caught her attention, and made her pause as she used her magic to sweep watercolour paints haphazardly across a page with lovely results. 'Did you hear that?'

'Hear what?' Annie said, hearing a snap in her voice that wasn't usually there. She felt . . . frustration. Maybe even full-blown, ugly annoyance. 'If some kind of tempestuous, ill-tempered spirit is about to attempt to contact you on today of all days, they're going to regret it, big time.'

'That!' Maeve said, louder this time as her chair squeaked back against the wooden floor and she shot to her feet. This time, Annie heard it, too. A faint, furious yowling that she'd recognize anywhere. That was enough to spark a little life back into Annie's numbed mind.

'Is that Karma?' she asked, running to join Maeve at the front door.

They could see movement among the long grass and could hear Karma's distinctly unimpressed caterwauls somewhere nearby, but the cat refused to show herself. Either side of the porch, the pair of them brushed their fingers together, clicked their tongues, *pss-pss-pss*'d, trying all of the usual tricks for Karma to show herself, but none seemed to work and Karma stayed determinedly hidden away in the meadow. Even a spoonful of custard came to no avail.

'She's being a madam,' Maeve said with a tut.

'Karma, what is it? What's wrong?' Annie said, at a loss as to why her familiar was behaving so strangely. It was then that Annie noticed the problem, finally spotting the tops of her cat's ears. They looked . . . soggy.

Karma was distinctly less groomed than usual. In fact, her fur was dishevelled, sticking out at all angles as though she'd been electrocuted and absolutely sopping wet. Her bright white coat was soaked with dark, muddy water, her signature pink bow and bell stained grey and brown. As Annie ran out to gather her into her arms, she gasped. She could have sworn that the cat's perfect downy ears had grown a fraction and now looked ever so slightly too big and tufty for her tiny head. Annie was not the only one who had transformed overnight.

'You fell in the stream, didn't you?' Annie whispered quietly, not wanting to embarrass Karma in front of anyone else, and earned an ashamed *mrow*. Her large round eyes gleamed with curiosity and confusion, staring at Annie with indignance, as though to ask what she thought she was playing at, throwing away perfection without consulting her familiar first. She looked entirely sorry for herself.

'Oh, Karma, it got you too? Don't worry, it'll be alright. Even princesses fall in streams sometimes.'

Karma gave a sorrowful, self-pitying whine and a headbutt to Annie's chin, clearly communicating that Annie must renew the spell at once or face her wrath.

'No can do, I'm afraid, darling. It's for Maeve's benefit and I know you love her enough to make the sacrifice. Mistakes and slip-ups are sadly now part of the deal. We're stuck like this for a while.'

The gathering storm couldn't have been the result of Annie turning her back on the hex. Her magic wasn't powerful enough to have impact on the elements – that kind of witchcraft only ever showed itself in highly charged, extreme circumstances. But the grim weather certainly added to the feelings of loss and hopelessness that had been plaguing her all day. It seemed suitably dramatic and reflected her mood rather well, as though the end of the world might be about to fold in over them literally, as well as the figurative way that it felt the case for her.

'Any more takers?' Hal called gruffly around the doorframe into the meadow. He gave it a few more moments, allowing a particularly slow pair of garden snails to finally cross over the threshold and nestle their way behind the shoe rack.

UNCHARMED

Annie hadn't had much choice in the matter, seeing as it was technically still Hal's home, when he asked whether she'd mind an open house for the woodland animals while the weather was so harsh. Not that she'd have protested anyway, but she had had to steel herself slightly at the sight of the entire downstairs of the cottage packed to the rafters with what felt like every single resident of the British woodland network. Among red squirrels, foxes, badgers, roe deer, hedgehogs, otters and the realms only knew what else, even Mage had been led underneath the spiral staircase to bed down and was currently giving Karma a very wary side-eye. The chaos had just about begun to calm slightly, after Hal laced a trough of berries and currants with a potent sleeping draught, mainly to ensure that no one ate any of the other guests under his roof.

Maeve had taken great comfort in knowing that she was surrounded by company for the night and had encouraged the entire family of wolf cubs to share her bed with her. It was the first night that Annie had seen the girl half keen to go to bed. She was already fast asleep, her chin resting on a snoozing cub, and the sight of her finally enjoying a good night's sleep was enough for Annie to think that this awful day might just have been worth it.

'That's the last of them,' Hal said, hands on hips and looking pleased. 'Thanks again for being good about this. They all know that they can come by whenever there's lightning. Rabbits in particular hate the thunder.'

'Of course,' Annie said, doing her level best to ignore the squeeze behind her ribs as he did a quick headcount across the new guests to make sure no one had been left outside. She had never met anyone quite like him. They stood side by side, looking out at the living area with the roaring fire and what must have been a hundred content creatures. 'I think it's wonderful. You're very kind.'

Hal gave a *'hmm'*. 'Or a mug.'

'Where do you normally sleep, then, when your couch is taken by snoring pine martens? Not a question I've ever contemplated before, I have to say,' Annie asked, laughing as she cast a sprinkle of magic over the scene to conjure a few blankets across the smaller creatures and tuck them in. Beside her, she sensed Hal's body language tense up just the slightest fraction. 'What is it?'

'Well, normally I'd be sleeping in my room,' he said quietly, his gaze determinedly fixed on Mage, who was finally starting to relax a fraction in Karma's presence as she made puddings on his flank. 'But it's just this moment occurred to me that there's a guest in there.'

Annie tensed to match as it dawned on her, too. 'Oh. Right. I see.'

'It's not a problem. There's no way you're staying down here with this lot. I'm sure I can find somewhere. I'll figure something out. Maybe Mage will have me. He snores like a bastard, but . . .' Hal rubbed the back of his neck, exhaling a resigned sigh.

'You can't do that,' Annie replied, horrified at the idea of him sacrificing yet another night's sleep out of kindness. She had turned this man's life upside down enough. 'Don't be ridiculous. We'll share.' The suggestion was aloud and out in the universe before she could stop it.

His head snapped around to her, brows shot high. There was a mild panic to his expression. 'Share?'

'Right, we'll share,' Annie said again, hoping that she sounded absolutely easy-breezy about the whole thing, even as her heart skipped several beats, flailed and then nosedived to somewhere around her ankles. Hal didn't say a word, but she saw his cheeks were flushing just as much as hers were. 'It's not a big deal. We've been living together for weeks. We're in a pinch and it's just a bed. One night.'

Hal seemed unconvinced. 'You're sure?'

Annie frantically smoothed her hair behind her ear and forced herself to focus on the practical matter at hand, not the extremely endearing way that Hal looked so concerned about the arrangement.

'It's settled,' she said briskly, drawing the last set of curtains downstairs before approaching the spiral staircase. 'Bagsey the side nearest the window.'

Hal's sheepish grin returned the slightest inch. 'Can't argue with the laws of bagsey. I'll give you some privacy to . . .'

'Oh. Yes. Absolutely. Thank you, I'll just . . . Mhmmm,' Annie squeaked, before rushing up the stairs as quickly as she could, feeling an incomprehensible combination of excitement and absolute mortification. Could this insane situation not possibly have arisen when she was a bright, glistening beam of perfection, rather than her current state of distinctly human dishevelment, still smelling slightly of the voles that she'd carried in from the meadow? At least her pumpkin latte-print pyjamas weren't news to him. She dashed around the room, hiding various lip balms, teacups and half-eaten chocolatey snacks at lightning speed.

By the time Hal joined her upstairs, Annie had almost made herself faint from the overthinking. She felt as though she was made of electricity, every nerve ending alight, like any moment she might just burst into hysterical laughter. But she did her level best to contain it all when he appeared at the top of the stairs with an extra blanket tucked under his arm, soft pyjama trousers hanging at his hips and a white T-shirt clinging to his stomach. He cleared his throat in the doorway.

'Well, after you,' he said gruffly, gesturing to the bed that Annie had fluffed up and smoothed as best she could, feeling treacherous as she stowed away her favourite teddy bear underneath the pillow. Now that they were both stood either side of it, the bed looked even smaller than she'd remembered it.

'This is going to be cosy,' she said, her voice squeaking with the optimism. 'And I love cosiness. I always try to be cosy at all times, cosy is a way of life . . .' She couldn't stop the words tumbling out of her mouth as she fumbled with the duvet, slipping in beside Hal. They both strained to keep their bodies tight and rigid, arms brushing as they tried to stay as far apart as physically possible. Hal's broad shoulders half hung off the mattress while Annie dangled one leg off her side of the bed. Both clasped their hands together above the duvet and stared straight up at the ceiling.

'You're sure this is okay?' Hal asked again, determinedly focusing on the light bulb above.

'Totally,' Annie nodded. 'Are *you* sure this is okay?'

'As long as you're okay.'

'Oh, I'm okay. Glad we're all doing okay.'

Annie wondered whether her pounding heartbeat might actually be audible over the sounds of the pouring rain on the thatched roof.

'Well, goodnight,' she trilled after a painful silence lingered for far too long. 'Shall we just . . . ?' She turned onto her side, facing away from Hal.

'Oh, right, sure. Good idea,' he replied, turning the opposite direction. Annie tried to close her eyes, but it was as though they had been pinned wide open. She felt like she shouldn't exhale at normal volume and was hyperaware of every single shift that Hal's body made pressed up behind her. She could hear the rise and fall of his breathing, every single faint brush of the blanket between them. She noticed the same scent that she'd experienced that day he'd first arrived – woody and amber, clove and chestnuts, even warmer now under the covers. She didn't dare to move in case it seemed as though she was trying to press closer. The thought was disastrous.

This ludicrous charade would never, ever have happened had the spell still been taking charge of her decisions. She scowled in the darkness and cursed her stupid mouth for landing her in this mess, her feet wriggling and kicking of their own accord. As bad days went, this one really took all the possible enchanted baked goods.

Annie thought she really was going insane when she felt Hal's body shaking behind her. It took a moment to realize that he was chuckling.

'What are you *laughing* at?' she asked, more stroppily than she intended, feeling like a brat as she threw off the covers. It was all too much. She had no idea how to handle this.

'Think I'd have been comfier next to the bloody horse,' Hal muttered between laughs. She couldn't help but join in.

At some point, Annie must have done the impossible and fallen asleep, because the next moment she was fluttering open heavy, sleep-soothed eyelids and nuzzling her head into the beautifully warm pillow. Except it wasn't her pillow. Her head was lying against something firm, that rose and fell in a slow, soothing rhythm beneath her. Coming around from the lull of sleep, Annie froze.

She was tucked snugly into Hal's side, her head resting on his chest. He had slung an arm across her whole body to pull her tightly into him. The peaceful, contented feeling that had enveloped her as she woke transformed into a flashing red alert. She could not let him wake up to find her like this, nuzzled up as close as she could possibly be, so Annie cautiously detangled herself from his limbs to slip away quietly. She fought against every part of herself to glance back and see how he looked first thing in the morning in her bed, all sleepy and dishevelled. That was not information that she needed to know.

Without even stopping to contemplate, she lunged for her dressing gown and sprinted so quickly down the stairs that she wondered whether some sort of involuntary magical transference had kicked in.

'Look who finally decided to join the land of the living!' Maeve was clutching a cup of coffee at the kitchen counter with an extremely amused look on her face. 'Let's ignore the irony of the girl who seems to inadvertently communicate with spirits using that old chestnut.'

'Good morning, sweetheart,' Annie said, flipping back her hair in an attempt to retain some dignity. 'Where . . .' She glanced around, noticing in her frantic state that this was not the scene she had anticipated. 'Where are all the animals?'

'Oh, I've been up for hours. I woke up fresh as a daisy again. Not a single haunted communication for two whole nights, can you believe it? So I saw them all on their way when the rain stopped. It seemed as though you two were busy, I didn't want to interrupt again.'

Annie gasped. 'Maeve, it's absolutely not what you . . . There's only one bed . . . We didn't have any other . . .'

'Take your time, have a nice relaxing morning. I'm off out for a walk, it's a beautiful day now that the storm has passed.'

Annie just whimpered, frozen to the spot.

'Shame neither of you are, y'know, like a witch or something,' Maeve said, shrugging on her coat and skipping out to join Mage in the meadow. She held on to the edge of the door as she turned back to Annie, an unmissable, mischievous glint in her eye. 'If only, hey? You'd think that magic could solve these kinds of logistical problems pretty easily.'

Annie's face burned the colour of her hot pink dressing gown.

Chapter Twenty

DON'T OPEN IT

Once Maeve had stopped cackling at the turn of events, Annie managed to cobble together what she hoped was a vaguely believable story to explain her transformation from perfection to distinctly imperfect.

'I assumed it was a mid-life crisis, but ditching caffeine also explains it,' Maeve said breezily, scooping the guts out of a pumpkin and plopping them into a bowl. 'I too would lose the plot within the first morning of such a decision.' Annie had decided that pumpkin carving felt like something that might calm her nerves and let her take out her frustrations on an unsuspecting gourd.

'A mid-life . . . ?! How old do you actually think I am? Actually, don't answer that,' Annie said grumpily, having managed to spill a bowl of cereal, break the vacuum cleaner and bang her head on the bookshelves before midday. It seemed that the spell had been carrying a lot of the legwork for natural clumsiness, as well as everything else. 'I don't think my ego can handle the answer.'

While her risk factor was seemingly in the red, it had been Maeve who'd suggested to Annie that perhaps they should let

Hal take a turn at magical guardianship. In the days since the storm, he and Annie had taken to communicating in sheepish looks and furious blushes. Both sides were yet to make any mention whatsoever of the compromising position that they had woken up in together.

One quiet Sunday afternoon, Hal dragged Maeve away from her sketchbooks to help in his search for a particularly uncommon form of ghost orchid running low in his Alchemy stash – an opportunity that earned an entirely unenthusiastic reaction. But, as a result, Annie found herself with a rare afternoon alone to decompress. To begin with, she wasn't entirely sure what to do with herself, pointlessly flapping from one room to the other, but soon found that curling up in the armchair with books and perpetually reheating mugs of hot chocolate was in fact very good for her soul. It was only when the warlock suggested to Maeve that the one thing missing from their autumnal setup was a bonfire, around which to share a conversation about the basics of healing magic, that Annie reluctantly surrendered her pillow fort. Annie may have felt different to who she was before, but she was still powerless to resist charred, gooey marshmallows. That was just a rule of the universe.

For a little extra warmth against the chilly night, she threw on a plaid shirt that had been left lying around over the top of her flowy pink dress. She may not have been perfect any more, but it would still always, always be pink. She pulled the long sleeves over her hands in a comforting way that made her feel like some kind of tiny soft creature. The exact, soothing sensation that she required to quell the puddle of feelings that sat so heavily in her chest: dread, regret, frustration, a selfish wonder whether she should just get it over with and inevitably return to the clutches of the spell already . . . They were all new, unfamiliar feelings to her touch and they glowed like white-hot coals when she brushed against them.

With a grumpy huff, she took a seat on a hay bale that Hal had placed around the small bonfire, which spat a spectacular spray of rainbow sparks, courtesy of Maeve's magic. She'd argued for fireworks, but Hal had argued back that Annie was too much of a risk factor to introduce any form of rocket for the evening. She was inclined to think he was probably right.

Hal's dark features were lit and shadowed in the glow of the fire. She noticed his Adam's apple bob as she sat down across from him and stretched her hands out to warm them. 'That's mine.' His voice sounded thick.

'The shirt? Oh, sorry. I just found it and it's freezing. Do you want it?' She went to shake it off her shoulders.

'Keep it,' he grumbled, then took a moment while he smooshed a melted marshmallow between two crackers. 'Looks better on you, anyway.'

In the dim fire light, neither of them noticed Maeve roll her eyes so hard that she almost toppled backwards off her hay bale.

Underneath the silver spyglass of a waxing moon peering down upon them, it dawned on Annie that she had no obligatory tug towards a midnight finish line any more. The hour didn't matter. She wasn't required to spend her evening watching the clock, counting down minutes instead of enjoying them. For tonight and the rest of her nights at Arden Place, she could just *be*. Hal was making Maeve laugh hysterically with an impression of a troll he'd encountered in the depths of Devon several summers ago and Karma was curled up by her side.

The gloomy, pessimistic feelings didn't disappear entirely. But Annie was slightly startled as she realized that, for the first time she could remember, everything in her felt . . . alive. Awake. Mixed. Musical. Her joy was like a blanket that she'd pulled out from a box in the attic – a little unfamiliar, a scent that smelled like a memory, but something soft and comforting to rediscover. A world away from the emptiness that she usually fought to bat away whenever she found herself standing still. While these early days without the hex were proving difficult, the quiet orchestra of flora and fauna that flooded the nocturnal meadow was a pacifying soundtrack for her to consider that, while many things appeared to have gone terribly wrong, this moment with Maeve and Hal somehow felt altogether right.

'Do you want a s'more?' Maeve asked, barely able to get the words out between the glue of stringy marshmallow that stuck her lips together. She grinned a chocolatey smile and Annie laughed.

'I would actually like several s'mores. These s'mores are about to solve every single problem in my life,' Annie said, summoning one of the long sticks that Hal had gathered for marshmallow-charring purposes.

'Why don't we do this every night for dinner?' Maeve asked.

'Because, contrary to popular belief in this house, you do need to eat a vegetable once in a while,' Hal said gruffly. 'Your shared passion for sugar is alarming.'

'I just care very passionately about all forms of sweet treat,' Annie said, twiddling her marshmallow in the flames. 'Also, s'mores is the best lip gloss flavour, so I have double the vested interest.'

'I didn't even know that existed,' Maeve said with a tone of wonder.

'Oh, I still have so much to teach you, child.'

Maeve responded by prodding Annie's upper arm with a cooled but half-melted marshmallow on the end of her stick, which earned a squeal in return.

Hal suddenly sprang up from his hay bale and rushed around the fire. 'Annie! Will you please be . . .' Coming up behind Annie, he reached a hand around her waist to move her arm away from the bonfire and grab her stick, which had promptly burst into flames while she was distracted by Maeve. She gasped – whether more at the flames or the proximity of him pressed against her again, she wasn't entirely sure. Hal gave a sigh of relief once he managed to extinguish the marshmallow.

He glanced at her with a lip twitch. 'Maybe a *little* burnt. Don't you own a bakery?'

'That's how I like them, actually,' Annie replied haughtily, trying her best not to laugh. 'It's still good, just . . . extra smoky.'

But the more she resisted, the more the laughter insisted on bursting out of her. And as laughter here always seemed to be, it was catching. The sight of Annie's charred black marshmallow smoking pathetically on the ground had Maeve snorting, then cackling so loudly and freely that it enveloped the whole of Arden Place in an echo. A moment later, Hal was bent double, too, a deep and hearty sound that made his eyes crinkle with fine lines. Soon, Annie was laughing so hard that tears began to pool. Happy ones. Real, happy ones. It was a moment that seemed to wrap warm arms around her. A twinkle, a glimmer, a memory that she would miss before it had even come to an end. Something precious and truly perfect.

Yes, she thought to herself between laughs. *This is it. This is how a life is supposed to feel.*

UNCHARMED

A spray of ash fragments blew from the top of the bonfire in a puff and fell like fireflies.

It took Annie a second to slow her laughing and register the way the ashes flickered as they landed on the grass. At first, she thought it was the night's cool breeze, catching the fragments like amber lights. But then they moved again. Further, more definitely. They were not just fire ash. Gradually, each translucent fragment pulled together, the scorched edges melting back into one another with trails of smoke. Eventually, a full piece of paper had unscorched itself to reveal an intricate silver star illustration as a rain of magical sparks scattered at her slippers. It was a letter. She glanced uncertainly at Hal, then Maeve. The laughter had stopped.

'Is that . . .'

Maeve swallowed down the end of her question. Silence strung itself between the trio as the letter levitated above the bonfire, the envelope catching its glow so self-importantly that it filled Annie with a quick hatred. It was showing off its power, its ability to make everything vanish. Finally, Hal spoke into the quiet.

'Don't open it.'

It might have been the bonfire smoke or the knowledge of what was inside that envelope that made Annie's eyes smart with sharp, stinging tears.

'I have to,' she said quietly.

'No, you don't. Who said we have to take any notice of them?' Maeve's voice was light and scoffing, but Annie recognized that slight, exposing shake to it that she used to hear when they first met all those weeks ago. The girl had frozen stock-still, a half-eaten s'more still between her fingers.

Usually, *Splendidus Infernum* would kick in at any moment,

intuitively fogging the scene to pleasantly temper things. Instead, Annie could see the reality with no rose-coloured tint.

Annie reached for the letter, grabbing it quickly to avoid the flames. The papers unfurled of their own accord and the handwriting glowed as intensely as the fire behind it.

Andromeda,

The magical monitoring department has informed me that there have been no significant spikes in Miss Cadmus's magic use for some time; twenty-one nights, in fact. As a result, I send the official decree that you may both return tomorrow to your usual circumstance within the non-wicche realm, on the trusting that Selcouth shall continue to maintain a close eye over her and her magic in a new placement for the endarkenment process. Please consider this an immediate conclusion to your guardianship responsibilities.

Some readings have correlated particularly strong magic use to the coordinates of Arden Place, but I have informed our watchman that this is due to three wicchefolk residing within one single accommodation and that you would have of course reported anything curious to me. I assume that I am correct, as I always am.

Morena

P.S. I do hope the unannounced arrival of one Mr Bancroft did not cause an overt amount of disruption and that he has not insisted on plaguing you with the same nonsensical, usually griffin-related requests that he so enjoys haranguing me with.

Annie swallowed, glancing at the others. 'It's from Selcouth.'

Hal simply shook his head, and returned to sit back down on his own hay bale.

'The coven says your magic is contained. We . . . we have to go home,' Annie said with a swallow. It felt surreal and uncertain to say it out loud, like a sting landing across her cheek from a slap. Memories of her other life, her real life, the life that she was supposed to be leading, came crashing back.

She had been sure they would have more time. It had felt as though this could be an infinite, a forever.

Maeve scoffed, the uncomfortable noise a plaster slapped against a new, raw wound. 'Well, that's a stupid decision. And obviously the wrong one. So, what, I go a few measly weeks without blowing something up or turning someone into a tangerine and they think I'm fine to go back to school with all of this . . . this magic?' She practically spat the last word.

Annie turned to her. 'Technically, they're right.'

Suddenly, the jaws of obligation and expectation bit back down. She had prised them open without realizing at some point between that moment and three weeks ago. Now, her arms gave way under the weight of keeping them at bay. She thought of the Sorciety. The coven. Her work. All of the expectation.

Maeve faltered, the treacherous answer evidently not what she was expecting to hear.

'I mean we've seen your magic do amazing things over the past few weeks,' Annie went on, taking a step closer to Maeve. 'You've achieved so much.' Her voice was too high-pitched. She tried her best to make it sound like good news, but it felt as though it would choke her. 'I'm so proud of you. You did it.'

'Then why are you sending me away?'

'Maeve,' Annie laughed – or tried to. It was dry, scratching. 'I'm not sending you away. Don't say that. We have to go home.'

'But . . . but this feels more like a home than anywhere I've ever lived.'

Annie had to close her eyes for a moment, not allowing the heartbreak to take hold. Instead, her hands flew to her hips in a pretence at some authority and she tried to give a light answer. 'Well, we can't stay here for ever, can we? This is Hal's house, for starters, and he doesn't want us here.'

'That's not true,' said Hal, who sat very still, his eyes narrowly fixed on Annie. There was cool determination across his face.

'See,' Maeve said emphatically, crossing her arms. The pair of them shot a conspiratorial look to one another across the fire.

Annie laughed at the ridiculous simplicity of Hal's reply, but it came out as more of an incredulous, angry breath. 'Oh, so all three of us are supposed to just abandon our entire lives and stay in this house together, are we? You're crazy. We already spend half of our time wanting to throttle each other. There's no way.'

'Why not?' Maeve hit back.

'Because life doesn't work like that, okay?' Annie's voice was rising, the temper that she had kept locked away for so many years choosing now of all moments to wake with an impatient lion's yawn. It wasn't fair. 'This isn't real life, the three of us holed up here together in a cosy cottage like all the realms' most mismatched, dysfunctional family. I have a job and real responsibilities. I already have a life, without the two of you in it making everything feel so completely confusing and . . .'

'Well, that's just charming, isn't it, Hal?' Maeve interrupted. He grimaced.

'I had a task to complete for the coven. And, look, we've done it.'

Annie brandished the letter, but Maeve snatched it from her grasp and promptly chucked it straight into the fire.

'I am not a task,' Maeve spat. Annie noticed the static of unbridled magic spark between the girl's fingertips again in a way she hadn't seen since their first days. But she quickly reeled herself back in and her powers' temper quelled. 'Annie, come on,' Maeve continued, her tone more bargaining. 'You've said it yourself that you're unhappy with the corner that you've been backed into. So am I. I know you wish that you could go back and change things for yourself. Maybe this is how we . . .'

'This is not a case of "we", Maeve. You have to go home and so do I. And Hal has to go back to his normal life without the two of us ruining it for him.'

Maeve stared at her, open-mouthed. She turned to Hal for support. 'C'mon, cowboy, back me up here.'

Even across from the bonfire, Annie heard Hal's deep sigh as he stood up to speak. 'Annie's right, Maeve.'

Maeve faltered. 'Since when have you ever called me Maeve?'

'Since I'm backing up your guardian on this one, kid. Neither of you belong here, holed up with me. That's just the way it has to be. It's the way that this was always supposed to go.'

Annie hoped that she was imagining the crack in his voice. She steeled herself to deliver the final word. It felt unnatural and ugly, to know that she was causing someone that she cared for anything other than happiness. And this wasn't just a someone, this was Maeve.

'I'm sorry, sweetheart, but the matter is closed. Our time here has finished.'

Maeve looked as though she'd been slapped; Annie could barely believe that she was seeing or hearing herself right. It felt as though she had been placed in a body that wasn't hers. She hastily brushed away a rogue tear that had escaped despite her best efforts.

'Go and pack your things, please.'

It felt as though her heart splintered when she noticed Maeve's bottom lip quiver for a fraction of a second, wavering like the shadows of the bonfire flames. But the girl quickly steeled herself, as she always did. Maeve stormed away and Karma leapt up hastily to follow her friend. Moments later, the sound of a slammed door crashed through the cottage with so much force that the entire house rattled.

Annie let out a heavy breath and slumped back down onto the hay bale, folding in half to hug her legs and rest her forehead against her knees. The silence, speckled with the angry spitting of the fire, felt so heavy.

Eventually, Hal dared to break it.

'Stay.'

He was hunched over, too, staring fixedly at his fingers that were laced together, elbows on thighs. Their bodies mirrored one another either side of the bonfire, silhouetting them both in orange and red.

'But you just said . . .'

'Well, I had to back you up in front of the kid, didn't I? But I'm serious, you should stay. For as long as you like.' Hal leaned towards her, his face illuminated by the flames. 'What is it exactly that you are trying to prove, Annie?'

She pressed her lips together, fighting the temptation to tell the truth but quickly buckled, the answer forming itself without any hexes or curses or spells to temper it into a more palatable, less startling truth. 'I don't even know any more.'

Hal didn't reply, simply raised his eyebrows to invite her to explain.

She picked at a cuticle before catching herself ruining the nail. She turned her distraction to the hay bale instead as she tried to talk sense into him, still not permitting herself to meet his eyes as she pulled at single strands. 'Things might seem okay right now, but a few more days and we'll end up driving you crazy. Maeve's scrunchies constantly lying around, my glitter everywhere . . .' Annie breathed an empty laugh. 'You already think I'm the worst.'

'Sometimes,' Hal nodded, leaning back and rubbing a hand roughly through his beard. 'Other times . . .' He paused, catching her eyes under lock and key. 'Other times, I think you might just be perfect.'

Everything in the current between them paused, the tiniest flecks of embers hanging in the air like fresh sparks of magic. Crackles from the flames snapped against the quiet. It was Annie who broke first, averting her gaze back to the bonfire and hoping that the flush across her cheeks looked only like a result of its warmth.

This wasn't part of the plan. She shot to her feet, clenching her fists and squeezing her eyes shut.

Hal tried again softly, looking up at her with his hands still interlocked, as though he didn't dare move for fear of frightening her away. 'Not just for Maeve, although I think we make a damn good team for the kid. This is . . . this is good. Why won't you give it a chance?'

She couldn't stand to hear another word. Annie spun on her

heel and followed the path back to the cottage that Maeve's whirlwind had scorched into the grass. She found herself in the kitchen and gripped the countertop to try to steady herself while her head spun. Her knuckles were white again. She hadn't seen that happen in weeks.

'It's a fair question, Annie,' Hal said quietly behind her. He had followed her inside but kept his distance, leaning against one of the wooden beams with his arms crossed. 'Give me one real, good reason and I'll understand it.'

'Because this is not the life that I am supposed to have. My real life is in London, my real life is at Celeste, my real life is at The S . . . at the city,' she said sharply, jabbing a finger into the countertop. 'A lot of people are relying on me and I can't just abandon them. I can't let them down.'

'Right, of course,' he nodded calmly. 'And what kind of happiness are you getting in return for that?'

He took a step into the kitchen towards her. Annie swallowed hard and stood her ground, jutting her chin out higher. 'That doesn't matter. I'm just fine.'

Hal simply nodded, eyes so fixed on hers that it felt as though he was looking directly into her soul. 'You're allowed to do it, you know. Why shouldn't you start again, for you?'

Another step closer. She mirrored it backwards.

'Why should you just be *fine*? Why shouldn't you be happy?'

Annie startled as she stepped back again and her shoulder blades touched the wall. She noticed Hal's jaw muscles tighten as he slowly moved his hand towards her face and tucked a stray tendril of hair behind her ear, which would never have been there if she was still under the spell. Such a perfect, tender gesture that he wouldn't even have had reason to do.

'You're too good to be tethering yourself to people out of fear instead of love.'

His voice was a thick, hoarse whisper. 'I know it's crazy for me to ask you to stay. I know you're too good and bright and brilliant for a small kind of life like mine. But I have to be selfish and unreasonable and ask it anyway. Stay, just for now, and we can figure it out a day at a time.'

Their eyes felt magnetized as he leaned over her, his arm above her pressed against the wall. Annie knew she should look away and break it, but there was a sincerity in his face. There was no sarcasm, no gruffness, nothing but a confident honesty and an inch of vulnerability that felt like a mile coming from him.

But this was not what was supposed to happen. This plan was messy and unknowable and chaotic. It couldn't even be called a plan. This wasn't the way that she did things.

'This is not real life!' Annie said crossly, something in her flaring uncontrollably.

'This is probably the most real your life has ever been, Annie.'

Hal reeled himself back in and took a breath with relenting, closed eyes. Annie looked at him blankly, a life of training taking over.

'This can't be real for me,' Annie said simply. 'Otherwise everything I've ever done, everything I've ever sacrificed, has been for nothing.' She spoke calmly and quietly enough that a numbness returned to her from head to toe. It was as though the harsh reminder of her old life had awoken some final, lingering dregs of the spell. Like it had sparked something at the pit of her stomach to fix things on her behalf, within the confines of her bones. She slid out from underneath his arm and made her way towards the staircase.

'Don't go.'

Hal tried one last time. She turned back to find he was still facing the space that she'd just abandoned, the back of his head low. With a sigh, he dropped his arm, but he refused to turn around to see her disappear upstairs.

She could only reply with the truth. 'We have to.'

Chapter Twenty-One

TIME TO GO

Arden Place was feeling its own heart break just the same as Annie was, a steady stream of rain pouring so heavily from dawn until dusk on their final day together that the clattering against the window panes transformed into a constant, aching background sigh. Karma wouldn't leave Maeve's side while she packed away her things, refusing to get out of her suitcase while shooting daggers at Annie that all the custard in the world would not be able to save her from.

It felt like Annie had been caught inside a snowglobe, as though some large, unwelcome hand had shaken her whole life up roughly and unexpectedly and now the fragments of it were tumbling down around her in slow motion. And she could only stand there in the drift, powerless and speechless, and watch while it faded away at her feet.

All she had ever tried to do was the right thing for everybody else. But somehow it had resulted in managing to make two very important people not want to speak to her any more, both irreparably disappointed and hurt by her decisions that were supposedly the right and proper ones to make. Annie had never felt worse.

Maeve finished her packing in a racket of furiously slammed drawers, shoved clothing and, to Annie's greatest dismay, a few sly sniffs of tears that were definitely not supposed to be heard. Maeve refused any and all forms of breakfast, leaving a stack of her favourite chocolate-chip pancakes untouched, and wouldn't even accept a cup of coffee from Annie. Instead, she briefly emerged from her room to make her own, ignoring all of Annie's desperate, sugar-laced attempts to try to patch up the rift that had sliced itself so suddenly between them.

Unsurprisingly, Annie hadn't slept a wink, but this time it couldn't be blamed on a twisted, sinister, generation-spanning hex. Her own guilt and tangled, complicated feelings kept sleep far at bay, as well as the pain and rejection that Maeve was emanating in the bedroom just below, rippling upwards to Annie's heart.

She had heard Hal treading the porch boards below as the sun came up, while she stared at the ceiling with bleary eyes. She had hoped that he'd accept a cup of maple coffee as a peace offering, just as he had that first morning. They could recapture that time and end whatever was between them on a peaceful, understanding note. But the moment she stepped onto a particularly creaky step in the staircase and revealed that she too was awake, Hal had promptly strode off into the woods with his hat pulled low. In the distance, she heard the canter of Mage's hooves. Hal didn't want to speak to her, didn't even want to see her. He probably never would again.

But what choice did she have? He would soon forget her. They had both agreed: they didn't go together and they didn't belong.

UNCHARMED

Following a hasty reply to Selcouth's letter so that Annie couldn't change her mind, it had been arranged that Morena would, at precisely 3 p.m. and not a moment before or after, call upon Maeve by summoned transference. Just as Annie had brought Morena to them all those weeks ago near the school, the Sage Witch would ensure that Maeve and her newly settled magic would transfer instantaneously to a new foster placement pre-arranged by the coven. Annie explained the plan as gently as she could, but Maeve only gave her a look that could have killed her if there was an appropriate, murderous spell to accompany it. Fortunately, Maeve settled for shoving past her on purpose with a sharp shoulder and heading out onto the porch to spend her final hours at Arden Place on the swing, gazing glassily onto the meadow with Karma nuzzling forlornly on her lap. Of course, the cat knew that something was deeply, deeply wrong – familiars always knew.

The devastating thought of Maeve being taken from her care and having to start again in yet another unknown place was almost enough for Annie to break. Maybe she could trigger Maeve to cause some kind of 'accidental' sorcery fire, just enough for them to sigh and tell the coven that they'd better stay at the cottage a couple more weeks . . .

That might keep them together for a while longer, but would still only be delaying the inevitable. Nothing this precious could last. And surely it was better for everybody to sever these ties today, before their strange little bond grew even stronger and more painful to pull apart. And who's to say that it was severed anyway? Maeve would come around, eventually. They could still be friends.

Deep down, of course, Annie knew that Maeve's fierce pride

would ensure that that would never be the case. She would see her around at Hecate House in a few years' time, when she had grown up into a young woman that Annie didn't know. They would give each other polite waves across the atrium and would both try not to remember the times they'd shared at Arden Place. There was no returning from this decision for the girl.

Annie finally managed to zip up her stack of suitcases that had accumulated through summoning spells over the weeks (even magic struggled to fasten them closed) and knitted together the weightless luggage spell that had impressed Maeve back in the canteen. Puffing her messy, falling hair out of her face, no longer big and bouncy, but hastily scrambled back into a claw clip, she realized the time with a jolt. It was mere minutes to three o'clock. She had desperately hoped that Maeve would come to say goodbye herself, concede to a truce so that their final moments together could be happy ones. But that wasn't very Maeve. There was still so much to make sure that she told her before they were apart for good.

Annie sprinted down the stairs, tripping over her own feet, hurtling around the spiral staircase at breakneck speed and skidding over the floorboards so quickly that she almost levitated (maybe she even did, a bit) before bursting through the front door.

'Thank the universe, you're still here,' she blurted out.

Reluctantly placing Karma on the ground, Maeve rose to her feet from the swing.

'Don't know why. I should have taken off last night.'

The two witches stood face to face, both unable to quite put into words how they were feeling. Annie, who had planned to say so much, couldn't find a single word that felt correct.

'Please don't make me go.' Maeve tried one more time, finally allowing her tears to fall.

'We both have to go home.'

'But this *is* my home.'

Maeve's shoulders rose and fell. She blew out a steadying breath, trying to be tough as she always did, but a sob changed into a hiccough, which morphed into a frustrated, angry sigh of resignation. As the buttercup-yellow sun slipped lower into a pocket of dull cloud, Maeve looked straight at Annie with the pain of a girl who had thought that she had finally found home.

'Maeve, I'm so sorry. But please, listen to me . . .'

As sun rays silhouetted Maeve in gold, the girl gave a resigned sigh of defeat. The faintest flicker of magic turned her translucent, with a waver like a waterfall, and three o'clock fell over the cottage at Arden Place. Annie could only watch through tears as the accidental, astonishing gem that she had found, like buried treasure, slipped away into someone else's hold.

One blink more and Maeve had gone.

Annie and Karma found themselves alone on the porch, only the cool, earthy October breeze for company, which picked up across the meadow as though it was trying to chase after the special girl who'd come to stay. Cascading its way towards the cottage, it caught Annie's hair on a gust and whipped away the scent of what now felt like home – a golden crispness and fireplace smoke and the sweetest cinnamon sugar. It stirred the long, pale grass and Annie swore that the faint sound of their laughter at the witches' ring was still carried along on the wind, wrapped around the cottage like a permanent friendship bracelet.

Annie waited for Hal to return until the sun went down. She couldn't even cry any more as she looked out, curled up on the swing, onto the horizon. She let the soothing motion rock her gently with her feet folded underneath her skirt and Karma on her lap, as dusk sank behind the trees and veiled Arden Place in the evening's lilac-grey.

'He isn't coming back,' she said quietly into the tear-damp tufts of newly scruffy fur on Karma's head. She gave her a small kiss, leaving a trace of pink lipstick behind, then popped her paws down onto the swing to begin her final preparations. Hal had taken himself far away, off on another adventure that was bigger and greater and more authentic than she could ever be.

Annie took a fond glance around the cottage: half-read spellbooks borrowed from the bookshelves left open, forgotten glasses of rainbow paint water, scatterings of coloured pencils, an always-open jar of biscuits, nests of blankets, matching slippers, discarded Stetsons, crumb-covered cake plates.

Hal would want his house as it had been before she and Maeve arrived and turned it upside down. Annie wriggled the fingers of her left hand to gather up a sprinkling of magic – a string of pale pink sparks carried itself around the cottage in a glittering loop. The magic tumbled through the gaps in the floorboards and passed in and out of each kitchen cupboard. It travelled the length of the shelves, across the carpets, trailed the table and chairs, ran up the staircase. One final trail tumbled from the ceiling beams and vanished away the 'Maeve's room' words she had inked onto the bedroom door.

A reminder that something so precious and sweet was also impermanent, impossible for her to keep. The stars took every last trace.

Moments later, Annie stood alone in the middle of the bare cottage, which looked just as it had before she had ever worked her magic. The only thing different was the kitchen window, which had been so full of warmth and promise when they'd first arrived. The glow had now gone.

Stepping out onto the porch, shutting the door behind her with a gentle click, Annie took one final inhale of the meadow air, trying her best to remember it as it had been when it was a happy place. She gathered up Karma, who had been weaving between her ankles, into her arms. Her familiar let out a single lamenting yowl.

'Don't give me that, Karma,' she replied softly. 'This was never meant for us.'

Like Maeve had once told her, perhaps the only thing to do was to let it go, like a balloon. She had to try and she had to forget.

Annie wriggled her toes in her patent shoes, feeling her transference magic awaken. She raised a hand to cast her magic, almost like a wave goodbye as her fingertips glittered pink. One moment more and the cottage was empty.

Arden Place seemed to give a curious, disappointed sigh, left truly alone for the first time in weeks, as though the wooden walls were wondering where the newly blossomed love that had filled it to the rafters had suddenly been snatched to.

Hooves galloped by, thudding at speed into the soft meadow before pulling up at the porch. The horse rallied onto his hind legs as two boots landed on the ground in a desperate hurry. The front door swung open, honest words ready to be spilled and insisted, but they tumbled out into an empty home. There was nobody to hear them, only the lingering scent of vanilla sugar that settled to the floor in a scattering of rosy-pink snow-like sparks.

Chapter Twenty-Two

SWEET HOME

Celeste was just as she left it, which brought equal parts comfort and dread to Annie's heart in the morning. A peachy flush spilled across the bakehouse floor as the dawn broke like a runny yolk. She was grateful to at least have a familiar routine to throw herself straight into. Nothing would help her come to terms with returning, other than just beginning again, not leaving room to think about all that she had left behind.

Everywhere looked pristine and beautiful, as it always did. The tables and counters were immaculate, the sconces and the coffee machine polished, the windows and chalkboards covered with Pari's illustrations. The Halloween décor was in full swing, too, feeling cosy and nostalgic. Annie wrapped her arms around herself, as though her body needed to feel something still and steady, to grip onto something solid before she completely disappeared. Celeste was inextricably linked with heart-quickening, spiked emotions now. It meant pressure that she hadn't intended to invite along, more deadlines than anyone should possibly have to match, expectations so enormous that only her magic could meet them.

Worst of all, Annie knew in her heart she would soon have to admit defeat and bring *Splendidus Infernum* back, to save her from herself and the impossible standards she had set.

Annie swallowed against the tightness in her throat and began to fire bursts of magic towards her tasks – turning on the ovens, reviving the wilting pink roses on the tabletops, levitating the sieve for the morning's flour sifting. She reminded herself that the golden cage was still golden.

Soon, the tinkle of the doorbell sprinkled through the bakery like hundreds and thousands. Annie leaned backwards from her work at the kitchen counter. Pari squealed and sprinted directly towards her, practically skidding across the tiles.

'You're here! We missed you!' Pari said, throwing her arms around Annie and squeezing her so tightly that it made Annie gasp. It felt as though the second Pari let go, she might unravel like a spool of thread. Faye soon followed behind, dumping her many bags on the floor.

'Glad to have you back,' Faye said, although Annie could already tell that there was concern in her gaze. It made her bristle, knowing that someone was looking too closely at her.

'You seem different,' Pari said, twirling Annie's lazy ponytail around her fingers affectionately.

'Oh, I know,' Annie said self-consciously. 'A bit of a shambles, really.'

'Not at all, you look so pretty!' Pari said brightly. 'You always look pretty. Like our own little macaroon kiss.'

Annie laughed, the brightness that perpetually radiated from Pari feeling like much-needed sunlight on her skin.

'Thanks, sweetheart. I really did miss you both. Can you believe how long I was away?'

'No time for pleasantries, I'm afraid. Time waits for no man and cake waits for no woman, so we'd better get cracking. I mean that both literally and as an egg-related baking pun,' Faye called as she threw an apron across the shop floor towards each of them. 'Annie, you will not believe the order sheet that we need to get through this week. I can practically feel the nervous breakdown radiating from you already. This should be fun!'

It only took those few moments for Annie to feel the temporary spark of joy from her co-workers drain away again. There was no *Splendidus Infernum* hanging around in the pit of her stomach, ready to buoy it back up artificially.

'No need to look so chuffed about it,' Faye said, rolling her eyes. 'It's a good thing. It's unbelievable. Celeste is taking over the world, Annie, one choux bun at a time. We've got this, don't worry.'

'I know,' Annie said with a quiet smile. Of course they did. She just wasn't sure whether she could say the same for herself.

'So how was it?' Faye said, simultaneously firing up the coffee machine, tying up her apron and chucking a rag over her shoulder. 'Did you get beaten up by a teenager?'

'Only emotionally,' Annie said with a fond smile. 'She was a superstar. I loved it.'

'Well, that's great,' Pari nodded, although she looked unconvinced. 'And how does it feel now that it's over?'

Annie bit down on her bottom lip and debated how honest to be. 'That's the part I'm struggling to work out.'

Her first days back passed in a blur of trying. Trying to settle back in, trying to be present in the here and now, trying to remind herself that this was where she was supposed to be and trying to be her very best self, even though she'd never felt worse.

Annie enjoyed being around Faye and Pari of course, but dragging her mood up to meet theirs took more energy than she could muster. She felt a tweak of appreciation in her chest, too, when regulars like Joe and Olive spotted her behind the counter for the first time in weeks. She made sure to take time to make each of them feel special, as she always would. Armed with personalized pastries and treats for each and every customer, she listened to their stories and asked the questions that she knew would make them feel lighter, opening a door for each of them to step through and slip off their shoes. But without the spell, Annie found that she needed reminding of things that she once knew off by heart. The jokes she tried didn't always quite land and awkward pauses of silence seemed to stretch for longer than could possibly be normal. Social awkwardness, as it transpired, was a terrible feeling.

It wasn't that she cared any less for those familiar faces. Of course not; Annie would always care deeply. It was simply as if she had less of herself to give in return. As though her heart had been left behind. She could no longer exist as an infinite well.

'If you'd told us it was this adorable, we might have come to visit sooner.'

Annie's eyes widened. She spun around on the spot so quickly that a spray of icing erupted from the piping bag that she was using to ink faces onto the pumpkin-shaped, chocolate-orange optimism macarons. Hal and Maeve would have liked them. She pushed them out of her mind.

Because here were Romily and Vivienne, side by side, with arms interlaced.

'You're . . . you're here! In my bakery?' Annie stuttered.

'Of course, babe. Wouldn't have missed your triumphant return, would we? We missed you terribly,' Romily pouted, then helped herself to a pumpkin to nibble on daintily.

Annie laughed, surprised by the warmth. 'I can't believe you finally came to visit. How did you know I was back?'

Romily shrugged nonchalantly. 'Just a hunch.'

'There's no keeping secrets from us,' Vivienne said. 'I can't believe you've spent almost the entirety of October doing voluntary work. Universe above, get a life will you, Wildwood? You could have jetted off somewhere glorious to get away from it all and hibernate for the winter, rather than sucking up to the coven even more than you usually do.' She smirked, examining her reflection in the back of the mirrored napkin dispenser. 'Hard work, I assume? You look dreadful.'

'Harmony,' Romily snapped, with a literal snap of her fingers to accompany it, as though her friend were a chihuahua to return to her heel. It was only then that Annie noticed Harmony, who had been distracted on entry by a handsome man enjoying a sandwich in the corner. There was a wave of iridescence floating between them, the man inhaling sparks of her siren-inherited allure without realizing. Harmony stuck out a sulking bottom lip and dropped the incantation, leaving the man to shake out his head as though it were full of cobwebs. Ruby had also joined the visit, but had launched straight into a hearty conversation with Faye about the difference between an Americano and a long black. She gave Annie a giant grin and a full, slightly chaotic wave when their eyes caught.

'Hi, Annie,' Harmony smiled brightly as she approached. 'Universe above, your roots! Are you prepping your Halloween costume already? The Bride of Frankenstein is such a fun one.'

Annie shot a self-conscious hand to her hair.

'You do look a little peaky, Annie,' Romily said softly, rubbing her upper arm gently. 'What did they have you doing, those awful witches, wherever it was that they holed you up?'

'The common coven have so little regard for personal maintenance. Everyone at you-know-where thankfully understands that image is everything in this realm and the next – something that Selcouth never cares to acknowledge,' Vivienne said.

'They're all desperately ugly, that's probably why,' Harmony said sadly and sincerely, as though discussing a heartbreaking charity campaign.

Annie gave them all a weak smile, but found that it felt like tugging a spoon through dark treacle to form one across her face. 'Why don't you take a seat? The window booth is the best spot. I'll bring you some tea and some treats. Just . . .' She lowered her voice to plead with them. 'No magic, please?'

'Wouldn't dream of it,' Vivienne said with a serene smirk.

While Ruby stayed chatting to Faye and Pari, the Fortune Four took elegant and poised position at the window, Romily whispering something as they sat down that made Vivienne snort and Harmony squeal with laughter. Although self-conscious, strangely sure that the comment had been about her or her bakery, Annie had to admit that they looked ethereally beautiful as the afternoon sun streamed in and lit them all in the golden hour. One of many tricks up Romily's sleeve was a spell for always finding flattering lighting wherever they went. The sight of their glow gave Annie that itch again, the longing to revert back to old ways, to be perfect once again. Perfect enough that she blended in alongside them.

'Tell us all about it, then,' Romily purred with concentrated eyes on Annie as she sipped at the delicate china mug (Annie had given them the very best of her vintage collection). She felt her brows raise of their own accord at the reality of Romily Whitlock asking yet another genuine question about her life and whereabouts that didn't involve some kind of gossip fodder. She smiled, surprised and touched. Every so often, Romily showed glimpses of the old version of herself whom Annie had grown up with. It felt exciting and heartwarming, like rediscovering a lost favourite toy.

'It was . . .' Annie struggled to find the words that wouldn't make the girls shriek with judgement and laughter. 'Wonderful. Rewarding. I was looking after a teenage you-know-what who was struggling to rein in her . . . "confidence".' Annie explained, before mouthing the word 'magic' to a slightly baffled looking Harmony. She got a drawn-out 'ohhhh' in return.

'Well, look at you. Should we have brought an apple for teacher?' Vivienne said dryly, adding a spoonful of sweetener into her cup.

'What was the girl like? A total nightmare? A right little witch, I bet,' Harmony asked, holding onto Annie's forearm on the table with spilling sympathy.

'What?' Annie laughed, shaking off a rush of hot defensiveness for Maeve. 'Not at all. I mean not the easiest kid in the world, but I've never known anyone with such a heart of gold. Apart from maybe the two that I work here with.'

'Oh? And what are we? Rotten nightshade? Pickled newt liver?' Romily said, with an air of offence.

'And you three, of course. That goes without saying,' Annie smiled. She felt her patience twitch in an unfamiliar, jarring way.

'How did her magic seem? Did you get it under wraps?' Vivienne asked.

'We made real progress. She's talented and so bright. It didn't take us long to realize that anything creative seemed to make it flourish, so we did all sorts of lovely activities to combine her art with her magic. She's a very special girl,' Annie said, carried away on the memories of those happy days before she could rein herself in as she normally would around them. As soon as she'd shared so much, she found herself regretting it.

'A "special girl", hey? Anyone would think you actually enjoyed yourself, holed up with some ghastly teenage girl with no manners and no money.'

Annie smarted and distracted herself by refolding the napkin on her lap. 'Honestly, I did, Viv. I think she managed to teach me far more than I taught her in the end.'

'Like what, how to prepare instant noodles and apply uneven eyeliner?'

'She was quite extraordinary,' Annie said, wanting to defend Maeve further from their harsh preconceptions. Their judgement felt all the more acute without the hex to blur her responses.

'Yes, yes, very special. Very precious. An absolute darling, by all accounts. So where is she now?' Vivienne said quickly. 'Have they found someone else to palm little Maeve off onto?'

Annie opened her mouth to reply, then closed her lips,

stumbling over an unwelcome, ugly thought. A thought that made her shoulders tense, her blood stop moving through her body.

'I . . .' She swallowed hard. 'I don't think I mentioned her name.'

Vivienne's eyes glittered, but for only a fraction of a second. 'Lucky guess,' she said, followed by a neat shrug.

'We heard mention of her at the first symposium, after you'd accepted the position,' Romily explained quickly on Vivienne's behalf. 'You can't expect a young witch to cause a minor disaster at school and for it not to make headline news at the club, Annie.'

'But it's nobody's business. Perhaps the coven's at a push, but . . .'

'The Sorciety *make* it their business to always know the unfolding of magic. You know that.'

Annie felt chastised, silly. She had always known that. 'Right. Of course.'

'Was her magic as extraordinary as they're all saying it was?' Harmony asked hungrily, her voice rasping a little. Annie let the moment hold in the air for a second. The small pause was all it took to realize that the three girls were, for once, hanging off her every word. Something wasn't right.

'Did you only come here to ask about Maeve?' she asked unsurely.

Romily laughed. 'No offence, babe, but we don't actually care all that much about the coven's latest charity case. We just wanted to hear all about the amazing things you've been doing and congratulate you on your achievements. We're your best friends, remember?' she added, with a smile that made Annie soften.

'We don't have to talk about her if you don't want to,' Harmony said.

'Indeed. I might suffocate myself with one of these cheese scones if we don't talk about something more interesting soon. And you know how I am with dairy,' Vivienne drawled.

Annie reeled herself back in. She was overreacting. Exhausted. The protective streak that she'd developed towards Maeve was running away with her, even when the girl was a million miles away. She was not hers to look after any more. Annie suspected that abandoning the spell was starting to make her instincts go a little haywire. It was almost doing the entire opposite of everything that it used to do. To test her, to spite her, to try to lead her back towards one more night's brew.

'What have I missed? Oh, pardon me there, shuffle up, will you, pal?' Ruby said, squeezing herself in beside Vivienne in the bay window and earning a look of pure loathing in return. 'Annie, I'm so excited to hear all about your time away. I just got chatting to your colleagues, they're so great! And did you make these? They're changing my life,' she asked, brandishing a maple pecan cupcake topped with crunchy, salty pretzel pieces.

'When you've quite finished walloping yourself across the table,' Vivienne drawled to Ruby, her mouth pinched.

'We were just about to tell Annie the big news,' Romily said, a little kinder, but with a sharpness to her eyes.

'Oh, fun! Sorry, Viv, my bad. You'll be there, Annie, right? I know you're not a gal who'd miss an excuse to get dolled up,' Ruby grinned.

'Sorry,' Annie shook her head, slightly baffled. 'Be where?'

'The Samhain Ball!' Harmony squealed.

'Oh,' Annie said, taken aback. With everything that had happened, she'd entirely forgotten about one of the biggest All Hallows events in the Sorciety calendar to welcome in the beginning of winter. 'I'm not sure I'm invited.'

'Annie, don't be so modest. Of course you're invited. Mummy specifically asked me whether you'd be there,' Romily said. 'You didn't hear it from me, but I may or may not have heard rumour that your Crescent status is part of the celebrations.'

Harmony gave a squeal and squeezed Annie's hand. Even Vivienne seemed pleased by the news. Ruby gave a sort of upturned frown, contemplating the revelation for herself.

Annie was so taken aback, she couldn't quite find the words. An invitation to a Sorciety ball, the biggest of the year, specifically from Glory Whitlock, the Supreme Herald. And, finally, the fully fledged membership she had always longed for. She had finally done enough to please them. She was finally good enough.

'You must come,' Romily went on with the same uncharacteristically encouraging, keen tone. 'It'll be fun. I mean it won't be all *that* fun. But Mummy has vowed for opulence above all else this year, with no expense spared, so at least the Tempest will be in all of its finery and we can wear some killer dresses.'

'We'll look better than everyone – and that's always enjoyable,' chimed Harmony.

'The drinks should be flowing, if nothing else,' Vivienne added.

'Yeah, c'mon, Annie. You have to come along,' Ruby said, dusting cupcake crumbs from her fingers without realizing that they were tumbling into Harmony's handbag. 'I have some wicked dance moves that need to be seen to be believed.'

Annie smiled, touched again by the way that they really did seem to have missed her. Coming back to her old life had felt like a rip in the universe, uncomfortable and jagged. But this had to be proof that she had made the right choice. It was all falling into place as it was supposed to. She had to stop questioning it.

'I'd love to go.'

They never included her as actively as this, not properly since her father had made his mistakes. Over the years, even with the spell to appease her feelings, it was always her, tugging at the ends of Romily's cloak, bargaining and promising her way into their plans in exchange for whatever she could give them. But here she was, going to the Samhain Ball with her best friends. Just like old times. The prospect brought the same hallowed thrill that she'd felt at fifteen. Old habits did die hard. Her heart reacted in the exact same way, like a trained animal responding to a call.

She would have to make sure that she was as perfect as she could be.

Chapter Twenty-Three

THE SAMHAIN BALL

The night before Halloween rolled darkly and wondrously across London like a charged storm cloud. The air felt thick with magic.

Annie had always thought of her home as a sanctuary. But now that she knew an alternative, had experienced what a home could and should evoke, she could barely stand to be there. The quietness and the stagnant air that hadn't been breathed back out by loving lungs, felt as though it bounced back off the walls to push at her. Karma wove her way in and out of Annie's ankles to reassure her that she wasn't alone.

Back in her bathroom, Annie clutched onto the colourful collection of clinking bottles, juggling each of the ingredients and holding them at arms length as though she wasn't quite sure she could trust them any more. Had life really been so bad before, allowing the spell to lead the way for her? It certainly hadn't proved itself to be any easier without the control of *Splendidus Infernum* to guide her. In fact, her life was actively harder since she had returned from Arden Place; it was tearing her in more directions than she could count.

Annie gingerly took a step closer towards the filling

bathtub, steam rising in wisps and coils that began to lull her mind with its invitation. Following expectation was simpler in so many ways. It kept pushing her along with a prodding, pointed finger. Had it really been so difficult, to live a life alongside those whispers of pain and regret? She had always managed to carry them all, she had never buckled. Perhaps she had been dramatic to consider it so utterly draining.

But she kept hearing Maeve, over and over, in the particularly pestering voice that she loved nagging Annie with. *This is your life and you're letting people make you unhappy in it.*

The bottles clattered to the floor. Pools of potion leaked across the tiles, ground herb powders and petal shards landing at her feet. The grasp of the haunted voices that came with the hex faded away into the distance.

'No, Annie,' she told herself firmly.

She owed Maeve at least this much. To let her own joy matter, to see what her heart was pulled towards. To try the hard way a little longer.

If she wasn't to turn back to the spell tonight, then at least that gave her a dash more time to consider her dress for the ball. She had to get it right and, without the guidance of the spell, she was holding on to the hope that just her own natural magic would be enough. Leaving the mess to deal with later (but closing the bathroom door behind her to ensure that paws didn't wander through puddles), Annie took a dubious seat at her sewing table in her pyjamas. She frowned. Normally, *Splendidus Infernum* would act of its own accord in these situations, reaching out from within her. It would tug her arms like marionette strings, lifting and dropping them with no thought required, until the perfect combination of outfit and accessories was created.

Annie tapped her fingers on her thighs. What did *she* want to let her magic do? Silence, except for the impossibly loud second hand of the clock on the mantlepiece. For once, not plagued at midnight with feelings and thoughts of others, she could hear her own breathing. Her own pulse. Her own fire. She barely dared to breathe, but it was then that Annie felt an impulse that seemed familiar. A pull to create and let her magic flow and flourish. Before she could second-guess herself, she fired up her trusty sewing machine.

Reams of fabric cascaded around her as though she were caught in a cyclone. Spools of thread flew and ribbons unfurled like ferns, dancing and dashing about her work space. Occasionally, Karma lost all dignity and pounced upon them with a waggling rear end and twitching ears that still hadn't returned to their normal size. Her paws landed unceremoniously with a chirp, but Annie only gave her a quick scratch of congratulations. She was lost in a flurry of focus, watching her own magic – her own talent – bring an imagined creation to life.

A thought occurred to her as she stitched fabric together in ripples and reams. Had *Splendidus Infernum* controlled her to the fullest extent that she had always assumed? How many elements of her carefully perfected personality were, in fact . . . really just her? She considered the possibility that her creativity had maybe even overstepped the spell sometimes, taken the reins all by itself with the confidence and reassurance that some other force would be able to reel it back in if anything were to go wrong. Had it been that way all along? Could some of her perfect self have been real and true? Magic tingled at her fingertips, pricking slightly at the enticing thought.

Hours later, with one final guide of the delicate fabric under the foot of the sewing machine, Annie rebounded against the back of her chair, as if waking from a dream. Between her thumbs and forefingers, she held the dress up in front of her as though it had appeared of its own accord, sent from somewhere else.

'What do you think?' Annie asked, chewing on the inside of her cheek. 'Is it enough for the Samhain Ball? Those witches don't mess around at this time of year.'

Karma leapt up onto her lap with a bell jangle and placed her paws together neatly on Annie's thighs. She glanced at the dress, her little head tilting one way in thought. After a moment or two of contemplation, she returned to licking the top of her left paw and fluffing up the fur behind her ears.

'You're right. Needs a little something.'

With a small flick of her wrist, Annie added what she suspected may be the finishing touch. She had lost her sparkle, left it behind at the cottage among the wildflowers and the long grass. She needed a reminder that perhaps it would one day return to her. A finely spun layer of her own magic coated the dress from top to bottom, a shimmer of starlight when the fabric moved. A faint smile tugged at her lips.

In Annie's experience, there was little else that could lift her spirits quite like slipping on a new dress. Granted, her spirits at present were lingering somewhere that felt like it must be the underworld, but this was a special dress that worked a small miracle. The layers of delicate tulle slipped over her skin and floated around her shape, billowing to the floor in light layers. It was, of course, a shade of pale pink that felt just right, but blended at the waist and down the sleeves into a spray of navy-dusted silver. Annie knew that her heart had been thinking of the dawn that bloomed over the woods each morning at Arden Place. From the top of the dress, which skimmed just off her shoulders, a trim of wildflowers, trailing stems and stars were embroidered by her magic, bringing the whole thing to life.

She swept her hair behind her shoulders and left everything else understated. As understated as a wondrous, magical gown could possibly be, anyway. This was a dress that would speak for itself and Annie knew the rules of fashion better than most – spell or no spell.

The steps into the Tempest Theatre music hall were peppered with the skeletons of leaves that had blown in on the gathering storm, but Annie permitted herself her princess moment on the grand staircase. Wearing her gown for the descent was too delicious a prospect for her to ignore. She took her time slowly on each step, hand gliding down the brass rail. Despite the nerves that were bubbling at the pit of her stomach, the weight of dread that pushed against her ribs before the start of every Sorciety gathering, for one moment she allowed herself to forget about it. As always, she could barely contain the excitable snort-laugh that escaped.

Having ascended the stage, mirrorball spinning above, Annie brushed her fingers against the ivory keys of the grand piano. The tune tinkled below her skin, cutting through the thick atmosphere until the sound settled across the tops of the theatre chairs like another layer of dust and moth wings.

The transformation was somehow slow motion and instantaneous as always, the magic that cascaded across the theatre bending time to its whim, bringing a tidal wave of enchantment with it. With that familiar spin of seating and spill of silver across the scene, the Tempest Theatre washed away the sleep from its eyes and revealed its truest, regal self once again.

Ball nights were something to behold even for the witch, warlock or wicchefolk who had somehow grown accustomed to the Tempest's usual splendour. Tonight, to celebrate All Hallows' Eve and the changing of the seasons, it was blinding in its beauty.

The theatre had become a grand ballroom, a richness to every aspect, from the high ceilings to the walls adorned with tapestries that depicted the six families at the helm of the Sorciety. The mirrorball wore a crown, orbs of its flames flickering in its reflection on a polished obsidian floor. The black glimmered with swirling movement, like a lake at night, symbols and shadows and faceless figures glowing faintly beneath the surface.

Tables were adorned with velvet tablecloths to match the drapes that veiled the windows, framing the silhouette of the park, which could just be seen through the thunderstorm that had finally broken. The only brightness came from the moon, a silver coin in the sky, perfectly circular in its pearlescence. It caught on fragile, ghostly cobweb decorations spun like silver thread and strung across the high ceilings. In a corner of the ballroom, an orchestra of spectral musicians played in front of a towering mirrored wall, giving the feeling that the space was infinite, like Annie might never leave, like it might hold her for ever.

Romily, Vivienne and Harmony were in the very centre of the hustle and bustle, enjoying their drinks but more so the pack of warlocks who seemed to have been pulled towards them like they had their own orbit. Annie politely excused herself through the crowd, leaving a trail of air kisses on various spellborn cheeks.

'So sorry I'm late,' she said breathily, flattening her skirts as she took her place beside them. All three of them took the time to examine her silently from head to toe, before shooting loaded looks at each other.

Romily's eyes trailed across Annie's dress. 'What is this?' Her normally serene face looked unusually pinched, as though she were straining to keep her features in place and under control. 'You were supposed to wear pink.'

'It is pink!' Annie gave them a self-conscious twirl, checking that the colour had remained how she'd intended. 'Of course it's pink. A little bit different but . . .' She faltered. 'Don't you like it?'

'I suppose it's fine,' Romily said tightly. 'If you like that sort of thing.'

'Maybe it is a bit much,' Annie said, suddenly wishing that she'd opted for something less eye-catching. Another wrong decision to chalk up with the rest. She folded her arms across her body, wishing that the gesture could make her shrink backwards, fade out to somewhere else.

'Since when do we not approve each other's dresses before a ball?' Harmony said to Vivienne, possibly intending it to be a private comment without actually lowering her volume in the slightest.

'Evidently, Miss Andromeda is feeling a little more confident in her own choices these days,' Vivienne said, eyes flashing in the candlelight. 'My, my. Things did change an awful lot while you were away, didn't they?'

Annie wasn't sure how to respond to that. She tucked her hair behind her ears, with an apologetic smile. 'I don't know what I was thinking. Sorry. It's all been a bit of a whirlwind since I got back. I'm not quite myself.'

'So we noticed,' Romily said, twirling the stem of her glass between her fingers.

'You all look sensational,' Annie said, practically tripping over herself to turn the focus away. It was amazing how quickly she'd fallen back into place next to the three of them. Her role had returned to her like a manuscript memorized.

'Quelle shock,' Vivienne said, as she turned her attention away to survey the room. 'Vintage Vespertine,' she added as an off-hand comment without even looking back.

Annie gasped, knowing the value of such a piece. In awe, she had to stop herself from reaching out to touch the buttery smooth silk that clung to Vivienne's frame and dripped around her like melted chocolate. Small capped sleeves fluttered at her shoulders, a string of black diamonds holding them together on an impossibly fine thread. She had paired it with a bangle in the form of a snake that slid its way around her right arm, its adder tongue flickering with a sparkling ruby before it descended back to her wrist. 'Exquisite,' Annie said, the admiration evidently audible, and Vivienne seemed momentarily placated by the compliment.

'What about mine?' Harmony chimed in as she shouldered forwards. Vivienne and Romily gave each other a look, Vivienne shooting across the circle to her side so that they could whisper. It was the one time that Annie always felt a genuine affinity to Harmony, when it was clear that there were tiers even within the Fortune Four.

'A little classier than yours, Annie, isn't it? Much more elegant,' Harmony preened, before realizing that she had perhaps gone too far. 'Not that yours isn't lovely, too.'

The affinity burst like a bubble.

Annie took a moment to admire Harmony's dress, an extremely dramatic affair that had all of the grandeur of Vivienne's, but not quite the effortlessness. Undoubtedly also expensive, the combination of orange silk, cascading in a floor-length bustled skirt, and the layer of glittering black lace beneath it was a little . . . Halloween. Granted, the corseted bodice was striking, as were the opera gloves and the enormous jewelled earrings. Annie could see that, in some ways, Harmony was trying just as hard as she was to compete for her place.

'Beautiful, Harm.'

Harmony looked pleased with Annie's assessment and promptly gathered herself around Annie's forearm in approval, leaning on her shoulder as though they were soulmates.

'Where's Ruby?' Annie asked, surveying the room for her. 'I thought she was coming tonight?' While she had only really felt determination to impress the Fortune girls and cement their favour, she had actually been looking forward to seeing Ruby with uncomplicated anticipation. Vivienne snorted and Annie frowned. 'Did I miss something?'

'With any luck, we shan't be seeing her again around here. The witch wears clogs, for stars' sake. I can't be seen near clogs,' Vivienne said before downing her drink, her tone so poisonous that it would have burned through the floor beneath them if it were to drip.

'Wait, what do you . . .' Before Annie could finish her train of thought, wondering what exactly Vivienne meant by that, Romily interrupted.

'Too right you're missing something, babe. What do you think of my dress?' Romily asked with an unflappable smile, picking up the train of her cape to ensure that it caught the light at just the right moment.

Romily was always the best dressed among them, but she had truly outdone herself tonight. The pale, champagne-coloured gown was finely glittered, a twirling design of leaves and tendrils that travelled their way around her body, with a precarious and plunging neckline. It was daringly form-fitting and had a sheer cream cape that cascaded from her shoulders to the floor. It was almost bridal, as though she were to marry magic itself.

'Rom, it's incredible. Belle of the ball.'

'I know,' Romily giggled, firing a wink back at Annie that felt so precious and earned that Annie wanted to grab at it and pocket it for herself.

This really was where she belonged, alongside these girls who had swept her up so long ago and shown her the way. This was the world that she was destined for. The sooner she accepted that and embraced it as best she could for everyone around her, the better.

There was one thing that would make all of this easier to slip back into, to quiet the tugging longing behind her ribs for something else.

Harmony beckoned to her and lifted Annie's hair, then leaned in closer. 'I have a secret,' she whispered excitedly, hiccoughing after finishing another glass of punch.

'Harm, we agreed that we weren't going to tell her. We were trying not to make her go all peculiar,' Vivienne said, tutting at their friend who was a sieve to secrets.

'Tell me what?'

'Mummy had a very important question for you. I'll let her know that you're here,' Romily said with a wink as she slipped away.

'You're the talk of the Sorciety, Annie,' Vivienne said knowingly, her voice plummy with information. She gestured with her black-tinted glass towards a tightly knit circle of witches and warlocks, the gilded snake sliding towards her hand as she moved. Annie recognized it as a gathering of the Heralds, the most important members of the Sorciety, including Glory Whitlock. Each of them were taking it in turns to peer at her. She was being discussed.

Annie swallowed hard. It was what she had been waiting for. It sparked something in her, though not necessarily joy or happiness. More of a gut-punch than a gentle squeeze. The reminder of the pressure to cement the fact that she truly belonged there, that she had earned her place, was a monstrous thing. It clung to her, made her gown feel ten times heavier, as though she needed to lift her hair from the back of her neck. She *had* to be perfect tonight. For them to accept her once and for all, for this all to be worth it. The pull towards *Splendidus Infernum* grew larger every moment, wrapping cold fingers around her arms. Perhaps it was impossible to exist within this world without the spell.

But this was finally it. She must have finally done enough. This was what she was supposed to have achieved.

Moments later, Romily reappeared with Glory on her arm, their mouths pursed in self-important pouts that hollowed their cheekbones. The Whitlocks all shared the same proud facial expression, a family who garnered admiration simply with their presence.

'Annie, darling.' Glory Whitlock made her way into the circle, a hypnotic and alluring forcefield seeming to waver around her. She held Annie at arm's length, before pulling her into a tight embrace. Annie exhaled, the bewitching feeling of something like a mother figure holding her in just the way that she needed.

'Glory,' Annie said in soft greeting.

'Word around the cauldron at symposium was that you've been doing us proud over at Selcouth, darling. A little errand for those Sage Witches at Hecate House, I hear? You should have come straight to me, Annie. Naughty thing.' Glory tapped her on the nose and winked at her in a way that so closely mirrored Romily, Annie found herself doing a double take. 'I simply must hear all about it.'

'We'll leave you two in privacy for a moment,' Romily said with a feline smile. She gave a small head nod to excuse herself, before Vivienne and Harmony immediately trotted behind her. Annie couldn't ignore the feeling that Romily was following an unspoken instruction.

'It's no mean feat to land yourself a role like that with Selcouth, Annie. As always, you continue to excel yourself. And I couldn't be prouder of you.'

Annie's heart gave a jolt. It was all she ever longed to hear, really. That she'd done right. Done just what she was supposed to do and someone was proud of her for it.

'You were always like a second daughter to me. And I don't know about you, but I suspect that that beautiful dress of yours would look even more sensational with a Crescent pin to accessorize it. It's only fair that we cash in a favour for all your hard work.'

Annie gasped. It was really happening. But none of it made any sense. She had clamoured and contended for this moment her whole life, ever since her father brought the prospect crashing down, but nothing had ever worked until now. Until this one, unsuspecting favour for the coven and a young girl.

'I'm so delighted, Glory, I really am. But I'm not quite sure what I've done to warrant it.'

'From what I hear, it sounds as though you may have identified a rude little hiccough for us to take a closer look at. Some young little thing from nothing and nowhere, who needs to be further examined?'

The world stopped moving. It was as though the sky had fallen and the earth had risen to meet it, claustrophobia binding Annie to the spot with a tight black ribbon. Panic bubbled in her throat, strangling her. This interest in Maeve from all sides . . . something wasn't right.

'Well don't look so surprised, Andromeda. You should know by now there's no such thing as secrets from the spellborn.'

'What do you want with her?' Annie dared to ask in a choked whisper. Everything else had sort of blurred backwards in Annie's vision, smeared around her. She had thought she had kept Maeve's talent hidden from the coven, from them.

'No need to make it sound so sinister, darling.'

'I . . . I'm afraid I can't help you, Glory,' Annie said, doing her best to maintain composure. 'I don't know where the coven have placed her. Wherever she is, she'll be safe and secure, as will her magic. It's under control now.'

At that, Glory scoffed. 'You have a lot of faith in a coven that continues to prove itself almost entirely useless. Not to worry, we have our methods of finding anybody we need to. I look forward to meeting her, intriguing little thing that she is. Could prove rather useful to us, my sources suspect, if she'd be interested in such a conversation. If not, well . . .' Glory grimaced.

Annie did her utmost to remain calm, even though it felt

like the thunderstorm outside was beginning to brew under her skin, too. She gave a breathy laugh with a dry smile, keen to underplay Maeve as much as she could to Glory. 'You've got this all wrong.'

As she often did, Glory reached out a tender hand to hold Annie's face – something Annie had always felt to be a caring, delicate gesture of affection for a second daughter of circumstance. But this time it felt different. She moved Annie's face left to right to guide it into the light, as though examining a chipped and spoiled vase and deciding how low to name her price. Her hand suddenly dropped.

'Need I remind you, Andromeda, of the . . . precariousness of your situation. Poor Romily and I have made great exception on your behalf, to keep you from being thrown away and forgotten altogether. It has not been easy to keep you in favour. And I should hope, if you are the girl I think you are, that you would understand. You owe us, Annie. And you will do what is required of you in return.'

Annie glanced behind Glory, noticing the tight circle of Heralds were all observing their conversation with great interest. She swallowed and did her level best to bring it to an end. She couldn't process the reality while Glory was standing so close by.

'I'm not sure who your sources are, Glory, but I think they may have their wands crossed. She's just a girl,' Annie laughed.

Glory peered intently at Annie, stony-faced with piercing purple-blue eyes. Annie was surprised to feel a sudden sense of palpable fury radiating from the Herald, as though it broke through a carefully restrained barrier.

'There is no such thing as "just a girl".'

Without excusing herself, Glory left Annie standing alone.

Reeling from the removal of such a powerful presence, Annie suddenly felt faint, as though she needed something to hold on to.

'How about we try some of those desserts?' Harmony interjected as she reappeared at Annie's side. 'I know I'm supposed to be on a sugar ban, but it is Samhain . . . Annie, those profiterole thingies sent from your bakery look frankly glorious.'

'Later, Harm. I just need to . . .' Annie was shaken. She couldn't think straight, couldn't hear her own thoughts. She felt unsafe, uncertain. She held her forehead, trying to stop herself from swaying. Was Maeve in trouble? Was *she* in trouble? Pressure clamped her temples. If she could just figure out the next right move . . .

'Actually, do you mind if we sit down?' Harmony interjected, looking slightly worse for wear in the ghostly ballroom light. 'Too much punch.'

It felt serendipitous. 'Of course, I need some air anyway,' Annie said, nodding in a haze as she guided Harmony to the edge of the ballroom and deposited her into a chair.

Chapter Twenty-Four

SERPENTS

Annie gathered up her skirts as she pushed through the throngs that flooded the dancefloor, a labyrinth of locked shoulders and sharp elbows. She broke through the crush and pushed open the theatre's rear saloon doors, gulping down a rush of cold air that cooled her bare shoulders. A long corridor, green walls lined with dark damask wallpaper and portraits of centuries of Sorciety members. Her heels clicking against the floor felt like ticking seconds, a countdown to match the beat of her quickening pulse.

She elbowed open the bathroom door and stopped short. 'Ruby?'

Ruby was slumped against the sinks, her knees pulled up to her chest, back rigid against the porcelain. Her hands were tightly clasped around her legs, head buried low. Annie was so taken aback by the sight that she had to consciously make her body move, to rush to Ruby's side. It was as though she'd been transported back to Arden Place, seeing Maeve in that exact fragile state, bundled up as small as she could make herself when she was afraid. But this was not Maeve. It was Ruby. Her friend, Ruby, who had, in the short time they had known each other, so often stood up for her and unwittingly acted as a shield. Tripping over her gown, Annie knelt in front of Ruby and grasped her shoulders.

'What is it? What's wrong?'

Ruby peered up from resting her forehead against her folded arms and glanced at Annie with swollen red eyes, mascara streaks staining her face in blotches. She rubbed her nose against the heel of her hand.

'This place, the pressure . . . I don't know how you do it, Annie.'

Annie struggled to understand. 'Do what?'

'The Sorciety. They're kicking us out – my family. Me, my brothers, my parents. They're throwing us away, like we don't even matter, and it's all my fault.'

Annie felt her heart plummet to somewhere around her guts, fires of empathy being stoked in the most ferocious way. She knew that feeling acutely well – the rejection, the questioning, the tender hurt. But there must be some mistake, for them to have decided that Ruby Wrathshade wasn't good enough? It made no sense. Ruby was one of the most vivacious, bright rays of sunshine that Annie had ever met. Her family were kind and humble and generous, keen to include everyone in the same ways that Ruby had with Annie.

Perhaps that was the problem.

'I couldn't care less what they think about me – never have, never will. But my parents? They just wanted to find their people, feel settled, and I've ruined that chance for them. How am I supposed to tell them? They'll be devastated,' Ruby said more quietly, barely able to make it to the end of the question before her words gave out to big, sorrowful sobs.

'I don't understand,' Annie said, shaking her head. 'How do

you know? And why would they expel you? You're . . . You're wonderful! Your whole family is wonderful.'

'Glory summoned me for a "delicate conversation",' Ruby said with added air quotes. 'Apparently someone told the Heralds I was disgracing myself, embarrassing Sorciety members. Not matching the standards that they expect the spellborn to exhibit. But . . .' she sniffed. 'I don't understand what I did wrong. I've just been myself.'

'Oh, Ruby,' Annie said, feeling her heart break in an identical, mirrored crack with Ruby's. She took a seat beside her on the floor, wrapping her up tightly so that she could rest her head on her shoulder. At least there had been a solid, tangible reason for Griffin and Cressida to be expelled. This was just plain snobbery and malice and judgement. 'You didn't do anything wrong, please don't think that you did.'

'Annie, I can trust you, right? We're friends?' Ruby, usually so certain in herself, so confident in her mannerisms and presence, so unfazed by the opinions of others, looked impossibly vulnerable as she asked the question. And something flipped in Annie as she saw it. The Sorciety was bringing out this exposed, sensitive part of a woman who, until she became an unwitting part of it, had probably never had to ask that question before. Annie hated them for it, for doing that to Ruby. It made her wonder what it had done to her, too.

'We're friends,' Annie said, giving Ruby a smile that she hoped was as reassuring as she could manage.

'I thought so,' Ruby said, returning the weak smile, wiping her nose again on her fluted sleeve. 'I don't know how to fix this for my family. There must be a way. They let you back in, right?'

Annie smoothed Ruby's hair, staring out at the bathroom.

'They did. But for how long this time? It's all so . . . superficial. So precarious. You can't make people like you, Ruby. That's a cold, hard truth that someone tried to teach me recently.'

'Well, that sucks.'

'Kind of,' Annie nodded. 'But the other side is that it makes the people who do like you, the ones who really understand you, feel like magic.'

Ruby was shaking her head, half-listening. '*Precarious*. What is it about that word? It comes up all the time around here. That's exactly right,' Ruby said, shaking her head. 'I've felt like I'm swimming upstream this whole time. I'm exhausted. It's damn awful.'

'It is. But the right people don't feel precarious,' Annie said. 'They feel solid and steady. They feel infinite.'

Hal flashed across her mind.

The bathroom door flew open and crashed into the wall behind it, so loud that Annie and Ruby both jumped. Romily, Vivienne and Harmony all stumbled in together, paused for a moment as they took in the scene and then promptly folded into fits of laughter. Romily was the first to compose herself, batting Vivienne, who promptly sent the gesture down the chain, smacking Harmony even harder.

'What in all the realms has happened in here?' Romily asked, unconvincing concern appearing on her face.

'Oh, darling Rubes, have they run out of finger food?' Vivienne said, pouting out her bottom lip.

'Annie, there you are! We were wondering where you'd gone, thought you might have fallen in,' Harmony added brightly, a slight slur to her words.

They writhed against one another, like snakes. The sheen of their glittered skin caught the chandelier candlelight so brightly it was as though they too were made of gleaming, immaculate glass.

Annie got to her feet, determinedly pulling Ruby up with her.

'Mummy finally broke the news, I take it,' Romily said, turning her attention straight to Ruby. 'Such a shame, we're all heartbroken, Ruby, honestly. But sometimes things just . . . don't work out.'

'Right,' Ruby said coldly.

'No hard feelings. Many witches have discovered that the Fortune Four have found them lacking. Most have lived to tell the tale,' Vivienne said, with a look so gleeful it burned Annie's skin.

'Speak for yourself. This is all news to me,' Annie replied. She didn't dare let any part of it show on her face, but she felt a deep-rooted anger take over everything else as she held Vivienne's gaze.

'Of course it is. Let me tell you, Annie, there's a lot that you don't know. You're not privy to as much as you think you are,' Vivienne hit back. 'You'd do well to remind yourself of that sometimes.'

'Oh shut *up*! It was you three, wasn't it? You're who had me thrown out,' Ruby shouted defiantly, although her voice cracked ever so slightly. It broke Annie's heart all over again and she tightened her grip around Ruby's shoulders. There had been no doubt in her mind who the 'somebody' had been who betrayed Ruby to Glory; the smug look on Vivienne's face confirmed it in crystal clarity. But Annie felt her friend stiffen at her side, as though forcing herself to stand taller. 'Of course it was. Y'know, the three of y'all are batshit bonkers.'

'Well, that's rude,' said Harmony, incredulous. 'What did we ever do to you?' She faltered. 'Oh, right . . . the frenemies thing.'

'If it had been up to me, we would never have fraternized with someone so bewilderingly vulgar in the first place. But philanthropy is a huge part of being *such* a good person, it's the least we could do. It's how Annie's stuck around like a bad smell, too,' Vivienne said, a lazy smirk draping itself across her lips.

'I can't stand to look at you three witches any longer,' Ruby grimaced. 'I'm out of here.' She rushed from the bathroom, shoving her way through Romily, Vivienne and Harmony.

'Ruby, wait . . .' Annie called.

All she could do was stare at them, astounded. It felt like standing face to face with three complete strangers. Perhaps they were. Perhaps she'd never known them at all, just a version of them that she had convinced herself of.

'Freak,' Vivienne cackled to Romily.

Suddenly Ruby was Maeve in the canteen all those weeks ago, and Maeve was Ruby, in all of her brilliant unique ways. Everything felt blurry. Annie could only identify a feeling of terrible, molten, defensive rage. She felt her magic crackle. It took everything in her to hold herself back, not to shove Vivienne in the chest, send her toppling into Romily. She could see their hierarchy of importance, one that she had always remained at the bottom of. It was a sharply contrasting relief to the fairness and patience and support that she had found herself held by at Arden Place.

She had suspected for a long time what her so-called friends were capable of. She had experienced bumps and scrapes from their impact her whole life. But seeing it so plainly felt like a bright, sharp, stinging slap.

She turned to Romily, trying to find a trace of her old friend, the younger version who was kind and compassionate and believed in something more than outward appearances.

'Rom, come on . . .'

Annie thought for one brief moment that a flash of something more passed behind Romily's brown eyes, but it was gone before she could even register it. 'If you don't keep up, you get left behind,' Romily said coldly. 'And you are trailing so far, far behind us all now, Annie. This . . .' – she gestured to the space across the room between them – '. . . well, I'm starting to wonder whether it's working any more.'

Vivienne spoke over her. 'Ruby's time is up, Wildwood. Careful you don't go the same way.'

'What's that supposed to mean?'

'The longer you remain on that side of the room, the longer we over here forget why it is exactly that you're still hanging by a thread of second, third and fourth chances,' Vivienne said.

'I didn't . . . I . . . I'm sorry.'

Annie could hear somebody apologizing with a quiet stutter, but none of them seemed to be talking. Romily's mouth was tightly sealed, Vivienne's brows were raised, Harm was distracted by her own reflection in the mirror opposite. It must be her own mouth; somehow she was the one apologizing. She was still saying sorry, atoning for the constant, blithe betrayal. The impulse was carved into her after all these years.

But, for the first time, she realized with fresh, furious clarity that she didn't mean a word of it.

'It's okay, Annie. You're always making so many silly mistakes, we're used to it,' Romily said gently. She stretched out an arm towards Annie, encouraging her to take her hand. 'Let's head back. We're missing the party!'

UNCHARMED

'C'mon, Annie, come and dance!' Harmony leapt across the room to tug at Annie's arm, but it fell limply to her side. Harmony returned to the pack like an uncertain animal.

'The party,' Annie nodded slowly, contemplating how everything could still be unfolding as normal just beyond the bathroom, while her whole intricate belief system fell apart. 'You want to return to the party. You want to pretend that everything is still perfect?' The volume of her voice rose of its own accord, until she was yelling by the end of the question.

Her hands flew up to her mouth, as though trying to cram the words back in. The earthquake sensation of her real, visceral anger and hurt felt so volatile, so unpredictable, and it seemed to be showing itself as such. Her shout made Harmony, Vivienne and Romily start, their brows shooting up to match one another. They shot each other an uncertain side-glance, unsure of the direction things were taking.

Annie reached for her composure and slipped it back on carefully like a silk robe. With a closed-eyed, serene breath, she returned her voice to softness. 'Why have you kept me around all these years?'

Romily giggled, then rolled her eyes when Annie didn't join in. 'I don't know what you could possibly mean. You're acting crazy. Imagining things.' As she shrugged, the glitter of her gown winked beautifully in the low lighting.

'I can't keep pretending that all of this is normal and okay,' Annie said. 'Keep pretending that you're not going to do the same to me as you have to Ruby, as soon as I put a foot wrong. Pretending, pretending, pretending. I can't do it any more.'

She looked up at Romily with pleading eyes. There had to be a sign that the girl she'd once known was still in there somewhere.

'Everyone else seems okay. Why are you the only one who's upset? We love you, Annie. You know that.' Romily reached out to hold her hand again, more insistent this time. Annie stared at it blankly, as though her own body part was disconnected from her. She willed her heart to sing as it normally would when Romily showed her any care. She willed it to feel better in that familiar, easy way. But this time it didn't.

'You're going to get rid of me, too, aren't you? When I refuse to help with whatever's going on with your mother and her fascination with Maeve Cadmus.'

Silence fell.

'Ah, and the penny drops into the cauldron with an almighty *thunk*,' Vivienne said with an eye-roll.

'Viv,' Romily said with a warning tone.

'Oh, give it up, Romily. I'm sick of this preening, pathetic conversation when there's a dancefloor full of warlocks waiting to be played with.'

Annie tried again, fists clenched. 'What does your mother want with her?'

Vivienne glared. 'You'd do well to ask fewer questions, Wildwood. The Sorciety has an exceptional talent for making people . . . vanish, should they stop proving useful.' Annie faltered. 'Heard from Mummy recently?' Vivienne asked, a fraction quieter, letting the leading question linger in the air.

Romily walked to the sink and slid herself up onto the countertop, gliding like water, then turned back to the mirror. She began to fix her tiara with a glimmer of magic. 'Annie, don't ask questions that you don't want to know the answer to, babe.'

'Tell me!' Annie shouted again.

Romily flinched, but this time she shouted back. 'I don't

know, okay?' She leapt to her feet again and approached Annie slowly, as though creeping up on prey. 'For one reason or another, my mother is utterly fascinated with you and your little loser friend. And yet here you are, even still, desperately flapping around in circles. *Poor me, poor me!* That's just like you to be so selfish!'

Romily's pouring confession was so sudden and forceful. Every word that came from these three witches was so weaponized, that the gentle quiet that filled the bathroom afterwards felt ill-fitting, incomplete. Annie supposed that this must be the space her anger was supposed to fill, but even then she couldn't summon it fully. It was like an engine that needed jump-starting, but she didn't have the strength.

Perhaps because she knew it was pointless, because this was always going to be the outcome sooner or later. She had known that, one day, she would take a wrong turn on her carefully laid course and uncover ugly, indisputable proof that none of these people truly cared for her. That none of them ever considered her further than what she might be able to provide in a one-sided exchange. She did her best not to be selfish, to never say no – even when she really, really wanted to. And all it had resulted in was being liked as far as she could be used. She was only ever what she could provide to them. Romily, Vivienne, Harmony, Cressida, the Sorcicty . . . None of them loved her.

But there were others who did. She was lucky enough that that was true.

'I wish it hadn't taken this long for me to realize it,' Annie said to herself.

'Realize what?' Vivienne said stroppily, jutting a knee as though she were bored.

Annie inhaled a small laugh. 'There is no amount of perfect in the world to please you, is there?'

The confession strung itself in the dim light like a constellation. Once she held it up in place, it shone brighter. She could see it there in front of her, the words real and important.

'You will never, ever know how high I tried to leap for you. All of you. You existed on pedestals for me, while I laid down and let you trample the parts of me that deserved to be up there just as much as you did. And why? For what? To feel as though there are wild dogs nipping at my heels for the rest of my life? As though one little trip or stumble will end the race and see me savaged?'

'Don't you think you're being a little dramatic?' Romily snarled.

'Dramatic?' Annie said calmly, a new glitter in her eyes.

The silence cascaded again as though someone had thrown a sheet of silk above them, the perfect quiet billowing. And, of all the times and places to think of in that moment, Annie found her mind rewinding back to her walk in the woods with Maeve, when they had been searching for Karma. She knew what Maeve – clever, strong Maeve – would want her to do.

'Be careful what you wish for, Romily.'

Annie took a deep breath. She balled up her fists, threw back her head and felt a noise erupt from her so brilliantly and wildly that it could have ripped her throat raw. She screamed, really screamed. Her rage scorched, a siren wail that was horrid and high-pitched, oscillating and . . . fantastic. Imperfect, ugly and free.

Before she could stop it, her magic reflected it all back from inside her to out. Intensity like this erupting from a witch would always show itself in her powers, too. Annie was volcanic, her magic white-hot and scalding. The stuff crackled between her fingertips as she screamed. Before she could even process or control the need to stop it, magic flew from her palms in blasts of kinetic energy. It had been pent up inside her, held under for so long that it was fit to burst as it came up to the surface. This was a lifetime of trying. The mirrored walls of the room cracked just as her voice did and then burst into shards.

Ribbons of glass cascaded through the air. Romily, Vivienne and Harmony flung their arms over their heads to take cover from the blast. Annie buckled, running out of breath, eyes streaming and hair wild as she stumbled against the bathroom wall.

Eventually, the last piece of glass tinkled unsteadily, then tumbled onto its side with a final note.

That was enough.

Annie inhaled deeply and a small, shy smile tugged up one side of her lips.

She let out a satisfied sigh. 'That felt good.'

Romily carefully rose to her feet, a disgusted, thunderous look in her eyes as she stumbled in her broken heels and ruined, shredded dress.

'Ew!' Harmony shouted.

'You lunatic!' Vivienne screeched.

'You could have killed me, Annie!' Romily yelled, livid.

'Don't you think you're being a little dramatic, darling?' Annie asked, smiling. 'It's just a little bit of a mess. You can fix this one for yourselves.'

Chapter Twenty-Five

MAGIC ALIGHT

Leaving everybody else to pick up the pieces, entirely literally, Annie gathered up her skirts and tore through the ballroom. She pushed aside Sorciety members and Heralds alike, for once with no regard for their opinion, no concern for what they thought as she ran in a blur of pink, smudged make-up and tousled hair. They would get over it. In a century or two. In fact, Annie knew all too well that the spellborn would be delighted to have more gossip about the Wildwoods to gorge on; the older matters were starting to grow stale. It was exactly what they had been waiting for, another chance to undo her seams like a ragdoll, and she was happy to oblige if it meant she never had to return to their greedy hold again.

Annie emerged from the Tempest Theatre and stumbled into torrential, bone-soaking rain. It fell in relentless sheets across the blur of Richmond Park. The Samhain Ball always brought fierce storms with it, the result of so much concentrated, high-level magic in one confined space. In previous years, she had revelled in the enchantment of it all, hypnotized by the feeling of being swept up in stardust, but tonight Annie couldn't leave it all behind quickly enough. Billowing, glittering skirts trailed in her wake as she tore through the park and through the storm, traipsing a pathway of mud behind her until she had run far enough that she could be confident no one was following.

She took a moment to catch her breath. Despite herself, a longstanding, deeply rooted part of her had still hoped that Romily might be running right behind, ready to spin her around and tell her what a terrible mistake she'd made by abandoning her for the others, how she should have chosen Annie all along. But that would never come. And it wasn't what she really longed for. Neither the apology, nor the sorry excuse for a friendship mattered.

Her heart had a home already. There were two people who *had* chosen her.

Annie fell against a stout oak tree and took shelter under its sprawling, knotted branches, a respite from the rain that was starting to flood the park. Her dress was sopping wet, her hair clinging to her face in ribbons, water droplets falling from her eyelashes and between her lips. She gasped for breath, wiping her face with the back of her hand that was equally soaking. She hadn't considered when she'd burned all of her bridges back there in such a vehement blaze that she would need a next move. She hadn't been thinking very much at all, until now.

She had to get to Maeve and keep her safe from what she now knew for certain was bad news. But for that she would need help.

Annie knew exactly where she wanted to go. The problem was . . . Well, there were several problems, but the most pressing was that she had no real idea of how to get there. Normally, transference required at least coordinates or a fixed location in mind, but Morena had never quite explained exactly where to find it. Annie could only hope that her magic would take the lead and complete a rather rickety transferral spell on her behalf.

A lightning bolt streaked its way across the night sky, a brilliant, definite white line. She had to be quick. It wasn't safe to be out in the open. Annie stepped back into the rain, tilting her head to feel the cold fall onto her face.

She called out into the air. 'Please, please. Magic, if you're listening. I need help. I need help,' she repeated, adjusting to the sound of the unfamiliar words. 'Take me to Arden Place. Please.' Annie could barely hear herself over the sound of the pouring rain slamming onto the treetops, even though she was shouting. 'I have to go home.'

She should have known that she could always trust her own magic. A witch's instinct was one of her greatest assets. Not only could hers fix things for others, but it could fix things for her, too. Annie felt her feet lift from the sodden ground, so wet and slippery that they slid right out of the crystal high heels that she had carefully selected for the ball. In the middle of the storm, the pink witch, alone in the park, vanished. Only the shoes remained behind, then a bright bolt of lightning struck them so precisely that they shattered.

Annie collapsed in a heap of soaked tulle, the weight of the water-logged skirts sending her balance askew. She huffed, shoving her hair out of her face and finding a streak of black mascara across the back of her hand when she pulled it away. This was all highly unglamorous and not how she would have imagined this moment occurring. Not that she had dared to let herself picture ever coming back.

UNCHARMED

There was the cottage across the meadow, just as she had left it, although distinctly more rain-soaked tonight, the wet grass clinging to her skirts and leaving filthy sketches on the tulle. A plume of determined smoke rose through the chimney despite the rain, the scent of burning firewood just about noticeable against the damp outdoors. Annie tried to decide whether that was a silhouette she could see behind those damned gingham curtains. Now that she had brought herself here, magic ablaze, the anger and passion was diluting to uncertainty. Fear that this had been the wrong idea. Because if it was, she wasn't sure what came next. There was only one place that she wanted to find herself, that might be a safe enough place to try to put her heart back together and begin again.

Cautiously, she made her way to the porch, trudging her torn dress through the mud. Towards the golden glow that was radiating through the window panes, reflecting on each rain drop like the meadow's own sparks of magic. A lighthouse, guiding her to safety after being lost at sea for such a long time. She felt detached from her body, could feel her bare feet sinking into the wet earth, sending splashes up her legs, and then the firm, familiar smoothness of the porch planks beneath her toes. The sound of the beating rain had grown louder, resounding against the thatched roof. She reached the front door, took a fortifying single breath and held it.

She was here. She was real.

It felt as though the world had stopped spinning as she raised a hand to knock.

Before she had the chance, the door flew open.

Her voice cracked. 'I had to come home.'

The moment hung between them, as though the universe

had glitched, like the air itself had become a solid thing that couldn't be moved and was waiting for them to decide what came next.

'You belong here, you know,' he said quietly.

Annie nodded. 'I know.'

Hal took a step towards her. Lit by the pearlescent moon behind the rain and the warm glow that tumbled out of the cottage, he moved slowly, to hold her face tenderly between his hands. She saw him swallow, his jaw visibly tense as he gently cupped her chin, lifting her face a fraction to meet his in the light, as though he had just uncovered a great treasure that he didn't quite trust to be real. Where he touched her, a crackle of his bronze magic sparked and hissed as it made contact with the rain. Backlit in the doorway, Annie could see his pulse hammering at the base of his throat. His breathing had turned heavy, chest rising and falling underneath his soft linen shirt. Another burst of visible, physical magic surged between them, sparks leaping from his bare skin onto hers and her own reciprocating, leaving behind tiny bursts of smoke and heat, embers in the rain.

Then, all at once, the fire caught.

The fragile calm of the moment was gone the moment their lips touched. Hal swept her up, gathering her as close as he possibly could, cutting the infuriating distance between them in one swift move and holding her in arms that felt as though they enveloped her body completely and weren't willing to let go. As though he'd decided to hold on to her for good, before she disappeared in front of his eyes again. It was lucky that his forearm was wrapped around her waist so tightly – Annie felt her knees buckle and her back arch as her whole body surged towards his. Her magic flared at the contact that she had been silently wishing on stars for since the first time he'd shown her his unwavering kindness.

'I missed you,' she managed to breathe out.

Their powers, alive and charged, coiled around them like invisible vines. Like climbing foxgloves and blooming dahlias, tendrils of static and sparks encased them as Annie's whole body hummed in response to his strong, charmed touch. She hoped that he could feel it, too, but the way his fingers tightened around a handful of her dress confirmed as much. Hal's hands pushed through her soaked hair, moving it away from her face so that his lips could cover every part of it, as though he were trying to kiss away each drop of rain. His lips travelled along her jaw, down her neck with ragged breath, back up to her mouth in a way that felt fitting against an October thunderstorm. The air around them shimmered like a heatwave, a mirage of magic flaring from witch to warlock and catching reflections, turning raindrops to fireflies.

Life was so beautiful when she let chaos take hold, even just for a fleeting moment.

Finally, Annie tore herself away to catch her breath, although she was fairly certain that she'd sacrifice something as unimportant as air to keep existing in that one moment.

'Are you even real?' Hal asked hoarsely, a haze across his eyes.

Annie laughed and nodded shyly. 'I think so. Are you?'

'Not sure,' he said. 'I've dreamed about this too much to know.'

She laughed again, suddenly self-conscious in a deliciously sweet way, both of them breathless with bright, wild eyes. He pulled her back to him with a kiss that was a fraction more gentle this time, less frantic but no less consuming. She could feel the care and concern behind it, just as passionate as the want and the need of the first.

Without breaking the kiss and while keeping an arm locked firmly around her waist, Hal spun them around and guided them over the threshold of the cottage with a stumble. He kicked the front door behind him, before crashing back against it and bringing her with him.

'Are you cold? You must be cold,' he murmured against her lips, voice thick with want. They stepped together, Annie lifting Hal's shirt away from his waistband to slide over his hipbones, making him hiss with her icy hands.

'Not any more.'

In the flurry of thoughts of Hal and home and heart, Annie wondered how she'd ever move on from that feeling. Maybe she never would. It would hold her for ever. Intoxicating in its equal parts of comfort and passion combined. How lucky they were to have found one another, to care so deeply and safely and to feel it returned in a way that set magic alight.

Chapter Twenty-Six

THE WEIRDEST THING

'I must look awful,' Annie laughed. She hurried to wipe the dark mascara trails from her cheeks, then immediately regretted it as she saw the sooty marks all over the sleeve of Hal's shirt that she had thrown on.

Hal gave a gruff '*hmm*' and leaned back against the arm of the sofa. He squinted down at her with one eye open. 'You were beautiful the minute I first saw you and you're beautiful now. If it's possible, you're even *more* beautiful now.' He brushed his thumb over her shoulder where the shirt had slipped.

She shook her head. 'I was immaculate a few weeks ago, now look at me.'

'Oh, I am very much looking at you, trust me. Maybe I'm biased to this moment because you're not threatening to kill me with a wooden spoon, I don't know.'

'The threat remains,' Annie said. 'At all times.'

She was lying with her head on his chest as though one had been made to fit the other, the same way that she had woken up that morning they had shared the bed. But this time she didn't have to run away. One of the blankets that she'd conjured all the way back on her first evening at Arden Place was draped over her. Now that her senses were slowly coming back, Annie noted that many of the touches that she had removed before she left had subtly returned. Perhaps her spell had unknitted . . . There were considerably more muddy boots by the door, several half-read open books lying around, horse paraphernalia discarded in inexplicable locations, but they were alongside her soft additions, the prettier parts. There was even a photograph that Maeve had taken of the three of them with Mage and Karma, in a small wooden frame on the mantlepiece. It all seemed to fit together, a lived-in, loved home. The feeling was made ten times bigger with the soundtrack of the crackling fire that Hal had conjured into the hearth. Annie had been unable to resist casting her own magic to add the scent of molten marshmallows to the room alongside the smoky wood. It smelled just like Hal.

She spoke quietly. 'I'm sorry. There's so much I need to tell you.'

'No "sorry"s. I want you to want to share your problems with me, Annie, rather than think of me as your last resort. Like I said before, we make a good team.'

'I do want to, I swear. This is all just very new, as a concept. I'm used to taking care of things myself,' she replied.

'Try me,' Hal said sincerely, raising himself up a little. 'Where do we start?'

'With . . . a spell,' Annie chanced, resting her chin on his chest and looking up at him. 'My spell.'

Hal's eyes pinched as he regarded her for a strange, quiet moment, then he let out a sigh of relief. He pushed his tumbling hair away and a twitch of a smile crept over his lips as he leaned back again. 'About time we finally talked about that.'

Annie blinked. 'Talked about what?'

'Your spell? The bathtub thing.'

Annie was fairly certain her heart had stopped beating altogether.

'I knew that something was afoot, the moment I laid eyes on you,' Hal said with a deep sigh and a hazy look, as though he were recalling the memory. 'Someone blew the door off my house and I walked in to find a princess and a little demon hiding behind my couch. I could sense that there was some supernatural stuff hanging around you, more than just the average witchery. Always been good at sensing when undisclosed magic's afoot. Think it comes from working with animals, who are generally a lot more straightforward than wicchefolk, but . . .'

He had known. Annie had assumed this whole time that Hal had been under the spell as much as anybody else. That her perfection had at least an early part to play in his patient, tender reactions towards her annoying ways. That it had to be the main reason for his unusual displays of kindness and tolerance. Even later, she had believed deep down that his feelings had only ever been some kind of residual effect from *Splendidus Infernum*. An enchanted obligation to stick around.

'You knew?'

'Sort of pieced it together,' he grumbled, a little self-conscious of the revelation. 'Took a lot of research to find out whether something like what I had in mind could even really exist. That's where I used to disappear off to when you were helping the kid, a lot of reluctant visits to Hecate House to use the library after I'd fed Mage. Told Morena I was thinking about embarking on a trip to the Outer Hebrides to hold a meet with mermaids. Not sure she bought it. Told me I was behaving like a . . . What was her phrase? "Lovesick nitwit", I believe.' A flush of pink spread across the tops of his cheeks above his beard.

'The night that Maeve was so upset, you rushed into the cottage so quickly to look after her that you forgot to drain the tub. First, I tripped over a load of invisible potion ingredients and then I saw the colour of it. Thought it had to be either an injured animal or . . . Pretty much confirmed my findings that such a potion really was possible. Didn't work on me though, did it? Never did. For . . . obvious reasons,' he said, gruff but soft. 'Thought you were perfect right from the get-go,'

'I . . .' Annie choked on the words, shaking her head, too moved and embarrassed to say much more. 'I don't know where to even begin with telling you about it.'

'Well . . .' Hal said hesitantly, a jolt of magic snapping inside his palm at the contact as he lifted her chin and leaned down to kiss her. 'We have time.'

Annie could feel her eyelids getting heavy, her whole body giving way to crash after crash of adrenaline. But she couldn't let sleep win yet. Returning to Arden Place had been a distraction, but ensuring Maeve's safety was her utmost priority.

'There's something else. Well, a lot more else, actually. But I think . . .' She swallowed hard, daring herself for truths that felt impossibly wild. 'I think I'm in danger, and Maeve, too.'

Hal frowned. The rain was drumming a murmur onto the thatched roof and the fire popped impatiently. The knocking sound of a woodpecker tapped against the side of the cottage as she steeled herself to tell him everything.

The knocking persisted.

It got louder, more solid. Annie shot upright, grabbing the

blanket to cover herself. She glanced back down towards Hal, whose brow had furrowed deeply.

'Are you expecting someone?'

'No,' he said uncertainly, tugging his T-shirt back on as he swung his legs over the side of the couch. 'But I also wasn't expecting to find a soaking wet, star-crossed princess on my doorstep tonight – and here we are. Stay there,' he said, his voice firmer with the last request.

He headed to the front door and, as Annie quickly conjured herself some jeans, she saw him steel himself a little to open it. It was the dead of night, the petrichor of the storm still clinging to the pitch-black sky. She couldn't blame him for being uneasy at the prospect of an unexpected visitor. Her own heartbeat began to quicken again with a sudden dread. Someone had followed her. Glory or Romily or anyone else from the Sorciety could have stalked her all the way here to find out where she'd run away to. The Sorciety wasn't something that you could just leave, turn your back on without repercussions. And they were full of sinister curiosity about her time at Arden Place. Annie shivered, despite the roaring fire. She should have told Hal straight away, should have broached the subject of the Sorciety with him weeks ago, confessed to *Splendidus Infernum* and every other messy part of her history. But that was like pulling at the end of a ball of yarn – it would unravel quicker than she could fathom. Hal threw open the door, his whole body tense and poised protectively.

'Well, can I come in or what?'

Annie let out something between a squeal and a shriek.

Maeve stood expectantly with her brows indignantly high, waiting impatiently for an answer as though Annie and Hal should not have been surprised to find her sopping wet on the doorstep, suitcase levitating next to her. She shook out the ends of her long coat sleeves, sending a splattering of dirty water in every possible direction.

Annie rushed to the doorway and practically snatched her up, squeezing the young, dripping wet witch into an impossibly tight hug, ignoring how soggy her clothes and Hal's shirt became in the process. At first, Maeve held herself rigid, still angry, a thoroughly peeved look stitched into her dark brows. But a moment later she relented, allowing herself to be held, and her arms flew around Annie in return.

'How in the universe did you get here?' Annie said breathlessly.

'Enchanted my suitcase with a copy of that navigation spell you used in the woods the day we met. Why did you even have a briefcase, anyway? And will you get off me?' Maeve said, her voice muffled by Annie's shoulder. Annie finally released her, but only so she could hold the girl by the shoulders and get a proper look. Panic suddenly overtook the joyful surprise.

'What's wrong?' Annie asked, feeling her senses spike and her grip tighten. The spell was long drained from her system, that much was evident by the way that her life had somewhat imploded. But her instincts towards Maeve were no softer. She could sense that Maeve was holding onto a secret. Annie felt its enormity, like an anchor slung around Maeve's neck.

Maeve, of course, just shrugged, which was answer enough. Annie ushered her inside, fussing with her wet coat and hair that left a dripping trail through the cottage.

'Good job I'm not precious about this place. Look at the

state of you,' Hal said grumpily, hands firmly lodged in his pockets. But he couldn't hide it, his voice softened as Maeve burst towards him in an uncontrolled, slightly flailing hug. Hal gave a half-smile down at the top of her head. 'Hey, kid.'

Suddenly aware of her mortifying burst of affection, Maeve broke free and took a step back, pushing up her glasses and tucking her hair behind her ears. She looked up at them both, trying to assess their true reaction to her arrival. A moment later, she frowned, eyeing up Annie in Hal's shirt. 'Why are you wearing that?'

Her mouth dropped open once the calculation was complete.

'Oh, pur-lease do not tell me I have just walked in on you two . . . getting it on,' Maeve said, grimacing.

'Maeve! Absolutely not. I got here moments before you did,' Annie said, her voice wandering into a high octave of embarrassment as she ushered the girl towards the kitchen. She conjured a fluffy towel into her left hand and wrapped up Maeve's hair into a pile on top of her head. Maeve promptly shoved it off and an effortless incantation dried her hair into its normal sleek, straight style.

'Thank the universe for that. I don't mind you two being together. In fact, it's about time you figured it out. But I absolutely forbid you getting it on while I'm in a two-mile radius of the house. Understood?'

'We're under the Cadmus dictatorship already, are we?' Hal asked, leaning against the staircase with folded arms. 'You've only just got here.'

'No time for that now, pirate cowboy,' Maeve muttered as she unceremoniously dumped her backpack on the dining table. 'We need to talk.'

'Is that right? Maeve, why do I get the feeling that nobody knows you're here?' Annie asked.

'All in good time, my friend. Can I get a cup of coffee? I've thought about that maple blend probably five times a day since we all went our separate ways. And it's been a long night. Transference really takes it out of you, doesn't it?'

'Did you . . .' Realization dawned on Annie's face. 'Did you transfer here unsupervised? Maeve Cadmus, you know that you are not allowed to do that without an elder witch conducting the spell on your behalf,' she said crossly.

Maeve scoffed. 'I think a slap on the wrist from the coven is probably the least of our problems right now. Any biscuits to go with that coffee?'

Annie rolled her eyes, then headed over to the kitchen. There was some unbaked ginger and chocolate-chip cookie dough that she'd prepared for the morning, currently unattended in the Celeste kitchen. The bravery-laced brown butter that she'd used in the mixture might help to encourage Maeve to tell the truth about whatever it was that she had come back to them for.

'Maeve,' Hal said sincerely. 'For once in your life, don't be smart. No pirate jokes or cowboy puns when I ask you this. I need a straight answer from you, because we care about you above all else.'

Maeve only tugged at her sleeves, earning a resigned sigh from Hal.

'Are you in danger, kid? Do we need to be worried?'

Maeve chanced a look back at him, knocked by his sincerity. She opened her mouth as though trying to figure out whether to give an honest answer, but then promptly closed it again. 'I'm not sure. Maybe.'

'What in the universe happened at the foster home?' Annie

called from the kitchen as the cookie dough arrived in a flourish of magic. With another, sparks falling like pastel-coloured sprinkles across the tray, the cookies rose, bloomed and baked instantly, bringing a warming scent of ginger with them. Annie scurried back to the table, heart racing.

Maeve began to fiddle with the petals of the pale blue hydrangeas that had been unceremoniously shoved into one of her old paint water jars in the middle of the table, a perfect, visual combination of the three of them. She kicked a muddy boot against the skirting board. Her reply was barely more than a mumble, but she was hiding a smile.

'The weirdest thing happened. Their curtains caught on fire.'

Once an appropriate number of cookies had been inhaled by all three inhabitants of Arden Place – and once its fourth had been summoned in a cloud of fur and whiskers – Annie steeled herself for a serving of tough love. She could sense that what Maeve required in that moment was belief, support and a promise that she would be taken seriously.

'We made a deal. Biscuits from me, the truth from you,' said Annie.

'And what does Hal bring to the table?' Maeve said sulkily.

'I seem to remember this was my house at one point,' Hal answered with a scowl. 'Although maybe I'm mistaken. Feels impossible to imagine it now without you two here, taking over my life.'

Annie noted that the latter part, which was probably intended to be a dig, sounded much more pleased than grumpy. Karma must have noted it, too. She gave him a *mrow* that might as well have been accompanied by an 'oh please', before she dismissively returned to grooming her exceptionally tufty ears.

'We're waiting,' Annie said to Maeve, sounding a little too authoritative for her liking. She softened her tone. 'What did I say when we first met? You can tell me anything.'

Maeve frowned harder. 'You're not going to like it.'

'I very rarely like anything you have to say and you're still here drinking all the coffee, aren't you?' Hal said. He nudged the plate of cookies over in Maeve's direction. She chewed thoughtfully for a minute while Annie and Hal exchanged increasingly worried glances over the top of her head.

'I made contact.'

Annie blinked. 'With who?'

Maeve looked miffed. 'The spirit. You know, the one that was haunting me day in, day out? The voice and the presence and all that other cool, slightly creepy stuff.'

'Maeve! What have I told you about dabbling in Necromancy?'

'I know, I know, keep your hair on. But at least hear me out before you completely flip your lid.'

Annie huffed. 'I thought that problem had improved once we talked about it?' It dawned on her that, even without the hex nearby each night, summoning spirits to haunt Maeve's deepest and darkest dreams, this particular presence was still evidently determined to remain close by. There might be good reason for it.

'It did, for a bit. But then it didn't. And I know what you're going to think, but something inside of me – that witch instinct that you're always banging on about – I just knew that I had to speak to them. Her. I knew that she had something to tell me.'

Annie faltered at this new detail. 'She?'

Maeve nodded.

Annie tried to jump from one logical stepping stone to the next.

'And what did she have to say for herself, then, this mystery spirit?'

'Well, that's the problem.' Maeve hesitated, frustrated. 'My intuition felt like it was on fire from the minute I left this place. I thought the presence was strong while I was here, but the first night I found myself on my own again, she followed me – and it was like everything was flashing red. Like she had a warning for me. I knew I needed to talk to her, that she had something to tell me. So I tried to make it happen, but I couldn't hold up the necromancy spell. I tried to follow the instructions in my grimoire, but the connection kept dropping. I had no clue what I was even trying to do.'

'You're telling me you've never had a casual chat with a haunted spirit before, kid? Sounds very unlike you.' Maeve shot Hal a look and he pulled a face back.

'I think . . . I think she's trying to tell me I'm in trouble,' Maeve finished uncertainly.

'Then we need to speak to her. Properly,' Hal said, slapping his thighs decisively. 'We've all learned that your intuition is something that shouldn't be taken lightly. So this is something we can orchestrate. Together.'

'And what are you proposing, exactly? A seance?' Annie squeaked as he rose.

The idea was entirely preposterous. She had always firmly believed that no good could come from that kind of sinister magic. She had experienced it for herself, dragged under in a sweeping sea of *Splendidus Infernum*. It had brought her nothing but heartbreak.

'Well, why not? The kid has already made contact, she's opened up the gate to whatever or whoever this spirit is. And they're not going to leave her alone until we figure out what their problem is. In fact, this spirit girl is probably already here,' Hal said, so casually that Annie felt like throwing her biscuit at his head.

'Absolutely not,' she said firmly, slicing the air. 'Out of the question.'

'But that's why I'm here, that's why I came back – for you to help me get it right. It's Halloween! The timing is fate,' Maeve said, her voice whining as she stamped her finger onto the table for emphasis.

Annie frowned, realizing that, yes, perhaps Maeve was right about that, as usual . . . But it wasn't as simple as that. She grasped at any possible reason as to why this would all be a terrible idea.

'Even if we wanted to,' Annie tried, 'we would need some kind of imagery or beloved connection to the spirit to guarantee success. A photo, an object . . . Seances never work properly without some kind of identifiable tie to the spirit – and we don't even know who she is. You can't just open up a random connection, Maeve. I understand you might like the idea of a ghosty gal pal, but . . .'

'It's her.' Maeve blurted it out. She promptly began to chew on the inside of her cheek, as though she regretted saying it out loud. Hesitantly, Maeve reached under the dining table to unzip her backpack and pulled out the fullest sketchbook of her collection. She dropped it onto the table with a thud that sent Karma's ears scooting back. She flicked through the pages, reams and reams of the same sketches, over and over.

The dark-haired girl she had drawn.

'That's who's been trying to talk to me,' Maeve said. 'That's why I've been trying to draw her for such a long time. I've always been able to see her in my mind, then it got stronger when my magic kicked in. I've spent ages trying to piece her face together as she's become more in focus for me. Then it all got sharper and clearer when we came to Arden Place and I saw her. I need to speak to her.'

Annie faltered. She had assumed the girl was a crush from school, maybe a book character that Maeve had a soft spot for. But this was the spirit who had, for one reason or another, chosen Maeve as her conduit.

The sketches had become even more detailed, more realistic over time, until the most recent rendered like a photographed portrait through Maeve's artistic talent. As she examined them more closely, a new suspicion began to creep in for Annie. It couldn't be possible . . . could it?

'Well, this is all very intriguing, isn't it?' Annie said, shaking her head effusively even as her cheeks began to turn red. 'But, young witch, if you think I am allowing you to hold your very first seance at fifteen years old for an unidentified, troubled phantom, I think you'll find that you are very much mistaken.'

An hour later, Hal and Annie were preparing as best they knew how for a young witch to hold her very first seance at fifteen years old for an unidentified, troubled phantom.

Chapter Twenty-Seven

INCOMING CALL

Hal had moved the dining table into the middle of the cottage, shoving the sofa aside (while Karma clung on with her claws) to make sure they had plenty of room. Annie wasn't sure for what entirely, but she suspected he just wanted to keep them safe as best he could and was kidding himself that 'room' would make any kind of difference when dabbling in communication with the dead.

Distracting herself from mountainous worry by making something look pretty was Annie's specialist subject, so she had conjured up a handful of extra sorcery regalia to complete the scene. A rich green velvet cloth was now draped over the table, stars and moons stitched into the tasselled hems. She had filled the cottage with candles across every possible surface, transformed the flames in the fireplace to an amethyst purple and had even switched out the gingham curtains for dark, heavy drapes, with a promise to Hal that they'd change them back the moment it was over. With a few scarves thrown over the lamps, Annie had to admit that, despite her fears, it looked just right for Halloween.

She had also, of course, provided suitable outfits for the

occasion. Hal had outright refused the smudge of black eyeliner that Annie had promised would darken his whole look, but had reluctantly accepted the fact that he would join the girls in wearing his coven cloak for a sense of formality. Annie had opted for a patchwork dress of pinks and purples, a little lavender woven into her braid for a dash of luck and calm. She insisted that Maeve at least tuck a small bunch into her scrunchie. While Hal and Maeve set about digging out an old crystal ball that he swore was in the shed somewhere, Annie threw together a simple dress for Maeve, black with giant bell sleeves. She strung a handful of lucky silver charms around the waist like a belt – a tiny artist's pencil, a stack of books, a star – and she hoped Maeve would find the poignancy in a little silver flame as the finishing touch.

The two witches – one eager, one apprehensive – and the warlock – ever-vigilant – sat at the table, all highly unsure of what they were about to enter into. Their faces glowed in the candlelight, a sheen from the fireplace highlighting the shadows in the cottage and turning them purple. In the centre of the table, Hal placed a dusty crystal ball and polished it up with the end of his sleeve, its surface swirling with the faintest wisps of smoke. Seeing them triggered something in Annie, their hypnotizing motion reminding her so strongly of being swept up in *Splendidus Infernum* that she had to look away.

'So what do we do?' Maeve asked, eager eyes wide behind her glasses, which reflected little glowing orbs from the candles. She shuffled her chair in closer to the table until her ribs were pressed tightly up against it, peering as closely as she could into the crystal ball.

'We start by placing our palms onto the table,' Annie said calmly. If they were going to do this, she would at least ensure that it was by the book, following every rule possible – a good girl's seance. 'And our fingertips need to touch.'

She lay her hands down onto the tablecloth, feeling the crush of the velvet, followed by the tips of Maeve's fingers placed against her own right hand. Hal's soon followed and touched her left. A moment later, perhaps feeling braver, he placed his full palm over the top of her left hand and squeezed it tightly instead. Annie felt her heart give a flutter at the comfort and she could have cried there and then when, a moment later, she felt Maeve make exactly the same decision. The smaller palm landed on top of her right hand. While it could never entirely quell her fear, it felt as though she had donned a suit of armour over her dress. The care of others was so powerful.

'Now, we close our eyes. Maeve, you'll speak the incantation just as we've been practising. And then we wait and hope that we don't encounter anyone . . . unseemly,' Annie said, apprehension catching her voice.

'I promised you a while ago, kid. No one's getting haunted on my watch,' Hal said. 'You're both safe,' he added firmly.

Annie slid her fingers properly between his. She squeezed his hand in a way that she hoped would communicate what she wasn't entirely sure how to say.

'We're good to go, then,' Maeve said, a wicked grin brightening her face in the candlelight. Annie had never seen her so excited, although she knew Maeve well enough by now to recognize that confidence came with a little bit of compensation. She gave her a weak smile and nodded for her to begin.

It would all be fine. The girl was extraordinary. They were safe. *Splendidus Infernum* was out of her system. Annie flinched slightly as Maeve cleared her throat and began:

UNCHARMED

> *Trace the air with silver breath,*
> *Souls that linger after death.*
> *We welcome you to speak with us,*
> *A magic threefold, hear it thus,*
> *We call you back to share a word,*
> *Know in good faith you shall be heard.*
> *Travel from the constellations,*
> *Appear unto my invitation.*

Maeve stumbled a little over the words and the rhythm of the incantation, but spoke it so defiantly that Annie felt proud enough to burst into a round of applause. She restrained herself so as not to ruin the delicate atmosphere.

For a moment, she thought the spell had failed. Maeve peeked one eye open at the same time Annie did, both surprised by the lack of action. Annie could feel Maeve's palm sweating into her own, the traitorous physical reaction giving away how much she was pinning on this moment.

All of the candles went out in a puff, so sudden and unexpected that it was almost audible. Their grey smoke trailed up to the ceiling, leaving only the light of the fire.

A soft breeze stirred through the drapes, despite the stillness in the meadow now that the storm had passed. Annie felt her senses withdraw in on themselves with pinpoint precision, on a knife edge. A quiet power hummed around her, as if the cottage itself had held its breath.

The crystal ball illuminated. It lit up like an electric switch, emanating a rippling white-blue glow so soft and hypnotizing that it was impossible to look away. The trails of smoke began to dance behind the glass as the active magic of their threefold spellwork came alive, until the wisps began to seep out from the crystal ball. Annie recognized the magic at work, just the same as the conjuring of the spirits within the hex that she'd called upon for so long. The smoke thickened and trailed its way to the ceiling above the table like ghostly ivy, sprawling out through the cottage to fill the room with a haze that turned violet in front of the fireplace. The perfumed scent was lulling and heady, almost sleep-inducing if it hadn't been for the movements that were starting to form a picture. A shape. A body. A spirit.

'You found me, Maeve.'

Annie had questioned whether there must be a deep, heartline connection between the spirit and Maeve, had even suspected what they might truly be to one another, but she hadn't quite been able to figure out how it all pieced together. Until that moment, the four of them entwined in ribbons of witchcraft.

She recognized the voice straight away. A voice that she knew so well, having spent night after night hearing her biggest regret, her deepest, most mournful sorrow. An impossible decision. A beloved child left behind.

And, now that she could see the face to match the voice, it was so obvious. Maeve had seen the picture and Annie had heard the sounds. In the cottage, the two came together perfectly, like two halves of a broken heart.

Maeve's mother.

Annie glanced sideways at Hal to see whether he'd managed to put the pieces together for himself and saw that it was written all over his face. He was frozen only in concern for the girl. How could they possibly explain this to Maeve?

'Hi, Mum.' Maeve's voice was a captivated whisper. Her eyes were wide and glassy. Annie noticed the slightest tremble to her chin. But the girl quickly steeled herself, as she always did, and soon the uncertain expression turned into one of childlike, joyous delight.

Of course Maeve knew. As if she would ever have been second to Annie in figuring out the truth about anything. Annie's heart swelled in a protective pride, having long ago resigned herself to the fact that Maeve would manage to outsmart her in all possible ways for the rest of time.

The ghost glided towards them from the fireplace, until she stood behind Maeve at the circle.

'I want to hug you,' Maeve said quietly.

'I know, darling. But don't lift your hands, you'll break the spell. Let me,' the ghost said in a kind, gentle voice. Maeve's mother took one final step closer to her daughter and wrapped cool, loving arms around her shoulders. Maeve closed her eyes, embracing the solid feeling that beloved, welcome ghosts could always provide, and let out a sigh of unmistakeable relief, a couple of stray tears releasing despite her best efforts. Her mother leaned over to place a firm and tender kiss on the top of Maeve's head as she squeezed her daughter close. 'I'm so proud of you.'

'Thanks, Mum.'

Annie tried her best to control the shaking of her shoulders as she cried, desperate not to ruin the moment for Maeve. It was the strangest mixture of overwhelming emotions – even by her extreme standards. Joy and delight for Maeve, finally being able to make contact with the mother who she had longed for. But a deep, etched river of devastation that these were the circumstances for it, that such a good kid had been dealt such a hard hand. Life was cruel across all realms. And, selfishly, which she hated herself for, there was a greedy longing of her own for a parent who would say those words to her daughter and mean them unconditionally.

'Annie, you okay?' Maeve asked, bringing her back to the moment.

'Of course! Don't worry about me, these are happy tears!' Annie beamed, sniffing.

'Sweetheart, there's not much time,' Maeve's mother said, softly enough so as not to interrupt, but with an urgency that made it clear there was a compelling purpose to her visit. She moved her way back around the table to face the trio. 'Enid Cadmus,' she said softly, introducing herself.

'This is . . . this is Annie and Hal.' Maeve stumbled over her own words.

'I will never be able to repay you for what you've done for Maeve,' Enid said, her hands wringing. She was only young herself; she couldn't be more than twenty-five. She and Maeve didn't look so alike at first glance, but something undefinable in their faces was noticeable now that they were both together, round freckled cheeks and determined dark eyes. 'But I'm afraid I must ask you for one more favour.'

'Anything,' Annie said to reassure her. 'I'd do anything for this girl.'

'We both would,' Hal said firmly.

'I know it,' Enid replied in a soft northern accent that matched Maeve's. 'It has brought me so much comfort to see.'

'Is she safe?' Hal asked with a stern gaze fixed on the visitor.

'I don't know, I . . . I don't think so,' Enid said, shaking her head and raising her eyes to the sky as though willing herself not to cry. Annie had heard the sound of her tears so many times before, but could hardly bear to see them for the first time.

UNCHARMED

'It's the Sorciety, isn't it?' Annie had to ask. She felt Hal's head turn towards her at her left, but she kept her eyes determinedly focused on Enid as she awaited the answer. The spirit nodded slowly.

'Word travels fast among the spellborn,' Enid said sadly. 'I have always known they'd come for Maeve, but I never dreamed that it would be so quickly after her magic came in. I thought we'd have more time, I thought she'd be older, more equipped to protect herself, to hide . . . But then she was paired with you, Annie, and everything sped up. I could sense that you were a keen necromancer and the chance was too great for me not to try to warn you both.'

'Keen necromancer? Have we met the same witch?' Maeve asked, bewildered. 'What do you mean? Have you two met before?'

'Annie has heard my worries for many, many years. You hold nightly communication, do you not?' Enid asked, faltering slightly as though she may have been mixed up.

'Yes,' Annie said quietly, then shook her head. 'Well, no . . . At least, I used to.'

'I've sensed that the bridge has closed in recent days,' Enid said gently, her expression kind and understanding. 'So I had to seize my last opportunity at contact. I have been watching over Maeve ever since I crossed over and left her behind. But there's only so much I can do beyond the veil.'

Annie swallowed hard. 'They're coming for her, aren't they?'

Enid nodded, closing her eyes as though the pain were too great to bear. 'The Heralds assumed that the Cadmus line was no more, that there was no one left to reveal their darkest secret. But the universe bringing you and Maeve together revealed otherwise. They know that Maeve is in fact alive and well – and powerful at that. They know it's her, that she is the surviving Cadmus.'

'Will someone please tell me what exactly is going on here?' Hal jumped in, his voice raised a little frantically.

'I second that. You're talking in riddles. What are you both on about?' Maeve said, exasperated.

'Do you want to take this one?' Enid said to Annie gently. Annie steeled herself for the whole truth to come tumbling out once the flood gates were opened.

'There's a lot more that I will tell you to fill in the gaps, I promise. But Enid and I, we're familiar with one another. We've talked before. Several times, in fact,' she said, turning back to Enid to find an encouraging look of camaraderie. 'And it would seem that there is a tie between Maeve and a certain underground magical elite, which is unfortunate and . . .'

'Underground magical elite?' Hal stuttered, his grip tightening on Annie's hand.

'Keep up, cowboy,' Maeve said with an eye-roll.

'Right, an underground magical elite,' Annie went on. 'Which my family were also previously a part of, until my dad ruined everything. But that's probably a story for another day.' Annie held her forehead for a quick second, then returned her hands promptly to the circle when Enid's outline wavered at the broken contact. 'Enid, you're going to have to fill in the rest of the blanks.'

'Of course,' Enid said, then turned her focus to Maeve. 'My love, the Sorciety has, for many centuries, existed in secret with certain families at the helm, those with the most longstanding and arguably most powerful magical heritages. Between them, they hold an inordinate amount of the universe's magic, and that powerful status is enforced by the deceitful nature of their club. They stockpile magic. They snatch it and they never share.'

Maeve blinked, then frowned. 'Right . . .'

'But there's more to it. The strength of those particular families isn't natural. It relies on a secretive ritual, the most abhorrent, twisted magic conjured by those at the head of the families. Spellwork that can bring wicchefolk close to the brink of death, just close enough that it blurs the lines of where their magic belongs, to upset the balance and confuse its direction. Then, while the ties to life are faded and the binds of magic are weak, they siphon off extra magic from the universe's supply. Their power grows through dangerous sacrifice.'

'There are six of those families,' Annie added, confused at the revelations but doing her best to help. 'Each with a Herald in charge at the Sorciety.'

'Six now,' Enid said cautiously. 'But once, there were seven. The Cadmus family.'

Annie startled. There was a pause.

'Hence the dead mum,' Maeve said, a tone of wonder in her voice.

'I would never, ever have left you behind willingly, beautiful girl,' Enid went on. 'I had long suspected my father was intending to push the ritual to its limits. He had changed, been mad with secrets and unexplained absences, obsessed with further research for more magical investment. So, with the full moon arriving and the Sorciety symposium looming, I stowed Maeve away safely, where I knew that whatever was to unfold wouldn't reach her.'

Annie sensed Maeve tense next to her.

'I'd seen the greed in his eyes when he compared himself to

the rest of the Sorciety Heralds,' Enid went on. 'Our family's magic was always the most naturally potent, it was capable of dominating all the rest, if only it was permitted. And my father wanted more. There would never be enough and I knew it would doom the rest of us eventually. It cost us all our lives. My mother, my siblings . . . For some wicchefolk, there is never enough. They will always be deserving of more, in their minds. Even if "more" risks the safety and security of their own family.'

Annie, in her confusion, knew at least that much for herself. Her own father had shown the same.

'Of course, the Heralds could never reveal what had happened to the Cadmus family. They could never confess that the ritual had gone too far in my father's hands, for fear of exposing what they themselves were conducting behind the curtain to keep such firm control. And so our existence was wiped from all records, the most mighty of memory charms exacted by the Heralds across the rest of the Sorciety, ensuring that no members could ask the wrong questions or wonder where we'd gone. The six families made us vanish from history.'

Annie's eyes smarted. That explained why she had been so blind to the truth, unknowing of the Sorciety's real malevolent secrets. But that was no consolation for everything else she'd caused.

Her worst fears were true, coming to life. She had brought all of this to Maeve's door, her family's twisted ties to the Sorciety and her own pathetic desperation to keep proving herself, to keep everybody needing her, whatever it took. 'I've led them right to her. It's all my fault.'

'No,' Enid said softly but firmly. The sentiment was echoed by Hal and Maeve.

'Sounds like giving me the . . .' – Maeve mimed cutting her throat – '. . . was always going to be on the cards eventually, Annie. If it wasn't you they used to get to me, it would have been somebody else.'

'The moment Glory Whitlock heard Maeve's name entwined with yours, it was written in the stars,' Enid explained. 'The last remaining member of the most powerful family, returned in a perfect twist of fate. And they've traced you here. They're coming for my baby. They're coming for you, Maeve.'

Annie's heart thumped, a crash against her ribs that made her want to flip the table, to grab Maeve in one hand and Hal in the other and run. She felt a forlorn ache for Enid, a wish with all of her magic to make such a young witch feel better about her decisions – they had been the right ones in the end. She had saved her daughter's life. The alternative was unthinkable.

In Annie's world, no one had protected her younger self. No one had ever cared enough to step in and sweep her up, to promise her that everything would be okay or that she could leave it to them to safely solve. But she would step up to protect Maeve. She would be the witch that her younger self had needed so desperately.

'They're coming. They're coming.'

Annie's eyes flew open, tears spilling as Enid's voice suddenly grew more frantic. Her octave had changed, the sound choked.

'I love you, Maeve. Whenever you need me, I'm always close by.' Enid's image flickered, fading into the haze of the room as she began to trail back towards the fireplace in a cloud of smoke. The connection waned. 'Annie, Hal, I beg that you protect her. Maeve, you must run.'

Chapter Twenty-Eight

CHAOS AND REVELRY

Hal's chair scraped back loudly against the wooden floorboards as he jumped to his feet. He shoved back his hair and began to pace the room, deep in thought as he did what he did best, putting together a pragmatic plan to look after them as best he could.

'Maeve, stay in your room,' he called over his shoulder as he began to gather his coat and boots.

'Oh, what? I just successfully hosted a seance, in case you missed that. I'm literally being hunted by the Sorciety because my magic is so bloody brilliant. Did you not hear that I'm the rightful heir? I think that earns me a free pass to the action!' Maeve shouted.

'Maeve, I'm not letting you get within one hundred million miles of any action,' Annie interrupted, casting a quick wave of magic around the room like a lasso to vanish the seance setup and pull the cottage back together.

'That's right,' Hal replied, still pacing. 'The only free pass you're getting is one to an early night in a locked room. Then we'll see about any rightful heir. You might not even have rightful air, if the Sorciety has anything to do with it.'

Maeve made an incredulous noise. 'I thought you guys were going to be cool parents. Do you want to skip straight to the part where you lock me up in an ivory tower so I can lob my hair out of the window for a handsome prince to shimmy up? Save us all a bit of time?'

'Now that you mention it, a tower is not a bad idea,' Hal said. 'Although no princes, handsome or hideous, will be getting anywhere near you until you're at least fifty years old.'

'If everybody could just take a breath,' Annie called at the top of her voice over their bickering. 'Then we might be able to actually hear ourselves think and come up with a plan that doesn't involve Maeve's unlawful imprisonment or my nervous system shutting down.'

The three of them paused, chests rising and falling in unison.

'Look,' Annie said softly. 'I fix things. It's what I do and it's what I've always done. This is no different. Granted, the scale is slightly larger than I'm used to, but . . .'

'And I look after folks, protect them. That's what I do,' said Hal. 'Granted, they're normally animals, but . . .'

'And *I* have extraordinary powers, the kind that haven't been seen among your average wicchekind for centuries. Granted, I might be even more talented and unrivalled than any of us could possibly come to terms with, but . . .'

'Maeve,' Annie said with a warning look.

'Kidding, kidding,' Maeve snorted. 'What I meant to say was that we're kind of a triple threat, right? Fixing, protection, ability . . . What kind of stupid, secret underground society could possibly stand a chance? Honestly, their whole vibe seems kind of embarrassing anyway. Like, just calm down and have a nice time, will you?'

Annie rubbed her hands together, pleased with the positivity. 'I like it. Less panic, more planning. Honing in on what we have to our advantage, playing to our strengths. Does anyone have any useful suggestions as to where we start with guarding ourselves against . . . well, whatever it is that might be coming?'

She could hear the desperation in her voice, even though she was doing her best to remain level-headed. She looked to Hal, who was frowning with determined thought. Maeve simply shrugged.

'Don't look at me. I'm the kid. Mostly here for quippy remarks.'

'We start by securing the cottage and the meadow, to make sure they can't surprise us,' Hal said at last, his voice decisive. 'Annie, you and I can work on strengthening the protection charms that I strung around the place. It's been a few weeks; they'll need bolstering. We can knit them fresh.'

'And while you two pull up the drawbridge, I'll do what I do best and dive into the books,' Maeve said, heading straight to the bookshelves to trail her fingers over the titles and pull out the ones that spoke to her. 'Anything around protection or talismans or lucky charms could be useful right about now.'

Hal threw his biggest coat to Annie. They hurried out into the pitch-black meadow and stood side by side, the woodland's rusty orange tones asleep and hidden under the cover of night. The pair shared a shy glance and Hal nodded for Annie to begin first. She tossed back her hair and shut her eyes, bringing her concentration to such an acuteness that it could have passed through the finest eye of a needle.

Keep Maeve safe. Keep her safe. Protect her. The motive was enough to feel her powers firing up, boiling with a ferocity that had no choice but to burst from her. Hot pink sparks flew from her fingers in jets and laced in intricate knots before her, like walls of chainmail. Hal's arms raised in the same way to mirror her spellwork.

'You don't have to do this, you know. You don't owe us anything,' Annie said quietly to Hal, keeping her gaze firmly on the magic as she worked.

A collision of pink and bronze sparks burst as their protective enchantments entwined.

From the corner of her eye, she saw him shake his head in disbelief. 'Thought you'd know by now. I care more about her than I've ever cared about myself. And you, Annie. You are my priority – and you have been since you both tried to take me out in the middle of the night in my own house. The minute I saw the two of you in that living room, it was like I knew you were supposed to be there.' He swallowed as though steeling himself. 'This magic, it's . . . it's strange stuff. But it's usually right about these things.'

They moved around the circumference of the cottage, following the path of the stream and, before long, a complicated tangle of magic had walled Arden Place, holding the house, the meadow and the surrounding woodland in a watchful embrace. The protection would block any and all transference spells into the area, buying them precious time. Annie felt her shoulders sink with relief that they had made progress, any kind of progress, and the feeling grew when a rough hand slid itself into hers. Hal cleared his throat.

'You think it'll hold?' he asked uncertainly.

'For now,' she nodded. 'But it's not enough with just the two of us. The Cinders, the Morningstars, the Whitlocks alone . . . You've never seen a wealth of magic like it.'

'We have to alert the coven,' Hal answered calmly with a slow nod. A strange sereneness had fallen over the scene, now that the protective magic was in place. Side by side, staring out into the woodland, they watched the inky trees, all studded with twinkles of their spellwork as though each was decorated with fairy lights.

Annie nodded, too. She had made peace with it. 'I know.'

It would mean ripping open yet another secret, one so huge and raw that life would never be the same again. It would mean alerting Selcouth to the existence of the Sorciety, complicating the magic system in ways that it hadn't faced for centuries. But none of that really mattered. It all came back to Maeve.

'I'll send a message right away.' Hal turned to her and softly stroked her face. 'It's Halloween, after all. They'll be ready for trouble.'

'There must be more we can do,' Annie said, frustrated.

'I have a few more tricks up my sleeve. When I first found Arden Place, when I was sad all the time and determined to be on my own, one of the things that drew me so strongly towards it was the sense that it was always looking out for me,' Hal said. 'This place is flooded with folks who can help us; it's like Maeve's own personal circle of safety.'

A thought flashed so brightly across Annie's mind that the words tumbled out of her mouth. And at the very same moment, Maeve spilled out of the front door of the cottage and practically levitated around the porch post, to leap down next to them onto the meadow. They spoke in unison.

'The witches' ring.'

UNCHARMED

Annie felt a flood of relief as she heard the canter of hooves approaching the cottage. It had only been minutes since Hal had run off towards the stables to gather Mage, but every moment she was uncertain of his safety had felt like a lifetime. She had, of course, refused to leave Maeve alone for a single second, following the poor girl around like a shadow.

'Will you just back off for a minute? I'm going to start smelling like a vanilla cupcake if you get any closer to me,' Maeve said crossly, peeved that she wasn't being entrusted with much of the mission thus far.

'Have you got at least two jumpers on? And your boots are comfortable? You can run if you need to?' Annie asked, travelling from kitchen shelves to cauldron in a whirlwind. One last hurried draught of basic healing potion had felt like a sensible use of time while they waited for Hal's return.

'Yes, yes. I'm ready,' Maeve groaned, her whole body charged with enough nervous energy that she could barely stay seated. Her knee jolted up and down so quickly that it shook the floorboards.

'And you've got your cloak fastened properly? I know you don't like wearing it, but it'll help the coven find us. Instincts will be stronger if we . . .'

'It's on, it's on. The blasted thing is itching my neck and keeps getting caught on my shoelaces, but it's on. Couldn't Selcouth have gone for something a bit more streamlined and aerodynamic than billowing velvet?'

'You'd like some skintight celestial Lycra as your coven uniform, would you?'

Their bickering stopped when they heard Hal whistle from outside. Annie hurriedly spooned a full ladle of the healing brew into a flask and Maeve practically bundled her out onto the porch, slamming the door behind them and running towards Hal and Mage. The horse rallied onto its hind legs and gave a loud, proud neigh, shaking out its mane as it landed.

'They're close by. Mage can sense it, too,' Hal said matter-of-factly as he jumped down from the horse's back to adjust the saddle and reins.

'How did they find us?' Annie gasped, rushing to help.

'I think we probably sent enough protective magic into the air to alert anyone of a magical persuasion in the United Kingdom as to our rough whereabouts. On the plus side, it'll help the coven locate whatever is about to unfold.'

'But they won't be the ones to find us first,' Maeve said grimly.

'Mage, transference is off the cards, so you're in charge of my girls,' Hal said, giving the horse a gentle stroke down his velvety muzzle. Maeve wasted no time, a glint in her eye as she seized the front of the saddle, threw a foot into the stirrups and launched herself up. Hal tossed a red apple up for her to catch and she presented it to Mage as a thank you.

'But what about you? We can't all fit on Mage,' Annie said, realizing that the logistics didn't work. 'Will you be able to keep up?'

'I'll meet you there. I stumbled across the witches' ring once; it'll show me the way again.' Hal spoke with determination, but Annie knew his face well enough by now to recognize the almost imperceptible but unconvinced furrow in his brow. 'I'm lucky enough to be loved by this woodland and, by default, that means you are, too. They'll keep you safe until I get there.'

'I'm not leaving you behind.'

'Yes, you are. These people have no interest in someone like me. I'll be alright.'

'Hal . . .'

'Please don't kiss,' Maeve grumbled from above.

Annie wasn't entirely sure how she managed to make her body move away from him, but her place was by Maeve's side. She felt Hal's rough hands find her waist and squeeze, before he gave her a lift up behind Maeve. With one last, lingering look up at both of them, Hal patted his beloved familiar decisively on his back leg.

'Away, boy. You know what to do.'

'You okay back there?' Maeve called, holding onto the reins as tightly as she could. Annie could just about make out the tops of Karma's ears, white fur sticking out over the flap of Maeve's satchel as the cat burrowed herself down into the bag.

Under the moonlight, Mage tore through the meadow in a streak of bronze and billowing pink cloak trailing from Annie's shoulders. She glanced back just in time to see the shape of the cottage and the faint silhouette of Hal disappear from her view. She had to trust that he would be okay and surrender to the unfolding of however this would end. She couldn't fix everything herself. They all had a part to play.

'No, I am not alright. I don't think I'll ever be able to brush my hair again. Are you?' Annie shouted back, fighting against the tearing wind. In return, she earned an unbridled, joyful cackle of a laugh from Maeve.

'This is the best night of my life. You know, aside from the imminent death that's hanging over us. Kind of just ignoring that part. I'm having a blast.'

Annie, despite herself, found that she cackled back. A big, loud laugh that caught on the trailing wind and surrounded them like a superpower, their laughter combining as it always did into something greater and better and stronger. Maeve's euphoric reaction was insane, all things considered, but it made a certain amount of sense that she'd be feeling even more untouchable than she normally did. There was so much magic in the air on Halloween night and Maeve had a proven track record of pulling the stuff like a tide to the shore. It was bolstering her, making her believe in herself. Her enchanted excitement was infectious.

'You are such a weirdo.' Annie had to yell to be heard.

'I thought we'd established that we both are,' Maeve yelled back. 'Together.'

Maeve whooped at the top of her voice and Annie had to smile at the absurdity of it all. This girl was braver than anybody she had ever known.

Eventually, having traversed what felt like the entire expanse of British woodland, Mage's pace slowed to a steady but alert trot. Picking up his hooves more cautiously through the leaves, he led Maeve and Annie into the very same clearing that they had stumbled across all those weeks ago. Detecting the same scent of concentrated magic that the horse was drawn to, Karma's fluffy head sprung up through the gap in Maeve's bag. She gave an inquisitive chirp of recognition.

They had found it. Well, Mage had found it. Annie was sure to conjure another red apple in the palm of her hand for him to snaffle as a reward. The toadstools lay in a pristine arc, untouched and unmoved, in splashes of garnet red and milky white that reminded Annie for one heart-tugging moment of jam and cream and Celeste. If she could return to that day when Morena had so unexpectedly summoned her from there, she wondered whether she would still accept the invitation so readily, if she could know then what she knew now.

She would, in every universe. It had led her to where she was supposed to be.

Feet firmly back on the ground, Maeve glanced uncertainly at Annie. 'Last time we were here, the golden rule was not to step inside it. Something about dance moves so dodgy that you literally die?'

'It's actually more a case of dancing for eternity even *through* death, a terribly lonely and unspeakably tragic demise,' Annie said lightly.

'Fantastic,' Maeve grimaced.

'Just . . . move slowly. Hal knows every inch of Arden Place and every last creature within it. Spirits like these are the guardians of the woods and he's certain that they'll want to help him – and us by association, just as they did with Karma.'

Hearing her name, Karma leapt gracefully out of Maeve's bag and landed with her front paws directly inside the fairy ring. Annie and Maeve both let out a simultaneous gasp, uncertain of what it could trigger this time around, but the cat simply shook out her fur with a tinkle of her bell and promptly began batting around an acorn.

'We shouldn't be standing unprotected; they'll be here any moment. Let me go first,' Annie said quietly, pressing a hand against Maeve's shoulder to hold her back.

'We'll step together,' Maeve said firmly. 'If you're about to burst into the merengue of death, then I'll try a Charleston, alright? On the count of three.'

With matching deep breaths, a glasses nudge from Maeve and a determined hair flick from Annie, they took one first step in unison and then another to join Karma in the witches' ring. A furious gust of wind picked up from nowhere, tangling their hair in a frenzied whip. Then it promptly dropped, like the woods had judged the outcome of their bravery and then sighed with relief. The finest, most iridescent of glitters blossomed at their fingertips and travelled up towards the tops of their arms, along their shoulders, down their backs. A subtle but mighty protective magic had been activated, courtesy of Arden Place.

Time ticked by, but there was still no sign of Hal. Annie had expected that Mage would canter back to the cottage the moment he safely delivered them to the circle, but the horse placed himself behind them, reversing his rear into the trees so that he could keep watch across the clearing. Hal must have instructed his familiar to remain close by.

Maeve gave a shiver, a spray of goosebumps prickling sharply on the bare inches of skin at her neck. Annie could feel them springing up across her own shoulders, too. She was about to make a dig at the girl, how she'd specifically told her to put on another jumper. But then a toffee-sweet scent carried on the wind, with a rich, earthy combination like embers and apples that was so distinctly familiar and autumnal, it took Annie a moment to notice it overpower the air. Her tongue was flooded with the taste to match, tangy and coppery, the faintest, sweetest hint of animal blood. Maeve began to pick at the skin around her nails and scratched at her fingertips absent-mindedly as though they were itchy.

'Do you hear something?' Annie asked, freezing to the spot the very same moment that Maeve suddenly held her position.

A brittle, crunching brush across the crackling carpet of leaves, somewhere not so deep into the woods. The murmur of voices.

'Something wicked this way comes,' Maeve muttered with a wayward smirk.

Annie flicked up her conjuring hand defensively and strained to tune in, to try to at least pick up on which direction they would show themselves. But the whisperings, growing louder and louder, were flooding in from every direction. Like they were falling from the sky, pulling up from the earth below them, laying in wait at the edge of the universe. They were using their magic to hunt Maeve and it could only be a matter of moments before they found where to aim their sails. They didn't have much time. Annie knew she had to seize the moment this time, and Maeve, too. She spun around to the girl and held her shoulders tightly.

'Before this all goes to complete chaos and revelry . . .' Annie began.

'My two favourite things,' Maeve said, eyes glinting excitedly behind her glasses. The voices were growing louder, more agitated. Annie could sense their angry desperation. Eager to play their ace, eager to arrive. They had found them.

'. . . I need you to know that meeting you has been the greatest happiness of my life, Maeve. I have been counting my lucky stars every night since we found one another. You have taught me so much about living authentically. About joy. About life. About myself. About what the point of anything and everything is.'

'Not too much, then?'

'And I know you think I'm cringey and bonkers and utterly hopeless,' Annie went on. 'And you're right, I would absolutely be the first one to die in a horror film. So, just in case that's where we find ourselves tonight, I need you to know how special you are, that you can take on the world. I need to make sure you hear that, because it wasn't something I ever heard myself. Maeve, you are capable of shining brighter than every star in the sky. And don't ever forget it, okay?'

Maeve pulled her bottom lip underneath her teeth.

'Okay?' Annie repeated, giving Maeve's shoulders a gentle shake.

'Okay,' Maeve said with an uncharacteristically serious nod. She opened her mouth to inevitably fire back something dagger-sharp, as always. But instead, she said quietly, 'Thanks for looking after me, Annie.'

Annie reached out to smooth her hair reassuringly. 'We've looked after each other.'

Maeve placed her own hands on Annie's shoulders to mirror her stance and give her a shake in return. 'And, Annie, we are not dying tonight, just so you know.' Her eyes twinkled. 'They don't know who they're messing with.'

They grinned at each other, sharing a camaraderie that had inadvertently rooted itself deeper than oak trees. Whatever was about to unfold, whichever tarot cards had been flipped by a greater force, whatever unworldly powers were about to erupt and crack open the atmosphere on Halloween night, Annie had learned that some things were deeply unshakeable. This girl was hers to protect.

Chapter Twenty-Nine

THE GLITCH

A whirl of thick, grey fog blew in through the woods and Annie knew that the sudden wind, tunnelling between the trees in smoky plumes, wasn't what it seemed. In a sickly, unnatural mist, it rolled in and unfurled itself, coiling around the trunks and whipping up piles of fallen leaves. She clung to Maeve as the path of the fog surrounded them, pulling the girl back as it brushed close to the edge of the witches' ring, but never quite crossing it.

Annie had known that the Heralds would find a loophole in their protection spells. Glory had promised that they had methods of finding anybody they needed to. But Annie hadn't expected such an unnatural, unsettling trick. Her and Hal's incantations may have forbidden transference, but the Sorciety had been carried here by other means. Efficiently delivered by elemental magic that had been twisted to their whim, to wrap them within the very winds of All Hallows' Eve. As the stormy tendrils of mist began to dissipate, they revealed themselves, stepping from the shadows.

Nine of them, Annie quickly counted up as she and Maeve spun on their heels; unwelcome arrivals surrounding the witches' ring in a whip-crack of scintillating magic. Mage reared up onto his hind legs and snorted furiously. Annie recognized every one of the wicchefolk who had taken it upon themselves to see to it that Maeve would no longer be the extraordinary threat that they perceived her to be.

Directly in front of them was Glory Whitlock herself. And . . . Annie's stomach fell to her feet at the sight. Romily. Another unthinkable betrayal from the girl she had once thought a firm friend, a kick to the gut so incomprehensible that Annie felt herself turn incandescent with rage. As though she hadn't caused enough pain already.

The potency of Whitlock magic landing so abruptly was overwhelming to the senses, like inhaling too-strong perfume over and over. Annie's head throbbed and she felt Maeve waver beside her, but she wouldn't be intimidated. She would not buckle to them any more.

To the Whitlocks' left, Vivienne and Harmony were arm in arm, already bickering, even mid-spell. Vivienne attempted to shake her friend off as though she were some kind of unpleasant octopus suctioned to her fur jacket. Harmony spotted Annie and gave her a happy wave, before Vivienne shoved her with a reminder that they were in fact on opposing sides.

The rest of the leading family Heralds, including Vivienne and Harmony's fathers, stepped out from the shadows and into the moonlight. They were surrounded.

Annie took a decisive side-step across Maeve to form a barrier, squaring her shoulders as she did so. It was time to play another part. The part of a witch who would never be bullied or browbeaten by such people. Inside she felt nothing but fear, but if she had learned anything from Maeve, it was how to keep that well-hidden.

'What an absolute motley crew you lot are. Took you long enough to find us. You could look a bit happier to finally get here. Was there a Buy One Get One Free on sticks up your arse down at the ol' Sorciety?'

'Maeve!' Annie hissed. Maeve was, of course, insistent on taking the first jab before anyone could rein her in. The older witch tugged the girl further behind her, a memory of that night when Hal had arrived at Arden Place and they had taken the same stance. Where in the universe was he?

'No, Annie,' Maeve said, shoving herself back to the front of the witches' ring. 'Let me talk to them. They've gone to so much effort to hang out with me, after all.' Her tone was mocking.

'She really is just as delightful as one would imagine,' Glory said, her face so tightly restrained that it came to a dagger-like pinch. Annie could feel a white-hot temper seething from the Herald at the mere sight and sound of the girl who inadvertently posed a threat to their existence. 'Stand aside, Annie. Do as you're told.'

Annie swallowed and shook back her hair.

'Annie, honestly,' Vivienne chimed in, sounding tired of it all. 'This is so beneath you, babe. It's beneath all of us. Why am I wasting my All Hallows' Eve traipsing through filth to come collect some spotty little tocrag who probably doesn't know a foxglove from a frogspawn?'

'Sure I do,' Maeve shot back. 'Frogspawn's the one that looks just like your face.'

'Alright, that's enough of that,' Annie said as Maeve jolted forwards, as if about to step outside the witches' ring. Harmony threw an arm out to stop Vivienne from launching herself at the teen.

'She's right, Annie,' Harmony said pleadingly. 'Just give us the bloody girl, will you? And then we can all go home. This is so boring and you're making me miss the *Spellbound Bay* special. I've never missed an episode and . . .'

'Both of you cease talking immediately, before I die of embarrassment on your behalf.' Finally, Romily spoke, taking a slow, measured step towards the witches' ring. Tension clung to the air, poised to break at the first swell of magic anyone dared to send.

'This isn't how any of us want this to go,' Romily said, her hands clasped neatly behind her back. 'But the fact of the matter is, Annie, your little friend here has been identified as a major, unfortunate glitch in the magic system.' She smiled as she moved, a frightening combination of poise and simmering violence. 'And no one likes a glitch, do they?'

Annie forced herself to answer calmly, although she could feel the sparks beneath her skin splintering into tiny weapons. These newly real, raw emotions were still proving difficult to keep caged. 'I do,' she replied. Her fists were trembling. 'I like this glitch very much. I happen to love this glitch.'

Maeve took her hand and squeezed it tightly.

Romily rolled her eyes. 'Oh, really?' She gave her a pitying, upside-down smile. 'As much as you loved your old life? C'mon, Annie. You know just as well as I do that nothing's going to change, even if you throw yourself on the bomb. The Sorciety doesn't allow for mistakes like this. What are you going to do, exactly? Bring down the whole system? This is how it *works*,' she said emphatically, laughing with a shrug.

'It doesn't have to be,' Annie said, although even she had to admit it was an uncertain declaration.

'Don't be ridiculous. It's better for everybody if this problem is simply . . . removed from the picture. We'll see to it that she's dealt with appropriately. It'll be as though none of this ever happened. Think how beautiful your life could be again.'

Romily had been taking slow steps closer as she spoke and now she reached towards Annie. She twiddled a loose blonde curl that had sprung from her braid. 'And, just between you and me, about all that "left behind" business: you know I'd never let that happen. I treasure our friendship. You've always been my favourite.'

'Oh, give me a break,' Maeve muttered.

'Don't you miss it, Annie?' Romily said, eyes sparkling. 'Us, thick as thieves? Just as it was supposed to be? And you, a part of something special. Your beautiful, charmed life. Don't you miss being perfect?'

Annie swallowed, eyelids fluttering. In some ways, she did. She did miss it all. Celeste and the pastries like pillows of spun gold. Her immaculate home, everything always exactly where she left it. Her time at Hecate House, buried in the library, always bettering herself to make everybody proud. Everything fitted together so neatly when she did what she was supposed to do. There was no confrontation, no awkward, difficult feelings, no bumps in the road. It was true that, in some ways, Annie really did miss being perfect.

As though she could see Annie's thoughts wander into the past untethered, beckoned by its rose-tinted embrace, Romily seized her chance. She snatched Maeve, tugging mercilessly at her hair and plucked her from the witches' ring with grabbing hands, stumbling backwards into Glory with Maeve firmly in her grasp. With a delighted laugh of pure evil, Glory threw a bolt of magic at Maeve's chest and sent her careering backwards into the tree behind them. Maeve hit the trunk with a sickening thud that made Annie feel hollow. Maeve winced at the pain, but her face quickly changed to a snarl as she realized she was trapped. The thick roots of the tree had bound themselves around her ankles, while the branches formed knots around her wrists.

'Don't leave the circle, Annie,' she just about managed to shout, her voice straining as Glory pulled her palm back and stretched the roots even tighter around the girl's body. The tree seemed to groan in reluctance at the cruel, unnatural entrapment it was being forced to partake in, a deep, creaking grumble that rattled the woodland floor.

'Let her go!' Annie screamed. She was mortified with herself, furious that she had allowed herself to be distracted by the promise of shiny, beautiful things again. Somewhere in her frantic mind, she heard Vivienne snort and Harmony cackle, then each take a dig.

'Sure, that'll work.'

'Worth a try, I suppose.'

Glory lifted Maeve's chin with one finger to stare straight into her eyes. Or at least attempted to, as Maeve refused to look back, keeping her own gaze firmly on Annie. 'Very like Enid, aren't you? She was a thorn in my side, too. Strangely talented, always questioning the way of things. Ask any of the other Heralds, they all want you dead like your mother. A most *unnatural* freak of nature, even for wicchefolk.'

'That's when you know it's really bad,' Harmony chimed in, still laughing as though not in the throes of chaos. 'When you're the weirdo of all weirdos.'

'But if she's fortunate and wise, as you claim she is, and she does as she's told like a good little pet, she could prove useful to us yet.' Glory turned from Annie back to Maeve. 'Seven is a luckier number than six. Perhaps she'd like to reignite the Cadmus heritage and join us, after all. Why wouldn't she crave a taste of unimaginable power?'

The prospect, hanging dangerously over them all now, was enough to make Maeve pause her struggle. Annie could practically hear the thoughts that were fighting each other in the girl's mind. A chance to save herself. Powerful people, who acknowledged that her magic was special, could maybe even compound it further. Annie had seen how much Maeve's confidence had improved over their weeks together. She couldn't blame her if the temptation of more was enough to sway her fifteen-year-old decisions. Maeve's gaze turned decidedly to Glory. Her mouth was set into a firm line before a smirk started tugging at the edges of her lips. Annie stilled, barely able to watch as her precious girl sold her soul to belong, just as she had.

But then she noticed the flex of Maeve's left wrist, the tinder-like sparks that glittered at her fingertips. The slow, secretive motion of the tree withdrawing its hold, followed by more crackles of the girl's magic. The branches loosened, the roots slithered back underground. Glory had been unwise to think that nature would be on her side, when it had always been so adoringly drawn to Maeve. The purest type of magic would always choose to protect that girl.

'Didn't you hear? I'm the weirdo of all weirdos.' Maeve jutted out her chin. 'Thanks for the offer, but unfortunately I would rather eat my own head than live a single day like you miserable lot.'

With that, Maeve shoved Glory. Hard, with both fists, followed by a blast of fiery gold magic and bright blue flames. The streams rebounded like firecrackers between all of the trees, splintering and sparking off in hundreds of different directions across the clearing. It all happened so quickly that Annie could barely process how it all unfolded, the scene in fragments that she couldn't put back together quickly enough.

She saw Romily lunge in an attempt to catch her mother from falling. But she wasn't fast enough. Instead, Glory savagely pushed Romily into the firing line of Maeve's magic, using her own daughter as a shield, as her right hand sent a cannon of power into Maeve's chest, so forceful and livid that the whole brutal motion looked impossibly, unknowably wrong. Something in Annie snapped at that moment and her powers seemed to act of their own accord. Jets of magic flew from her own fingers towards Glory. Blazing sparks exploded across the clearing, frantic as Annie and Maeve, Glory and Romily's magic rebounded between trees over and over in a glittering rain.

She saw Maeve fall to the ground, battered from all sides by magic, her small body curling inwards around the base of the tree trunk, dark hair tumbling and hiding her face from view.

She saw Romily waver, a red gash across her forehead and raw scrapes down her arms, caught horribly off guard by the merciless, reflex decision from her own mother. Yet she still managed to blast back again at Annie before taking cover, in an effort to protect herself where Glory had failed. Magic flew as attack and defence tangled together.

She saw Karma leap straight into action, pouncing from the witches' ring and directly onto Harmony's head to break her focus and block her attacking magic at Annie. Harmony was sent flying, stumbling around blindly with a shriek.

She saw Harmony's father yell and each of the Heralds falter. Furious, confused glances passed between them, uncertain of their next move and reluctant to go against what must have been Glory's strict original instruction. It was evident, in their hesitation, that they had intended to keep Maeve for their own gain after all – perhaps recognizing her value as much as Annie had, but in a very different way. At least they were occupied for now, each throwing arms up to protect themselves from the barrage of rebounding spells as they attempted to figure out how best to hone in on their target without entangling those on their own side.

Forgetting all about the incentive of protective charms, supernatural aids, promises of staying where she was supposed to, Annie bolted out of the circle. Nothing else mattered. She had to get to Maeve.

The moment she stepped out of the witches' ring, thick, choking ropes of magic whipped themselves with a biting sting around her wrists and tugged her arms back painfully. The shock caught her off guard. Where had they come from, these strange binds?

Battering the flying reams of magic away, Glory approached Annie with a fixed, sinister stare and a grin that seemed wild.

'This isn't you, Annie,' Glory hissed, sending a cold wash of fright down Annie's back. Her voice was different – or perhaps Annie was just hearing it accurately for the first time: cruel and unforgiving. She struggled to break away, determined to remove Maeve from the madness, but the binds held her rigidly. Glory's eyes narrowed as she realized that Annie wasn't going to bend to her whim this time.

'After everything I've done for you,' Glory said, a marvel to her tone like she couldn't quite believe her loss of control. She raised a hand and Annie squeezed her eyes shut, waiting to feel pain. But she stiffened when the hand only cradled her face.

'I know you, darling. What's gotten into you?' Glory said, her quietly unassuming, motherly words so jarring against the chaotic scene behind her.

All Annie could register was the desperate need to get to her own girl, to Maeve – an overwhelming feeling that she would give anything for it. Her own life, if needed. She supposed that was what a pure soul connection with someone other than her familiar was meant to feel like – true friendship or true love or the true feeling of family – and it had risen up so unexpectedly in her life, like a forgotten spring bud desperately determined to survive through any winter frost, through anything, all-consuming in its aim to carry on. A kind of love that was incomparable. Annie had no intention of letting that love leave this realm or any other.

'You belong with us, Annie,' Glory said, her smile fading. 'Nothing can change that.'

There was a ripple between the densely packed trees, a shiver that spread its way through the notches of Annie's spine. Because she knew, before the branches parted, before she saw him come tearing into the clearing.

Annie smiled. 'She already has. And so has he.'

Chapter Thirty

DRAW YOUR SWORD

There was Hal, breathing heavily, shoulders heaving as though he'd been running for dear life to get to them. He scanned the wild scene for a moment, taking in the blazing magic that flew between the trees, before his eyes found hers. Mage gave a frantic whinny and cantered to his side as Hal threw up a hand to grab his saddle, swing a leg over and mount his loyal familiar. Rearing Mage onto his hind legs, Hal backed him up several steps. Moments later, a stampede of billowing cloaks and furious, complex spellwork, aimed directly at every Sorciety member, came careering in from behind him.

Hal had very good reason for his late arrival. Not only had he brought a hearty contingent of Selcouth coven with him – a crowd of familiar faces spilling out through the trees not a moment too soon, pushing their way out of the bracken to get to the fight – but he was also accompanied by what appeared to be every animal that had ever graced the depths of Arden Place. Flanking him, among maybe a hundred creatures, Annie spotted the family of wolves that had scampered through the meadow all those weeks ago, the cubs still only half grown but baring razor-sharp teeth. Stags armoured with towering antlers pawed their hooves at the ground, poised to descend at Hal's whim. An army of bats swooped and loomed among the treetops, already disorientating the Sorciety as they struggled to retain composure against the swarm of wings. What must have been twenty foxes, screeching a battle cry, prowled between Mage's legs. And there were many more, too, all of whom Annie and Maeve had welcomed in during the storm – badgers, owls, lynx, red squirrels, stoats, weasels, wild boar and so many woodland mice that it looked and sounded as though the floor of the woods was beginning to crumble.

Every creature was charged with a protective energy, prowling around Hal and waiting for their favourite warlock to give the signal, so that they could rush to his defence.

'Don't get hurt, you lot,' he said gruffly. The warlock gave his one-fingered salute towards the Heralds. Hal's gang descended in a crush on the Sorciety, who tried to turn on their heels and run, but were met by a wall of coven members poised to fight. The last thing Annie noted before she turned back to Hal was a pair of antlers already lifting the trail of a cloak as they stampeded after Vivienne's father.

It had taken Hal a moment to register what was happening to Annie: Glory breathing down her neck, wrists and magic locked in her grasp.

'I would think very, very carefully about your next move,' he called calmly to Glory, although Annie could see a fire behind his eyes that felt foreign to his usual unshakeable calm. Mage picked up his hooves in a stutter, enough to make Glory falter, and, with a quick flick of Hal's wrist, a burst of bronze magic flew straight to the ties that Annie was bound in. They split and crashed to the forest floor like irons and she stumbled away as quickly as she could, shaking out her wrists so fiercely that sparks of her power exploded.

'Grab her!' Glory shrieked to the Heralds, all now locked in their own battles of ricocheting coven magic and the brunt of watchful wild animals. It was Barnaby Morningstar who was unfortunate enough to be nearest. Annie saw him hesitantly break his own fight to follow Glory's command. He sprinted towards Annie, wand outstretched menacingly in her direction, and smiled smugly as his hand closed around the trail of her cloak.

Hal had already galloped over. 'Don't even think about it.'

'Or what, you common brute? You'll set your little pony on me?' Barnaby shouted back, throwing up his pointed chin as he simultaneously sent out a blast of magic. Hal easily bent it away, sending it to the ground as he spun the horse around.

He shrugged. 'If you insist.'

Tightening the reins in a swift command, Hal brought Mage's back legs up to kick Barnaby hard and solid in the chest. The man folded in two, flew at speed into the darkness between the trees and disappeared from view. Mage gave a satisfied snort.

Annie reeled at the unnerving sight, but all she could think about was Maeve. Somewhere, buried in the brawl of Selcouth against the Sorciety, her girl was in need.

Hal swung Mage around again to gallop through the clearing and into the fight, aiming straight for Morena, who was locked in a collision against a Herald. Meanwhile, it was Vivienne herself who stepped into Annie's eye line.

'This is all your fault, you stupid bloody bimbo! Look at my *dress*!' Vivienne screamed, stomping her foot into the mud and sending even more splatters up her skirt. She let out a whine and her magic appeared in a fraught tangle between her palms.

'Oh, get it dry-cleaned, you unbearable crone!' Annie yelled back, startling herself with the viciousness that tumbled out of her mouth. Her emotions were roaring, all of them truer and more vivid than she could ever have dared to imagine. 'Did it ever occur to you that there are more important things?'

'More important than vintage Vespertine lace?' Vivienne squawked. 'I think not!'

'Perhaps like friendship! Your so-called friend and queen bee was just thrown to the wolves by her own vicious hag of a mother,' Annie shouted. 'Look at her! Why aren't you helping her?'

Pouting, Vivienne reluctantly turned to search for Romily among the frenzied, battling crowd of witches, warlocks and wicche. Eventually she spotted her, injured and cowering against a tree trunk, clutching onto the bark with terrified eyes. In that moment of chaos, it made Annie's heart twang with surprise sympathy to realize that Romily, in all of her self-preservation and determination to be admired, was only a product of her parents. And tonight, Romily had met the same startling reality as Annie once had, that her own mother would sacrifice life with her daughter to remain at the addictive, all-consuming helm of the Sorciety.

Vivienne huffed a final snarl at Annie, then ran to Romily's side, throwing an arm around her shoulders to carry her as she staggered and whimpered, clutching her side where Maeve's magic had hit with a painful blast. Together, they looked so weak, so feeble and cowardly, that they felt unrecognizable to Annie. How had she ever admired these people, feared their opinions, longed for their pointless, superficial approval? Shaking her head to clear the complicated thoughts, she threw herself into the mix once again, clawing to get to Maeve amid the fight.

'Karma, that's enough!'

Annie's familiar was still hard at work on shredding Harmony's up-do in the most efficient way she could manage, claws sinking into the sleek bun while Harmony flailed in circles. At Annie's command, Karma paused mid-swipe, gave her ear a quick clean, then leapt down from Harmony's head to run straight to Annie's side, altogether looking rather pleased with herself. Annie gathered her up and gave her a hurried but emphatic kiss on the head. 'Nice work. You'll be safe at home, I love you,' she whispered hurriedly, before quickly vanishing her familiar back to the safety of the cottage. This was no place for a princess like Karma – even if she had put up a grand fight for the cause of protecting their girl.

A scratch-covered Harmony staggered towards Romily and Vivienne, gratefully receiving their arms around her as they sobbed dramatically in unison. All three of them turned towards Annie, lit up by the fireworks of imploding magic that showed their matching hate-filled glares. The way that they rallied against her felt wickedly familiar. The trio gathered their magic to aim and screeched their final blows in unison.

'Look what you've done to us!'

'I knew you would always be trouble, I said it from the very beginning.'

'Stop!' Annie shouted, sending a wall of protective magic up in front of her like a screen, making their spells rebound back. 'I don't want to fight you all. We have too much history to end this way.'

'But we *are* the Sorciety! And you're ruining it all,' Vivienne screamed.

'You always put yourselves first. Why is this suddenly different?' Annie sighed, feeling broken. 'This isn't your fight, just because it's your parents'. We don't have to keep making their same mistakes all over again.'

At that, Romily faltered just the tiniest fraction, the bitterly vengeful expression that she'd inherited from Glory softening the smallest amount.

'Rom, please,' Annie begged, one last attempt to make them leave of their own accord. 'Get out of here. Be safe. There's still time to make different decisions of your own. Things can change.'

Romily looked away, furious, refusing to hold eye contact, but Annie noticed the way that she blushed. Her old friend frantically chewed on the inside of her cheek, a pained and uncertain look on her face that Annie hadn't seen there for years. Harmony and Vivienne only awaited instruction, wide-eyed and desperate, until Romily finally gave the most imperceptible and reluctant of nods. In a bright flash, the Fortune Four, minus one, huddled together with matching whimpers and vanished as a dark mist rolled in to carry them away.

'Annie!'

Somehow, somewhere in the melee of rebounding, snapping magic and exploding powers, Maeve had struggled to her feet again. She was grimacing and rubbing at her ribcage where Glory's magic had struck her, but there was a steadfast look in her eyes as she staggered.

Annie went to run to her, but an arm quickly swooped

around her waist and pulled her backwards. It was Hal. She would recognize his strength and warmth anywhere.

'What are you doing? Let me get to her,' Annie yelled, struggling to free herself.

'It's her time,' he shouted back into her hair. 'Let her fix this for herself. She's brave and she deserves it. She wants to shine.'

'But . . .'

'We're here to pick up the pieces if she fails. But she won't. Let her try.'

Annie knew he was right. Her whole body fell limp against him and it was as though the world stood still, stopped spinning on an axis altogether. This was Maeve's moment. Their eyes locked and Annie hoped the look that passed between them would remind Maeve that they were here, waiting in the wings, along with everything that she had told her before the chaos began. *Maeve, you are capable of shining brighter than every star in the sky . . .*

With her very last ounces of strength and determination, Maeve threw her casting hand directly upwards. Annie couldn't understand what she was trying to do. But then she saw that she was wielding something between her fingers.

A pink pencil. The one that Annie had enchanted with the silver tip of starlight all those weeks ago, which the girl had used to sketch the portrait of their funny family before any of them had recognized it for what it truly was. Annie couldn't believe she had kept it. The silver tip winked in a perfectly satisfying, magical way that, even in the chaos, reminded Annie of her special pink ribbons back at Celeste. Perhaps she really had passed on something useful to Maeve – even if it was only the importance of a momentary sparkle.

The last of the stars that peppered the dawn sky were lured towards her, recognizing her special magic – familiar in its uniqueness, beauty and creativity. Silver starlight met milky morning moonlight in beams that gleamed onto the girl. It all pulled downwards to her, allowing her to harness its power and light into the pencil, and she threw her wrist in wide, circling motions, dragging the starlight towards their battle ground to draw firm celestial loops around each of the Heralds. The starlight solidified in sweeping lines, just as it had that night on the meadow. Before they could even recognize what was happening, each of the Sorciety was trapped in an unyielding silver rope. A few of the bravest Selcouth members, including Hal, quickly acted to reinforce her grip.

But even starlight itself wasn't enough to hold Glory. The explosive rage of her unnaturally strengthened powers, the most poisoned, superfluous amounts of witchcraft gathered from years of dangerous sacrifice, allowed the Supreme Herald to break free. She sent the starlight reeling back at Annie and the coven to scatter them, then turned to the girl alone. Glory approached her in prowling, predatory steps.

'Almost gone and I've barely lifted a finger,' she said calmly once face to face with Maeve again, although venom poured from her voice. 'I can already smell the death on you. Normally, I'd insist on doing this the proper way to honour tradition, to save the ritual for when we'd returned you to the Tempest Theatre. But you haven't much time left and it would be wrong to waste it.' She towered over Maeve, who stumbled backwards away from her, groaning in pain as she spat out a glob of blood onto the woodland floor.

Glory brought her left hand to Maeve's throat and squeezed,

her right palm opening wide to summon her darkest magic. 'Your life lines are already blurred, your binds are weak. Your magic is ripe for the taking. Hold still, girl. Do as you're told and I promise this won't hurt a bit.'

'That's good.' Somehow, Maeve raised her head. 'Because this will.'

Annie couldn't fathom where the girl found any more strength, after everything she'd been through. But with one last punch of her fist, wielding the pencil like a sword, a deluge of her magic exploded in tangles. So beautiful and so bright was Maeve's tidal wave of incantation that every witch, warlock, wicchefolk and creature who had been watching on had to shield their eyes from the light.

Taken by surprise, Glory screamed and reeled, blinded by the astonishing silver starburst inches from her face. The Supreme Herald stumbled backwards, arms flailing and legs kicking out in front of her. One step too far. The moment her boot stumbled and slipped into the dirt inside the witches' ring, the circle of mushrooms set alight. It glowed indignantly at the unwelcome visitor who had dared to cross it, uninvited. A flash of undignified panic appeared on Glory's face, normally so poised, as the witches' ring caught hold. Her eyes went unnaturally wide as she realized her unfolding fate. In a blink, she was gone.

Once the starburst began to dim, the coven sprang into action. Each of the four remaining Heralds, caught so unaware by the surge of incendiary magic, found themselves with no choice but to surrender. Maeve's magic had bought precious moments that allowed Selcouth to finally seize them for good. Morena bound two of them, one in each hand, with only the slightest fraction of a satisfied smirk. Hal lunged for Vivienne's father, while a skinny rake of a warlock from the coven made light work of securing the fourth Herald.

Annie could barely believe it. They had really done it. They had won. Overthrown the Heralds and exposed the Sorciety, taken hold of a force so incomparably controlling, sinister and manipulative, its whispered secrecy the unforgiving bind that had held her life for so long.

'Maeve, we did it! You did it!' Annie squealed as she spun, her hands frantically clapping of their own accord, a wildness in her eyes and her voice that she had never felt before as the whole of Selcouth erupted into celebration.

Then she registered the fall of the silence.

She saw Maeve go limp and fall to the ground as the final glimmer of magic drained from her young body. She had turned grey, wilting in a way that Annie had never seen her do before as the last of the starlight, entwined with her own natural magic, emptied from the pencil with a stuttering jolt and returned to the sky.

Just as she always did – the reason that Annie had admired her from the moment they first discovered one another – Maeve had given every ounce of her extraordinary, authentic self to the moment.

Always. That was why Annie loved her. The girl knew no other way to live.

Chapter Thirty-One

A NEW HOME

Annie pulled at the loose threads on the patchwork quilt, knotting them all into tiny plaits, and waited. Occasionally, her vision blurred behind a film of tears, but she refused to let them fall. It had been hours since they had returned to Arden Place, but she would not admit defeat.

The moment that Maeve had hit the ground, Hal had run to her and scooped the girl into his arms. He had carried her to Mage, held her limp body close against his chest as they sped back to the cottage in a blur on horseback. 'This is my job,' he said gruffly when others tried to help, remaining silent for some time afterwards. Before they bolted, Annie had rushed to administer the hasty healing draught that she had shoved into her supplies before the fight, hoping that the basic brew would be enough to hold Maeve's broken pieces together in the interim.

The coven swiftly banished each of the Heralds to Hecate House, to be held under lock and key until they were fully informed of the goings on that had remained a closely guarded secret for so long. Annie's brief, hole-filled explanation of the

Sorciety's magic stockpiling system had earned a combination of extreme concern and curious fascination from the Gowden sisters. As the Sages in charge, they would prepare a case for trial and the entirety of the coven would decide together what the next moves might be. Wherever it was they had been sent, Annie knew it was safe to assume that it would be somewhat less of a luxury stay than they were all used to. Romily, Vivienne and Harmony would be thanking their lucky stars to have escaped when they did. Briefly, Annie wondered what would become of them. She realized she didn't care enough to find out.

The coven accompanied them back to the cottage, so the tiny house was standing room only, bursting at its low rafters with wicchefolk tending to wounds and nursing bruises in a serious, sombre quiet. By some miracle, everyone had escaped relatively unscathed in the grand scheme of the fight – apart from Maeve. It seemed wholly unfair that she, the youngest and most deserving of the winning feeling, had been the one to step up and take the final blow, particularly when the coven had treated her with such a lack of true care. Annie was seething, but her concern for Maeve was the only feeling that mattered in the moment. Perhaps recognizing the girl's sacrifice for themselves, all Selcouth members were refusing to leave until Hal and Annie were confident that they had returned Maeve to a stable condition. Morena and Bronwyn soon took charge of the situation and sent those able out across the meadow to gather fresh ingredients for healing potions. It was at least a comfort to know that the finest magical minds in the country were at work just past the porch and that several high-level brews were bubbling away on the stove, bringing a fragrance tinted with the scent of hazelnut chocolate.

Hal and Annie had not left Maeve's bedside. They were perched at the end of her bed, aching and filthy and exhausted, one on either side of the girl. Despite his drained energy, Hal was restless, launching to his feet every few minutes to pace the room, to stroke Karma, who had nestled in on top of Maeve's chest under the blankets, or to mutter quietly to the constant stream of animals who continued to visit at the window. Many had shown concern for Maeve's welfare and were bringing endless gifts of care. After an in-depth conversation with a red squirrel who left a tiny pile of sunflower seeds for Maeve as a gesture of goodwill, Hal returned to Annie's side and squeezed her shoulder gently.

'I've wished to dabble with time magic before, but never quite been tempted enough to take the risk,' she said quietly. 'But right now, I would give anything to be able to turn it back and stop her from knitting that enchantment.'

'Oh, and we both know the kid notoriously responds well to being told what to do,' Hal said, stroking Annie's hair. He squeezed again, the soft pad of his thumb against her neck, and placed a tender kiss on top of her head.

Annie bit firmly down on her lip. The overpowering guilt and shame had subsided to more of a general, aching numbness since the sight of Maeve out cold in her bed. She could hardly bear it. Hal took a seat next to her on the edge of the mattress and rubbed her knee absent-mindedly. The small, tender touches were the only thing that had stopped her from falling off the brink of madness with worry. She could hear the murmurings of the packed cottage outside, occasional cries of rallying enthusiasm from Bronwyn's endless positivity and the lower-pitched drawl of Morena's cutting sarcasm.

Annie dropped her head with closed eyes and shook it in

frustration; Hal's thumb still stroked her cheek. 'I was just trying to make everybody happy. I think I've broken my own heart in the process.'

Tears finally trailed her face and the few that weren't caught by Hal landed onto the quilt.

'Your heart works just fine. In fact, it's a million times bigger than anyone else I've ever met. You feel things so deeply and greatly and importantly,' Hal told her quietly. 'Annie, among many, many other things, that's what's perfect about you. And the rest really doesn't matter. Okay?' He gave her a gentle kiss. 'The kid isn't going anywhere.'

'I dunno, if my legs were working, I'd run out of here pretty quickly.' Their heads flew to the pillow, to where Maeve's eyes fluttered open and then promptly squeezed shut again at the sight of their kiss. 'I can't believe I lay down my life to save you lot and my first waking breath is going to be to vomit because of you two.'

Annie let out a noise somewhere between a startled gasp and a joyful shriek and threw her arms around the girl as she wriggled up against the pillows, forgetting that she was one great big battered and bruised injury. Hal tilted his head back in sheer relief and sprang to his feet, grinning.

'How are you feeling?' Annie asked keenly, holding the back of her hand against Maeve's forehead, then shimmying up her blankets, then adjusting the pillows behind her, then handing her a glass of water before starting the cycle all over again.

'Like I've been hit by a truck. Or a metric ton of starlight, I suppose.' A sprinkle of cuts and bruises had already bloomed like winter violets and she looked exhausted, but the glint in her dark eyes remained. 'Did you see my spell?' Maeve asked with a weak smile, squinting a little against the brightness of the first November day pouring through the curtains.

'No, I missed it,' Annie said with a disappointed frown. 'Can you do it again?'

Maeve gawped.

'Kidding,' she smirked. 'Of course I saw your spell. You were incredible, better than incredible.'

Maeve looked prouder than Annie could ever remember.

'But that doesn't mean that you're not also in seven hundred different kinds of trouble. You have to stop keeping secrets from me,' Annie went on. 'Since when have you known how to do that? And *how* did you possibly know?'

Maeve, of course, just shrugged. 'I read a lot. Don't underestimate me.'

As if she could, as if she would ever dare to again. 'Never.'

Hours later, after sipping on more varieties of *Salutaris Medella* healing potion than any one girl should have to stomach in a lifetime, Maeve was fortified enough to demand a trip out of bed. Not only was she feeling a little stronger with such skilled potion brewing on hand from the makeshift infirmary, but she had also heard that there was a rapturous audience waiting just outside her room to pile endless praise on her and generally go on about how much of a wonder she was. Annie had warned them to please stay quiet and to try not to overreact at the sight of the girl who had brought down starlight itself. Her warning was not noted.

Leaning on Annie's arm, Maeve slowly hobbled out into the living room and was met by enthusiastic cheers and applause.

'Hello, stray.'

With a billow of cloak, Morena stepped directly in front of Maeve just as she was attempting to take a grand bow, despite bruised limbs and sore muscles. Annie had conjured hasty baked supplies to boost everyone's waning energy and Morena was brandishing a cheese twist slightly like a magic wand, as though she wasn't entirely sure what to do with it.

'Here,' Morena said, handing Hal the twist and scattering a rainfall of flaky pastry crumbs across the floor in the process. 'Dispose of this, Mr Bancroft. Miss Cadmus and I have much to discuss.'

'Morena, can you give her a moment? She's only just woken up,' Annie said.

'Can Annie come?' Maeve asked, evidently unbothered by her injuries, but her grip tightened a little around Annie's arm as she asked.

'If she must.' With a sharp, subtle nod of her head, Morena gestured for the witches to take the lead and (rather slowly) they shuffled and limped carefully towards the front door. Before they'd quite reached it, they were intercepted once again, but Annie was delighted by the interruption this time. It was Ruby, with an impressive black eye and her arm held tenderly in a sling.

'You should see the other guy,' she said with a grin through her split lip. 'It was Vivienne's father and I hear he's now in a dungeon somewhere. Oh, I would pay big money to witness that.'

Annie pulled her carefully into a hug. 'You joined the other side,' she smiled.

'It's a much better fit,' Ruby said proudly. 'I went straight to Hecate House after those witches made it clear I wasn't welcome and – you know me and my big mouth – it wasn't long before I'd spilled a few secrets and opened up a whole can of worms,' she smirked. 'When Hal's letter came through and I heard you were in trouble, I had to come, didn't I?'

'Thanks, Ruby,' Annie said. 'You're a good friend.'

'It was nothing – most exciting Halloween I've had for a while. They're very welcoming folks at Selcouth. It'll take me a little while to learn the ropes of being part of a half-normal coven rather than a menacing elite club, but I think it suits me much more.'

'I have to agree. Don't get me wrong, they have their faults,' Annie admitted, too many examples to count on both hands all springing to mind. 'But they're the good side of magic,' she added reassuringly.

'Right, I can already tell,' Ruby said, nodding with a slight wince at her shoulder. 'I've just met my buddy Rune here, he's going to show me the ropes at ol' Hecate House.'

A slightly gangly warlock, all long limbs and towering height, the one who had managed to take hold of a Herald for himself, took a bold step towards them when Ruby introduced him. He pushed back a curl of dark hair as it fell into his exceedingly handsome face and Annie suddenly felt a little giggly as he removed his round wire glasses and gave her a lazy smile.

'Rune Dunstan. New watchman for Selcouth,' he said, shaking Hal's hand enthusiastically. 'A pleasure to meet you both, I've heard great things. Admired your work for a long time, Hal. And, Maeve, of course, that was really something special out there.'

'Thanks for stepping up,' Hal said, looking a little confused by all the human interaction. 'Congratulations on the role. Nice coat that, mate. You look the part, at least.'

'Oh. Right. Thanks,' Rune said, taken aback as he looked down at his long black leather coat. 'It was just a new thing I wanted to try, really. I wasn't sure . . . You think it works?'

'Looks cool,' Hal shrugged, turning himself back towards the porch and looking slightly unsure as to why he'd entered into a conversation about coats.

'Totally classic for a refined warlock,' Annie jumped in, keen to thank him herself. 'Effortlessly chic for autumn and winter. Really works for you with your beautiful bone structure. That should be your signature look,' she added, giving him an approving nod. 'I'll come and find you soon,' she said to Ruby. As she guided Maeve away, she noticed how a distinctly pleased smile tugged at the corners of Rune's mouth. She even thought she saw him punch the air ever so subtly.

After a couple more stops for congratulatory handshakes, Annie and Maeve finally made it out onto the porch with the Sage Witch, while Hal hung back to talk to Rune about his plans for magical security moving forwards. Annie and Maeve each took one of the wicker chairs that looked out onto the meadow. That left Morena with the swing.

'Why in this universe or the next would anyone require a chair that levitates? Is one's life really that dull?'

She took a rigid seat on the swing, billowing her cloak out behind her. She looked incredibly unsure, eyes bulging slightly as her feet floated just above the wooden floor.

'Obscure furnishing decisions aside, I wanted to talk to you, Miss Cadmus, about your display of magic back at the woodland. It was . . .'

'Dangerous and stupid and probably now a big, big problem. I know, that's always my thing,' Maeve said, wincing as she adjusted herself. She crossly chucked a gingham pillow out from behind her back and onto the floor.

'Quite the contrary,' Morena said quickly, causing Annie and Maeve to both startle at the same time. They shot each other a confused side-eye. 'It was in fact . . . rather brilliant. Highly creative, extraordinary magic. The stars don't bend for many. I hope you'll consider a future that works closely with Selcouth to hone your talents as they rightfully deserve.'

'Sorry?' Maeve snorted.

'Far be it from me to deny talent, Miss Cadmus. As Ms Wildwood knows from first-hand experience, I appreciate a witch who does not shy away from realizing her greatness and putting it to fine use. In fact, I rather admire it, particularly in a witch who has only completed as few orbital completions as yourself.'

'She means birthdays,' Annie whispered out of the side of her mouth.

'Ms Wildwood, this concerns you, too,' Morena carried on. 'You know I am not one to sweeten my words and, to be frank, I think you should consider relinquishing my incredibly generous hours of guidance to your charge here. I suspect she could benefit from your apprenticeship much more than you can these days. I suggest that you instead continue your work for Selcouth in a more permanent, respected position and I turn my most . . . nurturing attentions . . . to Maeve here.'

Annie's brows shot up. She hadn't given a lot of thought yet to how her work at Hecate House would continue, but she knew that it was just another part of her old life that she felt no pull to hold onto any more as she attempted to shed all of the expectations and obligations that had been placed upon her by others. Her years of apprenticeship with Morena had been enjoyable, but the motivations had only ever really been to secure her uncertain future at the Sorciety.

However, it was a huge compliment (especially from Morena Gowden, of all wicchefolk) to be considered valuable enough for a real position at the coven. And the prospect of saying no, of turning down something that she knew she should probably accept, seemed to stick in her throat.

'No, thanks,' Maeve said brightly.

'I beg your pardon?' Morena asked, practically spitting feathers at the gall.

'Nah, I don't think it's for me, this coven life – at least for now. No offence, I'm sure you have a great time. But it's all a little bit . . . controlled for me. And I'm doing just fine exploring my magic out here, with Annie.'

It was the bolster that Annie needed to hear. If it was what Maeve wanted, too, then all the better; that made her decision even more easy.

'Maeve's right, Morena. I'm so grateful for the opportunities that you've brought my way. But . . .' She hesitated, but shook back her hair to drag up some extra confidence. 'But I think I'm ready to take a step back. We'll still be a traditional part of the coven, of course, and we'll keep in touch. But I'm ready for my life to not be quite so broken up into so many different boxes. It's time to try something different for myself. So no. No, thank you.'

Morena breathed out sharply through her nose. Annie prepared to feel her wrath. But none came.

'As you wish.'

The earth didn't stand still. The realm didn't melt to the ground. She had said no and it had not immediately transformed her into a terrible person. She was still herself and the world continued to turn. In fact, she was perhaps even more herself for it.

'The other matter at hand is your living situation. You are still technically under the responsibility of Selcouth, Miss Cadmus . . .' Morena began to say.

'I want to stay here and live with Annie and Hal,' Maeve burst out, before immediately beginning to chew on one of her nails, as though attempting to control the exposing words and shove the confession back in. Annie glanced at her, then back to Morena, uncertain of the right response. Morena remained silent and pursed her lips, waiting for Annie to speak.

It seemed again that the only correct response was the truthful one.

'I would love to have Maeve,' Annie said quietly but firmly, squeezing Maeve's hand. 'Please consider it, Morena.'

Morena raised a single pointed eyebrow. 'You're sure?'

'I've never been sure of anything in my life,' Annie said. 'But I am very, very sure of this. The coven won't have to worry about her at all, other than to ensure she's provided with a solid magical education. I'll do the rest. I'll pay for everything. We'll move back to my house . . .'

'No, you won't,' Hal said gruffly, leaning against the doorframe with his arms folded. He stepped out onto the porch and closed the door quietly behind him.

'You'll both stay here, with me. If you'd like to, that is. Doesn't much feel like a home any more without you both in it, turning my life upside down. And the blasted cat, obviously,' Hal grumbled. He sent a small side-smile in Annie's direction and a silent nod that communicated everything she needed to hear. That he was sure. That he meant it. That he wouldn't change his mind.

'Well, isn't that just marvellous,' Morena said, before Annie had quite figured out the right words to reply. 'I do love when things are tied up with a bow, probably a ghastly pink one in this particular circumstance,' she said, turning to Annie. 'I'll draw up the paperwork once I return to Hecate House.'

Morena rose to return to the rest of the coven, stumbling from the swing as she landed her feet safely back down with an incredulous glare. Annie was fairly certain she heard her mutter the words 'idiot' and 'foolish furniture' under her breath towards Hal.

Hal took Morena's place on the swing and kicked off gently from the floor with his boots, sending it into motion. Annie looked out onto the meadow, November gilding the long grass. Maeve sprawled out next to her and Hal leaned back with his eyes closed and his hat pulled low, a deep sigh as he stretched out an arm to touch the tips of Annie's fingers, just for the sake of feeling her nearby. She had so much to say to them, to paint the picture of why this moment meant so much to her. But it wasn't the time to tell them how it felt. It was the time to let this moment be, to feel it trickle by like the stream that surrounded them and adjust to this beautiful, calm quiet being her real, authentic life – at least for now. How lucky she was to have found such sweetness.

'What would you like to do tonight, once everybody's gone?' Annie asked Maeve, absent-mindedly smoothing her hair and being careful to mind the cuts on her face. 'It's going to feel a little quiet when it's just the four of us again.'

'Anything that doesn't involve saving wicchekind would be ideal,' Hal grumbled.

'Maybe we could watch a video? And do face masks? And bake?' Maeve asked Annie hopefully, settling against her with closed eyes. It was precisely the evening that Annie had planned for them when she had headed to meet Maeve for the very first time.

Annie smiled. 'We can do that.'

Chapter Thirty-Two

APRICITY

The tinkle of the bell above the door of Celeste sang out. It was a softly mournful but fond farewell song, as it had been every time Annie returned since making the decision to give up the bakery. There was definitely a sadness, one that inevitably came with any kind of change or the start of a new chapter – even a happy one – but a loose-fitting, easy contentment, too, a feeling of peace that balanced the scales as though she were weighing out flour and sugar. Less of a harsh pain now that she had let go and more of a nostalgic, wistful ache that squeezed her hand and reminded her with tenderness that she was making the right decision.

Sometimes the right decision was a release, when it was tough to let go of something, but wonderful to let it float away. Like a balloon.

In that same way, it felt good to cross the threshold of Celestial Bakehouse, her name no longer above the door and the sign now painted a soft shade of cornflower blue, rather than pink. It felt good to enjoy the foundations she had laid and not feel dread about her day or worry about the workload or a pressure behind her eyes as she tried to prioritize everything she was struggling to spin at once. To know that she was free and that the place was passing into good, loving hands brought a serenity and lightness with it.

Annie had dragged Maeve away from her coffee and sketchbook time, only with the promise of coffee and sketchbook time *plus* freshly baked pastries. Life had slowed down considerably and they had plenty of time to stop by when Maeve wasn't doing something or other with her new friends, who she had made quickly and easily at her new school. Swinging by the bakery meant that Annie could gather up the last few things that she had left in the back room and give her friends a fresh start in their own space, which felt important. Plus she was fairly certain there were at least two pairs of shoes, if not more, lurking in her dressing area, which was also the last place she'd seen her favourite feather-trimmed blazer a few months ago.

After an emotional and frank conversation about her decision to leave, which left Annie and Pari both in tears and even Faye having to turn away to hide a wobbly bottom lip, they had come to the comforting conclusion that, although they would take over the rental agreement and make Celeste their own, Annie would always be at the end of the phone. For creative input, for secret recipes, for the inevitable collection of pink bows and hair clips that seemed to materialize of their own accord. And for firm friendship, above all else. They still had a very important Halloween costume tradition to uphold, after all.

'I can't believe I missed it,' Annie pouted, genuinely devastated to have broken their age-old tradition of trio Halloween costumes, despite having had arguably more important matters to handle. She wondered whether Maeve and Hal would be interested in joining the breakfast ensemble next year, but suspected she already knew the answer to that one.

'No big deal,' Faye said, wringing out the soapy suds from her dish cloth as she finished the last plate. 'We went as egg and soldiers instead, you would have approved. Right, let me just . . .' She threw off her rubber gloves and moved to empty the bin under the sink, just as there was a loud clatter. Maeve had been fiddling with the finely curated collection of vintage china cups. Three of them toppled from the shelf like dominos. She was just about quick enough with her magic to send them into slow motion, grabbing one in each hand, before the third hit the deck with a clatter and smashed into several shards.

'Oops.'

Fortunately for Maeve, still not quite used to keeping her magic hidden in the non-wicche realm, Faye's head had been stuck under the sink the entire time as she struggled to pull out the rubbish.

'Maeve,' Annie sighed from her favourite seat in the bay window, where she was arranging a big bouquet of white winter flowers. 'Make yourself useful. Take the bins out for your Auntie Faye.' Annie hit her with a daisy and a wink as she slunk past sulkily. Maeve rolled her eyes somewhere towards Alaska before taking the bag reluctantly at arm's length out to the cobbled back alley.

'You're still sure that this is the right call, Annie? It's hard to imagine this place without you,' Faye said, leaning back against the counter. She was searching Annie's face through investigative eyes to make sure that she was getting the truth, knowing that it was rare for Annie to speak up for herself or make decisions that felt truly right for her. She had always been able to read her like a book.

'No,' Annie said honestly with a breathy laugh and a rueful head shake that made her curls bounce. 'But I'm not sure of anything practical or sensible or expected any more . . . And I think I'm starting to learn that that's where the magic lies, when there's a little bit of room for spontaneity and the chance to stumble across happy mistakes.'

'You? Spontaneous?' Faye asked with an entirely serious face.

'I know, right?' Annie said excitedly. 'Who'd have ever thought it?'

'Well, in that case,' Faye said, wiping her fingers on the ends of her shoulder tea towel, 'we're thinking of having a party tonight. A bit impromptu, I know, but we wanted to celebrate our new venture and . . .'

'Tonight?' Annie gasped. 'C'mon, Faye, I said "spontaneous", not "last-minute, unscheduled socializing". I'm not a madwoman.'

Faye snorted. 'So what are you going to do instead?'

'Maeve's got homework, I'll help her out with that. Then I was thinking about trying this new recipe I . . .'

'Not tonight, you dafty. I mean with your life. Now that you're leaving Celeste behind, what's your next move?'

'For once, I have no next move,' Annie said, noting the pride in her own voice at the confession. 'I've played my whole life like a strategic game of chess and I'm exhausted. It's time to try a different way. All I know is that I want to keep baking. Hal says there's a tiny little place up for rent in the village near his cottage, all floral lampshades and lace doilies and frilly curtains. Low footfall, quiet days, peaceful . . .' Annie said wistfully. The moment that Hal had mentioned the empty cafe to her, she had felt a little tugging of possibility in her chest. A chance to bake for others, but back on her own terms, with the dials all turned down to low again. It sounded blissful. And really possible.

'Sounds perfect,' Faye nodded.

'Annie! Annie, look!'

Annie craned her neck to see what all the fuss was about or, more accurately, what Maeve had accidentally smashed this time. But the girl was dizzy with delight and excitement. Against the chest of her baggy hoodie, she clutched an impossibly tiny, jet-black kitten with a streak of ginger on his forehead shaped just like a perfect crescent moon, his fur so wildly fluffy that he had the overall appearance of a palm-sized pom-pom. He let out a high-pitched, screeching *meow* that sounded very pleased and snuggled himself in closer to Maeve.

'He was by the bins! Screamed so loudly at me that I thought I must have trodden on him, but on closer inspection I think he's just gobby.'

Annie rushed over so that they could speak quietly together. 'Imagine that, hey? Your familiar, a gobby little terror,' she whispered.

'You think he really is?' Maeve asked hopefully.

'No doubt about it,' Annie smiled, brushing a finger over the crown of the kitten's small head. 'Witches don't just stumble across kittens for no reason. That's fate up to her old tricks again. You're meant to be.'

'What shall I call him?' Maeve frowned, opening up the question to Faye, too. 'Trash?'

Annie gasped. 'You cannot call that adorable kitten Trash, Maeve. I forbid it.'

'How about Darkness? Death? Soul Stealer?'

'You are impressively grim, my child,' Faye called from behind the counter, shaking her head.

'Grimm . . .' Maeve said, her voice wandering off with quiet approval.

'He's totally your familiar,' Pari chimed in happily as she sauntered back onto the shop floor, arms laden with stacks of her new spiced apple crumble cookies that had recently taken Celeste by storm. 'Your auras match, both kind of crimson.'

Annie almost choked on her latte, the last dribble of it spilling out of her mouth and straight down her shirt as her brain short-circuited. This could not be real life. She exchanged a panicked glance with Maeve. They both stared at Pari in nervous confusion, unsure of the next move.

'What?' she asked off-handedly, placing the cookies in neat columns behind the counter glass with her tongs. 'All witches need familiars – and clever little Grimm has made it very clear to all of us this morning that he's Maeve's. Obviously.'

Annie spluttered a strange, incomprehensible noise.

'Oh, we've known since you moved in,' Faye said with a shrug, as though it were the most normal thing in the world to be identifying Annie's highly secretive magical existence as a witch in the non-wicche world. 'Pari is . . . of a magical persuasion, as you might say, so she smelt your magic among all the vanilla from a mile off. Knew those éclairs of yours were witchcraft the moment we saw them.' She turned back to the coffee machine and began to shine the steam spout. 'Sorry for the shock. Tricky one to just casually drop into conversation, isn't it?'

'Oh, I've known there's something going on with me for years, ever since I was Maeve's age. I seem to accidentally make things float, like . . . all the time,' Pari said, waving her tongs around. 'Kind of annoying, really. You don't know of any sort of covens or anything who might be able to help, do you?'

While Annie and Maeve were frozen mid-motion, it felt as though Celeste breathed a sigh of relief between its walls. It had grown rather used to having a witch in charge of things, serving the most beautiful, bewitching treats in all of London. The place would remain magical after all, as it rightfully deserved, with Pari's undiscovered witchery to take the reins. The bell above the door caught the peachy light that poured in through the windows as the day's queue began to form for opening, giving a charmed wink, thoroughly pleased with itself. Business as usual.

The girls returned to Arden Place together that afternoon with linked arms, Annie's transference spell landing them just on the edge of the meadow. Two dashes of silver jotted like a spill of metallic ink in the sky as the sun and moon sat together. Karma had been waiting for their arrival and, more importantly, her dinner. She leapt up from the porch swing and scampered over to them the moment their tumble of magic arrived on the grass. Annie laughed as her cloud of a tail bobbed through the heather. November was already proving extra beautiful.

Maeve skipped ahead towards the cottage, her bag of books slapping her side, the young witch laughing as she chased towards Karma with Grimm, her new familiar nestled in her arms. Mage gave a whinny at the side of the house, evidently feeling much braver around the cat these days – although he would not be pleased that he was now officially outnumbered by felines. Annie felt her heart flood as she saw Hal step out onto the porch, hands on his hips and his hat pulled low. Noticing their arrival, he threw an arm into the air and gave a wide wave with a shy grin that he appeared to be unable to control.

Annie waved back, but stood for a second to soak it all in. Never in her life had she had the time to press pause on any moments that deserved to be held and admired. To stop and feel, to appreciate the apricity – the warmth of the sun in winter – beaming down onto her face and around her body as though spinning her very own gown of liquid gold.

And she felt it, every inch of brightness in the moment. She felt it all, so grand and gorgeous that it seemed impossible that the moment could ever end. It felt as though her whole life was supposed to be this exact photograph, the shades of orange and brown and rusted red in the trees, the sky a brilliant, bold blue. And an all-important dash of pink from the wildflowers climbing up the beams of the porch like sugar decorations, framing their home together. But it would change and that would be okay. She would welcome whatever came next, too.

Annie marvelled at the moments that she must have missed, living for so long in a life that was never truly hers, and maybe she would mourn for them when the dust had settled. But she could have burst with golden gratitude for the ones that she had found for herself now.

Finally, Annie felt it. She felt it all, authentic and joyful and hers.

It felt perfect.

ACKNOWLEDGEMENTS

I'm writing my wedding speech at the same time as the *Uncharmed* acknowledgements, so I need to make sure that I'm thanking the right people in the right place. Mother of the bride! My bridesmaids! Catering! Oh, hang on . . .

Luckily, my husband gets thanks in both, so this one's easy. Adam, we'll be real-life married by the time you come to read this (at the time of writing, it's sixty-two days to go) and I am so excited to start our next chapter together. Thank you for holding down the fort when writing takes over. Thank you for being on the coffees. Thank you for always believing in me and for your overflowing kindness. With you, I found real magic.

I am so fortunate to have been dealt a publishing dream team, all of whom work tirelessly behind the scenes on these books. Thank you to Lucy Brem, who perfectly pulls out the spark of magic in these stories when they're still just an insane combination of bad jokes and therapy sessions. Sorry for always writing too much chat. I am over the moon that we get to keep working together on these weird little witches in windows.

Having my agent, Maddy Belton, on side for the *Uncharmed* era has been one of the best decisions I've ever made. Maddy, thank you for everything. You are the ultimate cheerleader, so hard-working and frankly a force to be reckoned with, while also contributing excellent pasta recommendations – a truly perfect combo.

Charlotte at Honey Plum Paper, who has managed to (yet again) create a book cover so stunning that I can barely believe it. I can only assume that you are in fact a genuine witch, with artistic powers that Maeve would be thoroughly impressed by. Thank you for your gorgeous ideas and the stunning work that captures these stories so perfectly.

Thanks to all at Pan Macmillan who continue to make me cry with their support and enthusiasm. I am so perfectly proud to be a small part of it. Chloe Davies, thank you for being the most organized human of all time and for taking my anxieties on board with such care and understanding. Thanks to Melissa Bond for all of your meticulous hard work and attention to detail across both books. Carol-Anne and the social media team, thank you for the joyful, clever content that worked wonders for *Rewitched*. Thank you, Jon, Mairead, Anna and the rights team: you have changed my life and made unbelievable dreams come true.

Thank you to each of the international publishers who have taken *Rewitched* and *Uncharmed* on adventures around the world, in so many languages and to so many countries. Especially Anne Sowards and the Berkley team: thank you for believing in these books – I gasp with excitement every time a magical email arrives from across the pond.

Thank you, Mum, my most trusted early reader and a constant source of magic. The Wirral girls, the Thundergirls,

UNCHARMED

Alice, Jenny, Jemma . . . Writing magical women, powerful girls and unhinged female friendships will always be my favourite thanks to a lifetime of being surrounded by you all. I love you fiercely, for ever.

Thank you to Sal and Stu for everything you do for us (allotment veg deliveries, cat visits, catching birds in the loft . . .) and for making me feel so loved and supported over the past ten years. I am so very happy and proud to be a part of your wonderful family.

Flo, my co-author and feline familiar. I know you're furious that you're not on the cover for this one.

The London Picklers: thanks for providing the fresh baguettes, morning crosswords and witchy vocab discussions while I slunk off to write a lot of this book on holiday. Having you all fill our tiny house (and put the coffee machine through its paces) is one of the most contented joys I get to feel. You're all the very, very best.

And, finally, thank you to the readers, reviewers and booksellers who found *Rewitched* quietly waiting for them on a bookshelf. I am endlessly grateful to you. Before I wrote that first page, I'd let my powers slip away and was desperate to rediscover them, but I had no idea just how much magic was waiting. I hope these books continue to remind you just how much your own magic matters.

It's time to rediscover her magic . . .

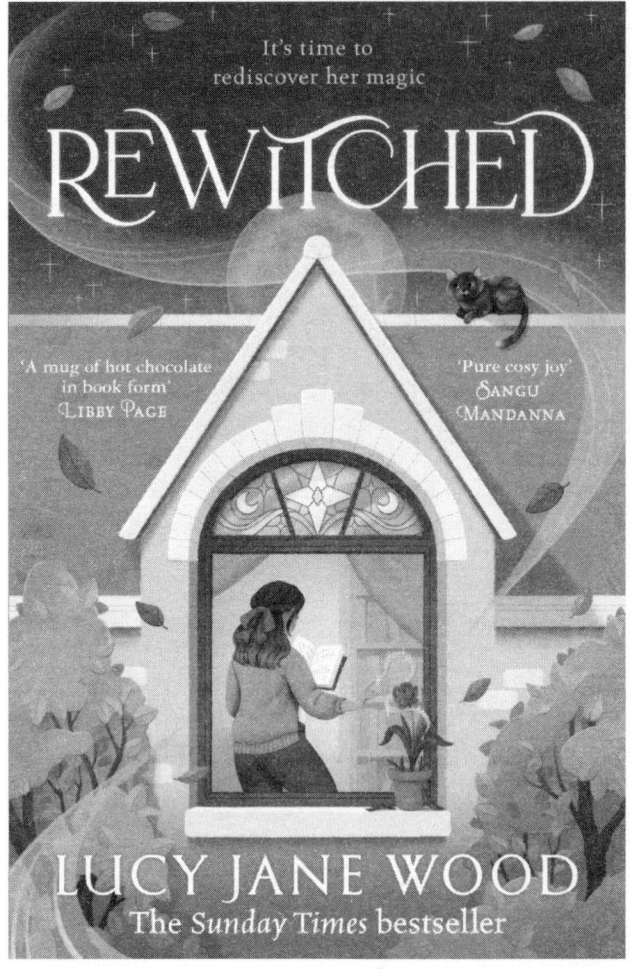

The instant *Sunday Times* bestseller

**A spellbinding cosy fantasy
about the magic of love in all its forms**

OUT NOW